ey come back? None of the others made it.

NO TRAV

Can t

NO TRAVELLER RETURNS

by
James S. Wallerstein

Illustrated by
Frederick J. Mackie, Jr.

Aurelon Tales
Mt. Kisco, N.Y.

International Standard Book Number
0-912388-05-6

Composition by
Darlene Wiederhold, Valhalla, New York

Printed in the United States of America

NO TRAVELLER RETURNS

THE COYOTES WERE HERE

BOOK I
KAAH NAGHALLAH
School of Fear and Mystery

BOOK II
BANE N'GAI
The Place of Evil Secrets

BOOK III
THE DOOM MACHINE
And the Siege of Glow Malomba

BOOK IV
THE INCREDIBLE TREASURE
And the Triumph of the Coyotes

To my Grandchildren
Jennifer, Brian, Kelly and Scott

BOOK I

KAAH NAGHALLAH

School of Fear and Mystery

Jaymie and Danny Larrabie

Students And Inmates At
The Kaah Naghallah Reform School

The Troublemaker......................Danny Larrabie

The Gifted Child........................Jaymie Larrabie

Juvenile Hood..........................Stevie Scanlon

Incorrigible Youth......................Keith Caldwell

The Cat Burglar.......................Cameron Westcott

Retarded Boy..........................Donald Turrentine

The Car Thief..........................Bobby Alliconda

The Shoplifter.........................Raymond Ridgeway

The Pickpocket.........................Troy Feroldi

The Runaway...........................Roger Newland

Throwaway Kid.........................Jody Kallinger

Wayward Urchin.......................Brandon Zuchtig

Tough Judge of the Juvenile Court..........Judge Tuffney

Parents of Jaymie and Danny.....Mitch and Pamela Larrabie

The Girl Next Door.......................Marjie Meyer

(continued)

The Masters Of Kaah Naghallah

Director of Kaah Naghallah Reform School....... Dr. Mehary
Teacher of the Naghallah Boys.............. Mr. Matthews
Drillmaster.......................... "Captain" Striker
Taskmaster.......................... "Captain" Smeer
Chief Correction Officer............. "Colonel" Lammington
Disciplinary Officer................. "Captain" Klayborne
Security Officer........................ "Captain" Craig
Chief of Naghallah's Private Police Force.... "Major" Powell
Assistant Chief........................ "Captain" Eberle

The Billionaire.......................... Karl Hasserman
His Money Man and Partner..... "Commander" Bartlow
His Scientist.................... "Captain" Vedemore
His Cooks...................... Minnie and Johanna
His Nurse.............................. Lyandra
His Caretaker.......................... Old George

Visitors, Guards, Keepers, Workers at the Hasserman Estate

'BYE, 'BYE, DANNY

When I first heard of *Kaah Naghallah,* it was a joke. One of those unfunny jokes that grown-ups tell to get a rise out of a kid.

"If you don't straighten out, boy, you're going to *Kaah Naghallah.* Do you know what they do to kids like you in *Kaah Naghallah?*"

The question was addressed to my brother Danny, who didn't answer. So I didn't find out what they do there to kids like us. At least not then.

Within a year, the place became a threat. "If you get into any more trouble, Daniel — just one more thing — you're going to *Kaah Naghallah.* And I mean it!" They called it *The school of last resort.* That's where "they take a kid apart and put him together — *correctly.*"

My brother Danny sure managed to get himself into a lot of trouble. He got put back a year in school and would have been in the same class as me. Except I got put in the stupid *Gifted Child* class. Then Danny got kicked out of Greenwood Junior High School entirely and sent to Greenwood Annex, "for problem youth". School at the Annex was very boring and Danny started playing hookey.

At the Annex, Danny met Stevie Scanlon and Keith Caldwell. Our father — Mitchell Larrabie — said they were a pair of juvenile hoods. He ordered my brother to stay away from them. That only made Danny like them better.

Stevie's father was a bank robber — the notorious Scug Scanlon, if you read the papers thirteen years ago. He got sent to prison for about ninety-nine years, escaped twice and was killed in a gun battle with the police. "No jail could hold him," Stevie boasted. "They couldn't take him alive. That was the only way they could stop him."

Keith didn't know anything about his people. "I guess they dumped me." Stevie and Keith were welfare kids, boarded out with foster parents who, Danny said, "treated them like shit". But I guess the boys gave the foster parents a rough time.

Danny brought them to the house a couple of times and Father threw them out. That was a shame. Keith and Stevie weren't bad guys.

The trio, Danny, Keith and Stevie, got busted nearly a dozen times, ending up in the police station or the juvenile court. For being rowdy in the park after curfew. That got Danny a J. D. card. For rioting, drinking beer, shoplifting, vandalism and "disturbing the peace". Danny said the cops kept picking on them. For "Habitual truancy", "Disorderly conduct" and then for stealing a car.

"That was lousy luck," said Danny. They got caught bringing the car back. But they did it five other times and didn't get caught. This time, their luck ran out. Danny was now on three different probations.

Danny was in trouble at home, too. Father claimed Danny had taken money out of his wallet. And he found *Crazy pills* in Danny's bureau.

Father got really angry. He took a strap and started to thrash Danny. But Danny, going on fourteen, wouldn't let himself be whipped. He fought back, and then ran out of the house. Father called the police, though Mother begged him not to.

Danny stayed away for three nights. Then late one night he sneaked back in, while everyone was sleeping. Danny wouldn't tell me where he went. Back in those days he didn't trust me.

Meanwhile, *Kaah Naghallah* had closed down in one place and re-opened in another. There were some nasty rumors about it, spread by a couple of former employees who had been fired. Some paper printed the rumors and was sued for libel by Dr. Mehary, Director of the *Kaah Naghallah Institute* "for the study and treatment of disturbed and delinquent youth".

The new site of the Institute was on the vast estate of a mysterious billionaire, Karl Hasserman, popularly known as *K. H.* Hasserman was ordinarily a very private man. He shunned reporters and was seen only by a trusted few. People wondered why he should lend his patronage to *Kaah Naghallah.* Was he truly concerned with public welfare—trying to turn incorrigible youths into law-abiding citizens? Or did he get a kick out of watching these unfortunate youngsters getting "taken apart and put together again *correctly?*"

The estate was way out in the wilderness. Karl Hasserman had purchased all the land for many miles around. Most of it belonged to a lumber company. K. H. bought the company. He also leased a large tract of State land. All of this was heavily patrolled and guarded against intruders.

Karl Hasserman was becoming more and more of a recluse. In his mountain hide-out, he met with only a small inner circle who reported to him on how his financial empire was going and received his orders.

K. H. had his fingers into everything. One of his conglomerates bought up Father's real estate and investment business. And now, Father's boss was a Mr. Bartlow, one of the few people who talked to Hasserman directly. They called him *Commander Bartlow,* though nobody seemed to know what he had ever commanded.

It was a bad day for the Larrabie family when Commander Bartlow came around. Father's new salary more than doubled his former modest earnings. He fixed up our ramshackle old house, bought two cars, hired a professional house-cleaning service and gave catered dinner parties. But his temper grew short and everything seemed to annoy him. Mother got a fur coat and a diamond bracelet. But she started feeling ill and getting headaches.

Danny could do nothing right. And Jaymie got yelled at for sitting around daydreaming, instead of exercising.

The Commander had a poor opinion of the Larrabie kids. "Your sons must be a big disappointment to you. Jaymie is good but weak. Daniel is strong but bad." They didn't quite know what to do about me. But

Bartlow recommended *Kaah Naghallah* for my brother.
"A boy learns discipline and obedience and comes out
without any criminal record."

Danny didn't go there yet. Mother wouldn't agree.
And anyway that new place wasn't quite ready. Instead,
Danny was sent to some psychiatrist, recommended by
Mr. Bartlow. The quack gave Danny all kinds of tests including brain waves and wrote a report I wasn't allowed
to see. Mitch wouldn't tell me and Danny wouldn't talk
about it.

"You want to know what he said about me? I'm sick in
the head." Danny didn't laugh. He wasn't kidding.

I won the math prize in school. That should have been
a happy day for me. But my brother Danny got busted in
an empty house, along with Keith and Stevie and a couple of other guys. The place was filled with stolen goods
and pot and crazy pills and burglars' tools.

Keith and Stevie were locked up in the juvenile clink
on their way to the State reform school. There was only
one reason why Danny didn't go with them. Father gave
his solemn word that within two weeks, Danny would be
sent to *Kaah Naghallah*. What started out as a bad joke
and became a threat was now a certainty.

*   *   *   *   *   *   *

"You can beat that rap," I told Danny. "All they can pin
on you is the trespassing. They can't prove you knew
about the drugs or stolen goods."

"They don't have to," said Danny. "I'm on probation for
three things already. I violated probation just by being out
at night. I'm fucked, Jaymie. And there's no getting out of
it. I wish, though, I was going to State reform school with
Keith and Stevie, instead of *Kaah Naghallah*. Now I may
never see them again."

Rudy Leone, a guy at school, said, "*Kaah Naghallah* is
one shitty place! Your brother Danny's going to
Naghallah? 'Bye, 'bye, Danny!"

THE KID WITH THE NOOSE AROUND HIS NECK

Jaymie came into the living room and couldn't believe what he saw. My brother Danny was standing up on a chair with a noose around his neck. The end of a leather belt was tied to a light on the ceiling. "Kick away the chair, Jaymie. Do this one thing for me! Come on! I want to get it over with."

"Don't, Danny!"

"Why not? Give me one good reason."

"Because you're my brother and I love you."

"Oh, come off it, Jaymie. Nobody in this family gives a shit about me. *And I ain't your brother.*"

I had heard this before, but wasn't sure *he* knew. Danny didn't think *I* knew.

"I know we're not blood brothers," said Jaymie. "But ——"

"We ain't any kind of brothers," retorted Danny.

Standing there with the noose around his neck, Danny poured out his tale of woe. He wasn't the son of Mitch and Pamela — Dad and Mother — but of a distant cousin, Peggy. "She was raped. They were going to abort me, but they waited too long.

"They gave me to the Martin family, who had no kid. But the Martins decided they didn't want me. I was abnormal or retarded or something. So they dumped me back on Cousin Peggy."

That wasn't the real reason. The Martins were getting a divorce. And neither of them wanted to be tied down with a baby. But Danny kept believing the worst about himself. Danny is a handsome guy. Or would be if he got a haircut. His long, yellow hair hung like a dirty mop onto his shoulders.

Danny continued. "Peggy dumped me again. This time, to her rich cousin, Pamela. *Thanks, Peggy. Thanks a lot for nothing,* says Pamela. She's having a baby of her own. Sweet little Jaymie.

"The Larrabies kept me as a painful duty. But they

didn't want me either. They *never* wanted me. I never got adopted ——"

"You never got adopted?" That and the rape I hadn't heard before.

"No, my dear brother. Or rather my not-brother. I never got adopted. I don't get any part of grandfather's estate. You get it all."

"I won't take it, Danny. Whatever I get, you get half. I swear it. If you do *one* thing."

"What's that?"

"Take that noose off your neck and promise you won't kill yourself."

Danny said, "It's too late, Jaymie. In another week, I'll be shipped off to *Kaah Naghallah*. And I won't be back for three years, if ever. Getting half your stuff won't do me any good. You can have *all* my stuff, which is next to nothing. Just try to do something for Keith and Stevie. They got nobody."

The grandfather clock showed five minutes to four. "If you won't kick the chair, I'll do it myself, Jaymie. When the clock strikes four, I'm doing it."

Jaymie pushed the clock back to *3:30*. "That clock ain't never going to strike four! I'll keep pushing it back forever!"

"Very clever, my sweet brother! Gifted Child! Honor student! Parents' pet! Two hundred I.Q."

"It's not nearly that much."

"You know what I. Q. I got? About fifty."

"You got a good mind, Danny. On practical things you're smarter than me."

"You got everything, Gifted Child. I'll bet you got a thousand bucks in the bank. I got shit!"

Danny's face was grey and unnatural. For nearly a year now he had been taking pep pills. But this time it was something new. *Sky powder.* It blows you sky high and then drops you into the dumps. Danny was in the dumps now. If I could only keep him talking!

"I'm a louse, Jaymie, I'm a no-good bum. You know what that psychiatrist said about me? I'm a dangerous psychopath!"

"That ain't true!"

"I hate you, Jaymie. I'm jealous of you. Twice, I tried to kill you. I threw you off the roof and I threw you into the lake."

"You didn't throw me off the roof, Danny. I slipped and fell. You didn't throw me out of the boat either. We were fooling around. Besides, you saved my life. When I fell through the ice, you pulled me out."

"They said I lured you on the ice to drown you. And then lost my nerve."

"That's stupid. We didn't expect the ice to break. It might have been *you* who fell in."

"You won't believe nothing bad about me, will you? If I come off this chair, I might decide to kill *you* instead of me."

Danny pulled the noose off his neck and pulled a knife out of his pocket. "I got a shiv here." It was a switch blade knife. When you pressed a button, a blade flew out.

"Let's see you tremble, Little Brudder. I'm gonna cut you up!"

"I won't tremble. I know you won't hurt me."

"Yeah? Why?"

"Because you never did a mean thing in your life. You did a lot of stupid things."

"Like what?"

"Like almost hanging yourself, because you're too chicken to go to *Kaah Naghallah.*"

"Chicken, huh? You can talk, Gifted Child. *You* ain't going."

"I'll go if you do, Danny. Either we both go or we both stay home."

"Mitch will never send his beloved Pet, Jaymieboy, to *Kaah Naghallah.*"

"He'll send me. If he splits us up, I'll make more trouble than you ever did."

The life was coming back into Danny's face. "I didn't mean that, Jaymie, about cutting you up. You're my friend, Jaymie. The only friend I got in the world. Except Keith and Stevie and they're going away."

"Danny, that thousand bucks I got in the bank. Or whatever it is. I'll give it to you, and my hi-fi, too. If you give me that shiv."

"I don't want your dough, Jaymie. You want the shiv? *Here!*" Danny tossed the shiv to me. "You want to cut me up? Go ahead." Danny was grinning now.

"You said you ain't chicken, Brother Danny. Will you do anything I will?"

"Yeah. If it don't take any brains."

I took the shiv and sliced my hand. And the blood flowed.

"What did you do that for?"

"Do it, Gifted Child!" ordered Jaymie.

"You're the Gifted Child, not me."

Danny cut his hand. We put our hands against each other and our blood flowed together.

"You said we weren't any kind of a brother. Now we're blood brothers."

"Okay. We're blood brudders."

"Now swear as I do. *I, Jaymie Larrabie . . . .*"

"*I, Danny Larrabie . . . .*"

"*I swear to be forever loyal and faithful to my Blood-brother, Danny Larrabie.*"

"*I swear to be forever loyal and faithful to my Brudder Jaymie.*"

"*We will defend and protect each other and share everything equally between us.*"

Danny said it.

"*The enemies of one brother shall be the enemies of both brothers.*"

Danny said that, too.

"*Our bond shall be unbreakable and everlasting.*"

Danny said it.

"*I swear this by my life and soul and by all that ever was or is or will be.*"

Danny looked bewildered.

"Swear it!" ordered Jaymie. And he did.

"*Now, Always and Forever!*"

"*Jaymie and Danny! Now, Always and Forever!*"

"You got my shiv now, Jaymiebrudder, so I'll take your hi-fi. That's fair, ain't it?"

"Yeah, You can have my color TV, too, Dannybrudder. But give me your crazy pills."

"What do you want them for?" asked Danny.

"To flush down the toilet."

He grinned. "Okay, sucker. The pills for the color TV." Danny added a bit sheepishly. "I wasn't really gonna hang myself. Jaymiebrudder. I was just putting on an act. I sure swindled you! I got a TV and a hi-fi and half your bank account. And what did you get out of it, Gifted Child?"

"I got a brother," said Jaymie.

*   *   *   *   *   *   *

That shiv cut deep. There was blood on our clothes and blood all around the room. Mother was alarmed and thought we had a knife fight. When we told her we were blood brothers, she was smiling.

"I'm glad you like each other. But what a peculiar way of showing it. Boys are foolish. Girls would never do a silly thing like that."

After that, me and Danny moved our beds together in the same room. Danny stayed in at night and didn't go night prowling any more. It was no fun without Keith and Stevie.

"I won't do it again, Jaymiebrudder. No sky powder and no crazy pills. If you ever see me with that stuff again, just beat the shit out of me. I won't fight back . . .

"Thanks for saving my life, Jaymiebrudder. It ain't worth much, but it's the only life I got.

"Don't tell anyone what happened, will you? Or they'll stick me in the looney bin for sure. Swear you won't tell, Jaymiebrudder!"

I swore. And I didn't tell.

CONFRONTATION

"Yes, Jaymie, you can talk to me. But the answer is *No.*"
So said Father. "Your brother has been enrolled in *Kaah
Naghallah.* I have paid his tuition. We are *not* going to
change that.

"Your mother and I are in complete agreement." Mother
said nothing. But she didn't contradict him.

"I have given the matter very careful thought, Jaymie.
And have received the best advice possible."

"From Mr. Bartlow?"

"From Commander Bartlow and others . . .

"No, I am not breaking up the family, Jaymie. Daniel is
not *kicked out.* He will be welcomed back when he has
learned how to behave in a civilized manner.

"*Kaah Naghallah* is not a concentration camp. It is a
strict boarding school. Kids are not beaten and locked in
cages. Where did you ever hear a thing like that?

"But they have strict discipline at *Kaah Naghallah.*
No namby pamby permissiveness. You don't get any
hand-outs there. No privileges, unless you earn them.
You have to toe the mark and show the right attitude.
There's no truancy and no fooling around.

"They take good care of you physically. They build
your body up with exercise and physical labor. No loafing. No drugs. No booze. No night prowling. They repair
your mind, too. The Head of *Kaah Naghallah* is a
psychiatrist — Dr. Mehary."

"The same guy who said Danny is a dangerous
psychopath?"

"Not *is,* Jaymie. He said Daniel might become one."

"Unless Danny gets three years of training and treatment at *Kaah Naghallah?*"

"It doesn't have to be three years. It could be con-
siderably less. If Daniel improves ——"

Mother had said nothing at all. Now she spoke. "Your
brother will be able to make home visits, won't he,
Mitch? Not right away. I'm sure Danny will be able to

make a nice long visit at Christmas. That's something good to think about, isn't it, Jaymie?"

Hardly. Since it was now just the beginning of February.

"Please, Jaymie," Mother pleaded. "Have some faith and trust in your father. He's doing the best he can for all of us."

Mitch added, "We're not throwing Daniel out of the family. This is the only way we can get him back into the family."

Jaymie said, "Why didn't you adopt Danny?"

"Perhaps it's just as well we didn't. Daniel is not a son to be proud of."

"What did Danny do that was so bad? You could get him out of it. You know you could. You didn't even get Danny a private lawyer."

"I'm not going to get him out of it. This time, he has to face the consequences."

There was a moment of silence. Then Mother said. "I think we should have adopted Daniel many years ago. We talked about it, but kept putting it off. We could do it *now*, Mitch. We don't have to wait until Daniel comes back from *Kaah Naghallah*. Would that make you feel better, Jaymie?"

But Mitch said, "Let's not rush things. Let's see how he turns out first."

Jaymie didn't know what more to say. I put on a sulk, like when I was a little kid. Then, if I sulked enough, sometimes I would get my way.

Mother said, "Jaymie will be a very lonely little boy without his brother."

Mitch said, "I'll make it up to him. I'll arrange to spend more time with Jaymie. Perhaps this summer we could make a trip to Europe. Would you like that, Jaymie?"

"No, I wouldn't!" I was acting more and more like a frustrated little kid. "I want Danny!"

"You're going to have to choose between Daniel and me," said Mitch.

"I choose the family. The four of us."

"That's not an answer, Jaymie. That's a cop-out."

"Okay. *I choose Danny!*"

Mitch was getting mad. I had lost all chance of changing his mind. Or Mother's either. She would never stand up to Mitch for very long. "You're a very foolish and spoiled little boy, Jaymie. You just sit around daydreaming in your private world. You have no idea what the real world is like.

"Stop dreaming, Jaymie, and face reality! Stop whining and become a man!"

Jaymie said, "Why don't you send *me* to *Kaah Naghallah*, too? *That* might make a man of me."

"I might just do that," said Mitch, grimly.

"You better, because if Danny gets sent away and I'm left home, I'll make more trouble than Danny ever did! I'll quit school! I'll get arrested! I'll get in the papers and disgrace the family! I'll smash the house up!"

Mitch stared at me. "You're not going to do anything, Jaymie. You just have a big mouth, that's all."

Jaymie picked up an antique chair. Danny got a whipping once for breaking it. It had been repaired and I broke it again. There was an empty vase on the mantel; fancy, expensive and ugly. Jaymie threw the vase against the mirror, smashing both of them. Then I walked out of the room and slammed the door.

CONFRONTATION II

Father called me into his study. This time, he was alone. "Are you going to apologize, Jaymie?"

"Why should I?"

In answer, Father handed me a brochure:

KAAH NAGHALLAH
The School of last Resort

"Read it," he ordered.

I must confess the illustrations were rather attractive. Woods and mountains; wild meadows and huge rocks; a vast vegetable garden and a tree nursery. Then, a white stone building; and inside, a schoolroom, an exercise room, a dining hall and a dormitory with a row of empty beds in it. No kids.

"The name *Kaah Naghallah* came from an ancient language and meant a ritual of some sort. A challenge. A test of manhood." It was a place where you would get *behavior modification, obedience training, corrective conditioning, character building, physical and mental improvement, counselling* and *motivation.*

"The student starts at the bottom of the ladder and works his way up. Every privilege has to be earned . . .

"A boy learns to face hardship and frustration and to conquer and control his feelings . . .

"In the end, when he is ready, each youth will face the ordeal of Kaah Naghallah and undergo transformation into splendid manhood."

"Sounds like a lot of bullshit," said Jaymie.

"Why do you think I am showing you this?"

"Because I either have to apologize or go with Danny to *Kaah Naghallah.* Is that it?"

"In some things, you catch on fast, Jaymie."

"Go ahead. Enroll me."

"I already have, Jaymie. You're enrolled, unless I cancel it."

"Good, Dad. Then I won't have to smash any more furniture."

Mitch looked frustrated. He had expected Jaymie to back down. "Maybe I ought to send *you* to that psychiatrist."

"That phony! You need him more than me, Father."

"You are completely under Daniel's influence. Why has Daniel such a hold over you?"

"Why has Mr. Bartlow such a hold over you?"

Mitch's voice became hard and cold. "All right, Jaymie. You can go to *Kaah Naghallah* with your blood brother."

Later, he told Mother, "Jaymie has become completely impossible."

"But you can't send Jaymie to *Kaah Naghallah!*"

"Why not? Let him get his belly full. It won't hurt Jaymie. It may do him some good. Jaymie is rotten spoiled and very soft. He always runs away from things. *Kaah Naghallah* may teach Jaymie to face reality.

"That kid would be a pain in the neck, if he stayed home."

THE TWO-BOY ARMY

"You're stupid, Jaymie. You're the stupidest kid I ever seen. Getting yourself sent to *Kaah Naghallah* on purpose. Only a jerk would go to that place."

"You're going, too," said me.

"I have to go. They got too many things on me. But at least I had some fun for a while. Now I have to take my lumps. But you, Gifted Child — Sorry, I keep forgetting. You're not in the Gifted Child class any more."

"I quit," said Jaymie.

"Yeah. Danny quits school, so Jaymie quits school. Danny goes to *Kaah Naghallah* so Jaymie goes to *Kaah Naghallah*. Monkey see, monkey do. What a dope!"

Jaymie was almost in tears. I thought Danny at least would appreciate my sacrifice. "I won't bother you, Danny."

"You ain't gonna bother me, Jaymiebrudder. I'm gonna have a lot of laughs watching you get your lumps."

"You'll get them, too, Dannybrudder."

"If things get too fuckin miserable, I might try to bust out of the place. I couldn't just leave you there. I'd have to take you with me. You'd be dead weight in a runaway."

"Maybe not," said Jaymie. "Maybe I'd be a help."

"Yeah? How?"

"Well, I'd say, 'Don't go down that path, Dannybrudder. The cops have an ambush there. Let's cut across the fields and hit the back road.'"

"And what do I say?"

"You say, 'You got sharp eyes, Jaymiebrudder. I sure am glad I got you for a partner.'"

"Want to bet I don't say that?"

"You might. You always give me credit when I deserve it. *Danny Larrabie, the boy hero, was a gallant youth. He led his gallant two-boy army on to victory!*"

"Some army!" Danny grinned. "Okay, army. If I'm the leader, that means I'm the boss. Right? When I give an order, you do it."

"Right, captain."

"Who is the boss?"

"You are, Dannybrudder."

He punched me in the shoulder. When Danny does that, it means he likes a guy.

I drew most of my savings out of the bank. The bank manager gave me a hard time. He said I'd have to get my parent's permission. I had to give him a story. My mother was sick and my father drunk and broke. We needed the money to pay the doctors' bills. I guess I ruined Father's credit.

"It's half yours, Dannybrudder."

"Hang onto it, Jaymiebrudder. Right now, I got nothing to spend it on. Any day now, that grey boy-catcher van is coming to pick us up."

"You and me could still run away."

"Are you kidding? It's February and cold outside. If we run away, it'll be in summer. That bankroll of yours won't last too long, if we're on the lam.

"We'll go to Naghallah. I don't feel so bad now that I got company."

'BYE, 'BYE, JAYMIE

"If you tell a kid something, stick to it! Never back down! Or the kid will walk all over you." That's what Mr. Bartlow told Mitch Larrabie and what Father repeated to Mother.

"I understand that. But couldn't Danny and Jaymie stay home for a few more weeks?"

"There's no sense putting it off, Pamela. The boys are leaving Wednesday."

Mother looked unhappy. "But a week from Saturday is Marjie Meyer's party. They invited both Danny and Jaymie. You know how terribly offended the Meyers get. Mrs. Meyer is such a gossip. If the boys don't go ——"

"That is quite impossible. The school has strict rules and the first thing the boys have to learn is to obey them. That bus leaves promptly at nine on Wednesday and the boys are going to be on it. *Period!*"

Mother pleaded "Please, Jaymie. Write Marjie a nice letter explaining why you can't come to her party."

I was going to laugh in her face. But me and Danny needed all the friends we could get. Maybe Marjie could do us a favor sometime.

I wrote: *Dear Marjie — We are sorry to miss your party, but we have to go away to boarding school. We will miss you.*

Fondest greetings,
Danny and Jaymie Larrabie
P.S. *Danny says, could you please send him your picture.*

Danny said, "What did you put that crap in for?"

"She's sweet on you, Dannybrudder. Marjie likes you a lot."

"Bullshit!" But he smiled a bit.

I thought Mother would be pleased about the Meyers. Instead, she began to weep. "Look," said Jaymie. "If you don't want us to go away, there's one thing you can do. Take me and Danny and *leave this house.* Find yourself a good lawyer. File for divorce and ask for custody of me and Danny."

Mother wiped the tears from her eyes. "You children grow up so fast, Jaymie. You know all about these things. But I couldn't do that. I couldn't leave your father."

She added weakly, "I'm sure things will turn out for the best."

As Friday drew nearer, Father became more friendly. He was even nice to Danny. "All charges against you will be dropped, son. If you make a good record at *Kaah Naghallah.* Judge Tuffney promised me that. And we'll put through the adoption papers. You'll be a full Larrabie and Jaymie's real brother." He had promised that to Mother to make her stop weeping.

"You'll look after your little brother, won't you, Daniel?"

"I'm not Danny's little brother. He just has fourteen months on me."

"I'll look after him," promised Danny and he punched me lightly.

"Don't look so gloomy, Pamela. The boys aren't going off to the wars. They're just going to boarding school. We'll be up to visit them, after they get settled down."

Mother continued to look miserable.

"The boys will be all right. Commander Bartlow has promised to keep a friendly eye on them."

The Commander was quite pleased that Mitch was sending his sons to *Kaah Naghallah.* Bartlow, we learned later, was Chairman of the *Kaah Naghallah* Institute.

The school was having trouble filling up its places. Disturbing rumors persisted. A number of tuition-paying students had been withdrawn. But the philanthropic tycoon, Karl Hasserman, was now offering scholarships to poor kids, so they too could benefit from the *Kaah Naghallah* program.

The care and correction of disturbed and delinquent youth cost the Greenwood taxpayers quite a bit of money. *Kaah Naghallah* was promising the city to take a goodly batch of juvenile trouble-makers off their hands for free. Not too many in the beginning. "But enough to show how well our program works."

Rudy Leone expressed his sympathy. "Hi, Jaymie! Hey, I heard that school is a nuthouse. What do they do? They turn a kid inside out there. Don't tell me *you're* going to *Kaah Naghallah*, too, Gifted Child? *'Bye, 'Bye, Jaymie!*"

A REAL SHITTY PLACE

A letter from Keith and Stevie:

Dear Danny and Jaymie:

We are still in the (can't read it) It aint too bad here. Nothin to do but play cards, watch TV and (can't read it) No skool. The teecher is sick.

But we got some bad news. Insted of reform skool, they are sendin us to some real shitty private place run by a bunch of Nuts. Kaah Naghallah. We herd its miserable. They experamet on kids and bust your ass. Any kid who gose there is muckled.

Kaah Naghallah is way out in the (can't read it) We wont come back for a long time. If we come back at all.

Nobuddy want to go the Naghallah. But the (something) Officer fingered us. That's cause we sassed him. He sed he wood fuck us up and he did. And the Jedge OKed it. He dont like us eider.

Can they fuck us up like that? Make us go to that shitty place where they experamet on you? We tole them we dont want to go, but they (Can't read it)

Can you get ahold of the Sivil Libaties peeple to try to stop it? Pleese help us!

Your freends,
        Keith Caldwell
        Steve Scanlon

"Keith wrote that letter," said Danny, with admiration.

"Stevie can't write for beans. He's even dumber than me.

"Keith is real smart. He could be in the Gifted Child class, if he didn't get in so much trouble."

It was too late to do anything, even if we wanted to. Tomorrow was *Kaah Naghallah* Day.

Nobody but a parent could get in to see Keith and Stevie. Me and Danny tried to sneak in, but we got chased. We dropped off a note, which they never got:

> *Don't try to get out of Kaah Naghallah.*
> *Me and Danny are going there, too.*
> *With the four of us, we'll have a ball*
> *No matter how shitty it is.*

KAAH NAGHALLAH   *February 20*

"You can't take all that stuff, Jaymie. What kind of a place do you think you're going to?"

"It's a school."

"*Kaah Naghallah* is a disciplinary school, not a summer camp. They will give you whatever you need and whatever you are allowed to have."

Me and Danny had the hall piled full of stuff. We might as well try to take as much as we could. Christmas before last, Brother Danny wanted a drum set. But Father wouldn't let Danny have a drum set until his school record improved. Instead, Danny got the illustrated *Children's Dictionary*. Parents' pet Jaymie then asked for a drum set and got one.

"Gee," said Jaymie, "I wish *I* had that dictionary instead of the drums."

"Want to swap?" asked Danny eagerly, fancying himself a real con artist. And we swapped.

Father grew wrathful. "That wasn't very nice, Daniel. Taking advantage of your little brother. I want you to give it back."

Meekly, Danny started to return the drum set. But Jaymie balked. "I'm not giving up my dictionary. Danny made a deal. Now he's trying to welch out of it."

All at once, Danny wasn't sure he wanted to trade the dictionary. He made me promise I would let him read it, when he wanted to. "It's a crummy dictionary," Danny decided. "It doesn't even have *Fuck* in it."

Danny had been trying to figure out how to smuggle the nine hundred dollars from my bank account into Naghallah. "They won't let us bring any money in. That's for sure. And they'll probably strip search us when we get up there." Danny decided to hide the bank money inside the drum. Danny knows how to hide things.

On the day of the departure, I felt blue. I got up when it was still dark and wandered around the old house, with its many rooms and memories.

There must have been tears in my eyes. Danny punched me. "Hiyah, Crybaby!" That's what I expected him to say. Instead, he asked, "Are you okay, Little Brudder?"

Jaymie nodded.

"You want to back out? You can still do it. Tell Mitch you changed your mind and apologize."

"No! We're sticking together, ain't we? *Now, Always* and *Forever!*"

He grinned. "Danny and Jaymie, *Now, Always* and *Forever!*"

THAT GREY BOYCATCHER VAN

We cooked ourselves a hearty breakfast, pancakes and cinnamon toast — probably our last good meal — and waited for that grey Boycatcher van to come and snatch us.

Mother was ill. Father had sent for a nurse and a doctor. He blamed me and Danny instead of himself for making her sick. "Let her sleep, boys, Don't wake her up!"

We didn't. We left a note for her.

"Commander" Barlow came over, carrying an attache case. He seemed real jovial today, now that he was snatching the Larrabie kids. "Your wife will be real lonely in this big house. Take her away, Mitchell. Give Pamela a trip to Europe. You'll have a real vacation with these little monsters off your neck. We'll call it *business*. The company can pick up the tab. Don't worry about the boys. I'll take care of them."

The Boycatcher van arrived right on schedule. In it, were five *"Guardians"*, who were to act as our Masters and Keepers. Bartlow warned us to treat them with respect and call them *Sir* or *Captain*.

Striker and Klayborne were large, powerful men who looked like professional wrestlers, somewhat out of training. Klayborne, we were told, had been a prison guard. Striker, a lion tamer. That was to convince us they knew how to handle juvenile punks like us.

Guardian Craig was red-faced and plump, with a drooping moustache. He looked like a bartender, but used to be a truant officer.

Mr. Matthews was a mousey little man with gold-rim glasses. He had been a teacher in a boy's school, but looked more like a sad clown in the circus.

The fifth guy was a man in a brown military uniform, whose name was *Major* Powell. *"K.H."*, the billionaire who owned *Kaah Naghallah*, had his own private police force. Major Powell was the head of it.

Like I expected, we got into an argument over our stuff. Powell laid the law down. "You can't take all that junk, boy!" No knife. No axe. Nothing that could be used as a weapon. That included hockey sticks and baseball bats.

No radio. No record player. No sleeping bags. No soccer ball. No football. "And leave that camera here!"

"Why?" asked me.

"Because I told you to!" No field glasses either.

When it came to my guitar and the drum set, I gave them a big argument. Striker bellowed, "Don't get snotty, punk! Get in the van *and shut up!* I'm counting *three* ——"

Danny gave me a warning punch, which said, *This is a reform school, not the Gifted Children's class. If you want to do something, do it sneaky. But never argue, if you don't want to be creamed.* However, to my surprise, Commander Bartlow said, "Let Jaymie take his stuff. There will be room. The other boys will have practically nothing."

We entered the van. There were two kids inside already. One was a thin kid with very light hair, even paler skin and strange yellow eyes. He sat there rigidly, without moving his head, staring at the ceiling.

"That's Donald," said Commander Bartlow. "He's a dummy. He can't talk."

I said "Hi, Donald!" but he just kept on staring.

Nobody knew quite what was wrong with Donald. He was "retarded", "autistic", "genetically defective" or maybe had some new and strange disease. Sometimes he acted like a wild animal and crawled around on all fours. But most of the time he just stood or sat where he was put and stayed there. Anyway, his caretakers got tired of looking after him and dumped him into Naghallah.

The other kid was a small boy who was weeping. "That's Jody," said Mr. Bartlow. "He bites people."

Jody's father was dead. His mother was living with some creep who didn't like Jody. The man claimed Jody bit him, kept stealing things and running away. Jody was a nuisance, so they shipped him off to Naghallah.

I said, "Hi, Jody!" but he kept on weeping.

Danny looked disgusted. He expected to get his comeuppance at Naghallah. But to be coupled in punishment with a retard, a crybaby and a loud-mouth kid brother was a little too much!

Donald and Jody
Donald sat there woodenly, while Jody wept.

THREE UNWILLING RECRUITS

We stopped next at the Greenwood Youth Shelter. "Major" Powell stood at the door to make sure nobody tried to run away. But that was hardly necessary. If we were going to split, we would have tried it already.

There was some snafu about the Shelter kids. Commander Bartlow went in and out a couple of times. Finally, they dragged out three unwilling recruits. Bobby Alliconda, Raymond Ridgeway and Brandon Zuchtig.

Bobby and Raymond were two wild boys who lived in the streets. Or did, until the Juvenile Squad captured them. They had eked out a living snatching purses, shoplifting, pickpocketing, rolling an occasional drunk and panhandling a meal. They lived in an abandoned building until the water pipes froze and the boys almost froze, too.

They had a great line for panhandling that almost always worked. "Please, mister. Me and my brudder lost our bus fare. Could you lend us a buck so we can go home?" They even collected from the cops until one day they hit the same guy twice. That's how they got busted.

Bobby and Raymond didn't look like brothers. Bobby had light hair. Raymond was dark with brown skin and black Afro hair. But they explained, if you asked them, they had the same father, but different mothers. That just might have been true. Their mothers were unmarried and their fathers were unknown.

Raymond and Bobby stuck together like Keith and Stevie. "I wasn't sorry when they busted us." said Bobby. "The Youth Shelter wasn't half bad. But this Naghallah place, I heard, is fuckin shitty."

Raymond said, "I heard it's a bughouse."

Bobby and Raymond had no folks except each other. There was no one to object when they selected the victims for *Kaah Naghallah*. All the Naghallah boys except me and Danny, it turned out, were welfare kids, without families and unwanted by anybody else. Bobby and Ray-

Bobby, Raymond and Brandon
Three Unwilling recruits.

mond agreed to go to *Naghallah* so they could stay
together. That much, the Judge promised them.

The boys looked scared as they got into the van. Like
they were going to the torture chamber instead of to
boarding school. Bobby just stood outside the door and
wouldn't move. "Major" Powell gave him a whack with a
club and shoved him into the van.

Raymond paused and took a final puff on a cigarette.
Powell knocked the butt out of Raymond's hand. The kid
cursed at him. Powell lifted up his stick to hit Raymond.
But at this point, a tall black man, one of the biggest
guys I have ever seen, stepped out from behind a
delivery truck and glared at Powell. Thinking better of
it, the Major lowered his arm and muttered a threat instead. "I'm putting my marker on you, boy! You'll get
yours."

Brandon hung back, too, and had to be pushed in.
Brandon was a skinny blond kid, gloveless and shiver-
ing, in a thin grey sweater much too small for him. These
Youth Shelter kids didn't have much in warm clothes.
Me and Danny had some extra sweaters and stuff that
we could pass around to the other guys.

Each Naghallah kid had a story to tell, but Brandon's
was the strangest of all. He was the youngest child in a
rich German family. But some pimp kidnapped him and
brought him over here.

That pimp was awful mean to Brandon. The kid ran
away, was caught and ran away again. This time, he was
picked up by the police and put in a foster home.
However, that pimp came after him again and snatched
Brandon for the third time. And he treated Brandon
even worse than before.

At last, Brandon managed to escape again. He wandered around, hitch-hiking, begging and stealing, ragged
and half starved. Then he met a gay poet who took Brandon into his home. This guy was real nice to Brandon.
"He bought me clothes and things. Even a TV and a
bicycle. He took me on trips and taught me math and
reading and playing the piano. He even wrote poems

about me and called me *a beautiful boy.*" But the juvenile people wouldn't let him stay with the Gay Poet. They stuck him in "that crummy Youth Shelter" and tried to trace his family.

Now comes the strange part. They told him no boy named Brandon Zuchtig, nor any kid like him had been kidnapped, either in Germany or over here. They dug up a birth certificate for him in California, but could find no trace of his parents who had disappeared. They wouldn't believe he came from Germany, although Brandon speaks German like a native. They couldn't find any trace of the pimp either.

The Gay Poet was the only one who believed Brandon. The social workers thought he made the story up.

The psychologist said it was a delusion about Brandon being kidnapped from a rich family in Germany. It was a day dream and never happened. But Brandon still believes it and hopes some day to find his family again.

THE JUVENILE CLINK

Next stop — *The Juvenile Clink,* also known as Youth House. For kids who are too tough for the Shelter, but not bad enough for the calaboose. Here, we collected two more prisoners. Or, to be optimistic, two more students for the *Kaah Naghallah* Academy. Yes, it was Stevie Scanlon and Keith Caldwell. Stevie, Keith and Danny fell into each others' arms.

Stevie had yellow hair and a rip in his pants. Keith had red hair and holes in his shoes. "Watch out for these two," said Klayborne. "They're bad actors."

Jaymie insisted on acting as the Master of Ceremonies, introducing everybody. Powell told me to *Shut up!* I ignored him. "I'm putting my marker on you, boy!" he told me. And Raymond laughed.

The seven of us were gabbing together. But Donald just sat there rigidly, like he was an exhibit in a wax museum. And Jody kept on bawling.

*We halted at the Juvenile Clink where
they gathered up Stevie and Keith*

"We have one more stop," announced Mr. Matthews. This one was at the city jail.

They aren't supposed to keep juveniles in the city jail. But this one was an escape artist and a first class trouble maker. Cameron Anthony Westcott, the Cat Burglar.

They brought in Cameron in handcuffs and legcuffs. "He broke out of Youth House and out of the police station."

"Keep the cuffs on him until you get to *Kaah Naghallah*. No big deal if he runs away there. At least Greenwood will be rid of him. He'll probably get lost in the mountains and won't be missed. This kid is a calamity."

The conscripts having been collected, "Commander" Bartlow took his leave.

THE CAT BURGLAR

Cameron, the one-boy crime wave, entered the van without persuasion. He swaggered in with a big grin on his face. "Greetings, comrades. Is this the express bus?"

"To where?" asked Keith.

"To the Naghallah school for wayward children?"

"Why?" asked Steve. "Are you in a hurry to get there?"

"Not at all, friend. I don't care how long it takes."

"This is the bus to the shithouse," asserted Brother Danny.

Cameron had been arrested seven times. "That's only when I got caught. I must have pulled about eighty jobs and got away with it."

Cameron never stole too much from one place. "Just enough to live on. I'm not greedy.

"I spread my thefts around." That way, nobody got too mad at him. They figured him for a nuisance more than a menace. When he was caught, Cameron sweet-talked the juvenile court into going easy on him. Probation, or, at worst, a couple of weeks in the Youth Shelter.

He claimed some older guy made him do it or put him up to it. A guy who didn't exist.

Even this last time Cameron got a break, going to Naghallah instead of the State Reformatory. At least the Judge said it was a break. Some tycoon was spending thousands of dollars to teach Cameron Westcott to become a good citizen. "Some boys have to learn the hard way. But at *Naghallah*, you'll learn."

"I'm getting my behavior modified," Cameron announced.

Two more guards from Karl Hasserman's private police force entered the van. They were both armed and took their places near the door. I was beginning to feel a bit like a desperate criminal on his way to the penitentiary. But I guess the guards were just hitching a ride back to *Kaah Naghallah*.

They made Cameron sit on the floor of the van with the cuffs on. The rest of us crowded together. The Masters spread themselves out comfortably, smoking or reading a newspaper. That was the difference between being a jailer and a jailee.

They kept Cameron's arms and legs cuffed up all the way. Poor Cameron kept squirming in his shackles. He complained and pleaded, but they ignored him. None of us spoke up for Cameron; which made me feel a bit ashamed. It wouldn't have done no good anyway.

We rode north at a fast pace. Naghallah was in the Grey Mountains, a goodly distance; far enough away to discourage visits from Greenwood.

After a few hours, we halted. They took us out two at a time to answer the call of Nature. Me and Donald were taken out together. At least, Donald was housebroken. Most of the time anyway. I talked to Donald and he sort of howled. I howled back and he laughed.

Cameron was housebroken, but they wouldn't let him out of the van. "You're the escape artist. We got orders to keep you in."

"I can hardly walk in these cuffs," protested Cameron. "How can I run away? I got to go bad!"

Cameron Westcott, Cat Burglar and Escape Artist
"Keep him shackled until you reach Naghallah. This kid is a calamity."

At last, Mr. Matthews, who seemed the most decent of the Masters, took Cameron out. "Too late," said Cameron sadly.

THE DEVIL'S SWAMP

For lunch, they gave us chocolate milk and peanut butter sandwiches. They tasted kind of stale to me. But the welfare kids consumed them eagerly. Like Dad said, Jaymie Larrabie is a spoiled brat.

We rode on for a couple of hours. The eight-lane highway changed to six, then to four and the four to two. All the while, Cameron had to sit on the floor in handcuffs and leg-cuffs. He complained about them being too tight, to no avail. Cameron begged for a cigarette, but didn't get one. Mockingly, the Masters bugged him and blew smoke in his face.

Finally, we reached Mountainville, the last town before *Naghallah*. Here, they took us to an Eaterie. Cameron, still in shackles, was left behind.

"I won't run away," he pleaded. "I swear I won't! I got no place to run up here." But the orders were to keep Cameron cuffed up in the van until we reached the school. "Quit yammering, will you! We'll bring you something back."

I had some money on me, and I bought Cameron a soda and a sandwich. Which was fortunate, because the Masters forgot about him.

We picked up another passenger in Mountainville. Somebody important. Captain Vedemore or Doctor Vedemore. He was a scientist and did experiments for Karl Hasserman. I wondered if he would do any experiments on us. Vedemore did look a bit like a mad scientist. All dressed in fur and with a wild-looking beard.

The Captain or Doctor took up enough room for two people. Jody and Brandon were put on the floor to make room for him.

We started up and turned onto a rough dirt road, winding between mounds of snow and ice on either side. We were going now into the deep forest, with endless rows of huge oaks and pines, gigantic boulders and clusters of silver birches. There was no sign here of any human habitation, except for the telephone wire strung next to the road. The light was growing dim.

Now the road turned and wound around a large hollow. Here, a black swampland was now masked by heavy layers of ice. The ice stared up like a thousand ghostly faces, extending as far as the eye could see. The van slowed down and then stopped.

"Take a good look," said Striker. "This is *The Devil's Swamp.*" Not long ago, a mass murderer had dropped his victims in here. Their bodies were sucked in and no trace of them was ever seen again.

The Master paused to see if we were all suitably impressed. "We put snotty, trouble-making kids in here too. They won't be seen again either."

Cameron said, "I hope you're kidding, sir."

"We don't kid around at *Kaah Naghallah.* This is not a joke. It's a warning. Most of you wouldn't be missed."

The guys all looked scared, except Donald with his yellow eyes and big-mouth Jaymie. I figured this bullshit was part of what the grown-ups called our "training and treatment". That's the trouble with being a "Gifted Child" instead of a street kid. You learn to put too much trust in grown-ups.

THE SCHOOL OF LAST RESORT

Soon afterwards, the dirt road ended. We turned onto another road with a tarred surface. Here, a metal sign warned:

Private Road
Trespassers Will Be Prosecuted

Here was the beginning of K. H.'s private domain. The rest belonged to a lumber company, owned by — K. H. of course.

We completed the ride in the twilight of late winter. The landscape was unchanged. Vast forests, studded with cliffs and boulders. A primeval wilderness. Except for those wires strung on poles, there was no sign of civilization.

Twenty-eight miles from Mountainville, we reached a high chain-linked fence. They had to open up a gate to let us enter. Inside, was a *Gate house* where we dropped off the security guards. Here, for the first time, we met "Colonel" Lammington. Everyone, it seemed, had a military title. Colonel Lammington was a member of Karl Hasserman's inner circle. Almost but not quite as important as Mr. Bartlow.

He counted us like a cattle dealer taking inventory. "Ten boys? What happened to the other two?"

"What do you mean? We got all ten of them."

"There were supposed to be twelve."

"There were two stupid little punks who ran away. They'll ship them up here, if they find them."

"We don't need them. Ten is enough to start with. Which two are the Larrabie boys?"

"The two with the blue sweaters. They're the only pay kids. The rest were all sent by the Juvenile Court."

Lammington surveyed us disdainfully. "A messy-looking bunch. I guess you can't expect much."

Jaymie was the only one who heard them talk. I got sharp ears.

The outer fence was about ten feet in height, topped with barbed wire. It ran on either side of the gate as far as the eye could see. Brother Danny surveyed the fence critically. "Easy to climb over, if we wanted to break out."

"Maybe it's electrified," said Keith.

Cameron said, "I don't think they're worried about keeping us *in*. I think that fence is there to keep something *out*."

The whole place looked like a fortified military compound under siege. A number of cottages were ranged in rows between watch towers. From the towers, powerful searchlights stabbed out into the darkness. The fence, we found out, ran all around the property and the towers had weapons.

Fancier bungalows were ranged in an inner circle. Here, the more important people stayed. Beyond, was a long white structure: The Administration Building. This is where the school was. Boys' dormitory on the third floor. Here was "The School of Last Resort", the *Kaah Naghallah Institute for the Training and Treatment of Delinquent and Disturbed Youth*. Also, the *Institute for Research on Juvenile Behavior*. All headed by that noted psychologist, Dr. Mortimer Mehary, and endowed by the philanthropist, Karl Hasserman.

Further back, on a high hill, was a red brick structure with white stone columns. *The mansion*. The dwelling place of the tycoon himself. It looked awful big. More like a museum.

"All right, boys, Get out!" At long last, they took the cuffs off Cameron.

"Pick up your stuff!"

I went to get the drums with the money taped inside. But they were missing. So was all our camping and sports equipment. They must have ripped it off at the gate house. I yelled about it.

Captain Striker grew very angry. Or pretended to be. "Are you trying to say we robbed you, punk?"

I looked at Danny. He signalled me to *Shut up*.

"No, sir," said Jaymie.

Danny just laughed. "You'll learn, Gifted Child."

Anyway, they forgot to steal the guitar.

On the third floor was a long room with a single heavy door. Here were twelve cots ranged in a row; two apparently intended for the missing runaways. On the right, was the lavatory. On the left, was a corridor lined with shelves, closets and storage space. This was to be the home of the Naghallah boys.

I noticed there was no lock on our side of the door, but a heavy bolt in the hall. The windows had steel frames and cross-bars. You couldn't climb in and out, like Danny did at home. Our dormitory could readily be turned into a prison cell.

THIS IS A REFORM SCHOOL NOT A HOTEL

In the lavatory, was a row of four toilets. All of them had signs taped on:

Out Of Order
Do Not Use

I tried one anyway and it worked. This was, I remembered, the *Institute for the Study of Juvenile Behavior*, where, as Keith said, "They experamet on kids". Maybe this was one of the "experamets." Hopefully, all the others would be equally silly and harmless. They must have forgot that some of us couldn't read.

I felt crummy and would have liked a hot bath. No baths here. There were three showers, but these really didn't work. No warm water. No soap. Just a trickle of cold water. Like the other guys, I skipped a shower and slept in my clothes.

No pillows. No sheets. And a sagging, lumpy mattress. But what did you expect, Jaymie? This is a reform school, not a hotel. You are an inmate, not an honored guest. The dorm was awful cold, too. But at least they gave us plenty of warm blankets.

Donald shrank away from the others and took the cot at the end. I chose the cot next to him. I howled and he howled back and we both laughed.

Brandon didn't choose a bed. He stood around looking scared and lost. Then Raymond called out, "Hey, Bran Bran! Want to bunk with me and Bobby?" Brandon smiled and came over.

Young Jody fell asleep with his shoes on. Cameron took his shoes off and pulled the blankets over him.

Donald's yellow eyes spied the guitar. To my surprise, he grabbed it. Rocking back and forth, be began strumming notes and chords. The notes became melodies. Just fragments that began in the middle and stopped before the end. Nothing I had ever heard before. When he stopped, I tried to take the guitar back. Donald clung to it. Danny called, "Let him keep it, Gifted Child. He plays better than you do."

"Captain" Craig, the night officer, came in suddenly and silently. "Lights out in five minutes, lads!" He counted our number. All ten here. They were always counting us or calling the roll, like we were dangerous prisoners who, they feared, might escape.

Outside, the wind was howling and the snow was heavy. I turned and twisted uncomfortably, unable to sleep; wishing I was in my bed back home. *This is what you asked for, Jaymie.* Like my old nurse, Miss Ferris said, "You made your bed. Now you got to lie in it."

February 21

"Captain" Vedemore, also known as Dr. Vedemore, was an important man. He was Karl Hasserman's scientific adviser and an engineer. You wouldn't think he would bother with the likes of us. But everyone seemed rather curious about us and took turns pushing us around.

Vedemore routed us up out of bed early in the morning. "Get up, you guys! Line up for inspection!"

We tumbled wearily out of bed. I didn't think Donald could understand the command. But Donald had learned to copy what the other boys did. When we marched, he marched. When we sat, he sat. When we were writing, working or exercising, he imitated us.

Nine guys lined up sleepily. Bobby Alliconda rolled over and closed his eyes again.

"You there, boy! I told you to get up!" The Master grabbed Bobby's long, tangled hair and pulled him roughly out of bed. Bobby yawned. Vedemore shook him. "What's your name, boy? Answer me!"

Bobby replied with a dirty word in Spanish. Unfortunately, Vedemore understood Spanish. He smacked Bobby.

"You're a real smart ass kid, aren't you? You know what we do to smart ass kids here?"

Bobby didn't. "You'll find out, boy. You'll find out!"

He thrust Bobby aside. "What do you sleep in your dirty clothes for? Why don't you wash, boy? *Comprende, muchacho?* Didn't they teach you to wash in that Youth Shelter?"

Bobby didn't answer. "Sir," interrupted Jaymie. "There's no hot water and no soap."

He turned on me. "I didn't ask your opinion, boy. You don't speak here unless you're told to speak."

He added, "This is a training school, not a vacation camp. You make do with what we give you. If you want any privileges, you have to earn them."

"Soap isn't a privilege —" I started to say. But Danny punched me. Instead, I said, "It's awful cold here. Could we get some heat?"

"It's warm enough," said Vedemore, who had a fur-lined jacket on. "Do you have anything else to whine about?"

"No, sir."

He then departed. At least I diverted him from Bobby. I guess I made the Masters' *Shit List,* as Danny called it. But I made a friend of Bobby Alliconda.

And what a surprise! Next day, we got both soap and hot water. We got bundles of clean clothes, too. Too small for the big boys and too large for Jody.

THE DIRECTOR OF KAAH NAGHALLAH

We had gruel for breakfast. That was the standard meal. Gruel for breakfast, hash or mush for lunch or supper and some powdered, condensed or dehydrated stuff for the third meal. It looked like we were guinea pigs to test how cheaply boys could be fed. The Masters and the staff ate well. It should have been easier to feed us their leftovers. Instead, they went to extra trouble to feed us something shitty. That was part of our *training and treatment.* We got the bare necessities. Anything else we "had to earn."

Nobody complained about the food, knowing it wouldn't do any good. This disappointed the Masters who were all set to give the complainer his comeuppance.

Even the gruel was in short supply. The cooks were two German ladies and Brandon spoke to them in German. He came back with a second portion of gruel for all of us and extra sugar and milk.

They put us to work cleaning and mopping. First our own quarters. Then the halls and other rooms. Mr. Matthews was supervising us. We learned he was rather a softy. Bobby and Stevie threw water at each other. Brandon went sliding down the bannisters. Keith and Raymond wrestled and Danny and Cameron fought a duel with mop and broom. But Mr. Matthews gave them no more than a mild rebuke.

"I'm going to write your name down and report you to Dr. Mehary." After a while, he had everyone's name down, excepting Jody, Jaymie and Donald. Young Jody was weeping as he scrubbed. Donald stood around holding a broom, but not doing anything. Jaymie was actually cleaning. It was less boring to do a good job than a lousy one.

Cameron said, "Don't work so hard, Jaymie. You're making the rest of us look shitty." I slowed down. I didn't want to get Cameron mad at me.

At the end, Mr. Matthews said he *wouldn't* report us to Mehary. "I'll give you all another chance."

In the late afternoon, we met the Director himself. I had

imagined him as a large, powerful man. But Mehary was dumpy looking and hardly bigger than me. His heavy horn-rimmed glasses made him look like an owl.

We were lined up in the hall, outside his office. Klayborne and Striker stood on either side of the line. Klayborne bellowed, "Stand at attention! Put your shoulders back! Brace!" He glared at our ragged assembly. "You there, punk! Take your hands out of your pockets. What's your name?"

"Cameron Westcott."

"You say *Sir* when you address a Master."

"How do I know who's a Master?"

"To be on the safe side, just say *Sir* to everybody. Yes, *Everybody!*"

"Does that include the ladies in the kitchen?"

"Don't be a wise guy!" Klayborne thundered. "We have ways of dealing with wise guys here. Now, what's your name, boy?"

"Cameron Westcott, *Sir.*" A confrontation was avoided.

Now, Dr. Mehary made his appearance. "These are the boys, Doctor."

Mehary observed us critically, as if to say *What a crummy bunch. They gave us the bottom of the barrel.* He read from a typewritten list. "*Alliconda, Robert.*"

"Here, sir."

"*Caldwell, Keith.*"

"Here, sir."

"*Kallinger, Jody.* Answer will you, boy! Stop snivelling! What's the matter with you?" Jody just stood there looking miserable.

"Here, sir," Keith answered for Jody.

Larrabie, Daniel.... Larrabie, Jaymie.... Ridgeway, Raymond.... Scanlon, Steven.... Down to *Turrentine, Donald.*

Dead silence. "That's the dummy," explained Striker. "He's the one who doesn't talk."

"He will learn to talk," said Mehary, sharply. "*Turrentine, Donald!*" he thundered.

"Here!" called Cameron, Bobby and Stevie all at once. Donald's wooden face changed like he was smiling a little.

They kept us standing around while we were called into Dr. Mehary's office, one at a time. He was nasty. Every guy except Donald got a piece of abuse. Donald went in wooden-faced and came out the same way, as if he couldn't understand what was happening. His clothing was messed up. Dr. Mehary had shaken him to no avail.

Not only Jody but Brandon came out bawling. Raymond and Danny came out angry, muttering silent curses. Keith and Bobby were shaken and red with shame. Cameron, who was in the longest, just looked relieved that it was over. Only Jaymie came out smiling.

Mehary looked at his records. *"Larrabie Jaymie?"*

"Yessir."

"You were committed here by your father because you were incorrigible and disobedient?"

"Yessir."

"You smashed furniture and refused to go to school?"

"Yessir."

"You used vile and filthy language?"

"Yessir."

"You threatened your father and threatened to disgrace the family?"

"Yessir."

"At the same time, *Larrabie Jaymie,* unlike any of the other boys, you received very good marks in school. You were an honor student in the Gifted Child class?"

"Yessir."

"Is that all you have to say, *Larrabie Jaymie?"*

"Yessir."

"Don't you have any sense of shame, *Larrabie Jaymie?* Any remorse or regret for your despicable conduct?"

"No, sir."

"Just what is it, *Larrabie Jaymie.* You can't be stupid. Is there something wrong with your brain?"

"Yessir."

He smacked me on the head.

"Are you psycho, *Larrabie Jaymie?* Are you a pathological case?" (More smacks.)

"Yessir."

"That's all. *Get out of here!*"
I decided I didn't like Dr. Mehary. But I had annoyed him more than he had annoyed me.

LYANDRA

At last, we met somebody real nice at *Kaah Naghallah*. The school nurse. Her name was Lyandra and that's what she told us to call her. She measured our heart and our blood pressure and found us all healthy. "Has anybody got any ailment?"

Nobody had anything real. But the guys all complained so they would get some attention. Lyandra looked tenderly at Donald, who had no ailments. At least he couldn't talk about any.

Brother Danny said he could really go for Lyandra. Cameron thought he had made a hit with her, although Lyandra was at least twelve years older than him. Stevie and Keith were both smitten. Everyone wondered why such a lovely lady would come to this desolated place.

Lyandra lived in the mansion. Her main job was looking after Karl Hasserman, the mysterious tycoon who owned *Kaah Naghallah*.

"What is K. H. like?" we asked her.

"He's a very unusual man," is all Lyandra would tell us.

HOWL AT THE MOON

I thought at first Dr. Mehary was a phony psychologist. We found out later he had written a lot of highfalutin books about Juvenile Behavior. What he did with us was what he called *Confrontation Therapy*. The idea was to shake a kid up and tear him down, so he would crack and spill his insides. Then you could find out what really ailed him.

First, you had to split a guy apart. You had to give him a shock or a couple of shocks. Then you could put him together again *correctly*. That was Mehary's cure for any juvenile mental ailment from autism to schizophrenia to drug addiction to juvenile delinquency. At least there was some reason for what he did, besides being nasty.

Mehary also wrote a book on *Victimology*. Most victims, he contended, sort of triggered their own abuse. The victim caused the bully, rather than the other way around. By acting frightened, the victim made the bully feel frightened. By attacking the victim, the bully felt his power and overcame his fears.

Mehary made a list of the Naghallah boys and divided them into bully and victim types. The older boys, including Danny, were all labelled "*bullies*". Brandon and Jaymie were "submissive-masochistic" personalities, inclined toward victimhood. Jody Kallinger was the *pure victim* type.

Jody was really acting like a victim, He was so miserable, he made everyone else feel lousy. Jody couldn't just weep quietly. He had to bawl out loud.

Very often in the world things that are good in the beginning change to bad. That seems to happen all the time in History. But here was one time when something *bad* changed to *good.*

The bad thing was we bullied Jody. We didn't do anything terrible. But we held him down and spilled a bucket of water down his pants leg. Then we did it again on the other leg.

Jody just lay on the floor like he was wounded. He

looked so hurt and helpless the guys had to figure out some excuse for what they had done. So Cameron said, "That's your initiation, punk. You have just been initiated into the Coyote youth gang. You are now a Coyote cub, Fifth Class, and can howl at the moon."

The guys all laughed like it was very funny. Jody just lay on the floor, all soaked. Then someone yelled, "Hey, guys, let's get Brandon!" And Brandon got soaked, too.

Then Danny yelled. "Hey, get Jaymie! Get the Gifted Child!" And the boys grabbed Jaymie and soaked him.

Then they got Bobby Alliconda. Each time, Cameron gave that spiel on how the victim was now initiated into the Coyote Pack, and could howl at the moon.

Then Stevie yelled, "Hey, let's get Keith! Put Keith in the Coyotes!"

Jaymie said, "You can't initiate nobody into the Coyotes."

"Why not?"

"Because you ain't a Coyote. Only me, Bran, Bobby and Jody are Coyotes. We've been initiated. You guys are too chicken to take the initiation."

"Who's chicken?" demanded Stevie. "You think I'm afraid of a little cold water? Go ahead! Initiate me!"

We initiated Stevie. Then Cameron and Danny had to let themselves get initiated, too. And Keith and Raymond. All the guys got the two-bucket water treatment.

We were nine wet Coyotes. And now that everybody had gotten their lumps, young Jody stopped looking miserable and began to giggle.

Donald just sat there watching. Nobody touched him or paid any attention to him. Donald looked sad. So Jaymie yelled, "Let's get Don Don. Make him a Coyote, too!"

The guys grabbed Don Don and poured two buckets of water down his trouser legs. Don Don didn't resist at all. He smiled a bit, like he wanted it. The guys cheered. "Y-a-a-a-y, Don Don! He's a Coyote!"

Donald tried to speak, but couldn't quite do it. It came out an animal howl. The guys all howled back. From now on, that would be *The Cry of the Coyotes*.

THE COYOTE BROTHERHOOD

Now that we had all been initiated into a youth gang, we decided we might as well have a gang. Thus was born *The Brotherhood of the Coyote Pack*.

We elected Cameron *Gangleader and Commander-in-Chief*. Stevie was elected *Deputy Gangleader* and Danny, *Adjutant*. Brandon, with a connection in the kitchen was named *Quartermaster*. Keith, *Chief of Intelligence*.

Jaymie was named *Recorder of the Sacred Scrolls* of the Coyote Tribe. That was a fancy name for secretary. The *Scrolls* were really a notebook.

Raymond was chosen *Guardian of the Treasure of the Coyotes*. Alas, we had no treasure to be guarded and no funds at all. Jaymie, however, had three silver dollars that my father once gave me, which the Masters hadn't had a chance to rip off. I gave these to Raymond as the Coyote treasure.

Donald, with the guitar, was named *Musician*. Bobby Alliconda was named *Mechanic and Trouble Shooter*. ("You mean *Trouble-maker*, don't you?" asked Bobby.)

Jody wanted to be a drummer boy. We had no drum, but we got him a pot and spoon to bang out signals. *Bang! Bang! Bang!* Three long bangs, repeated three times meant *Danger! Our Enemies are coming!*

Bang-ity Bang! Bang-ity Bang! A long, two shorts and a long bang was the call for a Gang meeting. *High Council. Everybody come!* Cameron said these were the signal calls of the Chippewa Indians. I think he just made them up.

Anyway, we made Jody *Communication Officer of the Coyote Pack* and he was pleased. No more weeping.

Then Danny said, "Let Jaymie write an oath and we'll all swear it. Write something, Gifted Child, and make it good!"

Jaymie wrote:

We hereby pledge eternal loyalty to the Coyote Brotherhood. To stand together against all threats and perils, come what may. The enemies of any brother shall be the enemies of all brothers. The Good of one shall be the Good of all.

We shall guard and defend each other and help each other with all our will and might and power. Our bond shall be unbreakable and everlasting. No terror or torture shall make us reveal the secrets of the Coyotes.

We swear this by our heart and life and soul. Now, Always and Forever.

The guys all liked it, even though they didn't understand the fancy language. And they all swore it.

Then Cameron made a secret mark which would be the sign of the Coyote Brotherhood. *The Shell and the Arrow.*

The shell and the arrow. The secret mark of the Coyotes.

FORBIDDEN SECRETS

Next day, we were cleaning and scrubbing down in the cellar. There were many locked doors here and many passageways. There was a stairway down to the sub-basement and another down to the under-sub-basement. It would have been a lot of fun exploring the place. But we were given strict orders to stay together and only go where we were told to go. "Don't go wandering off. It might be dangerous."

They didn't tell us why, but Keith asked.

"Dungeons," said Captain Striker. "That's where we put snotty kids who get too nosy. Do you still want to go down and look, punk?"

"Some other time, sir," said Keith and they both laughed. Some joke!

The grown-ups insisted Brandon had never been kidnapped from Germany. But he did speak German remarkably well. He made quite a hit with the two German cooks, Fräulein Minnie and Fräulein Johanna. They hadn't wanted any *Lausbuben* messing around in their kitchen. But Brandon was *ein guter Knabe;* a fine boy, not a nuisance. Accordingly, Brandon was drafted as a kitchen helper.

That was a big break for the Naghallah boys. Brandon could act convincingly stupid and accidentally on purpose bring us some of the food intended for the Masters and Staff. He also managed to smuggle snacks inside his shirt. Fräulein Johanna yelled at him and called him a *Dummkopf,* but she never reported him.

On Sunday, we had pancakes instead of gruel. When Dr. Mehary, who stuck his nose into everything, objected, Johanna told him, "We had a lot of batter left over. I gave it to the *Knaben,* instead of throwing it out." Mehary didn't notice Brandon had smuggled us a whole jug of maple syrup.

I wondered if they would have any religious services at *Kaah Naghallah.* There were none. Church goers had to drive twenty-eight miles into Mountainville or listen to the radio preacher.

Karl Hasserman and his people were not Christians, Fräulein Minnie told Brandon. "They have their own *Glaube.*" She added mysteriously, "I have learned not to ask too many questions. It would be well for you to learn the same, Bübschen." And she gave Brandon a curious warning. *"Erzähl deine Freunde das Maul zu halten. Die Wande haben Ohren."*

This, Brandon translated as, "She said to keep our fucking mouths shut. The walls have ears."

THE RUNAWAYS

February 24

Sunday night, the two empty cots in the dorm were filled. Major Powell thrust in two little kids. One looked even younger than Jody; the other was about like Jaymie.

They both seemed awful scared. Real terrified. It was hard to figure out why. There was nothing in our dormitory to be scared of. Then we found out they were terrified of *us.*

That Major Powell was mean. He and Striker picked the boys up at the Willow Creek police station. They kept telling the kids how cruel and brutal the Naghallah boys were. How they tormented and bullied little kids and did all kinds of nasty things.

The oldest kid was Troy, the other, Roger. They had been together in the same foster home. Their guardians dumped them and no one else wanted them. The *Kaah Naghallah School* offered to take them off the welfare rolls.

Troy and Roger didn't want to go to *Naghallah.* They ran away and stole a motor bike. But they had no money and very little gas so they got caught. They half froze, too.

Powell kept scaring the kids about how the mean, brutal Naghallah boys would abuse them. "We're going to lock you in with them and no matter what they do to you and how much you yell, we ain't gonna rescue you." By the time they reached the school, Troy and Roger were all shaky. They begged not to be locked in with us. Powell said whatever we did to them would serve them right for running away and causing so much trouble.

Gangleader Cameron interviewed the new boys. "Hey, kid. Come here!"

The kid was trembling.

"What's your name?"

"Troy Feroldi, sir."

"Don't call me *sir*. I'm a boy. The name is Cameron."

"Yes, Mr. Cameron."

"I ain't a mister, I'm a kid. Who's he?"

"That's my partner, sir. His name is Roger Newland."

"I'll kick your ass if you call me *sir* again. What are you guys shaking about?"

Roger just stood there with his mouth open. Troy stammered, "We're not shaking, sir."

Cameron kicked him lightly. "We got two empty beds over there. I guess they're yours and Roger's. Meet the guys — Bobby — Bran — Steve — Ray Ray — Keith — Danny — Jaymie — Donald — and Jody."

Troy and Roger looked like they had just been introduced to nine man-eating tigers.

Cameron smiled. "Did you ever hear of the Coyote youth gang?"

Troy and Roger stood there cringing, as if expecting the Coyotes to pounce on them.

"Do you know who the leader of this gallant band is?"

"Is it you, sir? I mean Cameron."

"Good guess, Master Feroldi. How would you like to be a Coyote?"

Troy looked surprised. "Do I have to?"

"No, but you're living in the Coyotes' den. You'll be a lot happier if you're one of us."

"What do you have to do to be a Coyote?"

"You get initiated. You take the oath. And you do three noble deeds. But the noble deeds can wait. None of us has done any yet either."

"Will it hurt?" asked Roger, anxiously.

We become twelve.

Troy and Roger meet the "mean, brutal Naghallah boys."

"The initiation? Are you chicken, Master Newland? The Coyotes laugh at suffering and hardship."

"It don't hurt," broke in Bobby. "All they do is spill water down your pants leg."

"Brother Alliconda! You are revealing the secrets of the Coyotes!"

"Well, they're going to be members anyway —"

"Blindfold the candidates! Get the bucket and funnel!"

Thereafter, first Troy, then Roger, received the Coyote ablution. It was so much less than the kids expected, they were both laughing.

"Now take ye the oath!" Troy and Roger took the oath.

"Now, kneel ye down!" Troy and Roger kneeled down.

Cameron gave them each a punch on the shoulder. "You are now a member of the Coyote youth gang. You have nothing to fear, now or ever. You have eleven brothers to defend you and answer your call for help.

"The Coyotes against the world!"

The guys all cheered. "A cheer for our new brothers! Y-a-a-a-y, Roger! Y-a-a-a-y, Troy!"

Troy and Roger looked bewildered. They couldn't believe these bad, cruel boys they had feared so much were now their friends.

*   *   *   *   *   *   *

We had to find an office for our new members. We made Troy *Supply Sergeant,* Brandon's assistant. And Roger was voted *Sergeant-at-Arms.*

"What does he do?"

"He has to keep order in a gang meeting. If any guy starts fooling around and acting disruptive, you have to beat him up and throw him out of the meeting."

"Anybody?" asked Roger, dubiously.

"Anybody," said Cameron. "Including me. If any guy messes around, give him the bums' rush."

That was really a joke. For Roger was the smallest kid in our gang.

The next day, we were working in the cellar again. We carried up firewood and vast amounts of trash and rubbish. Old George, Karl Hasserman's caretaker, was fixing the pipes. Striker said, "Watch these kids, will you." And left him in charge of us.

Old George was an easy-going guy and paid no attention when we fooled around. He took the trouble to show Donald how to sweep and clean and carry things. "Donald work!" said Don Don, proudly.

Troy was a dope. He was scared of a lot of harmless things like shadows or noises in the night. But he wasn't scared of the things he should have feared. Like going down the stairs into the Under-sub-basement.

Old George yelled at him. "Stay out of there, son! Anyone who goes down there may not come back."

"What is down there?" asked Troy, curiously.

Old George stared at Troy through his green, tinted glasses. "Let's hope you never find out, son."

NAGHALLAH SCHOOL DAYS

Up to now, Cameron had been a lone wolf. But he was a natural leader. He knew how to draw us together. Perhaps because Cameron could make a joke out of anything and make us laugh, even when things got rough. Or perhaps because he made each of us feel we counted.

Little Jody was no longer frightened. Overnight, Cameron had become the protecting father or big brother he had never known. "Can I put my bed next to you, Cameron?"

"Go ahead."

"I get scared at night. About things coming in the window to grab me."

"Well, I'm right next to you. Nothing's going to grab you."

Jody hero-worshipped Cameron. "I wish I had you for a brother."

"You have. I am your brother."

Jody woke Cameron up in the middle of the night. "I got to go —"

"Well, go ahead!"

"I'm afraid to go alone. Come with me, Cameron. Please!"

Wearily, Cameron stumbled out of bed and walked with Jody. What a difference it makes to have somebody need you!

Some psychiatrist had said Cameron was a psychopath with no sense of right and wrong; a guy who cared only for himself. That must have hurt Cameron, because he kept remembering it. "Is that true, *Gifted Child?*" he asked me. When you once get a name, it sticks to you.

"Of course not. Some jerks like to run people down to make themselves important."

"What am I really, *Gifted Child?*"

"You're a Gifted Child yourself," said me. "A great guy and a gallant leader of youth."

"Bullshit!" said Cameron. But he was smiling.

March 5

Our school room was at the other end of the hall. There were two rows of six desks, each with a chair attached. There was also a teacher's desk on an elevated platform. The chairs were too small for the big boys, about right for Jody and Roger. All the furniture at Naghallah was too small for most of us. This could hardly be a mistake. More likely, it was part of the Mehary *Training and Treatment,* designed to "cut us down to size" and make us feel lowly and inferior.

It looked like an ordinary school room, lined with blackboards, hung with maps and charts. There were bookshelves, a gigantic globe of the world, a slide projector, school books and a number of yardsticks stacked against the wall. Troy noted nervously they could be used for hitting as well as measuring. "They hurt, too!" Troy had been on the receiving end.

"There's not going to be any hitting in this school," Cameron declared. "The Masters could cream us one at a time. But they'll have a rough time handling the twelve of us, if we stick together.

"When I throw my note book, that means *Riot!*" So ordered Cameron Westcott, Gangleader of the Coyotes.

But nobody got hit. At least not then. Instead, Teacher Matthews gave us a math achievement test. I'm pretty hot at math. But I didn't want to get the guys sore at me. I asked Cameron, "Hey, Gangleader! What kind of a score should I get on the math test, high or low?"

"What are you asking me for, Gifted Child? Get the best mark you can, so they'll know we ain't all dopes."

Dr. Mehary corrected the papers and later announced we were the stupidest class he had ever seen. *Everybody failed!*"

Bobby said, "You flunked, huh, Gifted Child?" Everybody started calling me that.

I couldn't believe I failed and asked Mehary to see the paper. He didn't have it.

"How do you know I flunked then?"

"Because you cheated." He claimed I copied the answers from a paper on Mr. Matthews' desk. He was watching us through a peek-hole.

I sure didn't cheat. I didn't have to. And there never was a test I cared less about getting a high mark on. Dr. Mehary was determined not to give us credit for anything and make us each feel as crummy as possible. He barked, "Did you hear me, Larrabie, Jaymie?" He grabbed me by the shoulders. "You copied the answer sheet! Now didn't you?"

"Yessir. The answer sheet was all wrong though. I had to do the problems all over again."

He released my shoulders. "You think you're real smart? You're real bright in math? What's the cube root of 343?"

"Seven," said Jaymie.

He looked at me quizzically. "How did you get the

answer so fast?"

"I cheated, sir. I copied the answer from the blackboard."

There was nothing written on the blackboard. It had been washed blank.

"You're a wise guy, Larrabie Jaymie. Get out of here!"

From then on, I would never get a correct answer in a math test. I would do the problem right and then, for no reason, divide the answer by three or add 57. Mr. Matthews, who might have been a good teacher if they had left him alone, could never figure it out.

On the Social Studies test, I determined to get as low a mark as possible. You got *plus two* for each right answer and *minus two* for each wrong answer. So just guessing should get you a *Zero*. You really had to know your stuff to get *minus 100,* and get *all fifty* answers wrong.

"My brudder got minus 100!" boasted Danny, like he was real proud of me. Brother Daniel, who was trying to pass, ended up with an ordinary zero.

Dr. Mehary himself gave us a haircut. This was an important part of our "training and treatment" and he couldn't trust anyone else to do it properly.

Adolescent boys, he once wrote, have a *Samson complex.* "They fancy that heavy hair gives them strength." Since his aim was to make us feel weak and worthless, he had to reverse the Samson effect and take our hair away.

Troy and Roger got a complete baldy. That was their comeuppance for the runaway. The rest of us got only a two-thirds baldy. Which, however, looked even stupider than getting shorn completely. Danny and Stevie got a stripe down the middle. Raymond and Cameron got a stripe across. Bobby, who Mehary figured for a wise guy, got it both ways. The rest of us, Jody, Jaymie, Brandon and Keith got shorn just on top like a medieval monk.

Donald kept more hair than anyone else. He wouldn't stay still and kept squirming and jumping around. Donald, Mehary decided, was too backward to have a Samson complex. He was in an infantile state of development.

Mehary also designed the school uniform. Red shirts with long sleeves and bright purple pants that looked like pajamas. You could spot a Naghallah kid in that crazy outfit a mile away. Floppy yellow shoes, too.

If they aimed to make us feel small and shitty, it didn't work. After a while, we got to like our crazy outfit. It became the uniform of the Coyote Brotherhood.

THE LOCK-IN

Maybe they lost a great general when they threw Cameron Westcott out of military school. Cameron was a grand strategist. *Feint one way. Hit 'em another.*

Like I said before, we were locked in at night. Our dormitory door was heavily bolted — from the outside. "Brother Jaymie," commanded Cameron. "You will go to Dr. Mehary and complain about it."

"Complaining won't do any good," said me. "Why do it?"

"Gangleader's orders."

"Why me though?" I didn't particularly relish the assignment. Doctor Mehary could be awful sarcastic.

"You're the best talker. You won't go in alone. We'll all go with you."

Mehary cut me short. "Of course, you're locked in at night. That's to keep you where you belong."

"Are we students in a school?" demanded Jaymie. "Or inmates in a prison?"

"This is a reform school," declared Mehary. "You are inmates, not students. You're a bunch of juvenile thugs and we don't trust you any further than we'd trust a pack of rats."

"Suppose there's a fire, sir? And we are locked in?"

"There won't be any fire unless you boys start one. We're going to keep you under control, where we can handle you. *Now get out of here!* Go to your room. *That will be all!*"

Jaymie walked back sullenly. Cameron put his arm on my shoulder. "Nice complaining, Jaymie."

"A lot of good it did."

"You were perfect. Real good acting. Walking out mad like that."

"I wasn't acting."

"Now they won't suspect —" I looked at him curiously.

Cameron grinned. "I'm the Cat Burglar, remember. That old lock and that rattle-trap window wouldn't hold me five minutes, if I wanted to break out."

But Cameron had no plans for a runaway. "We couldn't just leave the little kids. We'd have to take the whole gang with us. We got warm beds now. And we're eating better, thanks to Brother Brandon. Things would have to get a lot shittier than they are now, before I'd go for a break-out. But we might want to scout around this place and case the joint. Like the Boy Scouts say: *Be Prepared.*"

"Were you ever a Boy Scout?"

"Cub Scout," said Cameron. "Den number *Three* in the Church. And you know something, Jaymie? That's about the only thing I didn't get kicked out of."

"You didn't get kicked out of the Coyotes," said young Jody, reassuringly.

A MESSAGE FROM HOME

March 9

A pair of letters arrived from Mother who had fortunately recovered. Both of them had been opened and re-sealed. Well, why not? Reform school kids like us could hardly expect our mail to be private.

First Letter: Dear Jaymie and Dear Daniel. How do you like the school? I am sure you will like it, if you give it a chance. Etc.

Second Letter: If you like the school and want to stay, could you boys please write some letters. *(It seemed Mitch had been getting a lot of flak from friends and relatives for sending his sons to "that outlandish school.")* Tell them you are happy at Naghallah and the people treat you boys well. If they do. I do hope they do!

There followed a list:

Cousin Katie Weisman and Cousin Michael in the hometown of Greenwood, who were offended because me and Danny didn't say *Goodbye* to them.

Our neighbors, the Meyers, who were offended because Marjie Meyer sent Danny her picture in a ballet costume and the school people sent it back with a rude letter that *the boys could not receive such unwholesome trash.* "I sure would have liked to see that picture!" said Danny.

Uncle Oscar and Aunt Rosa in California who said the Naghallah school was (several lines here were whitened out).

Uncle Leon and Aunt Laura in New York who said the school was run by (More lines whitened out).

Dr. Weinberger back in the Hometown of Greenwood who said he heard (Mind you, I don't believe this, boys. It can't be true. Mitch assures me that it isn't true.) But the Doctor heard--- (Here, a whole page of the letter was missing.)

Please write, Boys! Or at least Jaymie, write and get Danny to sign the letter, too.

P.S. *With love from Dad. Please do it for Mother's sake.*

The whole thing was really comical. Especially the part about Marjie Meyer in her ballet costume being mistaken for a street walker. I was going to tell my parents to "go jump in the lake!" Or not answer it at all. But if I didn't tell them I liked *Naghallah*, they might come up and take me home. With or without Danny.

I was beginning to feel excited about *Kaah Naghallah*. I really meant that stuff we put in the oath and wanted to stay here with the guys. Something big was going to happen here. We were on the threshhold of a great adventure. But whether for good or ill, it was too soon to tell.

So I wrote the letters on what a swell place Naghallah school was and how much we liked the other students. Me and Danny couldn't get ourselves to praise the Masters. But we didn't knock them. So there was nothing in the letters to make them mad.

SHADOWS OF THE FUTURE

March 13

Winter made a comeback with a twenty inch blizzard. They put us to work outside now. Snow shovelling, ice chopping, spreading sand, stacking firewood and especially moving the garbage around.

"We can't move the garbage, sir. It's frozen."

"Well, loosen it up, boy! Use your muscle!"

Karl Hasserman had snowblowers and all kinds of equipment to clear the more important roads and driveways. But the unimportant paths were left to us. It was hard work and rough. But I'll have to admit they gave us warm gloves and clothing. They even let Brandon bring us buckets of hot soup and cocoa. *"Strict discipline"* didn't mean freezing us.

"No sugar in that cocoa! That's not a treat. That's just to keep the boys warm." But Brandon dumped the sugar in accidentally on purpose like he always managed to do. Along with some cake intended for Karl Hasserman.

Nobody enjoyed standing around and supervising us. That job fell mostly on Guardian Craig, one of the least important of the Masters.

"Captain" Craig wasn't a bad guy. He accepted with thanks a cup of illicit cocoa and a purloined cake. If Jody and Roger made snowmen, instead of clearing the sidewalk; or if the big boys threw snowballs instead of toting the garbage, Craig looked the other way. He even laughed when a snowball hit him by accident and threw one back.

Still, you had to be careful. Maybe that friendly stuff was just a put-on. As Cameron says, *Never trust anyone over twenty.*

At *Kaah Naghallah*, we would always get to bed early. After supper, we got sent to our room. The Masters, I guess, sighed with relief. "Well, we got rid of those punks for the night."

No TV, of course, or radio or games or playthings. "The boys haven't earned any recreation." But we made up our own. A sneaker and two scrapbaskets became a basketball court. A tight bundle of clothes became a football. And instead of batting a baseball, we would throw a rolled up pair of socks.

Sometimes, the games would become too wild and noisy and the Masters would break in. "Just what do you think you're doing? Tearing the house apart?"

Silence.

"I guess we didn't work them hard enough. They still have too much energy."

"Tomorrow, we'll wear them out."

Then a look at Jody and Roger. "Are the big boys hurting you?"

"No, sir. We were only playing."

"Maybe those two young kids want a room by themselves?"

"No, sir. Please! We want to stay here!"

This always surprised the Masters, who expected the little boys to be tormented and abused.

Almost every night, we held a gang meeting. *Bang-ity Bang!* went Jody. "Hear ye! Hear ye!" called Cameron. "The punks of the Coyote Pack will now assemble.

"Recorder, *(That was Jaymie)* call the roll!"

Keith objected. "What do we have to call the roll for? We can count, can't we? We got twelve guys in the Coyotes and twelve guys here."

"You're out of order, Brother Keith. You ain't recognized!"

Calling the roll was a kind of ritual. It gave us a warm, cozy feeling that we were all here together. Outside, things were dark, cold and creepy. But here, things were warm and good. Danny was sure there were wiretaps in the room. The Guardians of Naghallah were watching us and knew everything we said or did. But we didn't care. We were confined in a place that was a cross between a boarding school dormitory and a prison cell. We called it *The Coyotes' Den.* It was begining to seem like home.

Jaymie called the roll. *Bobby Alliconda... Keith Caldwell... Troy Feroldi... All, Here... Jody Kallinger.* Jody was too shy to answer.

"Jody's missing," announced Cameron, sadly. "Sergeant-at-Arms there's a stuffed dummy here. Throw that stuffed dummy out!"

"Do I have to?" asked Roger, uncertainly.

"Sure. No stuffed dummies allowed in a gang meeting."

"Don't! Please! I'm not a stuffed dummy. I'm Jody."

The guys all cheered. "Y-a-a-a-y! Jody's here!"

Danny Larrabie... Roger Newland... Raymie Ridgeway... Stevie Scanlon...?

"I'm absent!"

"Don't be a clown. We'll dunk you in the shower."

The guys pounced on Stevie. He struggled. "Hey, lay off, will you!"

"Are you absent?"

"Nope. I'm here." And Stevie was released.

Donald Turrentine...?

"Here," called Donald, loudly and clearly and the guys cheered again.

Cameron Westcott...? Brandon Zuchtig...? All Present.

"That completes the roll call," said Jaymie, pompously.

Someone yelled, "Hey, fuckin' Jaymie. Hey, Gifted Child! You forgot to call yourself."

"Sorry. *I'm* here."

Cameron could always think of something to keep a meeting going "Tonight, my classmates, let us all say what we think about this place *Kaah Naghallah.*"

"I heard it was shitty," said Stevie. "But so far it hasn't been as shitty as we expected."

Bobby thought *Kaah Naghallah* was going to be miserable. "So far, it's just been crummy. And not too crummy at that."

"I don't know how long we have to stay here," said Raymond. "If I had to do ten years, I wouldn't jump with joy. But I could take it."

"Jaymie even wrote his folks he likes it here and wants to stay. Why?"

"On account of the Coyotes. I want to stay with you guys."

"We're a crummy bunch of rotten turds. Right?"

"Nope! The Coyotes are the best."

Cameron turned to Troy. "What do *you* think Brother Feroldi? You sure didn't want to come to Naghallah. You and Roger ran away."

Troy didn't want to talk about it. "They might be listening."

"Who?"

"The Guardians. The people who run this place."

We had searched the place for a bug and didn't find one. "I don't think they bother listening. They figure they got us under control."

Troy looked cautiously over both shoulders. Then he shivered a bit. "We heard the Naghallah kids would be used in some experiment."

"What kind of an experiment?"

Troy didn't know. "But it must be something bad. They kidded us and told us it would be a one way trip. That's what they said. *We won't be bothered with them any more.* Right, Roger?"

Roger nodded.

"They said me and Roger wouldn't make very good material."

"For what?"

"For the experiment. Whatever it's gonna be. That's why we tried to run away. We got scared of Naghallah and scared of the boys here. They said you were——"

"You're not scared of us any more?" asked Danny.

"I'm not afraid of the *boys*," said Roger. "They're my friends."

"Maybe you don't have to be scared of the place either."

Something had happened to Troy and Roger, when they

first came to *Kaah Naghallah*. They were taken into a room and Striker wanted to put a collar on them. It was a weird-looking thing, a metal ring with horns and wires and buttons on it that locked around your neck. Maybe electric. And Vedemore said not to put these things on yet. It was too early.

"You mean they're gonna stick electric collars on all of us?"

"They're not gonna put any collar on me!" declared Raymond. He put his hands on Troy's shoulder. "And we won't let them put any collars on *you!*"

That made Troy feel better.

Cameron asked, "What good would it do them to put these metal collars on us? Anybody got an idea?"

I could think of quite a few unpleasant things they could do with the collars to track us down and control us. But I didn't talk. The guys were jittery enough already.

"What'll we do," Keith asked, nervously, "if they start putting collars on us?"

"We'll do what we have to do. Fight back!" said Cameron. "But let's not go off half cocked. They got all the power on their side. First, let's probe and see if we can find a weakness. And if we're going for a break-out, pick a time when it ain't so fucking cold."

"Will the little kids ——?" asked Roger, anxiously.

"Sure, we'll take you! The Coyotes stick together. We all break out or none of us do."

WHIRLING BOY

Most of the time in school, Donald just sat there. Sometimes, he talked to himself real softly. Words that nobody else could understand. When we were supposed to write something, Donald would draw pictures. Weird stuff. Animals with human faces. People with horns and wings. Some of his stuff wasn't bad.

Usually, Teacher Matthews paid no attention to Donald. And he didn't hardly bother with Jody and Roger who couldn't read or write at all. He made them copy the alphabet and copy words out of the lesson book.

Now, Roger was writing *cat, fat, bat, sat* and *hat.* Jody was writing *jug, rug, bug, hug* and *dug.* Brother Danny had his eyes closed and his hands in his pockets. Joke player Raymond made a rubber band sling shot. He shot a paper wad at me and hit Troy.

Mr. Matthews was talking about Columbus and the explorers. Keith gave him an argument. Columbus didn't discover America. The Indians did. Teacher Matthews was pleased that somebody was paying enough attention to contradict him.

Something set Donald off. Maybe it was the red bird just outside the window.Or maybe it was the grey mouse that scurried across the floor.

Suddenly, Donald gave a yell, and leaped out of his chair. Donald swung his arms and spun about like a whirling dervish. Whirling one way, then suddenly reversing, changing course suddenly, he always managed to keep from hitting anything. Now, without missing a step, Donald began throwing off his clothes.

Donald's shoes came off first. Then his shirt. Mr. Matthews cried out in dismay. "Somebody stop him!"

Donald kept whirling. Still dancing gracefully, he threw off his trousers.

"You can never tell what Donald will do." explained Keith. "He's artistic."

"You mean autistic."

The guys were all yelling and clapping. Donald threw off his shorts. Mr. Matthews rushed to the door and latched it, trying at least to keep Donald in the classroom. Donald spun his arms and Teacher Matthews had to duck out of the way. Now Don Don threw off his socks. Still dancing, he tore at the lock trying to open it.

"Please! Stop him!" implored Matthews, fearing for his reputation as a teacher, if Donald got loose.

Now Stevie and Cameron grabbed Donald. They pulled him down onto a green scatter rug. "Okay, Don Don, that was a great show.

"We'll book you in a night club for *The Dance of the Seven Veils*. Whirling Don Don, the Strip Tease Kid."

Donald went limp and made no resistance as the guys put his clothes back on. Then he climbed under the green rug and pulled it over his head. He lay there quiet, all curled up, like an unborn baby inside its mother.

"We'll leave him there," Teacher Matthews ordered. "Thanks, fellers."

Donald stayed like that until school was over. Then he got up and followed us, like he usually did.

SHADOWS OF THE FUTURE II

March 21

It was after *Lights Out*, but we didn't feel sleepy. We gathered around in a circle, in the darkened room.

What a great time for telling scarey ghost stories! Only Brandon told us a real one. . . .

Brandon had become a favorite of the kitchen ladies. "But, they're afraid. They tell me things. Then later they tell me never to repeat them."

We listened eagerly. "There were people here last year," said Brandon. "Not kids. Young men and women. *They disappeared!* Nobody ever saw hide or hair of them again."

"They couldn't just disappear," protested Jaymie. "The cops would come around and look for them."

"They came. The State Troopers thought they had gone hiking in the mountains. They searched for miles and miles around, but found no trace of the Missing Ones.

"Johanna said they never left the house. They went downstairs. Below. Whatever is down there. They were *betrügen* — tricked."

Johanna and Minnie said nothing. "But they're afraid the same thing may happen to us."

"You mean *disappear?*"

"She said *Verschwinden*. We must be careful and ready. Never believe what we are told. However, the time is not yet."

The ladies said, *"Die Knaben sind noch nicht in Gefahr."*
The boys are not in danger *yet.*

BEHIND THE LOCKED DOOR

More snow and we were working inside again. We cleaned the cellar, which was about as big as a football field. It looked like it hadn't been cleaned for years. Full of rubbish, mud, shit, ashes, tar, half-burned crap, useless junk and smelly chemicals. A dirty job! But we earned at least a weak compliment from our Keepers. "For the first time in your life, boys, you earned your keep."

Next, we started in on the *sub-basement,* which was even filthier. We were all a bit leary of going down there, after all the rumors and warnings. All twelve of us stuck close together. But we found no dungeons or torture chambers here. No man-devouring monsters. Just some very large rats.

There were some weird looking gadgets, generators, energy collectors and mysterious regulators. Karl Hasserman was among other things an inventor and an engineer. The whole place was heated by geothermal heat drawn from steaming underground springs. They gave a lot of heat.

Old George was directing the Naghallah boys in the *sub-basement* clean-up. The smell was too much for the finicky Masters. As long as Old George could handle us, they let us alone.

If anyone asked Old George where the hot water came from, he replied, "Straight from Hell, boy. Want to go down and look?"

At the far end of the sub-basement was a heavy door with a tricky lock. Here, a spiral stairway went down into the *Under-sub-basement.* None of us had been there. All we had seen was the stone stairway curving downward. Old George warned us: "Keep out of there, boys! Leave that door alone!"

I think we all dreamed about that stairway and had

nightmares about it.

Stevie said maybe there was nothing down there really. Just more muck and crud and dirt. If we could know for sure, we wouldn't have to worry about those bullshit stories.

If anyone went down, the door might lock and the boys wouldn't be able to come back out. Maybe the Masters would rescue us. Maybe they wouldn't. We would have to be careful.

Cameron laid out a plan. Two guys would go down with stolen flashlights. (Danny and Stevie). Two guys (Cameron and Keith) would guard the door and keep it open. The rest of us would create a diversion. To keep Old George occupied while Stevie and Danny explored.

Old George had a fear of snakes. There were, he told us, some awful big ones in the cellar. He enjoyed scaring the Naghallah boys, but scared himself in the process. "Watch out for the pythons, boys."

"How big are they?" asked Troy.

"Big enough to swallow a snotty kid."

"What about a kid who isn't snotty?"

"They'll swallow him too. But they'll go for the snotty kids first."

We put our plan into operation. "A snake! A snake!" yelled Bobby in the upper basement.

"A big one!" cried Jaymie.

Roger and Jody screamed. Brandon and Troy shouted. Don Don joined in a series of wolf howls.

Raymond yelled at the other end of the basement. "It's here! It's here! Behind the boiler."

Old George ran from one place to another, brandishing an axe and searching in vain for the phantom snake.

Cameron and Keith guarded the door. Danny and Stevie got back up safely. But all our maneuvers led to nothing. At the bottom of the spiral stone stairway was a heavy metallic door, bolted and impassible. There was no way of telling what was behind it.

Stevie and Danny looked relieved. I think they were just as glad the door was locked.

SNEAKY, ROTTEN, STUPID KIDS

March 27

The weather had turned fair. The snow was melting. They took us out to work. We were digging a trench along the roadway for the water to drain off, removing rocks, picking up wood and filling in holes with pick and shovel. They could have done the job twenty times as fast with machinery. But that wouldn't be giving us *Training and Treatment.* They took our winter gloves away. No work gloves. "Don't be a baby. Let's see some honest blisters on your hands."

Brother Danny got himself a name. *Shovelbuster.* He busted three shovels. It's a good thing Old George was in charge of us instead of Klayborne or Striker. They might have taken it out of Danny's hide. Old George said, "We'll take that out of your pay." Which was a joke because we weren't getting any pay. All we were getting was blisters and sore backs.

Bobby was pushing a wheelbarrow. He kept tipping it over. Bobby got himself a name, too. *Bobby, the Dirt Spiller.*

They roto-tilled the fields and we had to go making piles of rocks, then moving the piles around. Brandon got out of it at first by working in the kitchen. But Dr. Mehary determined that *all of us* should have the benefit of *"corrective conditioning"*. Brandon was sent to the rockpiles, too.

It really wasn't as tough as I've been describing it. For one thing we boys learned at *Kaah Naghallah* was how to goof off and do nothing; yet look like we were working.

We cleared the lawn and driveway of Karl Hasserman's mansion. I wondered if K. H. was watching us from behind those drawn curtains. I wondered why he financed this odd school, then hid himself from its students or inmates. A man with as much mystery as he had money.

They had us cleaning out briars and brambles and fallen trees, seeding and fertilizing, planting and raking and building a wall.

They didn't have many animals at Kaah Naghallah. But they had riding horses. The security guards used them for scouting the woods and maybe for tracking a runaway. We cleaned the stables and scattered the manure over K. H.'s garden. We weren't allowed to ride the horses. That, like so many other things, was a privilege we had to earn, but never did.

Manure makes the best fertilizer. We fertilized the lawn and shrubs around the mansion. K. H. was having a big shot visitor in a very fancy car with red upholstery. Joke player Raymond fertilized the car, too. (We didn't get caught.)

April 10

Up to now, we had been working inside the wire fence that surrounded the compound. Now, for the first time, we were taken outside. At the north end of the compound, there was a tremendous mass of rubbish, scrap metal and broken glass. This, we had to load onto hand-carts, lug down a narrow trail and dump into a swampy gully. We hauled an awful lot of rubbish into that gully, but there always seemed to be more.

Security guards, in their grey uniforms, kept watch over us. They had clubs and guns, which made the boys a bit nervous. I was sure they wouldn't shoot a kid, even if he tried to run away.

"Don't count on it," said Brother Danny.

"Major" Powell, however, told us the guards were there for our protection. "There are some nasty things in the woods." And he told Troy, who believed it. "We lost one bunch of juvenile punks who tried a runaway. All we found was a few bones and pieces."

"What is out there, sir?" asked Cameron, who could be most respectful, even while scheming up rebellion.

Powell gave a crafty smile. "The kind of things you see in horror movies. You see them once and don't get a chance to talk about it. *Grivets... Mandrils... Peccaries...* and *Krakens.*

He rolled these names off in a low sinister voice. The

brave big boys trembled a bit. But Jaymie turned away, trying not to laugh. Usually, I am a coward. But you learn something in the Gifted Child class.

Grivets and *Mandrils* are a kind of monkey. *Peccaries* are wild pigs. None of them very dangerous. The *Kraken* was a sea serpent. If it existed at all, it would be in the ocean, not the woods.

The rest of the guys, though, kept on feeling nervous. They were city kids. In this wild country, anything seemed possible. Stevie said, "Gee, Jaymie, how can you be sure there's no sea serpent in the woods? Maybe there's a big lake there."

"Maybe they can come out of the water and prowl around," said Bobby, shivering.

"Do Krakens eat people?" asked Raymond, anxiously.

"Maybe they do," said me. "But they'll eat Powell ahead of us. He's got a lot more meat on him."

Officer Powell got a big kick out of scaring kids. He scared the shit out of Troy and Roger, telling them about the mean, brutal Naghallah boys — that is, *Us*. Now he scared them again with his people-hunting monsters. Roger was sucking his thumb. Troy was biting his nails and trembling.

Cameron kicked them both in the ass. "Some Coyote you are! All shaky just from hearing about something that isn't true. What would you do if you ran into a real monster?"

"I'd die!" said Troy.

"No, you wouldn't. You're a Coyote and you'd fight. If we ever decide to break out, we'll stand up to whatever we meet."

Cameron had no plans for a break-out. "Right now, I can think of a whole lot worse places than *Kaah Naghallah*." He grinned. "You know something? I rather enjoy getting my behavior modified."

Nevertheless, urged Cameron, let the Masters believe we're afraid of the Forest. Then they wouldn't watch us so closely. Thus, we pretended to be quite terrified of the grivets, mandrils, peccaries and krakens. Keith even claimed the creatures chased him. Bobby spotted the monsters' tracks. Brandon heard them roar and bellow.

The Masters never caught on. They took us to be *"sneaky, rotten, stupid kids."* Well, we weren't *stupid.*

THE NAGHALLAH CADETS

April 16

In the middle of school, we received an urgent summons to Dr. Mehary's office. They lined us up, Cameron and Don Don at one end, Roger and Jody at the other.

Dr. Mehary surveyed us silently. We wondered for which of our misdeeds we were being called to account. *"Westcott, Cameron!* Step Forward!"

There was something about Dr. Mehary that inspired fear. Cameron quavered and looked uncomfortable.

"I understand you boys have formed a youth gang. Did you receive permission for this?"

"No, sir. We didn't think we had to. It's not a gang really. Just a club."

"And what is the purpose of this — *club?*"

"Just to be friends, sir. And help each other. And have a little fun. We didn't do anything bad."

"So far, you haven't. We know all about the Coyotes, Westcott, Cameron. We know *all* about *everything* you do. Now who is the leader of this — *club?*"

"I am, sir. The boys elected me."

"Very well, then. We'll let you be the leader of what I have in mind. We're going to form a Boys' Brigade. *The Naghallah Cadets.* Captain Striker and Guardian Craig will give you military training. Without weapons, of course. Now let's see you line your men up!"

Cameron got kicked out of military school. But he still remembered a few things. "Form column of twos!"

Stevie and Danny ... Keith and Raymond ... Bobby and Brandon ... Troy and Jaymie ... Jody and Roger. Cameron leading, with Donald by his side.

Forward March! ... Halt! ... Right about face! Mehary

had us march up and down several dozen times, until we were all in perfect step.

"From now on, wherever you go, you boys will march in formation!"

"Yessir," agreed Cameron.

"Yessir," echoed the Naghallah boys.

"You're not very promising material. But I might be able to make something out of you yet. *Dismiss! To your classroom, march!*"

Captains Striker and Craig gave us what they called "Military Training." With wooden guns. *Right shoulder arms! ... Present arms! ... Porte arms! ... To the left flank, march!*

At first, it was a bore. But after a while we began working real well together. Everybody in unison, like a chorus line, and it felt good. Roger and Jody had a bit of trouble following. But Donald did everything the rest of us did, without an error. We began to enjoy it.

Less enjoyable were the exercises they made us do. Push-ups, sit-ups, bendovers, knee bends, jumping jacks, running-on-the spot. Our performance was always "pretty sloppy". "Do them over again," commanded Striker. "*And this time do them right!*" Craig said they were getting us in shape. He didn't say for what.

We stood at attention, while Dr. Mehary reviewed us. "Pretty sloppy, I'd say. But not as bad as I expected. The boys are improving. Not quite the wild savages they were when they came here."

Sundays, we had no school and no ordinary work details. We were supposed to clean our quarters, clean our wash and do our homework. We were given piles of work sheets filled with problems and questions. Nobody ever did them. We used the sheets for making paper airplanes and passing notes.

No Sunday recreation. (We hadn't earned it.) "But it's not good to let the boys hang around idle. Scheming up mischief and maybe doing it. You have to keep these kids moving." So Sunday became drill time for the *Naghallah Cadets.*

On Sundays also, Dr. Mehary received a number of important visitors, to whom he expounded his theories of Behavior Modification and the correction of juvenile delinquents.

Controlling wild boys wasn't too different from breaking in any savage beast. You had to exhaust them physically and overwhelm them mentally. Break the old thought patterns of rebelliousness and install new thought patterns of obedience and submission. You didn't have to be harsh or cruel. "Just very firm."

Then the visitors would be taken to observe the Naghallah Cadets, as evidence how the most difficult juveniles could be handled.

Captain Craig was our drillmaster. "Come on, lads," he implored. "Show your stuff!" We were lined up. "Count off, lads!"

"One!" shouted Cameron. *"Two!"* hollered Stevie. *"Three!"* yelled Danny. *"Four!"* called Donald, without any prompting. All the way down to Roger, *Twelve.* Loud and clear.

We paraded around. *Right oblique, March! Left oblique, March!* We should have had band music . . . *To the rear, March! Double time, March!* We high-stepped and goose-stepped, turned and reversed. Real sharp and snappy.

Captain Craig beamed. "Excellent, lads!"

The visitors looked bored.

A PYRRHIC DEFEAT

April 22

Brandon would go wandering around by himself. When the opportunity came, he would grab choice foods intended for the grown-ups and bring them to us in the dormitory. Brandon got too bold and too reckless. Taking goodies right out of the Masters' buffet. Vedemore and Klayborne caught him.

Brandon got an awful beating with the rubber hose. Then they pushed him into the Boys' dorm room and told him. "If we ever catch you again, you're gonna get it three times as bad!"

Brandon lay on his bed, moaning and sobbing. He had welts and bruises from his shoulders to his knees. The other guys all got mad. This was the first time a kid had been beaten at *Kaah Naghallah* and we determined it would be the last.

"We got to stand up and let them know we're not going to take it!" So spoke Ray Ray and Stevie and Danny and Bobby. And they started shouting and yelling. "Riot! Riot!"

"Hold it, guys!" Cameron held his arms up. Then he turned to Jaymie. "What do you say, Gifted Child? What can we do?"

I figured our position was pretty weak. We didn't have much to bargain with. The Masters could smash any outright rebellion. But we could wage guerilla war and make an awful nuisance of ourselves.

They could make more trouble for us than we could for them. But the Masters might give us *something*, just to make things easier for themselves. If we didn't ask for too much.

"What do we ask for, Jaymie?"

"Just two things. We'll sit through their stupid school. We'll do their shitty work. We'll go through their silly drills. *But we don't want to be beaten and we don't want to be separated.*

"No guy gets hit or hurt. And they don't split us up. Those are the two things we'll fight!"

Cameron said, "Methinks the Gifted Child talks good sense."

"You got brains, Jaymie."

"He's just got a big mouth," said Brother Danny.

Cameron determined to talk to Mehary. He started toward the door. Keith yelled, "Hold it, Cam! You go in there by yourself and you'll get what Brandon got. Only worse."

"You'll come back with your ass busted," warned Bobby.

"Let's all go," urged Ray Ray.

"Maybe we'll *all* get our asses busted."

"Okay, guys. Form column of twos." Roger, Troy and Jody all looked frightened at the forthcoming confrontation. Brandon arose slowly from the bed. He was stiff and sore.

"You don't have to go, Bran."

"I don't want to stay here alone!"

"Nobody has to come, if they don't want to. Don Don, you want to stay?"

Donald gave a curious smile. His yellow eyes flashed. "Donald march with brothers," he announced.

"Jody, Troy and Roger can stay."

Jody said, "No, I'm going with Cameron!"

"Me, too," said Roger.

"You're gonna protect me?" Cameron grinned.

Troy said. "We won't be much protection. But we're sticking with the Coyotes. If we get beat, we get beat."

We left our dorm room without permission and ignored a direct order by Captain Eberle to halt and go back. Then we broke into Mehary's office without permission and without knocking. That was three serious violations of the rules, before the confrontation even started.

Dr. Mehary was at his desk and arose angrily. "What is the meaning of this intrusion?"

"Please, sir——" began Cameron. "May I have your permission to speak?"

Dr. Mehary sputtered, "You break in here and then ask permission. What's the matter with you, boy? If I tell you *No*, will you leave?"

"No, sir."

"Well, speak then. And be quick about it!"

"One of the boys, sir — Brandon here — was given a beating today. He has bad bruises on him. Look, sir ——"

"I'm not interested in Brandon's bruises. You were wandering around where you were forbidden to go. You broke into the Masters' Common room and stole things. The whipping you received was thoroughly deserved.

"Incidentally, you are *all* out-of-bounds right now. You have *all* violated a direct order. You all deserve to get the same thing."

Cameron looked uneasy. He opened his mouth several times, but nothing came out. Then he said, "Sir — We have always obeyed your orders and will do so in the future. But there is one thing, sir, we won't stand for. We won't let any Naghallah boy be hurt or beaten——"

Mehary cut him short. He pounded on the desk. "Now listen here, Westcott, Cameron. You were sent here because you couldn't get along in the world outside. You, Westcott, were a thief, a burglar and a check forger; as well as a liar, a pickpocket and a public nuisance. Zuchtig, Brandon was a street boy."

"No, I wasn't!"

"Don't deny it! You have been sent here to be corrected and disciplined. Not only Westcott and Zuchtig, but all the rest of you.

"When I agreed to take you here, I was given power to handle you. When you deserve punishment, you will be punished. If you need to be whipped, you will be whipped. That goes for any and all of you."

He glared at each in turn. "Do I make myself clear, Scanlon Steven?"

Stevie started to say, "*Fuck you!*" But somehow the answer came out, "*Yes, sir.*"

"What did I tell you, Alliconda, Robert?"

Bobby's face grew red. "That you have a right to whip us, sir."

Mehary picked up a ruler and pounded on the desk. "Any arguments?"

Everyone was silent excepting stupid Jaymie, who couldn't keep his big mouth shut. "We have some rights——"

"You have *no* rights, except those I give you. Which I can take away at any time."

There was an alarm bell on Dr. Mehary's desk. He fingered it lightly. "I'm giving you boys one minute to get out of my office. And five minutes to get back to your room. After that, I'm going to ring this bell and you will be twelve very sorry little boys."

Confrontation and Defeat

Dr. Mehary quashes the Youth Rebellion.

Cameron sounded the retreat. *"Form column of twos. March!"* Out of the office ... Down the hall ... Up the stairway ... back to the Boys' Room.

A Pyrrhic victory, they say, is a victory that is really a defeat. You could call the battle of Dr. Mehary's office a Pyrrhic defeat for the Naghallah boys. A defeat, that is, which was really a victory. After the confrontation, there were no further beatings.

*   *   *   *   *   *   *

Later

There was a knock on the door. The Masters didn't knock. They came barging in, trying to catch us at something. There was no lock on our side, so we blocked the entrance off with a heavy bureau. The blocked door made the Masters pound and shout in an angry voice. "Open up, you boys! Open up there!" We finally did, but we took our sweet time about it.

This time, there was a gentle knock. It was the nurse, Lyandra. She had come to look at Brandon and put healing ointment on his injuries.

Lyandra said it was a shame to treat Brandon like that. We did right to go to Dr. Mehary. He wasn't as bad as he seemed. "His bark is worse than his bite." *But there were others.*

Lyandra treated and bandaged everybody, though they really didn't need it. Roger claimed he had a sore toe. Jody had a sore knee. Raymond had a bad ankle. Stevie had an injured elbow. Cameron pretended he had a stiff neck and she massaged it.

"And how is Donald?"

"Donald good," he said.

Lyandra put her arms around him and kissed him. Don Don blushed. It was the first time I saw his face red instead of pale.

Still Later

That wasn't quite the end of the matter. We had another visitor — Major Powell. He barged right in. We forgot to put the bureau back against the door.

We were lying in our beds, half dozing. He switched the light on. "Get up!" he ordered. "Line up in formation. Did you hear me! *Move!*"

We lined up sleepily in a ragged line. "Your behavior has been disgraceful," he declared. "You're a rotten bunch of ornery punks. And don't think you're getting away with anything. We keep a record of everything you do."

Dead silence

Now Powell added in a stern voice. "Fifty bad conduct markers for all of you!" A scornful look. Then he turned and departed, locking the door behind him.

One by one, the Naghallah boys flopped back onto their beds. They sighed with relief and then began to laugh.

Brother Danny said, "Dear, dear, Gifted Child! You got yourself *fifty* bad conduct markers. No gold medals for you in this school."

TWELVE JUVENILE HOODS

Nearly everybody at *Kaah Naghallah* had to be called *Sir,* or something fancier. Mr. Matthews, however, permitted himself to be called, "Hey Teach!" Teacher Matthews was once on the faculty of some exclusive private school. Why should he leave that good job to teach twelve juvenile hoods like us?

"Maybe he got kicked out," said Keith. "And this is the only job he could get." Matthews did take a nip of brandy every now and then and kept a bottle in his desk.

Mr. Matthews didn't really expect to teach us much. He handed out photostated lessons in Science, English or History. We were supposed to read them, then answer the questions at the end.

"I can't read the big words, Teach," complained Roger.

"Help him, Troy."

"I can't read 'em either, Teach."

"Help them, Jaymie."

Strangely, both Troy and Roger listened to me when I showed them how to figure out the sounds of the letters. No one else ever showed them how to sound the letters out before. Just called them *stupid*.

Teacher Matthews leaned back in his swivel chair with his dark glasses on. You couldn't tell if his eyes were open or shut. We had school or work or both every day, including Saturday. No playtime for the Naghallah boys until we *earned* it and our shitty behavior improved. But we took our playtime right in school. Right under the teacher's nose. But quietly.

Mr. Matthews wasn't really asleep. Suddenly, he would break out. "Daniel Larrabie! Sit up properly and do your lesson!" . . ."Jody Kallinger! Get back in your seat!"

"Steven Scanlon! And Keith Caldwell! Are you playing *cards* in school? Give me those cards! I will report you to Dr. Mehary!" (But he didn't.)

"Stay here, Brandon. Back to your seat! You can't go to the bathroom again!" (But Brandon went anyway.)

"Cameron! Cameron Westcott! Don't take your shoes off in school!"

"My feet hurt, Teach. The shoes are too tight." Donald, imitating Cameron, took his shoes off, too.

Now a cry of anger and indignation. "Robert and Raymond! What are you doing? Playing *dice* in school?"

"No, sir."

"Come up here! Both of you. Give me those dice! Empty out your pockets."

Bobby and Raymond came forward and let themselves be searched. Matthews found nothing. For by this time the dice were safely hidden on Troy.

Matthews sighed. "Go back to your seats." He looked around the room. "Now who will read what you wrote about the lesson, *Transportation and Communication?*" Nobody volunteered.

"Jaymie Larrabie," he said, hopefully. "Suppose you

Teacher Matthews

read the lesson."

I looked at Cameron. I didn't want to get the guys mad at me. Cameron said. "Go ahead, Gifted Child. Read it."

I did. I knew how to sound real serious and important, yet get the guys all laughing.

Matthews always called on me when visitors were present. Some of the Masters brought people around to gawk at us. It made us feel like we were in a freak show.

Matthews hoped the visitors would just gawk and go away. But this seldom happened. "Caldwell and Alliconda," ordered Dr. Mehary. "And you, Westcott. Bring some chairs for the visitors."

Sullenly, the three youths dragged in some comfortable folding chairs from the next room. These were reserved for the visitors and masters only. The visitors settled down and began to smoke. Teacher Matthews looked distressed.

"Proceed, Matthews," ordered Dr. Mehary. "Show how you handle the boys."

Teacher Matthews sighed. Then he said, "Jaymie. Give your report!"

I gave one of my reports from the Gifted Child Class. *Comets and Meteors . . . Earthquakes and Volcanoes.* It made the other kids laugh and the visitors yawn. After about ten minutes, they got up and left.

We could have raised havoc in Mr. Matthew's class. But we didn't. As Brother Danny said, "School is crummy, but it ain't miserable. It could be a lot worse." Mr. Matthews was the least shitty teacher we could expect at *Kaah Naghallah.* We kept our misbehavior within limits and took part in only minor mischief.

Mr. Matthews, I think, was surprised. He got credit for being able to control "these juvenile hoods". When the term ended, he told us, "You all passed in school". But no vacation for the Naghallah boys. The new term started the day after the old one ended.

GREAT PLANS FOR THE NAGHALLAH BOYS

We had almost forgotten about Commander Bartlow. K. H.'s money man and Father's boss. He came up in a chauffeur-driven limosine. It looked rather like the one we put horse manure in. We didn't get caught on that one. But Raymond promised no more funny tricks, unless we voted for them in a gang meeting.

Bartlow called me and Danny into a fancy green office, ordinarily out-of-bounds for the Naghallah boys. Danny clammed up and let me do the talking.

"Well, boys, you're both looking strong and healthy. I can tell your parents, you're in good shape. The school is benefiting you."

"Yes, sir."

"Do you have anything to tell me? Any complaints?"

"No, sir." I was sure if a kid complained to Mr. Bartlow, it would be worse than useless.

"Your mother was worried about you. Especially Jaymie. She thought Jaymie might be lonely and not be able to make friends with the other boys — from such different backgrounds.

"But I can tell your mother not to worry, I understand you twelve boys are thick as thieves together.

"Do you like your schoolmates?"

"Oh, yes, sir," said Jaymie.

"You don't talk much, do you, Daniel?"

"Yeah. I like the other guys."

"And how about the Masters? Do you respect and appreciate what they are doing for you?"

"Well——"

"I hope you have no ill feelings against those who are trying to correct you. Remember *Discipline* is a special form of love. It shows we care about you. Sometimes we have to hurt before we can help."

He talked on and on. Danny gave me a look. "Let's get out of here!"

Jaymie said, "May we go now, sir? We have to get back to school."

"I am glad you are so interested in your school work. How do you find Guardian Matthews as a teacher?"

"He's a fine teacher," lied Jaymie. "We are learning a lot."

"Are you learning, too, Daniel?"

"Yessir. About (*Aside*) What's that shit, Jaymie? *Comets and Meteors . . . Earthquakes and Volcanoes.*"

Bartlow dismissed us. "All right. Go back to your school now, boys. I will talk to Dr. Mehary and the other Guardians. (*Doubtfully*) I hope I can give your parents a good report."

A week later, Commander Bartlow summoned us again. He was quite jovial and had a camera. "Your mother wants me to take a picture of you boys. Stand up there now. I want to get the two of you."

Danny pretended to punch me in the face.

"No! No! Not like that! Let's see some brotherly affection."

Me and Danny put our arms around each other. "That's better." He snapped several pictures.

"You look well and healthy, boys. Do you have anything to ask?"

"Yes, sir," said Jaymie. "Did you see K. H. ?"

"Yes, Karl Hasserman." (A curious smile) "He is very interested in you boys. He watches everything you do. I hope you never make him angry."

His voice was hard and menacing. We were both silent. Then Bartlow smiled again. "We have great plans for you. You can tell your friends. Karl Hasserman has *great plans* for the Naghallah boys."

I remembered a sad story we read in the Second Grade. The Fox had *great plans* for Chicken Little and his friends when he called them into his cave. They didn't come out.

URCHIN BOLD WITH HAIR OF GOLD

April 29

Dr. Mehary kept picking on Brandon. That gay poet Brandon used to live with somehow found out his address. He sent Brandon a load of gifts and wrote a poem to him.

Bran never saw the poet's gifts. The Masters ripped them off. Dr. Mehary read the poem out loud in school in front of the other boys, with sarcastic scorn. Brandon got all red and miserable.

Lovely Brandon, urchin bold,
Elfin smile and hair of gold.
Joyful eyes of azure blue.
Gleaming like the morning dew.
Graceful, like the leaping deer.
How I wish that you were here!
Far away though you may be
You're always in my memory.
Oh, youth of wonder, shining bright,
I'll meet you in my dreams tonight!

Dr. Mehary halted and stared at Brandon, who flinched and felt like crawling through the floor. Mehary expected us to laugh with scorn. Instead, there was dead silence.

Mehary looked annoyed and disappointed. "Well, what do you think of this poem — Larrabie, Jaymie? *What?* Speak up, boy! We can't hear you."

"I don't think the poem is altogether accurate, sir."

"*Accurate?* Just what do you mean by that?"

"I don't think Brandon looks like a deer, sir."

"That's a pretty stupid criticism. And what is your opinion of this poem, Westcott, Cameron?"

"I don't have one, sir."

"Do you think Brandon's eyes gleam like the morning dew?"

"I don't know, sir. I never seen the morning dew. It was

always gone when I got up," said Cameron with a straight face.

"And what do you think about all this, Alliconda, Robert?"

"I didn't understand the poem, sir."

"And just *what* did your feeble brain not understand, boy?"

"About that *shining* stuff. What's Brandon supposed to be shining? And how can the poet see it, when he ain't here? Anyway, Bran ain't shining now."

Indeed, Brandon had crawled under the desk and covered up his face with his hands.

Dr. Mehary gave us a disdainful look. "I thought I had *one* retard in this class. It looks like we have *nothing but retards. Twelve* of them!"

He arose disgustedly, knocking over his chair. The laughter we had been suppressing broke out loudly. We laughed and laughed and couldn't stop. Angrily, Mehary ripped up the Gay Poet's letter and stalked out of the room.

Brandon must have liked that guy. He retrieved the torn fragments and put them together with Scotch tape. Brandon said the Poet was good to him. "It wasn't like they said. He never touched me. Not in any dirty way. And he didn't take my picture with no clothes on. I had my swimming trunks on." That Investigator had a dirty mind.

But Brandon did admit the Poet gave him massages and alcohol rub-downs. "He gave a real good massage, too. I had a sprained shoulder and a bad back ——"

Privately, we kidded Brandon, calling him *Urchin bold, with hair of gold.* And *Brandon, Brandon, shining bright, see you in my dreams tonight.*

Some guy would ask, "Hey, Bran Bran, how about giving me one of them poetic massages?"

At first, Brandon squirmed and got all red. After a while, he just grinned.

The Poet's name was Rodney Desmond. Brandon did write him; and Minnie, the cook, mailed the letter for him down in Mountainville. About the school and Brandon's

Coyote gang brothers.

This is a crummy place, but it could be worse. We get kicked around here, but we have a lot of fun, too. The Masters are shitty, but the boys are tops. Always joking and kidding around. We have a merry time with a lot of laughs.

Thanks for the presents. But don't send no more. The Masters steal everything.

Hope to see you soon for real, not just in your dreams.
Your friend,
Brandon

A BRAWL IN THE HALL

May 3

Most of time, Donald was real quiet in school. You would hardly know he was there. But now, Donald started to burst out laughing. All of a sudden and for no reason at all.

Don Don kept laughing through the math lesson, while Teacher Matthews was writing on the blackboard. Finally, Mr. Matthews grabbed Donald by the shoulders and started shaking him. We all began yelling and he stopped.

"I didn't hurt Donald. Did I hurt you?"

Donald kept right on laughing and got us laughing, too. Mr. Matthews stood there helplessly while the laughing continued. Finally, he told us some stupid old jokes. We laughed still more and Teacher Matthews looked pleased.

Don Don got another fit of laughing in the Mess Hall. "Captain" Striker wasn't as restrained as Mr. Matthews. He smacked Donald. Donald laughed again and this time Vedemore smacked him. Then he got slapped again by Striker and we started yelling.

The meal was a mushy concoction served in a soup plate. Donald shoved his dish right into Striker's face. Then he grabbed Jody's dish and tossed it at Vedemore.

The two large guardians closed in on Donald and dragged him out of his seat. Vedemore held Donald's arms while Striker began to whack him. Donald struggled helplessly. The Naghallah boys all jumped up, shouting, "Lay off him! Leave Donald alone!"

Officer Eberle tried to push us back. "Stay out of it, boys."

Danny knocked Eberle out of the way. Cameron grabbed Striker's arms as he started to smack Donald again. Stevie, Keith and Danny piled into Vedemore, trying to break Donald loose. The rest of us joined the melee, shouting and yelling. Bobby, Troy, Brandon, Raymond and Jaymie all piled in. Roger and Jody were jumping up and down, cheering and yelling. Striker and Vedemore went down under an avalanche of kids. We broke Donald loose and surrounded him with our bodies.

There was a sudden silence. Everyone froze as Dr. Mehary entered the room. A deadly pause. Then he spoke. "Just what are you doing here? *Answer me!*" His voice was high and shrill. More like a woman than a man.

"Sir," said Cameron, boldly. "They were beating Donald."

"Who?"

"Mr. Striker and Mr. Vedemore, sir. Donald didn't do a thing. The were beating him for nothing."

"Donald was being disciplined," said Vedemore. "He was behaving very badly."

"They all have been behaving very badly," said Striker. "They should all be punished."

We gathered together in a shield around Donald, prepared to fight. Stevie, Keith, Danny and Cameron were in the front. We might be able to stand off these four grownups, Vedemore, Striker, Eberle and the Director himself. But Mehary could readily call in reinforcements. He could surely muster at least one, maybe two, grown-ups to handle each kid. Even without weapons, they could clobber us.

Another long, deadly silence. Mehary let us stand there and sweat for a while. "Your behavior is inexcusable," declared the Director. "You will be disciplined."

Another pause. "You will have no more supper. Go to your room!"

Since we had already eaten about as much as we wanted, that wasn't much of a punishment. We didn't care for the crummy mush anyway.

"Form column of twos," called Cameron. We marched in formation out of the mess hall, up the stairs, back to our quarters. Don Don had a big smile on him.

"Donald get brothers in trouble."

"Yeah, Don Don. We got muckled on account of you."

"Brothers help Donald. Donald help brothers."

"No more laughing like that, Don Don. You'll make the Masters blow their top and next time we'll get creamed."

All the Masters' shaking and slapping didn't curb Donald's wild laughter. But he stopped cold when Cameron gave him a light punch on the shoulder.

That was another Pyrrhic defeat for the Naghallah boys. Don Don didn't get hit any more and the rest of us got no penalty except losing our unwanted supper. Some day, the Masters are going to flip their lids and whomp us. But it hasn't happened yet.

* * * * * * *

Later

We had a night visit from Major Powell again. We all stood at attention and *Yes-sirred* him, while he called the roll. Cameron says, *"Don't sass the Masters or get them mad over something silly. No rebellion or confrontation, except over something big. Then we got to fight with all we got."*

We expected to get our fifty bad conduct markers. Instead, this time we got *double*. *"One hundred demerits for all of you."*

Nothing has happened about our bad conduct markers. Most of the boys think they're a big joke. But some of the guys are nervous. They figure some day we'll have to pay our demerits off.

NAGHALLAH SCHOOL DAYS II

May 8

Mr. Matthews seldom talked in class. He handed out sheets with problems or questions which we were supposed to answer. The boys complained, "This is too hard, Teach!" But we soon found Mr. Matthews didn't expect us to do the work. The guys used the question sheets to mark up or throw around.

"And here's something for you, Jaymie . . . " Figure out the correlation between the average rainfall in the State and the average temperature.

There were pages of measurements and it took many hours of figuring by a complicated formula. I found there was *no* correlation between the rainfall and the temperature. Mr. Matthews didn't seem surprised or even interested. I guess he just wanted to keep me busy.

For days now, Teacher Matthews had been writing furiously into a notebook, which he hid away inside his desk. He paid no attention even when Bobby and Raymond got out of their seats and began to wrestle.

We were all real curious about that mysterious notebook. That evening, Cat Burglar Cameron broke into the desk and stole it. We didn't really mean to snoop. We thought Mr. Matthews had been writing something about *us*. Instead, we found our teacher had been writing a novel. About a young college professor of Ancient History who fell in love with a beautiful actress. First, she led him on, then she threw him over.

The poor guy lost his job, too. And the only work he could get was to teach a bunch of juvenile delinquents in a boys' reform school. Here, he wrote:

"The boys weren't the horrors I expected. I found them poor, pathetic creatures . . . "

So ended the novel. At least that's as far as Matthews got. Cameron put the notebook back in the desk. I don't think Matthews ever knew it was gone.

COYOTES LOYAL AND TRUE

The Masters of Naghallah had a fondness for military titles. Most of them were addressed as *Captain.* Powell, Chief of Hasserman's private police, claimed the rank of *Major.* Now there was Lammington, K. H.'s Chief Executive, who had assumed the rank of *Colonel.* This made him top man on the totem pole, except perhaps for *Commander* Bartlow.

Lammington hadn't been around much lately. But now he was back, sticking his nose into everything. We were warned to be very polite and respectful, if he came into our quarters.

"What'll we do," asked fresh Bobby. "Bow or salute him?"

"Just stand at attention. *Brace.* And don't put anything in front of the door. That door must be open at all times, unless we lock it."

Most of the Masters had a lot of meat on them. Lammington, however, appeared gaunt and lean, almost like a skeleton. His face, I thought, looked like he was wearing a rubber mask.

We stood at attention in a sloppy line. Lammington gazed at us disdainfully and spoke complainingly to Craig and Vedemore. Lammington was dissatisfied with the way the Naghallah boys were being handled. Too creampuff. "This place is being run more like a play school than a disciplinary institution."

The boys, he thought, were much too cheerful and contented. They ought to be more subdued. "They look like they're scheming up something." However, there was nothing he could really pin on us. We did our work. We went to school. We marched and drilled and kept our quarters reasonably clean. The trouble was we seemed to enjoy it. We were noisy and laughing, instead of looking suppressed.

He seemed determined to get something on us. Lammington and the other Masters made sudden sweep searches of the dormitory, looking for crazy pills, weapons, pot, liquor, cigarettes or stolen stuff. Or something dirty. They found nothing, not even the food we stole. We ate that up fast, before the Masters could grab it.

When we first came to *Kaah Naghallah*, they strip searched us. Danny had that shiv in his boot. But the shiv was on Stevie when they stripped Danny and on Keith when they stripped Stevie. Then back on Danny when Keith got his going over. The shiv was never hidden on Jaymie. "It ain't that we don't trust you, Gifted Child. You're just too clumsy."

Now, the shiv was hidden out on the roof. Along with wire cutters, wrenches, pliers, our silver dollars and other stuff the Coyotes might need some day. Unless somebody snitched, the grown-ups were unlikely to find them. To reach them, you had to crawl dangerously along a narrow, slippery ledge. Only a fool kid would do that. Besides, the Masters didn't know we had found ways to get in and out of the window. They thought they had us locked in securely.

Determined to catch us at something, Lammington, along with Striker and Klayborne, made a raid on us one Sunday morning. Nobody snitched and they didn't look on the roof. But Lamington found several packs of butts and forbidden matches in Stevie's drawer. We were sure Lammington planted them. In the beginning, Stevie was crazy for a butt. But by now he was used to being without tobacco. And if Stevie got his hands on any butts and matches, he would hide them better than sticking them on top of his drawer.

The four youngest kids, Jody, Roger, Troy and Jaymie, were questioned separately. They thought we four would be the most likely to snitch. Were the big boys mean to us? Were they planning any trouble? Was anyone giving them smokes or pills and other stuff? Did the big boys have any hidden weapons? Did they fool around sexually and play dirty games?

The big boys worried a bit about what we might say. Especially about Roger and Jody. But they had no need to worry. We were all Coyotes, loyal and true.

Said Jody, "The big boys are good to us. They take good

care of us. They never do anything dirty or mean!"

"I'd take a thousand beatings," declared Troy. "But I'd never snitch. *No torture or terror would make me reveal the secrets of the Coyotes.*"

The Masters were disappointed. But at least they figured they had nailed Stevie Scanlon cold. Stevie was ordered to report to Dr. Mehary. He felt nervous about it. Maybe they would lock him up and stick him in solitary. This had happened to him once. In the misnamed *Children's Protectory.* We decided we would all go with him. When Lammington and Company came to escort Steve, the rest of us followed.

Mehary eyed us angrily. "I sent for Scanlon. The rest of you go back to your room!"

Nobody moved.

"I gave you a direct order!" thundered Mehary. "I'll repeat it *just once.* After that——"

Still, nobody moved.

Mehary's long arm reached out and grabbed the nearest kid, who happened to be Jaymie. "Did you hear what I said, Larrabie, Jaymie?"

"Yessir."

"What are you doing here then, when I told you to leave?"

"We're here as witnesses, sir. Stevie is innocent. He didn't take any butts or matches."

"How do you know that?"

"Because we all live together. We each know what the other guys are doing."

"Then how did those cigarettes get into Scanlon's drawer?"

"Somebody put them there, sir. But it wasn't any of the boys."

Mehary bellowed angrily. "What are you trying to say, boy? That Colonel Lammington is lying? That *he* put these things in Scanlon's drawer?"

"You said it, sir. I didn't."

A grateful look from Stevie and a furious one from Lammington.

Mehary released Jaymie with a smack in the face. He grabbed young Roger, the kid, he thought, most likely to tattle. "Roger!" he roared, "I want you to tell the truth."

"Yessir." Roger was trembling.

"Have you ever seen Steven with cigarettes or matches? Or any kind of pills?"

"No, Doctor. Never."

A crack in the face and a shaking. "I want you to stop lying!"

"I'm not lying, sir!"

Two more smacks. An angry yell from Stevie and a shout from Cameron. "Leave him alone!"

Mehary lowered his voice and put his hand on Roger's shoulder. "Now Roger. I want you to tell me. Have you ever seen Steven, or Cameron, or any of the other boys, with any liquor or weapons? Or things they're not supposed to have? Or stolen things that belonged to somebody else?"

"No, Doctor. Never."

"Tell the truth, Roger! Did they take any hammers or axes or saws or knives?" Another smack and a shaking. *"Did they? Answer me!"*

"No, Doctor. Never."

Mehary threw Roger aside. The kid turned toward Cameron with an adoring look. His face said, "I passed the test. I'm a loyal and true Coyote."

Mehary went down the line and questioned each kid. Everyone said the same thing, excepting Donald who just made noises. Everyone got a smack in the face, excepting young Jody who just got a shaking.

"These little punks all stick together," said Klayborne, disgustedly. "They cover up for each other."

At the end, Mehary looked a little weary and puzzled. He knew we would resist getting beaten or separated and didn't want to spark a riot. At the same time, he was determined to "give the boys a punishment that would make an impression on them" and would impress the other Masters with his firmness.

"For three days," he ordered, "you will be given bread

and water. Nothing else." Orders went out to the kitchen.
Nothing but bread and water for the Naghallah boys. For
nine meals. "And you will eat in your room."

It's good to have connections in the kitchen. Cook
Johanna followed orders. But the word *bread* was inter-
preted very broadly. Rolls, buns, special loaves of rye and
wheat with heavy crusts; biscuits, raisin bread, honey
bread; even gingerbread and cinnamon toast. And the
cooks looked the other way when Brandon spiked our
water with tea, sugar and lemon flavor and our bread with
a spot of butter. I think we never ate so well at Naghallah
as those three days on a punishment diet.

What a peculiar place *Kaah Naghallah* was. A cross between a juvenile penitentiary and a merry boarding school.

We hoped it would stay that way.

*   *   *   *   *   *   *

Later

Once again, we had a night visit from Major Powell and
got ourselves a load of bad conduct markers. *Two hundred*
this time. I'll bet we hit a thousand before the year is over.

We were supposed to hang our heads in shame. Instead,
Roger started to giggle. Not about the demerits, but
because Powell had his shoe laces untied.

"Newland!" bellowed the Major. "Do you think bad conduct markers are comical?"

"N-n-no, sir!"

"If you keep on piling up demerits," said Powell,
ominously, "you're going to be twelve very sorry punks."

He turned and walked to the door. As he was leaving,
young Troy let out a loud and long Bronx cheer.

Angrily, Powell turned and glared at us. Donald started
making animal noises. Some of them sounded rather like
the Bronx cheer did. The Major gazed at Donald, then
shrugged and departed.

A VISIT FROM HOME

May 19

That first, wonderful green of Spring was bursting out all over. *Kaah Naghallah* was beautiful now. The gardens, fields and borders were replete with multi-colored blossoms. But no summer vacation for the Naghallah boys. A little less school and a little more work.

That week-end, a most unexpected thing happened. Our parents came to visit. Commander Bartlow was with them. Also, a white-haired gentleman, Judge Tuffney. He was the Juvenile Court judge in Greenwood. Cameron knew him well. "I was up before him at least seven times. I guess he gave me a break — sending me here, instead of to the State Reformatory."

Judge Tuffney was the one who had signed permission for Brandon, Raymond and Bobby to be sent to *Kaah Naghallah* from the Greenwood Youth Shelter. Stevie and Keith, Jody and even Donald had the Judge's signature on their placement papers. So, it turned out, did Troy and Roger. Judge Tuffney, the guys thought, got some money out of it. Karl Hasserman, our sponsor, may have paid him off to get some welfare kids for Naghallah, when they couldn't get any regular pupils. Though why he wanted us boys was still a mystery.

After Donald was dumped by his guardians for being hopeless, he became a ward of the State. The Juvenile Court then, for no apparent reason, committed him to *Kaah Naghallah*. Now Don Don was really improving. But not because of anything the grown-ups did.

Jody was likewise dumped, and became a ward of the State. So, indeed, were Troy and Roger. Cameron, Stevie, Keith, Bobby, Raymond and Brandon were all placed or committed here by Judge Tuffney's youth court. Only me and Danny could be withdrawn by our parents. Come to think of it, the Court had its zingers on Danny, too. He had that stolen car rap and the house breaking rap hanging over him.

I was the only kid free to go home. The others, if we split, would have to keep on the lam. If they got caught, they might be sent to a place a lot shittier than *Kaah Naghallah*. Here, at least, we were in good company.

Dr. Mehary was a bit nervous about the visitors. And about me. I was the one guy not completely in his power. For the first time since we came here, he gave me a compliment. "You have a high potential, Jaymie. I may have been hard on you. But that is because I hold you to a high standard."

We were dressed in our new blue uniforms of the Naghallah cadets. Danny said, "Little boy blue! You look cute, Jaymiebrudder."

"So do you, Dannybrudder."

"I heard what Mehary told you, Gifted Child. You're Mehary's pet."

"Fuck you!" said me.

"Is that nice?"

We were marched out to where the visitors were assembled. They put us through our paces. *Squad right! Squad left!* With wooden guns. It felt stupid, but the visitors were impressed. "You're doing a fine job on these boys," said Judge Tuffney.

We broke rank. Me and Danny greeted our parents. Mother hugged us. Father shook our hands. "You look mighty well, Jaymie. Mighty healthy. I think *Kaah Naghallah* is doing you good."

"Daniel looks good, too," said Commander Bartlow. "I told you boys, *Naghallah* will make a man out of you."

"I got a good report for you, Daniel. From Dr. Mehary," said Dad. "He said you have improved a lot."

"Your son is Dr. Mehary's pet," said me.

"You're talking about *yourself,* Gifted Child."

"They're still acting like they did at home," said Mother, pleased about it.

We introduced our parents to the other ten guys. Our friends and schoolmates. Mother said, "I think the boys are very nice. I'm surprised. I thought they all were——"

"Juvenile delinquents?"

"Well, something like that. But they don't seem bad at

all. That Donald, he doesn't talk?"

"He talks with the guys. But not when grown-ups are around."

"He's so light, that Donald. He's an albino. And his eyes are all yellow! Do the other boys make fun of him?"

"No. We all like Don Don."

"Twelve boys in one room? That seems awfully crowded. Does it bother you?"

"No. It's okay."

"Do you fight a lot?"

"Not seriously. We just kid around."

"Of all the boys, which one is your best friend?"

"Danny, I guess. But I like all the guys."

Mother pulled me aside. "Do you like it here, Jaymie?"

"Yes, Mother."

"Do you want to come home?"

"No, Mother." She seemed disappointed.

We told Mother about the Coyotes. Mother likes to be told things. That gave her something to report to Cousin Katie, Uncle Oscar, Aunt Laura and the rest of the family. We said nothing about the strange and frightening stories we had heard.

"What do you boys do all day?" asked Dad.

"We go to school. We work indoors. We work outdoors. We drill for the Naghallah cadets. And we fool around."

"What do you do mostly?"

"We fool around."

"What do you do at night?" inquired Father.

"We hold gang meetings of the Coyotes."

"Do they let you boys form a gang like that? I thought they would be very strict here."

"Not too strict. We get pushed around a little. But not much."

"It's not as bad as you thought, is it, boys?"

"No, sir."

"They're having the time of their life," said Mr. Bartlow.

"How is the food?" Dad wanted to know.

"It's crummy. But we steal stuff meant for the grownups."

"I won't tell on you," promised Dad, who was in a good mood.

Our parents had brought us several boxes of goodies. Fruits, chocolates, cakes and concentrates of soft drinks. Dr. Mehary let us accept the stuff. But later he came around to confiscate it. By that time, however, we had consumed most of it and hidden the rest. Mehary wasn't too mad. He was pleased with us.

Mother, Dad and the Judge got the V. I. P. treatment. They were wined and dined at the mansion of the mysterious K. H. It was a fabulous meal, said Dad, with caviar, *filet mignon* and the finest cigars and brandy. Served on golden plates in a mirrored dining room with tapestries and crystal chandeliers. Commander Bartlow played host. The mysterious tycoon never did appear. But they met his "charming and beautiful" nurse, Lyandra. "She spoke well of you boys."

The billionaire sent his apologies. He was "indisposed".

Judge Tuffney, with Commander Bartlow at his side, interviewed the boys he had sent up to *Kaah Naghallah.* That is, he talked and the boys listened.

"Well, *Cameron Westcott,* you are learning to do honest work. No more burglarizing and check forging. No more stealing and swindling. Right, boy? Crime doesn't pay, does it? . . .

"*Raymond Ridgeway.* You don't rob any stores here. Or snatch any purses. Let's see your hands . . . Good . . . You have honest blisters on them.

"*Robert Alliconda.* No cars to steal here. Or was that *Steven Scanlon?* I think both of you. No more shenanigans. We'll make good citizens out of you instead of criminals . . . Right, boys?"

There were some cars here but we never thought of stealing them. It would be easy to block us off along that narrow thirty mile track to Mountainville.

"*Brandon Zuchtig——*" A very severe look. "You don't have rich men here to give you a hand-out. You will learn to live a clean and decent life and earn what you get . . . Right, boy?

"Keith Caldwell and Daniel Larrabie... You don't play hookey from this school. And you don't take pot and crazy pills here. No more night prowling and housebreaking ... No more brawling and silly pranks. No more gambling and joy riding ... Right, boys?"

The Judge never waited for an answer, but went on to the next guy. *"Troy Feroldi...* and *Roger Newland...* You don't pick any pockets here. Or dump over garbage cans. You two are the runaways and motorcycle stealers. You don't want to run away from here, do you, boys? ..."

"No, Your Honor," said Troy.

"Why not?"

"We have a lot of friends here."

"The Guardians of Naghallah are all your friends," said the Judge, pompously. "Even if they seem harsh at times. Sometimes you have to be harsh in order to be kind. Right, boys?"

"Jody Kallinger, you don't bite people at Kaah Naghallah. Or throw mudballs and break windows. You're learning to act like a human being, instead of an animal ... Right, boy? ...

"And, let's see ... The retarded boy. *Donald Turrentine.* Do you know your name?"

"Yessir," said Donald.

"You're learning to talk."

"He's learning to play the guitar, too," said Jaymie.

"Really? You boys are all going to be very grateful some day for coming to Kaah Naghallah ... Right, boys?

"And Jaymie ... *Jaymie Larrabie.* You are Daniel's brother?"

"Yes, Your Honor."

"You weren't sent here by me. Why were you sent here?"

"I am psychopathic, Your Honor. And emotionally disturbed."

"Really? Have you improved any since you came to Naghallah?"

"No, Your Honor."

Dr. Mehary broke in. "I think Jaymie *has* improved. He

is much more cooperative and helpful with the other boys."
Judge Tuffney patted me on the head. "That's good to
know. Keep up the good work, Jaymie! . . . Your methods
are working, Dr. Mehary. I shall report that twelve out of
twelve boys in your custody have shown substantial improvement. An excellent accomplishment!"

Back to the mansion for high tea. Then our parents and
the Judge departed with Bartlow in his limosine. Dad said,
"Goodbye, boys. Keep up your good record. I am proud of
both of you."

THE STRANGE LAWS OF THE COYOTE TRIBE

There wasn't much Spring at *Kaah Naghallah*. A few
weeks and it changed from winter to summer. Real hot
now.

They put us to work weeding. We had to weed around
thousands of small seedlings planted in K. H.'s fields and
the flowers and vegetables planted in the tycoon's garden.
We were told to "shape up" the orchards and meadows
and woodland groves; and the network of paths and road-
ways that criss-crossed the compound. Pulling up briars,
thistles, vines and nettles. Moving fallen logs and brush,
and gathering up rocks and stones and piling them neatly.
All the guys got sore hands, mosquito bites and poison ivy.

Everyone grumbled. Troy said, "There ought to be a
law——"

"There is," said Keith. "There's a law against child labor
and we're child labor."

Raymond said, "We ain't child labor. Child labor is when
a kid gets paid for working, even if it ain't much. We get
nothing."

"We're slave labor."

But Dr. Mehary said we weren't *any* kind of labor. We
were getting "training and treatment", "behavior
modification", "corrective conditioning", "work therapy",
"motivational redirection". . .

The purpose of weeding wasn't to get rid of the weeds. It was to give us good work habits and overcome our laziness and anti-social attitude. They were trying to help us poor, sick children. If we wouldn't work, maybe we'd rather get locked up and sit on our butts and do nothing?

Cameron said, "Don't rock the boat, fellers. There are a lot worse things than weeding. We'll keep doing it. But everybody go real slow and goof off."

From now on, every loyal Coyote had to goof and fuck around. Any guy who got praised by the grownups for doing a good job would be dunked in the shower with his clothes on.

We held a gang meeting and voted 11 to 0 to make that a *Boy Law:* that is a law of the Coyote Brotherhood. The Coyotes are a democracy and everything has to be voted. One boy, one vote and everyone is equal. Don Don didn't vote. He just laughed.

Cameron got the first praise for doing good work and, Gangleader or not, he got dunked. One thing about the *Boy Law.* We enforce it. Sooner or later, every guy got praised by the growups and dunked by his brothers. Excepting Donald. We dunked him anyway, so he wouldn't feel left out.

We made a number of other Boy Laws:

(2) *No stealing from each other.*

(3) *No stealing from the grownups without the Gangleader's permission.* (If one guy got caught, we would all get muckled.)

(4) *No snitching.*

(5) *No mischief or trouble-making without the Gangleader's permission.*

(6) *No fighting, except in fun.* No matter who started it, BOTH guys get dunked.

(7) *No guy can show off or get high marks in school, unless the Gangleader tells him to.* Danny punched me. "That's for *you.* Gifted Child. No one else can break *that* Boy Law."

(8) *Share everything.*

(9) *Stick together.*

(10) *Defend and help your brothers.*

(11) *Bullshitting is okay usually. But in a gang meeting you have to tell the truth.*

(12) *No one can quit the Coyotes and no one can be kicked out.*

The Boy Laws were enforced better than any rules made by the grown-ups. A dunking in the shower or getting cold water down your pants leg wasn't anything terrible. But nobody jumped with joy when they got it.

That *Boy Law Number Six* stopped a lot of fights.

Troy and Jaymie were about the same size. I washed my shirt out nice and clean and then Troy snatched it.

"Hey, Troy! That's *my* shirt!"

"No," said Troy. "*This* is yours." And he handed me a dirty, messy shirt. I grabbed for the clean shirt. Troy pushed me. I shoved him back and started swinging.

"A fight! A fight!" yelled Jody.

"They ain't kiddin'," said Bobby.

Cameron yelled. "Get the bucket and funnel! Two brothers are fighting."

Then me and Troy decided to settle our dispute peaceably.

Cameron arbitrated. "How about ripping the shirt in half?"

A howl of protest from both Troy and Jaymie.

"Well, then——" Cameron dug up a pack of playing cards stolen from the Master's Common room. He dealt out two poker hands. Troy got himself a pair of *8's;* Jaymie, a pair of *5's.* So Troy got the clean shirt.

Cameron's judgement was fair enough. I don't think King Solomon could have done any better.

A LETTER FROM MOTHER

May 29

Dear Jaymie and Danny:
I am glad you boys like Naghallah and are making such excellent progress. Keep up the good work!
Your father has to go to Europe on business for a few months and I am going with him. But I couldn't go unless I felt sure you boys would be all right.
Commander Bartlow has promised to watch you and take care of you, and keep us posted.
All my love, MOTHER

Mr. Bartlow was about the last person me and Danny would choose as a caretaker. If there was something wrong at *Kaah Naghallah*, he was surely involved. We didn't know yet if it was just a kooky boarding school with a lot of nutty *Behavior Modification*. Or if the school was a front for something else. Something creepy and frightening.

This is your last chance to go home, Jaymie. Maybe you should go home while you still can and tell them there is something very wrong here.

But none of the grown-ups would believe me. And none of the other guys could go home. Whatever happened, I wanted to be in on it . . .

Mother's letter also enclosed a picture for Danny from Marjie Meyer. This time, she had her regular clothes on.

A BULLSHIT LETTER

June 1

Cameron also received a letter, addressed to *"Tony Westcott"*. Cameron's full name was *Tony Cameron Westcott*. But he didn't like to be called *Tony*. "That's the name they busted me by and whipped me by and expelled me by and jailed me by and threw me out of the family."

"Did *Cameron* bring you any better luck?" asked Troy.

"Sure it did," he insisted. "I came here and met you guys."

The letter was from his aunt and uncle. "Tony" read it aloud:

We thought you were in jail. But we learned now that you were sent to a home for wayward boys. That was good news. If you work hard now and do well, you can come out without a record.

"We hope for your sake they don't let you out too soon, until you are really better.

Our noble and popular leader was a bum to his family!

"Do me a favor, will you, Jaymie? Answer this garbage."

Amazingly, an intelligent guy like Cameron still printed instead of writing script. If I printed the letter, they would think he wrote it. "And don't try to be funny, Jaymie. They got no humor at all."

"Fuck 'em," said Danny. "Why answer it?"

"They're my only relatives. Some day I might need them to ask for a hand-out."

"You want a bullshit letter?" asked me.

"That's right."

So I wrote, or rather printed a bullshit letter. I described and praised Cameron's eleven roommates; reported how we formed "the Coyote club for self-improvement"; and avoided insulting the Masters who would probably read this letter. Then I told how hard we worked and studied and drilled for the Naghallah cadets.

"Write sloppy and make some spelling mistakes," advised "Tony". And I did.

GUNS AND INSULTS

June 4

A wonderful summer day! They took us out of the compound to work on the trails. There were a lot of trails, branching out into the forest. We were supposed to mark them, widen them and clear out the rocks and unwanted vegetation.

We would have liked working on the trails. Except that Captain Klayborne and some other guys were sent along to guard us and keep us in line. They didn't trust us for nothing.

Klayborne had a gun on him and waved it around. "Don't go off the trail!" he warned. And to show he meant it, he fired a couple of shots into the air.

Klayborne had a nasty scar on his face. According to Johanna, he had been a guard in a reformatory and was attacked by a couple of kids, trying to escape. Klayborne got slashed and hit over the head and spent several months in a hospital.

Klayborne was always perhaps a bit cracked. But that knifing made him worse. He hated the youths who attacked him. Not only *them,* but all young guys, including *us.*

When Stevie had to take a leak, he started to walk behind a rock. Klayborne pulled his gun on Stevie. "Come back here, boy, or I'll let you have it!" He might have, too. Klayborne was shaking with anger and his face was twitching.

Shooting a kid would require a bit of explaining. But it wouldn't be too hard to figure out a cover up. "The kid tried to jump me, and grab the gun." Or, better yet, it was an accident.

Klayborne made Stevie stand there with his toes against the rock. He kept waving his gun around. "You want to run away, boy? Go ahead, try it and see what happens. Make my day!"

The guys started yelling. Klayborne called us *"Trash"*, *"Scum"* and *"Guttersnipes"*. And he called Raymond a nasty, racist name. That made us all mad.

Bobby retorted in kind. He called Klayborne "a queer" and "a weirdo". We were heading for real trouble when Guardian Craig intervened.

"I'll take over the boys, Klayborne. Come on, lads. Line up there. All of you. You too, Steven. In formation!"

He marched us in formation all around the compound and then back to our quarters.

There was no use complaining to Dr. Mehary. In his book, the Masters were always right and the kids wrong. Captain Craig was basically a decent guy and had pulled us out of a hole. But that was all we could expect from him. Craig wasn't going to get into a hassle with Klayborne for our sake.

When we were ordered into the forest the next day, we refused to go. Thereupon, we were summoned into Dr. Mehary's office.

"I understand you guys disobeyed a direct order to work on the trails."

"No, sir, we didn't," said Cameron. "We'll work the trails. But not if the kook Klayborne is in charge of us."

"I won't *have* that kind of language," snapped Mehary. "Captain Klayborne is a Master of Naghallah. You will speak of him respectfully."

"He almost shot Stevie!" broke in big-mouth Jaymie.

"You are out of order, Larrabie, Jaymie. Scanlon here looked like he was trying to escape."

"I was just taking a ——"

"Silence!" commanded Dr. Mehary. "You boys were placed in our custody, and we're going to keep you here until we are ready to release you. Don't get any ideas!"

"Sir," said Jaymie. "If we ever do run away, it won't be just one guy. It will be all twelve of us."

"Thanks for telling me that."

Troy broke in. "He called Raymond a name. He said ——"

"I don't want to hear it. We thought we were giving you a real privilege, letting you work in the forest. But I am now taking that privilege away.

"There is plenty of work inside the compound. And that

is where you will be kept from now on. Dismiss!"

So what? Working inside the compound might become a bore after a while. But at least you wouldn't get shot there. There were too many witnesses.

We made a bad enemy out of Captain Klayborne. He had his own private Shit-list of bums and rascals who were due to get their comeuppance. The Naghallah boys were all on his list. So he told us. *"All twelve of you."*

Old George laughed about it. "You boys loused yourselves up again."

A ROUGH AND READY CREW

June 14

Believe it or not, our Drillmaster, Captain Craig, is a song writer. He made up a song for the *Naghallah Cadets*. We sang it in our blue uniforms, loudly and somewhat off key:

We are the Kaah Naghallah boys.
A rough and ready crew.
People come and cheer for us
In everything we do.

You can tell us by our gallant deeds,
And by our fighting heart.
We never quail and never fail
In anything we start.

When we are challenged
And they put us to the test,
You can hear them saying,
"The boys of Kaah Naghallah are the best!"

Dr. Mehary didn't think much of the song. More suited to a summer camp than to a reform school. But visitors were impressed.

THE LION TAMER

I don't know if Captain Striker was ever really a lion tamer. But he treated us like we were a bunch of wild animals. He walked around with a long-handled whip and cracked it on the ground in all directions. Never quite hitting us, but coming uncomfortably close.

Striker would exhort us to work harder! "Come on, boy! Put some pep into it!" And while we could weed just as well sitting down as bending over, Striker wouldn't let us sit. "On your feet, boy! No loafing!" Then a crack of the whip, for emphasis.

Once, swinging wildly, he laid a lash across Stevie's legs, leaving a red welt. "Oh, I'm so sorry," said the Captain. "That was an accident. Did I hurt you?"

Stevie responded with a curse. Striker raised up the whip and I thought he was going to strike Stevie on purpose. Cameron gave a low whistle, which meant *Get ready for trouble*. Striker, however, cracked the whip on the ground again, just inches from Stevie's feet and walked away.

Striker realized if he whipped one kid, the rest of us would riot. But he walked around dishing out just one lash accidentally on purpose. Almost every day, at least one guy got hit. "Oh, I'm so sorry," murmured Striker. "Did I hurt you?"

Stevie, Keith and Danny, then Cameron, Troy, Bran and Jaymie were all targets. Roger and Jody scrambled out of his way. Jody, not quite fast enough. Hot-blooded Raymond got a hold of a kitchen knife. "If he whips me, I swear I'll cut him!"

Cameron told Raymond to *cool it*. "And get rid of that shiv. If anyone gets abused, we'll defend them. But just one lash, ain't worth a riot and getting us *all* creamed."

Raymond chucked the knife. Maybe we were "incorrigible, rebellious juvenile hoods," but when Cameron gave an order, we obeyed it. Raymond got himself a lash, too. "Sorry, boy, Did I hurt you?"

"Oh, I'm so sorry, Sir! It was an accident!"

Stevie was up in the tree, cutting dead limbs with a bucket of pruning sealer tar. And he dropped a load of tar on Striker's head. "Oh, I'm so sorry, sir. Did I hurt you?" It was an accident, Stevie insisted.

And Troy, who was watering, turned the hose on Striker, right in the face. "Awful sorry, sir."

In the confusion, Jody hit Striker with a mudball. And Danny threw his whip into a jungle of briars and poison ivy.

After that, Striker let us alone.

"THIS AIN'T THE GIFTED CHILD CLASS"

June 18

Karl Hasserman's silver spruce trees were infected with gall. They put us to work taking the gall off. Bare hand. With cutters that didn't cut. They were small and dull. But we were "dangerous juveniles" and weren't supposed to handle anything that might be used as a weapon.

Tree by tree, we took the gall off. But no matter how much infection we removed, there always seemed to be more.

"You ought to spray with Koraldine," suggested Big-mouth Jaymie. "You should have done it back in April. The gall is caused by an insect ——"

"When we want your advice, we'll ask for it," said "Colonel" Lammington, sourly. "Just do what you're told *and shut up!*"

"That's stupid ——" began Jaymie. And he gave me a rap in the mouth.

Big Brother Danny was watching. I thought he might try to defend me. And get in trouble himself. Instead, Danny was laughing.

"You haven't learned yet, have you, Little Brudder? You still think you're in the Gifted Child class."

One week later:

More and more gall. The infection we cleared kept growing back again. And spreading onto the healthy trees. We cut off whole branches to get rid of the stuff. Lammington looked mad, as usual. He said we cut off too much and ruined Karl Hasserman's magnificent silver spruce trees.

Jaymie said our pruning would make the trees better. The limbs we cut would all grow back stronger and healthier. I think I won the argument, but ended with another rap in the mouth.

Danny said, "Please don't argue with the Masters, Jaymiebrudder. Especially not with Striker and Lammington. They're a couple of S. O. B.'s. And that Klayborne is a maniac.

"I don't like to see you getting smacked around. I'll end up getting my own ass busted. You're my kid brudder and I'm supposed to protect you."

"Then why didn't you?"

"I couldn't stop him from giving you *one* smack. If he started giving you fifty cracks, I'd have butted in."

"Thanks a lot," said Jaymie, rubbing his jaw. "Thanks a lot for nothing!"

"Aw, what are you mad at *me* for?" asked Danny. "I didn't hit you."

RIOT!

June 28

"It looks like Old Matthews got the gate," said brother Danny. Matthews wasn't in school. Instead, they had a new teacher whose name was Mr. Smeer or something like that. You could see he didn't think much of us. He sat as far away from us as he could, like we were polluted.

We weren't dirty. We took a shower every day. Though they never gave us enough soap or clean clothes. We had to steal extra soap and wash our dirty stuff in the sink. We found out Donald liked to wash clothes. Naturally, we let him do it.

However, our being dirty wasn't the reason Mr. Smeer sat so far away from us. Mr. Smeer figured us for a bunch of hoods. He had an alarm bell on his desk to sound off, if he couldn't handle us. He wanted to be sure we didn't get close enough to jump him before he could ring it.

Mr. Smeer carried a long, thin cane. It wasn't the kind you use for walking. He swished it through the air, then laid it down on the desk for us to see. "I don't want any trouble in this class," he declared. "But if there is any, I know how to deal with trouble makers."

Roger gave a nervous laugh. Smeer glared at him. "What's your name, boy?"

"Roger Newland."

"You say *Sir* when you address a Master. Didn't you learn that boy? I want respect and courtesy in this class."

Silence. Mr. Smeer proceeded to call the roll. *Roberto Alliconda.*

"Bobby Alliconda, sir."

"It says Roberto on your record. Are you Spanish, Roberto?"

"My grandmother was Spanish. I lived with her."

"Alliconda is your grandmother's name. What was your father's name?"

Bobby shrugged. "Dunno. I never seen him."

Bobby expected us to laugh, but nobody did. Bobby looked so sad and hurt. Smeer, however, persisted in the interrogation.

"You lived with your grandmother, Roberto. But you were committed to Naghallah from the Greenwood Youth Shelter. Why was that? Did your grandmother throw you out?"

"She died," said Bobby.

Smeer continued the roll without comment . . . Caldwell . . . Feroldi . . Daniel Larrabie . . . *Daniel!* Brother Danny was dozing.

"Here," called Jaymie. Then Danny, waking up, said he was Jaymie Larrabie. Smeer glared at me. "Daniel Larrabie!"

"Yessir," said Jaymie.

"You're the one with the bad record. How many times were you in juvenile court, Daniel?"

"I didn't count them, sir," said Jaymie.

That got a laugh from my classmates and a stern look from Teacher Smeer. "I won't have any silliness in this class," he warned.

"Roger Newland!"

Roger giggled instead of answering

"Did you hear what I said, Roger?"

Roger pinched his nose, trying hard to stop laughing.

"Donald Turrentine." Don Don was silent as usual. Keith answered for him. "Here, sir."

Roger pinched his nose harder, but he couldn't stop the giggle.

Mr. Smeer gave him a look. "All right, Roger. That's *two* for you. I won't tolerate any fooling around in my school. We're going to have discipline here!"

Mr. Smeer considered himself a stern disciplinarian. Matthews was a milksop. He had let these boys run wild. With these punks, you had to crack down right from the beginning.

"Now let's see how much you know. Or rather how stupid you are."

He passed out some sheet with arithmetic problems. Mostly, fractions and long division. Only me, and maybe Keith could do them. I wrote the answers large so that

Danny and Raymond, on either side of me, could copy.
Stevie then copied from Danny. Bobby copied from Raymond. Donald was drawing snail shells. Troy, Roger, Brandon and Jody in the front row could just stare at the paper.
Roger pinched his arm to stop a giggle.

"Why aren't you writing, Jody Kallinger?"

"This is too hard, sir."

"You are eleven years old, aren't you, Jody? Surely by this time you shoud be able to do a simple problem in fractions. One fourth and one fifth. Come, come, Jody. You should do that in your head . . .

"I'll give you a hint." He wrote on the blackboard. *L.C.D. The lowest common denominator.* "Now what is the L.C.D. here, Jody?"

"I don't know, sir."

"You there. What's the L.C.D.?" He pointed to Jaymie.

"I don't know, sir."

"If you're that stupid, the boys next to you better copy from somebody else."

Roger's pinching failed him and he broke into a giggle. "All right, Roger," thundered Smeer. "I'm giving you the last warning!" He wrote *20* on the blackboard. "Now what is the answer, Roger Newland?"

"I don't know, sir."

"*Roger Newland!* Just what have I been talking about? What is the L.C.D.?"

"Twenty," whispered Jaymie. But Roger didn't hear me. His giggle turned into a look of apprehension.

"I can't believe you are that stupid. What is the *Lowest Common Denominator* of five and four?"

"Fifty-four," stammered Roger.

"Do you have sawdust in your brain, boy? What is a denominator?"

"I don't know, sir." Roger was shaking.

"You don't know what a denominator is? You are an imbecile, Roger. I'm going to have to smarten you up."

Smeer reached for the cane. "Come up here!"

Terrified, Roger clung to his chair.

Mr. Smeer looked at his hands as if he didn't want to soil

them. He wanted us to do his dirty work, bringing Roger to justice.

"You there, Keith Caldwell," ordered Smeer. "Bring Newland up here to me!" He swished the cane back and forth. *"Do it!"*

Keith placed his arms lightly on Roger's shoulders. Roger clung even tighter. Keith rocked the kid feebly back and forth. "I can't move him, sir." Keith sure wasn't trying very hard.

I looked at Cameron. He had his book ready to throw. That meant *Riot.* But he didn't throw it yet.

"Roberto Alliconda," commanded Smeer. "Bring Newland up here!" Bobby just sat there and shook his head stupidly.

"What's the matter with you, Roberto? Talk Spanish if you can't speak English. Bring Newland up here!" He pointed.

"Bese me anca," said Bobby.

Smeer didn't speak Spanish and didn't know Bobby had told him to "Kiss my ass."

"You two. Larrabie and Scanlon," commanded Smeer. "Help Caldwell. You three big, strong boys ought to be able to bring Roger up here."

Stevie and Danny came forward. But instead of seizing the culprit, Roger, Stevie tackled his friend Keith. And Danny tackled Stevie. The four became a pile of wrestling, struggling youths with Roger in the middle. Angrily, Smeer grasped his cane and descended upon them.

Now Cameron threw his book. *Riot!* And joined the melee. So did Raymond, Bobby and Jaymie. So did Brandon, Troy and Jody. Only Donald remained aloof.

Mr. Smeer charged in, swinging his cane on any boy in sight. I guess he was aiming at our butts. But at least half the blows landed on our arms and legs and back. Smeer landed about a dozen blows, one of them on me. Then Don Don caught him by the legs and tripped him up.

Smeer struggled to his feet. He was swinging the cane wildly and violently. One stroke caught Brother Danny across the face, leaving a red welt. Once again, the urchins tripped him. They tore the cane out of his hand and broke it.

Smeer was shouting for help. He tried to reach the desk and sound the alarm. He went down for the third time. We pulled off his shoes and tore off his coat and shirt. He kept yelling and the boys ripped off his pants and undershirt. At length, the shoeless and trouserless teacher regained his feet and fled out of the room.

Smeer was shouting for reinforcements to quash the youth rebellion. "Let's get out of here!" shouted Cameron. "Follow me. On the double!" On our way, we tossed Smeer's pants and shoes into the garbage.

About five minutes later, a group of guards with rubber sticks charged into the classroom. But it was empty. They charged into the Boys' Dormitory. But that was empty, too.

We sprinted through the kitchen, grabbing some bread and cheese. Cameron led us out into the fields. "The Naghallah boys reporting for work, sir."

"You're early," said Old George. "No gall today. Weeding." We weeded with a good deal less goofing around than usual.

It took them over an hour until they found us. Major Powell and his men rounded us up less violently than we expected. We were prodded and pushed, but nobody took a real swing at us. Maybe they tired themselves out hunting for us. "Dr. Mehary wants to see you. *Now!*"

We were marched to the office. To our surprise and relief, Smeer wasn't there. Mehary eyed us silently for several minutes. Finally, he spoke. "I have been informed about your disgraceful behavior. Just what do you have to say for yourselves?"

Cameron gave me a look that said, "You talk, Gifted Child. You're the champion bullshitter."

"Sir," said Jaymie, "we didn't do anything but defend ourselves. Mr. Smeer started hitting us with a stick."

"I don't believe that."

"Yessir. He started hitting Roger just because Roger didn't know something."

Smeer laid his cane on every boy within reach.

Then Donald came up from behind and tripped him up.

"Is that true, Roger?"

"Yessir. I didn't know what a *Denominator* was."

"And what *is* a denominator?" demanded Mehary.

"I still don't know, sir," said Roger trembling.

"He hit me, too," broke in Jaymie. "And he hit my brudder, Danny. Look at Danny's face." The welt from the cane
was large and red.

Complaints came from all sides. Everyone said they had
been hit, *"for nothing"*. Mehary threw up his hands. "I
don't want to hear any more. You hoodlums won't get any
sympathy from me. Go to your room. *No supper. And
three hundred bad conduct marks for all of you!* Dismiss."

We marched out with relief. The lost supper didn't matter. We had enough stolen biscuits and stuff stacked away.
And the bad conduct markers didn't give us any sweat.
But one thing was sure. We weren't going to get any time
off for good behavior. "You fellows really loused up this
time," Old George told us.

However, the rebellion had one unexpected benefit. They
put Mr. Matthews back again as our teacher.

"Matthews knows how to deal with these punks."

"Matthews is the only one who can handle these juvenile
hoods."

They equipped him with an alarm bell, but he never rang
it. We never gave him any reason to. Mr. Matthews was
the least shitty teacher we could expect at *Kaah
Naghallah*.

The guys were always making up crazy nicknames.
Jaymie was stuck with *The Gifted Child*. Brandon,
celebrated by Gay Poet, was *The Urchin Bold, With Hair
of Gold*. Donald was *Strip, the Whirling Boy*. Cameron was
The Cat Burglar and got meowed at. Danny was *The
Shovel Buster*, Stevie, *The Pants Ripper*, Bobby, *The Dirt
Spiller*.

And now Roger became forever more *The Denominator
Kid*.

Later

They put us to work weeding thorn bushes. Real prickly and stingy. No gloves, of course. I guess this was supposed to be a punishment. But we did a real sloppy job of it.

A TEST OF MANHOOD

June 30

It took a while for "Commander" Bartlow to get around to me and Danny again.

"I have a message for you and your — youth gang. Is that what you call it?"

"It's a club, sir."

"Do you know who this message is from? It's from Karl Hasserman himself. I told you once he had big plans for you. And now the time is coming near——". He paused. Me and Danny remained silent.

"You need have no fear, boys. No harm will come to you. *If, that is, you do what you are told.* Everything has been carefully planned to insure your safety. You will be safe, if you follow our instructions. But if you disobey orders — if you go off on your own — things may happen that we cannot control.

"There must be absolute obedience. *Do what you are told to do and nothing else!* Tell that to the other boys."

"Just what is this thing we are supposed to do?" asked Jaymie.

Bartlow hesitated. "Let us say it is a kind of test. A test of manhood. To see if you are ready to graduate from *Kaah Naghallah.*"

"You mean they'll let us out?" asked Danny. "I thought we were supposed to be here for three years."

Mr. Bartlow smiled. "We're not going to dump you out on the street. I know most of the boys have no home to go to. You will remain at *Kaah Naghallah.* But no longer inmates. You will be honor students. You will share and enjoy all the privileges the Masters have. Would you like that?"

If that ever happened, the Masters wouldn't like it at all. They thought we were a bunch of worthless punks, and would be piqued at having to treat us as equals.

Jaymie asked, "What will happen if we flunk this test, sir? Will we get a chance to take it again next year?"

Commander Bartlow frowned. "No, Jaymie, I'm afraid this is a one-shot thing. If you flunk, the consequences could be — most unpleasant.

"You may go now." That was all that he would tell us.

THE INVESTIGATOR

July 4

The staff of *Kaah Naghallah* and their families held a big picnic and celebration. Feasting, fun and games. We boys weren't included. We didn't expect to be. We got out of school though and slept half the morning.

Later, we were conscripted for the clean-up. There were lots of eats left over. Guardian Craig was real friendly. "Dig in, lads. Help yourselves!" We ate a lot and stole all the leftovers we could carry.

The next day, a Police Inspector visited the Institute. He was investigating something. He wanted to talk to "the boys" privately. Colonel Lammington said. "Sure. Talk to them all you want."

The Inspector asked us, was there anything wrong at *Kaah Naghallah*? Was there some mystery going on here?

Cameron said be real careful. The guy might well be a phony. The Masters might just be testing us to see if we would blurt out something bad about the school. We told him there was nothing wrong here that we could see. But to make it seem real, we griped a little. They made us work too hard. And we got no recreation.

The Inspector said he didn't run the school and couldn't change their policies. But hard work never hurt anybody. He went away a bit disappointed that he didn't get more out of us.

ANCIENT CIVILIZATION

Dr. Mehary was expecting some important visitors. A delegation of behavior-modifying psychologists to whom he would show off his successful methods for *"the correction and control of delinquent and defective juveniles."*. They would visit the school where Mr. Matthews was ordered to put us through our paces.

Teacher Matthews was somewhat nervous about it. You could never predict what the Naghallah schoolboys would do. Especially in front of visitors who came to observe us like we were a bunch of circus freaks. We might act up and embarass Dr. Mehary. And maybe get Teacher Matthews fired again.

Matthews decided the best way to get through the visit was to call on Jaymie and have me give a talk. The talks I give either bore the guys or make them laugh. I figured it would be better to make them laugh.

My last talk was on *The Creatures of the Sea*. This time, Matthews suggested *Ancient Civilizations*. "There's a book in the library, Jaymie—"

The library was *out-of-bounds* for the Naghallah boys. But Matthews had a key and let me in. It was a huge green room filled with important-looking books covered with dust. One of the few places we hadn't been made to clean.

The book, *Ancient Civilizations*, was by Karl Hasserman, the mysterious benefactor and sponsor of our school. Translated from the German and still replete with German words and phrases.

Strangely, the book appeared to run backwards. The first chapters dealt with familiar lands. Egypt, China, Persia and Mesopotamia. Then on to still earlier times when reality was mingled with myth and make-believe. *The Lost continent of Atlantis. The Golden Empire of Antarctica.* Back in the days when the South Pole continent was warm.

Move back now to still earlier times, many centuries before Atlantis. These were the days of *Die Alten*, the Old Ones. "A superior people of great power". Their's was *Die Erste Gesittung*, the First Civilization.

"How did they come to Earth, these Beings who were more than human? Perhaps in starships or through a Gateway from another world. When did they come? Perhaps in the days of the dinosaurs and like the dinosaurs they vanished from the face of the Earth . . ."

There were *Uralte Runen* (Ancient writings) hidden in caverns, tombs and secret places. The writer claimed he had deciphered them. There were pages of illustrations showing "this ancient language". It looked like a lot of squiggles with a ball pen made by a blind-folded monkey.

At the beginning of the book was a quotation from Fichte. *Reality is stranger than the wildest imagination.* The final pages of the book had been removed.

Inside the jacket, were some handwritten notes:

Nothing has been heard of the second Bane N'Gai group for more than a month. Nor is there any trace of the first group. If there are any survivors, they are lost and unable to return.

HOW TO HANDLE INQUIRIES: *It would be best to make a complete denial. Any investigation would be disastrous to* (can't read it) . . .

A THIRD BANE N'GAI ATTEMPT?

Lammington has determined that boys of an early adolescent or pre-adolescent age would have the greatest chance of success. They are more adaptable and would be better able to survive the crossing.

We could recruit a group from Dr. Mehary's Institute. If properly controlled, these street kids would be well suited. They can withstand a high degree of stress. Avoid those youths who . . .

That was the end of it. But I could guess at the missing words. *Avoid those youths who would be missed if they did not return.*

None of the Naghallah boys would be missed, excepting me and Danny. And Mr. Bartlow could doubtless find a way to handle our parents. "Crazy, reckless kids! They ran away from the school. You couldn't control them. But don't give up hope. We're doing everything we can to find them."

Was this thing for real? Or was it a hoax? Finding the notes by chance was too unlikely. Somebody must have meant for me to find them. But why? Was this part of our "training and treatment" to scare us and make us feel fear? Like the Krakens and the Mandrils, the Death swamp, the underground dungeons and the gun pointed at Stevie's head? Or was it a warning?

From who? From Teacher Matthews? Was he our secret friend? Why didn't he tell us outright? Perhaps he didn't dare. I made a copy of the notes on the library duplicating machine and gave them to Cameron.

Matthews said nothing. He seemed a little nervous. He took a couple of swigs from that brandy bottle he kept in his desk, when he thought nobody was watching.

I made up a talk from Karl Hasserman's bullshit and added some bullshit of my own. The visitors, however, didn't hear me. A couple of people stuck their noses in and gawked at us. When they heard a boy was going to give a talk, they walked out.

I talked just to the class. I spoke real serious, like a professor lecturing. That way, I can always make the guys laugh. I even got applause.

THE MASTERS OF NAGHALLAH

Cameron called a gang meeting. For some time, we had worried about our dormitory being bugged. Were the Masters listening in on us? We searched the Boy-room all over, even in the shower. There was no trace of any recording device or unusual equipment.

Keith had an idea. The Masters of Naghallah were very concerned about getting *"respect"*. If we insulted them enough, they were unlikely to ignore it. One of them would get mad and rap on us.

We formed a circle. Each guy in turn had to insult one of the Masters:

"Striker is a piece of shit," began Bobby.

"Klayborne is a fucking queer!" declared Stevie.

"Dr. Mehary is a kinky screwball," ventured Keith.

"Vedemore is a scumbag," said Raymond.

"Mr Smeer is a smelly pig!" giggled Roger.

"Major Powell is a prick!" asserted Cameron.

"Mr. Bartlow is a fucking ass hole!" proclaimed Danny.

"K. H. is a crook," suggested Brandon.

"Lammington is a louse!" continued Jaymie.

"Captain Craig is a clown," declared Troy.

"Mr. Matthews is a funnyman," chuckled Jody.

Craig and Matthews were the least unpopular of the Masters and their insults, accordingly, were the mildest.

Donald stuck his tongue out and made animal noises. "Oink! Oink!" "Squawk! Squawk!" And he thumbed his nose at the window.

We went around the circle several times. After a while, we ran out of insults and started repeating.

Keith put on an imitation of Dr. Mehary, with his high voice and a bit of a lisp. Keith was a scream. He went prancing around with a pair of phony glasses falling off his nose. Bobby and Stevie were his victims. "Poor sick boys!" he lamented. He grabbed Bobby. "A pathological, pixilated puerile punk."

"Dr. Mehary" grabbed Stevie. "I'm going to modify your shitty behavior. Some adversive conditioning for you-hoo!"

Keith pretended to beat them all over the place while lecturing on the *Mehary Method* for treating *"these miserable, maladjusted, messed up misfits."*

"Now I'm going to take these sick children apart and put them together *correctly.*"

He picked up an imaginary needle about a foot long and tried to stick it into Stevie and Bobby. He broke one needle on Bobby and two on Stevie. The fourth time, "Dr. Mehary" stuck the needle into himself by accident and collapsed.

The next day, we were called into Dr. Mehary's office. But not about the insults. Actually, Dr. Mehary praised us

for once. He said he had received a good report on us from
Old George and another good report from Teacher Matthews.

No one seemed mad at us or gave any sign of having
heard the disrespectful insults. Cameron concluded that
maybe we weren't being bugged after all. The Masters of
Naghallah held us in contempt and ignored any silly
schemes we might engage in.

IN THE COYOTES' DEN

Reassured that we were not being bugged, Cameron called a High Council of the Coyotes. "Those notes Jaymie
found, those warnings we got, all might be bullshit. But
where there is a lot of smoke, there might be fire."

Almost all the guys had heard something frightening
about the *Kaah Naghallah* school before they came here.

"I heard some stories about this place, too. 'We could
send you to the state reformatory, Westcott. Instead,
we're sending you to *Kaah Naghallah.*'

"'What kind of a joint is that?' asks me.

"'It's an Institute to study the behavior of punks like
you. They break you down into little pieces and then stick
you together again. If they mess you up, that wouldn't be
any loss.'

"I thought of a place run by mad scientists where they
operate on your brain. I said I'd rather go to the Reformatory. But they said, 'Tough shit, punk! You're headed
for *Kaah Naghallah.* You're muckled, screwed and fucked.'

"But when I got here, I couldn't believe it. Getting locked up with a lot of little kids."

(Derisive cries and jeers from Cameron's brothers.)

Cameron threw his hands up. "Okay! I'm the oldest guy
here — I think. Anyway, I'm the biggest and the
toughest." *(More yells and jeers.)* "Well, maybe Danny and
Stevie — or maybe Ray Ray could take me. I don't want to
fight my friends.

"What I mean is nothing really bad has happened at *Kaah Naghallah*. We got kicked around a little. But no worse than in any boy reform school.

"Maybe these nightmare stories were all bullshit. I sure hope so. But maybe they just haven't happened *yet.*"

There was a moment of chilly silence. The guys all looked at each other. We all had the same feeling. Some invisible evil hanging over us. I thought of K.H. as a tremendous spider in the center of a gigantic web. Somewhere inside the web, we twelve youths were trapped, guarded by the Masters of Naghallah until K. H. was ready to use us. *For what?*

Cameron said, "We'll have to find out something about Karl Hasserman." That meant spying in the mansion. It would have to be at night, when they think we're asleep.

"We'll send out just one guy," Cameron decreed. "Two guys would be ten times as likely to be spotted. *The Coyote Scout.* That'll have to be *me.*"

"Why you?" Both Stevie and Danny wanted to be The Coyote Scout.

"Because I know how to move quietly. And I can see in the dark. I wasn't The Cat Burglar for nothing."

"You got caught, didn't you?"

"I got careless and got bad breaks. And I got greedy. But you should have seen the loot I collected."

"What did you do with the loot?"

"Pissed it away," said Cameron, sadly.

Cameron gradually collected the tools he needed. A couple of screwdrivers, a turnblade, wrench, pliers, microcutter, nippers. Bobby and Raymond, accomplished shoplifters, carried out their assignment fully, while we were cleaning up around the tool shop.

"Don't *you* steal nothing, Jaymie. You're too clumsy. You'll be caught for sure."

We hid the stuff out on the roof. The Masters were constantly searching our room, but never looked out there. We found an extension cord in the cellar and smuggled it upstairs. Cameron really didn't need it to climb up and down. He could climb like a squirrel.

The night was dark and foggy, with drizzling rain. A shitty night for most people, but just right for the Cat Burglar. The only trouble was the Masters who kept breaking in on us to make a "bed check". Everybody got in the act. Striker, Vedemore, Craig, Lammington, Klayborne, Powell and even Teacher Matthews and Dr. Mehary himself. At least, not Smeer. He kept away from us.

We rigged up a dummy in Cameron's bed. Two stuffed laundry sacks under the blankets, with a sleeve sticking out. Easy to spot up close, but the Masters usually just flashed the light around.

"Move your bed up real close, Jody." That would half block the Master's view.

"I don't want to sleep next to a dummy," objected Jody.

"That's not a dummy. That's your brother, Cameron."

Jody giggled. "What'll I say if they ask me ——"

"Don't say nothin. Pretend you're asleep."

"How do you do that?"

"Keep your eyes shut and suck your thumb, like you usually do."

Loyally, Jody sucked his thumb and snuggled close to the dummy. Cameron removed the window guards and frames and descended to the ground. Then Keith and Stevie replaced them. Gradually, the guys grew quiet and went to bed.

About an hour later, the hall light went on. Then a sliding bolt and a jangle of keys. Stevie, on guard, had just time to duck under the blankets.

The door of the dormitory opened. A flashlight moved around the room, pausing an instant at each bed. Then the voice of Teacher Matthews. "You guys all right? Everyone asleep?"

No answer. Jody bit his arm to stop a giggle. Now the door was locked and bolted again. Retreating footsteps.

Feeling safe at last, Jody released his suppressed giggle. But he muffled it under the blankets.

Stevie, the watchman, returned to guard the window, now joined by Keith. The silence was broken only by the light rain falling on the roof. Finally, you could hear the call of an owl. *Too whit. Too Whooo.* Repeated three times. The window opened and the cord dropped down. Then Cameron climbed back into the room.

RECONNAISSANCE

July 19

"Gather ye in a circle," ordered Cameron. "But keep it low. No lights."

"Did you get in the mansion?"

"Did you see K. H.?" We piled on the questions.

Cameron smiled a bit wearily. "You didn't expect me to do it on the first try. I had to case the joint first.

"Anyone but the Cat Burglar would have gotten caught. Everything around the mansion is wired for an alarm. They got infra-red lights that set off a signal, if anything comes through."

"You mean we can't get in the mansion?" cried Raymond in dismay.

"Oh, we can get in. But first we got to get in the guard box and shut off the alarm. It opens with a triadic megakey."

Only Keith knew what *that* was. "The one with the three points. There's one on the key board in the tool room closet.

"Our last foster father was a locksmith. He had all kinds of crazy keys."

"Yeah," said Stevie. "He kept everything locked up. Even the bread box and the refrigerator." Keith and Stevie never got a full meal. Until they stole the master key. That got them into trouble. "That's one reason he decided to dump us."

Keith said, "Me and Stevie opened up the wine cellar. We stole a split of brandy. What a ball we had! Scanlon passed out."

"You did too, Caldwell."

"Okay, we both did. But you went first."

"I drank more than you did."

It shouldn't be too hard to get into that closet. Take the door hinges off, then put them back on again. Cameron could be in and out in maybe ten minutes. But the chances of getting caught were great. At night, the alarm system would be on. In the daytime, the Masters and guards were always snooping around.

"Anybody got any ideas?" Cameron looked around the circle.

"Create a diversion," suggested Jaymie. "How about a fight?"

"Hey, that's good," said Cameron. "Who's going to fight?"

"Me and Danny," volunteered Jaymie.

Danny said, "That fight wouldn't last long. There'd be just two hits. *One* when I hit Jaymie and *Two* when Jaymie hit the floor."

Cameron said, "Sorry, Jaymie. You got a great brain, but you can't fight for beans. You do the scheming. Let Stevie and Danny do the fighting."

THE DIVERSION

The next day, it was still raining and we were put to work cleaning the cellar again. At the appropriate time, Stevie Scanlon and his pal and buddy, Danny Larrabie, squared off. They shouted curses and insults at each other. Then they began to slug. The Coyotes all gathered around them, screaming and yelling and making unsuccessful attempts to pull them apart.

Guardian Matthews came running over, joined by Old George and another guy. The slugging and yelling continued. A signal from Cameron. He had the triadic key. And the battling youths let themselves be separated.

Teacher Matthews bawled them out. "Shame on you! Calling each other such vile names." Determined to show he was no milksop, Matthews tried to act like a stern disciplinarian. He ordered the boys each to stand on an inverted bucket facing the wall of the cellar. Danny looked at

Cameron, who signalled *Do it.*

"For how long, Teach?"

"Until I tell you to stop."

Stevie and Danny stayed on the buckets for about fifteen minutes, until they got tired and bored. Then they walked away. Teacher Matthews, however, was determined to show his authority. "You will shake hands," he ordered, severely. "And you will apologize to each other. Otherwise you will go back on the buckets."

So Stevie and Danny shook hands and traded apologies. Matthews prided himself on how well he was able to handle these juvenile hoods. Stevie had a black eye; Danny, a cut lip. "We had to make it look real."

Stevie said, "I'm sorry, Danny. I didn't mean to muckle you, like that."

And Danny said, "You got muckled a lot worse than me, Scanlon. *I'm* the one who has to be sorry."

Stevie retorted, "You're full of shit, Larrabie. You got the worst beating. *I'm* the guy who ought to be the sorriest."

And, believe it or not, Danny and his pal, Stevie, started fighting about who should be the sorriest for beating up the other guy the worst.

Cameron warned them. "If you have a real fight, that's breaking the Boy Law and we'll dunk both of you."

"Yeah?" said Stevie. "Who's gonna dunk us? You and what army?"

"Me and the Coyotes."

"Those squirts are gonna dunk me and Danny? They couldn't even dunk a doughnut."

We did dunk both Stevie and Danny. But everybody else got soaked in the process.

Mr. Matthews wanted to know how our clothes got so wet. "We got caught in the rain, sir." volunteered Raymond.

"How could you get caught in the rain when you didn't go out of the building?"

"I don't know, sir. It must have rained right through the roof."

Mr. Matthews sighed and shrugged. He had long since ceased to expect any sense from the madcap urchins in his screwball class.

RECONNAISSANCE II

Jack Eberle — Captain Eberle to us — was second in command of Major Powell's police force. Lots of tools and stuff were reported missing. He came around and searched our dormitory, pulling everything apart.

We were real careful to replace the frames and cross-bars on the window, just like they had been before. They didn't think we could get out on the roof and didn't look there, but everything else got a going over, from the toilet bowl to the bedding. All our drawers were emptied out. Our clothes and things were thrown around. In the end, our room was in shambles and he found nothing.

Eberle lined us up. Then he pulled Jody out of line. "What do you know about the missing tools, Kallinger?"

"Nothing, sir."

Next, he pulled out Roger. "What happened to those tools, Newland? I want the truth now!"

"I don't know, sir."

Finally, he pulled out Jaymie. He must have figured me for a weak sister, too.

"No, sir. I don't know nothing."

"You don't know nothing? What kind of grammar is that, boy? *Dismiss!*" He walked out, leaving us to clean up the mess.

We were real proud of Jody and Roger. They had learned to lie with a perfectly straight face. No twitching or quavering. *Coyotes loyal and true.* Cameron tied a shoe lace around each of their necks, pretending it was a medal.

The Cat Burglar made three more reconnaissance trips before he broke into the mansion. Cameron was being real cautious. He discovered an underground passageway that connected our cellar with the cellar of the mansion.

"There's a door in the wall, covered up with some sheets of plywood. Just a spring lock. You can open it with a penknife. I figured there was a door there."

"How?" asked Troy.

"Muddy footprints, Brother Feroldi. Just going one way."

"You're a detective."

"I'm a thief. A good thief has to detect on the cops."

But you couldn't break into the mansion that way. Cameron tried it and set off an alarm. "I scooted back fast and replaced the plywood." Cameron then set off another false alarm on purpose. That was part of his strategy. Set off a lot of false alarms. Then they wouldn't pay attention if a real alarm went off.

Cameron also scouted the office of Dr. Mehary, the Director of *Kaah Naghallah*. "He yells at us for being messy. But his place looks like a garbage dump." Crammed with files and cardboard boxes, old journals and nutty books.

Dr. Mehary was writing a book himself. *On the Control and Correction of Sociopathic Juveniles.* "That means trouble-making punks like us. Right?"

The twelve Naghallah boys will all be in that book. "But he changed our names around. Brandon is Bradford. Me, I'm Tony. There's a whole chapter on him. I really *am* Tony. *Cameron Anthony Westcott.*" The bastard brat of an old southern family that had gone to seed. So said Cameron.

He almost got caught, too. Cameron was so busy reading a book, *The Sexual Problems of Adolescent Girls,* that he didn't notice Dr. Mehary coming in. He just managed to hide behind the files.

Cameron's last excursion almost ended in disaster. That nosy Jack Eberle made the bed check. He wasn't satisfied just to flash the light around, as usual. He began to examine every bed.

Donald rose up silently. His long arms were stretched out in front of him. His hands touched against Captain Eberle and then pulled away. Once again, he touched the

Captain, then yelled as if he had burned his fingers. Slowly and stiffly, he started for the door.

"Hey, you! Where are you going? Come back here!"

Donald didn't answer. He kept on going. His yellow eyes were frozen in a glassy stare.

"Stop, you!"

"He can't hear you, sir," said Jaymie. "He's sleep walking."

"Is that the retard?"

"His name is Donald Turrentine, sir."

"Stop, Turrentine! You stupid dummy!"

Donald had opened the door and entered the hall. Eberle went after him and seized him. He slapped and shook Donald. but the kid's face remained rigid and frozen.

Eberle kept shaking and slapping the youth. Cries of anger came from the other guys. The Captain thrust Donald back into the room. "Here, you take him. Put him to bed." He closed the dormitory door and locked it. Cameron's bed remained unchecked and unnoticed.

If that sleep walking was put on, Donald sure could act! For a moment, Donald's face softened into a faint smile. Then he became the retarded boy again, making bird calls and animal noises.

The guys clustered around Donald, patting him on the back and punching him playfully. "Thanks, Don Don. You saved Cameron's ass and everybody else's, too."

Donald's yellow eyes gleamed. He lifted up his hand and pointed to the window. There was a moment of silence. Then the chirping of the crickets and the rustling of the wind through the trees. More silence. Then the familiar hooting of an owl. Cameron had returned.

THE PLACE OF EVIL SECRETS

July 26

"Form ye the circle," ordered Gangleader Cameron. The other eleven Coyotes sprawled out on the floor. "I was in the mansion. That's quite a place. Full of beautiful stuff to steal, if I still was The Cat Burglar." We all began jabbering and asking questions. "Keep it down," ordered Cameron. "One guy at a time. We don't want the Masters breaking in on us. Hold your hand up if you want to talk. Yeah, Ray Ray?"

"Did you see Karl Hasserman?"

"Nope, I couldn't find what room he's in. There are a couple of rooms that are locked and have a curtain in front of the window. He might be in one of those. Yeah, Stevie?"

"I didn't put my hand up. I was scratching my ear."

"Downstairs," continued Cameron, "they were holding a meeting. I think Bartlow and Lammington were there. And Vedemore, Striker and Klayborne. I could hear their talk, or some of it, through the air vent."

"No sign of Hasserman?"

"Nope. They were talking about tunnels. And a labyrinth. You know what a labyrinth is?"

Keith did. "A whole bunch of tunnels and underground passages running into each other. A big maze. A guy goes in and he can't find his way out."

"I heard about a labyrinth," said Troy. "There was a monster in it."

"Yeah? What happened?"

"When anyone went into the labyrinth, the monster ate them up."

Jody looked scared and bit his nails. Roger shivered. "I hope it ain't true. There ain't really a labyrinth, is there, Cameron? Not around here?"

"We don't know. There just might be a labyrinth behind that locked door in the under-sub-basement."

"With a monster in it?"

"You can't tell what's in a labyrinth. You have to go inside to find out. There was something in this labyrinth the men wanted very much to find. People went down to look for it, but didn't come back.

"Vedemore started talking about tunnels. There are ways of measuring tunnels — empty spaces between solid rock — by vibration patterns and electromagnetic waves. They can do that in ordinary mines and caves. But there's no way of mapping these tunnels. The patterns always keep changing. The real tunnels are never like the instruments show.

"You had to go in by the passage way. They couldn't dig down. I didn't make out why. Maybe they feared digging would cause the tunnels to collapse. Or maybe ——" Cameron paused — "*they're afraid whatever Things are down there might get out.*"

Something Cameron did triggered an alarm. "I tried to think of a story to tell in case they caught me. How I seen a guy skulking around and followed him into the mansion. They wouldn't believe me, but it would be better than nothing. I hoped they wouldn't do anything worse than beat the shit out of me."

For a while, everybody was running around in circles. Then they decided there was no intruder. "That fool alarm just went off again by itself". Finally, Cameron was able to make his escape.

"I found out one more thing. The name of the labyrinth. It is called *Bane N'Gai.* That means *The Place of Evil Secrets.*"

THE MAN WHO WASN'T THERE

July 30

Cameron continued his reconnaissance, trying to find Karl Hasserman. There were three locked rooms on the second floor of the mansion, with the windows covered by curtains. "Two of the rooms were empty." The Cat Burglar climbed up and gained entry through one of the windows.

"I got a look in the third room." Cameron paused for dramatic effect. He couldn't resist being a bit of a ham actor. "There was a guy in it. But it wasn't Karl Hasserman."

"How do you know?" asked Danny.

"Because, Brother Daniel, it was your friend. The tall guy with the little moustache. Commander Bullshit."

"You mean Commander Bartlow? He's no friend of mine. He did everything he could to muckle me. And Jaymie, too."

"How did he muckle you?" asked Bobby.

"By sending us here to *Kaah Naghallah*. Only it turned out he done us a favor."

"We hope," said Keith.

"Well, you're not going to be bored here," predicted Cameron. "You guys wanted excitement and it looks like we're going to get it."

"What makes you think so?"

"Because there's a big mystery about this place. Hasserman is supposed to be running it, but nobody sees him. Visitors just disappear. And there's something behind that locked door in the under-sub-basement."

Just thinking about that place down below made us all shiver a bit.

"That Bartlow made himself right at home, like he owned the place." continued Cameron. "It began to rain and I was getting soaked. I figured I better get out of here. Nothing's going to happen. Then this other guy came in. He was an old German with a heavy accent. But it wasn't Karl Hasserman, the billionaire."

"How do you know?"

"I didn't at first. Bartlow called him Hasserman, and this old German did look something like *K. H.* in that picture. But the real Karl Hasserman was a big man. This guy was sort of shrivelled up and a lot shorter.

"The big reason though was how he and Bartlow talked to each other. The real K. H. would be giving orders to Bartlow. But Bartlow was giving orders to *him.* He was real polite, this old German. Not just polite, he was — you know, bowing and stuff. What's the word for that, Gifted Child?"

"Obsequious," suggested Jaymie.

"Yeah. Like Bartlow was a king or something. Called him *Eure Gnaden Kommandanten.* What's that?"

"Most Honorable Commander," translated Brandon.

"Were they speaking German or English?"

"Sort of mixed up. I couldn't understand most of it. What are *Dreckige Lausbuben?*"

"Dirty no-good juvenile punks," translated Brandon.

"I figured that must be *us,*" said Cameron. "Bartlow was trying to tell the old German not to stick his nose into things. We were *dreckige Lausbuben,* not worth bothering about.

"Then the German showed Bartlow a sheet of paper and Bartlow looked pleased. He stuck the sheet in a drawer. I wanted like anything to get a look at that sheet and I hung out there in the rain, getting more and more soaked.

"At last they both left the room." Cameron got a fast look. "And do you know what was on that paper?"

Nobody even tried to guess.

"Just a name written on it. The same name twenty times.

Karl Hasserman
Karl Hasserman
Karl Hasserman

"He was practicing forgery," concluded Keith.

"We got something on Bartlow then," said Danny, happily. "The big shot model citizen is a forger. We could blackmail him."

"Maybe we could," said Gangleader Cameron. "But did

you ever think, Brother Daniel. It might be rather dangerous — *for us?*"

The Next day

Cameron hung his wet clothing up to dry. It was, however, one of Mehary's snooping days. After inspecting our dorm, he confronted us in the school room. "Westcott, Cameron! Why were your clothes wet?"

"Were they wet, sir?" asked Cameron in pretended surprise.

"You know very well they were wet and I want to know why!"

Cameron looked blank. Mehary glanced around the classroom. "You want to tell us, Feroldi, Troy?"

"Tell you what, sir?"

"Why Cameron's clothes are wet, of course, you stupid little punk."

"I don't know, sir!" cried Troy in alarm.

Mehary stared at the assembled youths again. "Is your hand up, Larrabie, Jaymie?"

"No, sir."

"Suppose you tell us anyway why Cameron's clothes are wet."

"We put him in the shower, sir."

"With all his clothes on? But *Why?* What did Cameron do? Was that a punishment?"

"No, sir. It was sort of an initiation. To celebrate Cameron's birthday."

"You put Cameron in the shower with his clothes on to celebrate his birthday? That was rather childish, wasn't it?"

"Yessir. But it was fun."

"Fun?" demanded Dr. Mehary. He picked up a ruler and slammed it on the desk in disgust. Then he walked out of the room.

Later, the guys decided to initiate Jaymie as the world's champion bullshitter. I got stuck in the shower with my clothes on, naturally.

A BIG MEETING AT THE MANSION

August 3

"Form ye the circle!" called Gangleader Cameron and the Coyotes gathered around him. Roger and Jody hastened to grab a place on either side of Cameron.

After a couple of night outings in which he saw nothing and nothing happened, Cameron had finally hit on something important. "There was a big meeting at the mansion. Commander Bartlow was there. And Dr. Mehary. And Colonel Lammington. And Striker, Klayborne, Vedemore, Craig and Powell. And Smeer and Eberle. They were all there. They drank a lot and ate a lot. First, they were all laughing. Then things got nasty.

"There was a big argument. About *The Boys* — that is, *Us*. Mehary did most of the talking. Everyone else seemed to be against him. Lammington finally told him to *Shut up!*"

"He told Mehary to *Shut up?*" The Coyote kids laughed.

"Yeah. Whatever they were planning, Mehary didn't like it. Mehary said *he* was in charge of us and *he* would decide things. Lammington told Mehary he was just hired help. 'You're being paid and paid well, so don't go shooting your mouth off.'

"Mehary started talking about his reputation. Klayborne told him he didn't have any reputation. He was a big windbag and a phony."

The Coyote kids all laughed again.

"Mehary talked about his responsibility. Eleven of the boys — all except Jaymie — had been sent to him by Judge Tuffney, of the Greenwood Juvenile Court.

"Then Vedemore broke in and said, 'You know why the Judge sent those punks here instead of to the State reform school? He was paid off, that's why. And don't tell me you didn't know it.'"

"Judge Tuffney was paid off to send us to *Kaah Naghallah?*" cried Bobby, unbelievingly.

"That's what Vedemore said. I wish I'd had a tape recorder. I don't think Bartlow and Lammington liked to have him blurt it out like that.

"Anyway, Mehary got up pale and shaking and said 'Do you want my resignation?' And Bartlow said, 'Of course not. You are still the Head of the School. We will consult you about everything.'

"Mehary left then, not quite so mad. The others began to talk about him. Bartlow said 'We still need him to keep the boys in line and keep the busybodies off our back.'

"Somebody thought Dr. Mehary might cause them trouble. 'He won't,' Lammington assured them. 'I'll have a private talk with him.'

"Powell thought Mehary was just shooting to get himself a bigger payoff.

"Bartlow said, 'I think we all deserve a bigger payoff. Karl Hasserman can afford to be generous, gentlemen.' The Masters all laughed and drank a toast to Hasserman."

There was a split in the ranks of the Masters of Naghallah. But in the end it looked like they made up.

Cameron said, "I tried hard to discover what they were planning. All I could find out was that Mehary was against it. He said he wasn't going to stand there and let *The Boys* be —— Not after he had put so much into them."

"Let us be *What?*" asked Keith.

"I don't know. I didn't get that last word. But it's something I don't think we're going to like very much."

That proved to be the understatement of the century!

BOY LAW NUMBER THIRTEEN

August 6

Cameron was a nocturnal animal. He liked to prowl around at night and rest during the daytime. He would sleep in school and sneak off and take a nap in the tall grass while we were supposed to be working.

"Are we boring you, Mr. Westcott?" asked Teacher Matthews.

"Yeah — I mean, no, sir. I can listen better with my eyes shut."

Cameron could sleep anywhere. Sitting in a chair, or even standing up. At night, he became alive. With his triadic mega-key, Cameron had cracked the dread door of the under-sub-basement. Only to find there was another door behind it. A heavy bronze metal door, like in a bank vault. It opened not with a key but with a combination dial.

Cameron had an idea that he could crack it. "I got stuck in jail with an older guy. He told me how you could bust a safe. No explosives. If you have real sharp burglar's ears and fingers, you can tell when the tumblers turn and spot the swing numbers." Cameron tried it, but it didn't work. "It never works the first time."

Keith said, "We better let well enough alone. I wouldn't go in there for a million bucks."

Cameron said, "I'd rather go in than get *put* in. If we find out what's inside, then we'll know what to do."

Troy said, "Please, Cameron, don't go *in*! You might never be able to get *out.*"

The guys all thought we should leave that door alone. It was too risky and might start something that we couldn't finish.

We held a gang meeting and made that a Boy Law. *Nobody, including the Gangleader, shall touch the metal door in the under-sub-basement.* We voted that 10 to 1. Donald was silent.

"That's *Boy-Law Number Thirteen*," announced Jaymie.

"Well, fuck Boy Law Number Thirteen!" said Cameron. "You want to kick me out? Okay, *I quit!*"

"No, Cameron! Please don't! We want you." The guys were all pleading and yelling.

"Besides," declared Jaymie. "We all agreed: *No one can quit the Coyotes and no one can be kicked out.* That's Boy-Law Number Twelve."

"Well, fuck Boy-Law Number Twelve!" said Cameron. "Okay, I'll stay in the Coyotes. But not as Gangleader. Elect somebody else."

We held a new election. This time Donald spoke, loud and clear. "I vote for Brother Cameron." Everyone else did, too. Cameron was re-elected 11 to 0.

We were afraid Cameron wouldn't accept. He just sat there a while, without talking. Then he said, "Okay, guys, if that's the way you want it. We'll leave the door alone for a while. But if I'm Gangleader, I got to do what I think best."

The next night, Cameron stayed in. We all felt real happy and contented. Twelve kids in one room, but we didn't feel at all crowded. We felt real close to each other and glad to be together.

We played some of our crazy games, throwing rolled up socks at each other. We shoved two bureaus against the door to keep the Masters from breaking in on us. They yelled and pounded, but we ignored them.

Major Powell finally did break in and was disappointed to find that nobody was missing. He made us line up and bawled us out. Then he pronounced sentence. *No recreation period for one week.* He forgot we didn't get any recreation now.

He also forgot to give us the usual bad conduct markers.

THE COLLAR OF BONDAGE

August 9

Up to now, *Kaah Naghallah* hadn't been too bad. We got kicked around on occasion, but most of the time we rather enjoyed the place. Now, things started to get rough.

Brandon got it first. He was the cooks' pet and would bring us extras from the kitchen. Even caviar sandwiches intended for the guests at the mansion. Sometimes he would go wandering around the fields when he was supposed to be working.

We had supper, but no Brandon. No one had seen him for a couple of hours. Supper was even shittier than usual. We were supposed to get a minimum diet until we earned something better. Which never seemed to happen. However, Minnie or Johanna always stuck in something tasty. Today's stuff was really garbage.

The Masters were watching us. The guys got restless and started walking around. Striker ordered us to stay in our seats.

Cameron got up, defiantly. "Where is Brandon?" he demanded. We all got up and started shouting, too.

Striker bellowed, angrily. "You boys are through eating. No more supper. Go to your room!"

We walked out without cleaning up the table. Being deprived of that shitty garbage was a punishment all of us could readily endure. We hoped that Brandon would be in the dormitory. But he wasn't.

Cameron called a gang meeting. Moved, seconded and unanimously carried that we march over to Dr. Mehary and demand Brandon's release. They must be holding him somewhere. Brandon wouldn't take off by himself.

"Maybe he had an accident."

"No accident. The Masters know where he is. Otherwise they would be questioning us."

Cameron called out. "Form column of twos. To Mehary's office, march!"

The Coyote youth gang marched to the door. But now

we found we had been locked in. About an hour earlier than usual.

We could break out through the window. But that would reveal our secret escape route. "Wait on the window," advised Cameron. "Let's try something else first."

"Make a lot of noise," urged Troy.

We started yelling and pounding and jumping on the floor. Roger cut a whistle from a willow branch and shrieked like a fire alarm. Raymond could make a noise with his mouth like a police siren. Donald howled like a wolf. The rest of us kept yelling *Brandon! Brandon! We want Brandon!!* Karl Hasserman, we had been warned, was very disturbed by loud noises. If K. H. was still around, we made enough noise to make the old buzzard jump out of his wheel chair. *If* he was still around.

Maybe we didn't annoy K. H. but we did annoy somebody. In less then ten minutes, Captain Striker unlocked the door. "You want Brandon? Here he is."

Brandon looked different now. Subdued and frightened. They had shaved all Brandon's hair off. And around Brandon's neck, they had fastened a weird-looking collar. Made of some white, metallic material and studded with knobs and projections.

"What happened, Bran?"

Brandon kept jerking his head and shoulders. Wearing this collar gave him the shakes. He was on the verge of bawling.

"Two guys grabbed me and stuck this thing on me. And they slapped me around and shaved my hair off and called me a thief."

"What did you steal?"

"Just some food. Olives and fruit. Johanna lets me take things. But she wasn't there and they said she isn't coming back!" Brandon began to sob. Johanna was almost like a mother to him.

The guys examined the collar. Danny said, "Maybe we can get that fucking thing off." But Brandon was afraid to try. The men had warned him. "Leave it alone, or you'll be very sorry." It looked awful solid and hard to remove.

"Does it hurt?"

Brandon felt around his neck. "It don't bother me now."

Stevie said, "There must be some reason why they stuck that collar on. Maybe they can control a guy that way."

Brandon shuddered. "You mean turn you into a robot or a zombie?"

We all touched Brandon just to make sure he was still a human boy. Brandon looked miserable. He shivered with shame and fear. Tears welled in his eyes. Cameron said, "You got a collar on you? So what, if it don't bother you? And your hair will grow back. We're still your friends and brothers. So quit bawling."

"I ain't bawling."

"Maybe Johanna just went on a vacation. Maybe she'll come back, too."

Brandon hung his head. "I'm a creep."

"No you ain't! The guys all think you're tops, Bran. They were ready to tear the place apart until they found you."

Cameron punched Brandon on the shoulder. The tears stopped and Brandon gave a faint smile.

"We started to march on Mehary's office. We'll do it in the morning and make them take the collar off."

Donald came over. He put his finger on Brandon's collar and felt all around it, as if it stirred some memory. Then he moved his fingers around his own neck. "Friend! Brother!"

"Yeah, Don Don. I'm your friend, too." Brandon clasped Donald's outstretched hand.

There was a strange glow in Donald's yellow eyes. I always thought Donald had a lot more brains than people gave him credit for. It was just hard to understand him. Donald sometimes talked in sign language and he did it now. He touched Brandon's collar. Then he put his hand on Troy's neck, Then on Cameron's neck.

Cameron said, "You mean me and Troy are gonna get a collar? Not on your life, Don Don! They'll never stick one of those fucking things on me!"

Donald with those yellow eyes that had no whites in them was staring into space. His lips moved without making a sound. Then he spoke. "It is coming. Brother Cameron. *The time of the Nightmare.*"

Donald stood there straining as if trying to remember. "The *collar* comes first. Then the *cage*... The *Door of Darkness*... The *Labyrinth*, ... And the journey into the *Land of Fear*... " He halted and became silent.

"What shall we do, Don Don? What did we do in that dream of yours?"

Donald didn't answer. He had become the retarded boy again. He sprawled out on the bed, muttering and making animal noises.

NEVER IS A LONG TIME

In the morning, we all felt better. Even Brandon, despite the collar. We had a crummy breakfast of watery gruel, then steeled ourselves to march on Dr. Mehary's office and make him take that thing off Brandon. No collars for the Coyotes. We were going to run free.

The office was locked. We pounded on it and started yelling. Captains Vedemore and Striker appeared. "Dr. Mehary is not here."

"When will he be back?"

"Later. Now go to your work."

"Doing what?" asked Cameron. He left off the *Sir*.

"Report to Captain Craig at the tool shed. He wants you to pick berries." That was good news. We could eat the berries as we picked them.

"You will each get a bucket. We want those buckets full!" K. H. was having a birthday party. So they told us. And *he* liked raspberries. "Let's see you boys get out there and hustle."

There were endless thickets of raspberries and other thorny and prickly stuff all around the property. But most of the berries were still unripe and tasted sour. The birds carried off the ripe ones. The Naghallah boys ate two for every one they gathered.

Nobody hustled for *that* birthday dinner. None of *us* were invited. The guys threw berries at each other. And bundles of grass. And pieces of dirt.

Stevie and Danny, instead of working, climbed up an enormous oak tree. Guardian Craig yelled at them, but they paid no attention. Roger and Jody went searching for four-leaf clovers instead of berries.

Donald caught a hop toad, talked to it in a croaking voice, then let it go. Then he found a turtle in a swampy pond, crooned to it, then put it back in the pond. Only Brandon sat there solemnly. Wearing that collar must take all the fun out of everything. Once in a while, Brandon picked a few berries. But mostly he was just staring up at the blue, cloudless sky. It was a glorious summer day.

Me and Keith found a big patch of ripe berries and got our buckets almost full. Cameron lay down in the tall grass and fell asleep. Bobby and Raymond filled half a bucket and then were playing some game, pitching pebbles. Troy climbed up over a rock and disappeared. An hour later, he was still gone.

Captain Craig got tired yelling and started yawning. At last, he blew his whistle. "Line up, lads! And bring your berries in!" Eleven guys lined up. No Troy.

"Troy Feroldi is missing, sir. May we search for him?" Craig said *No*. We did anyway, but didn't find him.

Now Striker, Eberle, Smeer and a couple of other Masters appeared. "Back to your room! *On the double!*" So far, the Masters had never used the clubs they carried. But so far we had never out and out defied them.

"Troy is missing, sir," said Jaymie. They didn't seem to care. I figured they already knew where he was.

We felt mutinous, but we marched to our rooms. There was no other place to go. The door was locked and Troy was inside. Like Brandon, his head was shaved and he had that weird collar on him.

Troy's story was the same as Brandon's. He had gone wandering around. Klayborne and Lammington grabbed him. They yelled at him for loafing and gave him the works. Everybody was mad about it, excepting Brandon.

He seemed just a bit glad that someone else had been collared, too.

Raymond called it a slave collar, like his Black ancestors had to wear back in the days of slavery. They had bells on them, those collars, so they could find you if you ran away. You could hide in a swamp or a bramble and they could never spot you. But when you moved, those bells would give you away.

These collars didn't have anything on them that made a noise. But maybe it was the same idea. All those weird gadgets were a way of tracing us and controlling us.

Raymond swore they would never get a slave collar on *him.* "Never! They'll have to kill me first!"

Never is a long time. Before the sun had risen three times again, Raymond's neck was in a slave collar, too.

MURDER MOST FOUL!

In the morning, we marched on Dr. Mehary's office. We marched in lockstep in a manner to gladden the heart of any drill sergeant. Lyandra was watching us. She waved and smiled a little, then turned away. Dr. Mehary wasn't there.

The food was shittier than ever. We were used to getting leftovers, but these leftovers tasted like they had been standing around for a month.

Captain Striker ordered us to report for weeding. Instead, we marched back to Mehary's office.

"What do you want to see Mehary for?"

"We want him to take the slave collars off Troy and Brandon."

"He isn't going to take them off."

"We want a chance to talk to him."

Striker got mad. "I'm giving you a direct order. Report to Captain Eberle for weeding!"

"Not till we talk to Dr. Mehary."

"You're disobeying a direct order. You're going to be twelve very sorry punks!"

Colonel Lammington came and repeated the order. We repeated our defiance. Then, surprisingly, the two Masters went away.

We broke into Dr. Mehary's office. It was empty. We flopped down on the chairs and on the floor and waited. I wondered if we hadn't been too rash, openly defying the Masters. Maybe not. If we did nothing, we'd get the slave collars on us one at a time. After that, we wouldn't be able to defy them. Brandon and Troy seemed to have lost all their spirit.

They let us sit there. That made us sweat. The Masters sure as hell weren't going to let us defy them and get away with it. Naghallah was supposed to be a tough disciplinary institution. You would have expected them to call out their reserves and put down our juvenile rebellion, give us a beating and lock us up without food until we submitted. That's what they would have done in the old Naghallah. That would almost have been a relief. In this new Naghallah, with its slave collars and sinister mysteries, we faced something more terrible and more dangerous.

So reasoned Jaymie, the worrier. But the other guys were joyful and carefree. Happy that they had stood up to and defied the Masters. Even Brandon and Troy were smiling again.

In the back of the office, was a heavy white door that led to Dr. Mehary's living quarters. It was locked, naturally. But Cameron had that master key that he carried around in his boot, just in case they should search the dormitory. Boldly, he thrust it in the lock.

The first room was lined with books and pamphlets, many of them written by Dr. Mehary himself. Here was, *Behavior Modification of Defective Juveniles, The Training and Treatment of Delinquent Youth, The Mehary System for the Control and Correction of Boy Criminals.* And other shit.

The next room was crammed with files and cardboard

boxes, old journals and notebooks with unreadable scrawl. The walls were hung with diplomas and awards given to Dr. Mehary. From the Behavior Research and Study Institute and other high-sounding organizations.

The third room had more boxes, crammed with news clippings mostly about juvenile crime and violence. Mehary's desk was in this room, covered with junk. A bottle of rubber cement had been knocked over and spilled on the mahogany surface. From the floor, there was a faint humming sound. The electric typewriter had been knocked off the desk, but was still going. A waste basket had been overturned. The desk drawers had been pulled out and their contents emptied on the heavy green carpet.

"Holy crap!" cried Keith. "Somebody broke in here and searched the place!"

Raymond said, "Was it *you*, Brother Cameron? You wanted to steal that chapter he wrote about you?"

Cameron said, "You should have seen the stuff he wrote about *you*, Brother Raymond. But this break-in wasn't me. I'd never do a messy job like this."

Bobby held up his hand. "Listen!" From behind another door you could hear the faint sound of music, followed by unintelligible talking.

"He's in there! Dr. Mehary's in there. We better get out of here."

"We came to talk to him, didn't we?"

Cameron pounded on the door. "Dr. Mehary! Dr. Mehary! It's the boys, sir. Can we talk to you?"

No answer. Just silence. Followed by more faint music.

Cameron tried the door. It was locked, but yielded to the skeleton key. We walked down a corridor past the marble-tiled bathroom.

"Dr. Mehary!" called Cameron.

"Dr. Mehary!" echoed the Naghallah boys.

Again no answer. Then the mournful strains of an old-time country ballad:

*"Seven girls a-going to the graveyard.
And only six a-coming back."*

There was one more door. To the bedroom. It was unlocked. Vainly, Cameron knocked and called again. Then turned the handle.

The portable radio was still going, but the bedroom was empty. A single white sheet was spread over the king-size bed. There was something underneath the sheet. A big lump. It didn't move. We looked at each other, no one daring to touch it. At last, Danny stepped forward. He seized the sheet and pulled it back ...

Clad in his night clothes, the Director of *Kaah Naghallah* lay there with his eyes toward the ceiling. Dr. Mehary's body was cold and rigid. He had been dead a long time.

Was it a heart attack? Or something else?

Dr. Mehary didn't die naturally. On the side of his head, above his ear, was a puncture wound. A sharp, pointed object, like a dart, had been thrust into his brain. There was a ring of dried blood around it and the skin of his face had turned blue. As we looked at him, he seemed to be staring back at us, his face frozen in terror and surprise.

In the presence of the dead, we were all silent. Cameron raised his hand and beckoned. Silently, we followed him. Cameron relocked the two doors and led us back to the dormitory.

Keith finally broke the silence. "Mehary was wasted. Why did they do it?"

"He knew too much about *Something* and they were afraid he was going to talk."

Cameron said, "Look, they know we were in the office. But they don't know we were in the bedroom. We couldn't have gotten in there without the master key. No one must let on that we know Mehary's dead. *Our lives may depend on it.*"

DEAD MEN TELL NO TALES

Later that night, well after midnight, a grey van with almost no lights moved down the driveway. Maybe they were taking Mehary's body and dumping it in that swamp on the road to Mountainville. *The Devil's Swamp.* I remember Striker telling us, "We can dump trouble-making kids there, too. This isn't a joke, it's a warning."

Most of us had seen death before. But the violent death of someone we had known left us in shock. None of us liked Dr. Mehary. But we wished to have him go away and leave us alone. Not get murdered.

Mr. Matthews, our teacher, was gone, too. He was the Master we liked best or disliked the least. Johanna and her sister, Minnie, were gone. Had the cooks and teacher shared the fate of Dr. Mehary? Or, hopefully, fled because they feared it?

And those young people who were here last year "just disappeared." Were the twelve inmates of the Kaah Naghallah reform school destined to disappear as well? What would happen if we did? A lot of people might say *Good Riddance.*

Cameron called a gang meeting. We held it in the shower in case the room was bugged. We couldn't find any trace of any listening device. But I had a feeling they knew everything we said and did. Maybe they wanted us to find Mehary's body. To strike fear into us. Perhaps those slave collars on Troy and Brandon were transmitters and told them everything they wanted to know. But we kept on acting like we were very clever and had kept all our secrets hidden from our Keepers.

We took a roll call, which seemed rather unnecessary. But it had become a kind of ceremony and made us feel good. Then we recited the oath. Anything to put off as long as possible the real purpose of the meeting. *To decide what we had to do.*

There were three things we could do, said Keith. We could run away into the mountains. We could make our way to Mountainville and tell the police. Or we could stick around and see what happened here. And maybe be very sorry afterwards.

Stevie and Danny were for running away. But Cameron was against it. How long could twelve city kids survive in the woods with no equipment or supplies? Maybe, if we were lucky, through the summer. But sure as hell not in the winter. And, if they wanted to, they could track us down and knock us off easier in the forests than here.

Bobby said there was no use going to the police. They wouldn't believe us. We're a bunch of trouble-making juvenile delinquents, making up lies about our Keepers. By the time the cops got here, there would be no trace of anything wrong. Then they'd probably break us up and ship us off to different shitty juvenile institutions. We wouldn't be the Coyotes any more.

"No one's going to believe a bunch of kids anyway."

"Unless we could give them proof. If we had a camera and took photographs of Mehary's body ——"

The Mountainville police are probably paid off anyway," declared Raymond.

"What'll we do then?" asked Steve. "Stay here and maybe end up in *The Devil's Swamp?*"

Cameron said, "They didn't go to all that trouble bringing us here just to waste us. They got something they need us for. If we could find out *What,* we could decide—"

We ended up taking a vote:

Go to the police for help —— Nobody.
In favor of a runaway —— Stevie and Danny.

Then Stevie and Danny changed their minds. "If it was just the big guys, maybe we could do it. But we can't run off and leave the little kids."

"Who are the big guys?"

"Well," said Danny. "I'd say the big guys are me, Keith, Stevie and Cameron. And maybe Raymond and Bobby. Us six might be able to take the woods."

"And who are the little kids?" demanded Jaymie.

"You are, Little Brother. And Brandon, Troy, Roger and
Jody. And Don Don wouldn't be much help."

The "Little Kids" all yelled and shouted. Danny tried to
calm them down. "Don't get me wrong now. You guys are
okay. You're all my Bloodbrothers, *Now, Always and
Forever,* But ——"

Donald very seldom talked. But he did now. His yellow
eyes flamed with anger. "You say Donald no help. Donald
always help brothers."

"Yeah. Sure, Don Don. I didn't mean ——"

"Donald fight for brothers! Donald save brothers!
Donald has power!" He pounded his fist into the wall.
"Donald will protect you all."

"Sure you will, Don Don." Danny put his hand on
Donald's shoulder. "You'll help us when we need it. I know
you will."

Donald was smiling again. He spoke more words in that
one minute than he usually did in a week.

"We decided what *not* to do," said Cameron. "We ain't
running and we ain't going to the cops."

There was a timid knock, repeated several times. It
wasn't our Keepers. They would just barge in. We removed
Bobby's bed that had been propped against the door.

It was the nurse, Lyandra. She smiled at us. What a
beautiful lady she was! Even in her white nurse's uniform
and funny cap. We needed some grownup to confide in. I
was tempted to pour out my heart to her. Young Roger
started to speak. Cameron sternly punched us both.

Lyandra looked at us expectantly. But Cameron's warning glance silenced us all. She smiled again. A radiant
smile. "How are you boys getting on?"

"Not so hot," said Keith. "Look at what they done. They
stuck a slave collar on Troy and Brandon."

"I see it. Oh dear! Does it bother you?"

"It's miserable," said Troy. "I wish I knew how to take
it off."

"I don't know how either, but I will speak to Dr. Mehary
when he comes back," said Lyandra.

Speak to Dr. Mehary when he comes back! Either she

didn't know Mehary had been murdered or she was trying to deceive us. Make us believe the whole thing was but an ugly dream. But then, Lyandra must be working for *Them.* She was a spy, perhaps an enemy.

"What happened to Dr. Mehary?" asked Jaymie.

"He had a heart attack. He was taken to the hospital."

"When will be be back?"

"Soon, I hope." Lyandra's voice was soothing, but her hands were twitching nervously.

She must know that she was lying. But perhaps Lyandra wasn't an enemy. Perhaps she was warning us. *Dr. Mehary is in the hospital. That is all you are supposed to know. Speak and act as if you believe it. Your lives may depend upon it.*

Cameron caught on fast. "Sorry about the Doc. We didn't like him much. But we hope nothing bad happens to him."

"I hope so, too," said Lyandra. "Now come and have your lunch."

"What about our collars?" demanded Brandon.

"Have patience. There is a reason for everything. Now wash your hands and faces and come to the dining room." She said that like a governess addressing a group of bratty six year olds.

"This afternoon you will be given an assignment weeding the vegetable garden. You will do what you are told and do it well. *Trust me.* And don't ask any questions."

Cameron complained. "All we get to eat is a lot of shit."

"Don't say that. I made your lunch today myself." She took Cameron by the hand, like he was a kindergarten toddler and the rest of us followed meekly.

The lunch was surprisingly good. Scrambled eggs and fried potatoes, grape juice and chocolate pudding. Lyandra gave us that smile again. "Now be good boys! Go out and do a good job!" But behind that smile I sensed there was a threat. *Don't make any trouble! Don't get them mad! If you do, things will really get rough for you!*

We weeded a little and fooled around a lot. The guys

threw clumps of dirt at each other and wrestled and climb-
ed trees. Cameron warned, "Don't work so hard, Jaymie.
Remember the Boy-Law. You want to get dunked in the
shower?" It was so hot, I wouldn't mind it at all today.
However, no grown-up praised me for doing a good job. So
I escaped a dunking.

CAMERON VANISHES

Danny woke me up. It must have been just before dawn.
"Cameron went out last night. He didn't come back."
The Cat Burglar had planned to search the cellar of the
mansion. "He wanted to find out about those collars. Me
and Stevie told him not to go. It was too risky right now.
Wait a couple of days. Cameron said we didn't have a couple of days to wait."
The Cat Burglar thought he had a charmed life and
couldn't fail. But the cops got him on his last job and now
the Masters of Naghallah got him again.
"Maybe not," said Jaymie. "Cameron may be holed up
somewhere. Or maybe he couldn't get back, because they
were watching the window. Get some sleep anyway, Danny. If Cameron is really missing ——" I didn't dare think
about it.
In the morning, Cameron still didn't show. We ate a shitty breakfast and felt miserable. We all realized how
helpless we were without Cameron. Like a car without a
steering wheel.
We were ordered to report for weeding. Instead, we went
to our room. Eleven of us started up the stairs. When we
reached the dorm, we were nine. Brother Danny was gone.
So was Stevie Scanlon. Cameron's first lieutenants who
were supposed to lead us when Cameron wasn't there.
"They were right next to me," said Bobby, in a scared
voice.
I had a queasy feeling in the pit of my stomach.
Something was grabbing us off, one at a time.

Next in line for Gangleader was Keith and then Raymond and Bobby. Keith and Raymond were brave and true. But now they seemed completely lost and helpless. Bobby Alliconda appeared stunned and in a daze. And Donald had become the retarded boy again. That flash of power and understanding was gone. That left the five "little kids", as Danny called us, Troy, Roger, Jody, Brandon and Jaymie. They were all scared and shaky. Somebody had to be the leader. I decided it had to be *me*.

"Gang meeting," I announced. "What'll we do now?"

Nobody had any ideas. "You're Gangleader now," said Raymond. "You name it. We'll do it."

"We'll wait one hour for Stevie and Danny," said me. "If they don't come, we'll have to act alone."

"Doing what, man?"

"We'll march on the mansion," I resolved. "Right up to Karl Hasserman himself. Or whoever is in charge there now. We'll have to bluff, saying we sent a message. To my parents and relatives. They'll come down here looking for us. They'll bring the police, the State Troopers, the F.B.I. and maybe the marines. . . ."

"And then what?"

"We'll offer them a deal. We'll keep our mouths shut, *If* they release Cameron, Stevie and Danny!"

The hour was up. I tried to act like Cameron. "Form column of twos and follow me! *Forward, march!*"

Now the door opened stealthily. Danny and Stevie came in. Nobody had grabbed them. They had been on reconnaissance and had procured a flock of weapons. Five kitchen knives, two axes, a hammer, a machete, a crowbar, a broomstick. And some lead pipe and glass bottles. Broken glass could be a mean weapon.

"Who made *you* Gangleader, Gifted Child?"

"The guys chose me."

"Where do you think you're going?"

I told them.

"Go ahead and lead, Little Brudder," said Danny. "We don't have any better ideas."

Still, they called for a new election. "We weren't here when you voted." To Jaymie's surprise, he was elected Gangleader 11 to 0. Modestly, he voted for himself.

MARCH ON THE MANSION!

August 12

I thought we shouldn't take any weapons. It would give them an excuse to shoot us, if they needed one. *The kids went berserk. They had a whole armory of knives and axes. What could we do? We had to defend ourselves.*

Stevie said, "If they want to shoot us, they'll do it anyway. They'll say we attacked them, even if we didn't."

"As Gangleader, I'll walk first," said me. "Without any weapons."

"Except your big mouth," said Danny.

We had a stolen flashlight hidden away. That would give us all the light we needed. I tied a white towel to the broomstick and carried it. That would show we wanted to parley. Strangely, the whole place was empty. None of the Masters, guards or attendants could be seen. But we had the feeling of being watched.

We marched down into the cellar. From here, that underground passageway led to the cellar of the mansion. That way, they wouldn't spot us until we got there. We hoped! We passed the grim door that led downward into the nether regions. Maybe Cameron had gone inside on a one-way trip. I tried not to think about that.

I looked around. Stevie and Danny were in back of me. Then Bobby and Brandon, Troy and Roger. With Donald and Jody tagging behind. Raymond and Keith were missing. Maybe they were out on reconnaissance. But they could have told me. When Cameron gave an order, the guys obeyed. When Jaymie gave an order, everyone did what he felt like doing.

I tried to keep the guys quiet, so we could surprise the enemy. But they were all shouting and yelling, "Cameron! Cameron! We want Cameron!" Still, there was no one around.

We were approaching the underground tunnel. Brother Danny raised up the crowbar, ready to smash the tunnel door, if it was locked. It was open.

The passageway was dark and damp and had a musty odor. Suddenly, a huge figure loomed up before us. "Stay right there, you!" It was the trigger-happy ex-reform school guard, "Captain Klayborne". One of the men who put slave collars on Troy and Brandon. We halted.

"We want to talk to Karl Hasserman," said Gangleader Jaymie.

"No, you won't! You're gonna turn right around and go back where you came from."

The guys started shouting again. Klayborne pulled out a gun. "Listen, you punks. I've shot about a dozen guys in my time. They went down and they didn't get up. I've shot a couple of kids, too. Real mean, nasty kids who came at me with knives and axes. I gave them *one* warning and that's all I'm giving you. *Now turn around and get out of here!*"

Stevie was edging sidewards. Klayborne released the safety catch, "I warn you! Stop!" They weren't going to let us reach the mansion. "I'm counting *three,*" warned Klayborne, *One... Two...*"

A shadow was moving directly behind the big man. Two shadows. Two knives flashed and were pointed into Klayborne's back.

"Drop that gun, Muckler!" Raymond made his voice sound deep and fierce. "Drop it and don't turn around!" The knives were razor sharp. They cut into the Master's shirt.

Klayborne's face had a nervous twitch. He was surrounded and couldn't stop all of us. Klayborne had been attacked before by a mob of reform school inmates. "Vicious punks", like the Naghallah boys. Juvenile thugs could be as dangerous as men, if there were enough of them. For a moment, he just stood there. Then he threw down the gun and Raymond grabbed it.

"Put your hands behind your back, Muckler." Keith tied Klayborne's wrists with laundry rope. Our captive appeared just a bit relieved. He had expected to be violently assaulted.

"You go first, Captain," ordered Jaymie. "Into the tunnel. Remember we got the gun now."

Klayborne was a head taller than any of us. He gazed at the rebels with a mocking smile. "You won't get into the mansion that way, boys. It's closed up at the other end."

Maybe. And maybe he was lying. Anyway, we could smash our way in. We had a hostage now. We could trade him for Cameron.

"Move!" ordered Keith. "Walk!" If there was a hidden peril in the tunnel, one of the Masters would be the first to get it.

The flashlight was fading. It yielded but a dim light in the darkened tunnel. "Count off," I ordered. We were all here, all eleven of us. Only Cameron, Number One, was missing. Donald's yellow eyes were glowing in the darkness. I never noticed that before.

We traversed the tunnel slowly, momentarily expecting a trap or an ambush. But there was none. We emerged into a wide space lined with pipes and tanks. This must be the cellar of the mansion. Here, according to Cameron, four or five different stairways led to different parts of the huge, sprawling house. We found one spiral staircase leading upwards. We didn't quite know what to do with our prisoner. He was getting restless. No longer frightened; rather embarrassed at being captured by kids. At the first chance, he might try to break loose.

We put him in the middle and started up the stairway, Gangleader Jaymie in the lead. The dark cellar was suddenly flooded with light. "*Stop!*" The Voice, magnified and distorted by some mechanical gadget, seemed to be coming right out of the wall.

"Put your weapons down and release Captain Klayborne!" This was spoken with a certain derision; contempt for the unfortunate Master who had let himself become the prisoner of children.

Despite the distortion, there was something about the voice that was oddly familiar. One of our keepers and rulers. Not Bartlow, with his broad *a's*. Lammington, perhaps. This voice had a growling, gutteral sound. The boys were all looking at me. I remembered I was supposed to be the Gangleader. I tried to keep my voice from quavering. "We will release Captain Klayborne, sir, and put down our weapons, if you will release Cameron Westcott."

"*Cameron Westcott?*" A short. pause. "Who is Cameron Westcott?"

"There were twelve boys here at what you called a school ——"

"Eleven, I think. You are eleven now."

I had a horrible feeling they were going to pretend Cameron never existed. Cameron had vanished. Or rather he had never been. Was there any way we could prove that Cameron was real?

"There were *twelve* of us here," said Jaymie. "Cameron was sent here by Judge Tuffney who visited *Kaah Naghallah* a few weeks ago. My parents were here, too. They have pictures of Cameron."

"Do they, Jaymie? But your parents aren't here any more. They went away and dumped you. Daniel, too. Worthless trash!"

I replied, "My parents are on their way home, sir. They didn't dump us. They sent us to school here. Commander Bartlow suggested we come. My parents know all about our ten classmates. And so do the rest of my family. We write them every week ——"

The Voice seemed a little less contemptuous. "Tell, me, when did you last see your missing friend?"

"Cameron was with us in the dormitory. He went out for a walk and didn't come back."

"Really? You mean he was spying on me? I don't like people who spy on me." The Voice sounded ugly. But at least he no longer denied that Cameron existed.

Bobby yelled, "Where is Cameron? What happened to

him?"

"You will find out in time. Now lay down your weapons."

Our prisoner had been edging forward. Keith and Raymond pulled him roughly back.

"Where is Cameron? We want Cameron!" The guys were all shouting. Raymond pointed the gun at Klayborne's head.

The big man was sweating. "Watch out, boy! Those things are dangerous. Point it, *away*."

Raymond tightened his grip on the trigger. Or pretended to.

"Your friend is alive!" cried Klayborne. "They didn't hurt him. Don't point that thing!"

"Is that true?" demanded Keith.

"Yes, Keith," said the Voice. "Cameron is unharmed."

Stevie yelled, "We ain't taking your word for it. We want to see him."

"You will in time, Steven. Now lay down your weapons. *And do it promptly!* I have been very patient with you. But now my patience is running out."

I tried to think what we could do. We could shoot Captain Klayborne, or pretend to. But he seemed quite expendable as far as the Masters were concerned. They could stop us easily if we charged up the stairs. If we tried to retreat, they could block us off in the tunnel.

I said, "Sir, we know you brought us here for some purpose. There is something you want us to do. And we will do it, if you let Cameron go."

Apparently, I had hit a responsive chord. The Voice was no longer angry — just a bit amused. "Does Jaymie speak for all of you? Hold your hands up, if Jaymie speaks for you."

Every hand went up. Still, he called our names one at a time. "Steven?"

"Yessir. I'll do whatever you tell me, if you let Cameron go."

Everyone agreed, excepting Donald who made animal noises. Rather like the braying of a donkey. "Donald means *Yes*," assured Troy. "He has his own way of talking."

"All right, then. Pile your weapons against the wall."

"Wait!" cried Jaymie. "We want to see Cameron first."

The Voice laughed. "Don't you trust me, Jaymie?"

"No, sir. We don't trust *anybody.*"

A muffled cough. "Very well then." Now there was a series of clicks and buzzes. "This is *Number One.* Put me through to the boy." A mumble at the other end. "The prowler. The trouble-maker down in the lock-up. Yes, Cameron Westcott."

The wall had become like a television screen. Flashes of light and darkness, blurred and out of focus. Now the camera moved down a dark corridor, halting at something that looked like a cage with heavy bars. A youth lay sleeping on a pile of rags.

"Cameron! Cameron Westcott!" The youth raised up his head.

"*Stand up!*" Yes, it was Cameron, with neither shirt or shoes. His head had been shaved and around his neck was fastened what Raymond called "a slave collar". Like the ones on Troy and Brandon. His belt had been taken away, too.

"Cameron!" I yelled. "Are you okay?"

"Yeah. I'm okay. I prowled around once too often."

"We're going to ask you some questions. Just to make sure you're live and not a video-tape or a hologram."

Bobby asked, "Who are the Coyotes?"

"A nutty youth gang. Eleven jerky little punks and me."

Stevie asked, "Who is the leader of the Coyotes?"

"I used to be. But I'm an ass hole. You can have the job."

Raymond asked "What happened to the Cat Burglar?"

"*The Cat Burglar?* You mean *me*? I got muckled."

Jaymie asked, "What is *Boy-Law Number Thirteen* and what did Cameron Westcott say about it?"

"Boy-Law Thirteen? That's the one about not touching the metal door in the Under-sub-basement. Cameron said, '*Fuck Boy-Law Thirteen!*' I was a dope!"

Jody asked, "What thing did Cameron get thrown out of?"

"I got thrown out of military school. I got thrown out of just about every organization I was in, except the Cub Scouts and the Coyotes."

Danny asked, "Who was the *Shovel Buster?*"

"That's you, Danny. And your brother's *The Gifted Child.*"

Keith asked, "Who is *Whirling Boy?*"

"That's Don Don. Brandon is *The Urchin Bold.* Bobby is *The Dirt Spiller.* And Roger is *The Denominator Kid.*"

We were all convinced it was Cameron live. Down, but unbeaten, he could still joke. "How do you like my haircut? A real nice baldy, huh? I joined the club with Troy and Bran Bran."

I said, "We are convinced, Sir. We accept your terms."

"I told you, stack your weapons against the wall."

"Will Cameron come up here then?"

"No, boys. You will go to *him.* Through the bronze door. Into the Underground. You wanted to see what was down there. Now you will."

Cameron had bruises on his face and body. But the Voice said, "That's your own fault, isn't it, Cameron? You resisted arrest and started to fight?"

"Yeah," said Cameron.

"They have been treating you well? Giving you food and fresh water?"

"Yeah," agreed Cameron. "I could use a coat or a blanket though. It's chilly here."

"Give him a coat," said the Voice. And the picture faded.

The Voice continued. "We have been watching you the whole time, boys. You thought you were being very clever. But we knew everything you did. Your tool stealing and your night prowling and your silly youth gang . . .

"You will each submit to wearing what Raymond calls *a slave collar* and to getting what Cameron calls *a baldy.*"

"Do we have to get our heads shaved?" asked Bobby, sadly. His long, brown hair had finally grown back.

"Yes, Robert. I'm afraid so."

"And if we don't submit?"

"Then you will make me very angry. When I get angry, things happen. Most unpleasant things. Both to you and to your friend, Cameron. I have been extraordinarily patient with you boys, because you amused me. But now I am getting a little tired of you."

The guys all looked at me. Stevie said, "Go on, Jaymie. You're the Gangleader. Decide!"

I remembered something from the Gifted Child class. What the Egyptian Pharaoh said, when Alexander invaded. "*If you are facing certain defeat, surrender on the best terms you can get.*"

"We agree to your terms, sir," said Jaymie. We stacked our weapons and released our prisoner.

"You have made a fortunate choice, boys. You will go to your friend."

The Voice was warm and friendly now. So friendly that I dared ask the next question. "Who are you? Are you Karl Hasserman?"

"I'm *Number One*. That's all you need to know."

He added, "We won't keep you locked up for very long. We have a mission for you. What you must do will be explained to you in time. If you succeed, you will be well rewarded."

"And if we fail, sir?"

The Voice became harsh and cold again. "In my vocabulary, there is no such word as *Fail.*"

*　　*　　*　　*　　*　　*　　*

That was Jaymie's last act as Gangleader. For better or worse, I had arranged the surrender of the Coyotes. Any dream of rescuing Cameron by cleverness or bold bravado had been shattered.

Maybe we had saved Cameron's skin. Maybe we had put all our skins in peril. At best, we had avoided disaster. Or at least postponed it.

"You be Gangleader now, Dannybrudder."

"Stay with it, Jaymie. You did okay."

"I don't want it!" Jaymie's eyes were filled with tears.
"What's the matter with you, Little Brudder? Hey,
you're *crying!*" Danny punched me in the shoulder. "I
told you *Kaah Naghallah* was going to be rough. Quit
bawling, will you!"

Jaymie kept on sobbing.

"Okay," said Danny. "I'll be the fuckin' Gangleader."

"Form column of twos," Danny ordered. And we
marched back through the tunnel. Into the sub-basement
and down. Through the dread metal door into the Underground. *And the Gate to the Inferno closed behind us.*

[End of Book One]

BOOK II

BANE N'GAI

The Place of Evil Secrets

Conscripted Slave Boys. . . . . . . Cameron, Danny, Stevie,
Donald, Brandon, Bobby,
Raymond, Jaymie, Keith
Troy, Jody and Roger

Seekers of the Power Thing. . . . . . . Colonel Lammington
Major Powell, Captain Striker,
Captains Klayborne, Vedemore,
Craig, Smeer and Eberle,
Commander Bartlow

Doomed Travellers in a
Nightmare World. . . . . Dean Harlow, Alice Harlow,
Jerry Golding

Monsters, Horrors, Wonders, Creatures
Denizens of the Otherworld

The Thing-Without-a-Name

STUDENTS INTO SLAVE BOYS

Through the bronze door, we entered *Bane N'Gai, the Place of Evil Secrets.* I don't know quite what we expected to find on the other side. But it was just another tunnel. Then a flight of stairs, a ramp and still more tunnel. This one was a wide corridor with side branches. The whole thing looked man-made. The floor was covered with wooden planks. The walls re-enforced with bricks and cement and illuminated with fluorescent light.

Major Powell and several of his guards met us at the entrance. They walked before and behind us. Powell spoke no word, just beckoned with his hands. The guards kept looking around nervously, fearful not of us surely, but of *Something* that might be lurking in the tunnels. We passed several doors. Major Powell opened one and told us to go inside.

We waited in the dim light. After a while, several of the Masters entered. Captains Vedemore, Striker, Smeer, Eberle and Craig. We expected them to gloat over us. Instead, their faces were solemn and a bit sad.

"Where is Cameron?" demanded Danny.

"You'll find out in good time, lads." Craig was the one who called us *lads,* instead of *punks.*

To Smeer, our one-day school teacher, was entrusted the task of shaving our hair off. He performed this task with efficiency and a good deal of relish. The red hair of Keith, the yellow hair of Stevie, the black hair of Jaymie, Raymond's Afro and Bobby's brown hair lay strewn together on the floor.

Then they put the collars on us. No one resisted excepting Raymond. He balked at the "slave collar" and received a punch in the mouth. It was Smeer who hit him. Raymond has a hot temper and would have hit back. But Bobby calmed him down. "Cool it, Ray Ray! We all have to wear them."

"Okay, I'll be a fucking slave boy," said Raymond, resignedly.

"*Number One* gave us his word," said me, "that we would join Cameron."

"That you will, lads," promised Captain Craig. "Just follow me." He led us down a curving side tunnel, unlocking and relocking another heavy metal door.

"I feel real sorry for you lads. I hope you make it."

"Make what?" asked Brandon.

He didn't tell us.

Now we could see the cage or cell just as we had viewed it on the television screen. Cameron's face was peering through the bars. "Well if it ain't the Naghallah children! All the Coyote cubs got their collars on!"

Craig unlocked the cage door. We had a wild idea of freeing Cameron and escaping through the tunnels. But this tunnel ended right at the cage. The only way out was the way we came in and that was surely blocked. Too late to run away now!

Captain Craig gave us a cheerful smile. "Go inside, lads. You won't be as comfortable here as you were above. But you won't be here for very long."

The way he said that gave us the shivers. Young Roger was trembling. "Where are we going?"

"You are going on a journey, lads. It will be a great adventure."

"Will we —— come back?"

"Of course you will. You will be doing an errand for *Number One.* The Headmaster will be pleased with you. We will welcome you home."

Jody was the first to go in. He embraced Cameron, his adored hero. Raymond was the last. Craig put his hand on Raymond's shoulder. "Sorry you got hit, lad. Good luck to you!" And he locked us in.

The place, as Stevie said, was "shitty" but not terrible. It was bigger than we first thought. Still, with twelve guys, rather crowded. No beds or mattresses. But there were sliced up old carpets and scatter rugs to lie on. No toilets; but some holes in the floor. No bath or sink. But a faucet with luke warm water.

They brought us soap and buckets. Later, hot soup

and a jug of milk. Even toilet paper, tooth brushes and a change of clothing. On a scale of one to ten, *Bane N'Gai* youth prison would probably rate a zero. Still there could be worse places.

Anyway, we were all together and that meant a lot. Troy said he'd be willing to stay here forever, if he could be sure nothing worse would ever happen to us.

"This is the Coyotes' den," cried Jody, happily, turning a cartwheel.

"The Coyotes' cage," said Keith, dolefully. "And cut the cartwheels, Jody. There ain't much room. You almost kicked me."

"Sorry." We'd have to learn to live like a can of sardines. Or, as Raymond put it, like captives on a slave ship. Though they had to take better care of us than of those old-time slaves, because we were not replaceable.

Strangely, what was happening fulfilled Donald's nightmare. *The collar comes first. Then the cage ... The Door of Darkness ... The Labyrinth ... And the journey into the Land of Fear ...*

"Can you remember, Don Don, anything more? How did the dream end?"

Donald didn't remember. He didn't even answer. His yellow eyes glowed and the few hairs that the clipper had missed were standing upright on his head. Donald had gone autistic again. He was crawling around on all fours like a wild beast about to spring.

Donald started making goat-like noises. He acted like a goat, too, leaping around the dungeon. *M-a-a-a! B-a-a-a! M-y-a-a-a!* I called to Donald. He charged at me, butting me in the stomach and almost knocking me down. Then he charged at Bobby who jumped out of the way. All at once, Donald turned and began banging his head against the stone wall of our cell. Real hard.

"Cut it, Don Don!" Cameron and Stevie pulled him away. Donald was struggling fiercely. Danny and Keith had to help hold him.

Donald strained and twisted. Cameron started talking to him. "You're our brudder, Don Don. You bang your head against the wall, you hurt yourself. We don't want you to be hurt."

"*Glug! Glug! Yeeeee! Yeeeee!*"

"No bump head, Don Don?"

"No bump head." He spoke those three words clearly. The guys released him.

Donald lay on the floor and kicked at the wall with his feet. Cameron said, "Let him kick. Maybe he can knock the wall down."

After a while, Donald stopped and curled up into a ball. He pulled a piece of carpet over his head.

"What's wrong with Don Don? He ain't been this bad for months."

Keith said, "Maybe it's the slave collar. One by one, we're all going nutty."

Or maybe it was something they had put in the milk. Nothing sinister. Something to quiet us down. We all started feeling woozy. Each of us grabbed a strip of carpeting and sprawled out on it. That wasn't much of a bed, but good enough for slave boys.

THE COYOTES AGAINST THE WORLD

I worried at first about us freezing here, without blankets. But the place was real warm now. They must have turned the heat up. Too warm and we sweated.

"Half way to Hell," said Bobby and he was only half kidding.

Cameron told me not to feel bad. In my few hours as Gangleader of the Coyotes, I did as good a job as anyone could. Everything was stacked against us.

"They put the slave collars on us," lamented Jaymie. "And we let them do it!"

"They could have collared us any time they wanted," answered Cameron. "We're no worse off. And we're all together. For *that*, let us give thanks to the *Kee-Kereekee.*"

"What's that?"

"The Guardian Spirit of the Coyote youth gang. The Great Coyote, *Keekereekee.*"

"Sounds more like a rooster," said Troy.

"He is a Great Coyote," Cameron insisted. "I ought to know. I made him up.

"Bow ye all. And salaam to the North. In grateful homage to the *Keekereekee.*"

"Which way is North?"

We bowed and salaamed in all four directions. Cameron made us all feel good again. Cameron was a clown. He ripped off two strips of cloth and tied one around my neck, the other around Danny's "for our services as gallant leaders of the gallant Coyotes". The guys cheered. "Y-a-a-a-y, Danny! Y-a-a-a-y, Jaymie!" Though we had only led them to disaster.

When he put a collar on me, Striker said, "So you were the leader of these hoodlums? I put this marker on you as your badge of office." And he stuck a clothes-pin on my nose. It was real tight and pinched. But I said, "Thank you, sir. This is a great honor."

Now I put the clothes-pin on Cameron's nose. "Now that you are Gangleader again, I confer on you this badge of office given me by Captain Striker."

The guys cheered again. They cheered about anything. "Y-a-a-a-y! Cameron's Gangleader again!"

Cameron said, "I don't know why I should be. I was a shitty Gangleader. I got you all muckled, fucked and loused."

"Just temporarily." said Brother Danny. "We are coming back!"

"The Coyotes will rise again!" cried Stevie. And we all shouted, "On to victory!" We cheered and marched around the narrow dungeon cell. Maybe our captors were moved by the indomitable spirit of youth. But more likely, they marked us down as a bunch of noisy idiots. At least the collars hadn't silenced us. Not yet, anyway.

We leaped around, yelling and shouting, "The Coyotes against the World!" Seeing how helpless we were, that seemed a rather one-sided contest.

"We're down, but not out. The Coyotes will rise again!"

"On to victory!"

Captain Craig brought us our food. Bread and milk and some stale peanut butter. The milk wasn't spiked, he insisted. "See, I'll take some myself." He took a very small sip. This concoction was made from a powdered mix and had a funny taste. However, he promised us our next meal will be "a real feast."

Craig apologized for keeping us "in this hole here." But they were still preparing for our great adventure.

"We ain't in any hurry," said Bobby.

"Anything I can do for you fellers?" He was trying real hard to be agreeable.

Jaymie opened his big mouth. "Can I ask a question, sir?"

"Go ahead. But I don't promise to answer it."

"What happened to Karl Hasserman?"

The Captain didn't expect *that* question. "Karl Hasserman? You mean the man in the mansion?"

"Yes. Where is he now?"

Craig looked nervously over his shoulder. "That's what a great many people would like to know."

Had Hasserman gone the way of Dr. Mehary? The world's richest man wasted by his own henchmen? And now they were taking over his empire in bits and pieces.

Cameron had tried to penetrate the secret of *Bane N'Gai*. He failed, but stumbled on to something else. That the tycoon wasn't around any more. That was dangerous knowledge.

"I'll get you some more soap, lads. And some towels," promised Craig. "The apples are getting ripe now. I'll bring you a sack of them." He locked the cell door and departed. Craig wasn't a bad guy. The best of the Masters, excepting maybe Matthews. If it were up to *him*, he'd let us go.

But Captain Craig wasn't going to put his own neck on the line or take any risks for us. Anything we told him, he would report to *Number One* to cover himself.

Craig brought us some cold pizza and warm orange

juice. Also some small and sour apples. Not exactly a feast. But you have to give the Captain credit for trying. We ate every scrap. By now, we were hungry enough to eat the carpets.

THE GIRL IN BED

We hung around for a couple of days with nothing to do but gab. The guys all talked about their adventures. Everyone was bullshitting. It wasn't a gang meeting and you didn't have to tell the truth.

Cameron was a great story teller. He was burglarizing what he thought was an empty house. And he ran into a girl in bed. She started to scream. And Cameron said, "Please don't yell. I'm a burglar, not a rapist. I promise I won't touch you."

"Still, she tried to scream. And I said, 'If you don't yell, I promise I'll go away and won't steal nothing'."

Cameron found her handbag. It was stuffed full of cash. He asked permission to steal just five bucks, because he was broke.

"You'll do it anyway," she said.

"No, I won't. Not unless you let me."

"Well, go ahead," she said. And she smiled a little.

"And can I steal some stuff from the refrigerator? I'm awful hungry."

"'This is ridiculous,' she said. But she smiled again. What beautiful teeth she had!"

"Like Red Riding Hood's grandmother," said Troy.

"Please!" asked Cameron, "Can I meet you sometime when I'm not stealing?"

"She put out her hand and touched me. 'Are you for real?'

"'No,' said me, 'I'm really a prince looking for Sleeping Beauty.'

"'You came to the wrong house,' said she and yawned.

"I asked permission to kiss her. 'Just one kiss and then I'll leave.' She didn't say *No*, so I did."

"You kissed her or you left?" asked Keith.

"Both," said Cameron. "She had a private telephone number and I wrote it down."

Cameron called her up two days later. "This is the Cat Burglar. Remember me?"

"'I'll be home tomorrow night,' says she.

"'Alone?'

"'At eight o'clock. I'll wait for you.' And then she laughed, like a silver bell."

Cameron went to the house. But the lady wasn't waiting for him. Waiting instead were two detectives from the burglary squad.

"What did you do?"

"I handed the dick a package. It contained the flowers I was going to give *her*. Then I got out real fast, before he could decide to shoot me."

Cameron sighed. "I thought she loved me. I never seen her again. Right after that, I got caught."

"Lucky for the Coyotes," said Brandon. "She might have turned you into a good boy and you might never have come to *Kaah Naghallah* with us."

IN THE CAGE

The days dragged on and we were still in the lock-up. I guess any grown-ups who were crowded in like we were would have gone nuts and blown their top. But the Naghallah boys were used to living close together and we could live with it.

We had only one fight and *that* of all people was between Jody and Roger. All of a sudden, they started swinging at each other. Jody claimed Roger pushed him. Roger said Jody kicked him. I think the real reason is they both sort of hero-worship Cameron and are rivals for his attention.

We threatened to invoke the Boy Law and douse their heads in the water bucket. So they shook hands and made up.

I had my thirteenth birthday in the slave-cage, or whatever you'd call the place we were locked up in. Last year, I had a party on my birthday and a table full of presents. This year, I got nothing. Not even a greeting card. Maybe the family sent something and the Masters ripped it off, like they usually did.

Brother Danny, however, remembered my birthday. He even gave me a present, a pair of shoe laces. My old laces were all busted and tied together with knots.

"Thanks, Danny. I sure can use these. Where did you get them?"

"Stole them. of course. From the supply room. When me and Stevie got the weapons. I picked up a pair for you." Then Danny yelled, "Hey guys! It's Jaymie's birthday. Can you imagine this little squirt is now a teenager!"

The guys all cheered and they all socked me. Everyone took fourteen punches. Thirteen easy socks, one for each year, and a hard one for luck. I hated that last one. It was the only punch that hurt. And it didn't change our luck at all. We were still muckled, fucked and loused.

Anyway, the guys decided to give me a party. We drank water, pretending it was beer and jumped around, pretending we were dancing to a rock band. In our crowded cell, using a sneaker, we played football, leap frog and monkey-in-the-middle.

We made so much noise, Captain Craig came to see what was going on. When he heard it was Jaymie's birthday, he brought us some cookies and lemonade.

Every day, Craig would bring something for "his lads". An apple pie, a box of fruit, potato chips, chocolate bars, disinfectant. We should have been more grateful than we were.

"How long do we have to stay in this fuckin shit hole?" demanded Stevie.

Craig didn't know. They were still preparing.

August 29 (?)

Two and a half weeks have gone by. Seventeen wake-ups in the Cage —— if I counted right. It's always like night down here. There's just one dim light in the ceiling.

Striker took my watch, after we were captured. He said, "You don't have to know what time it is. You ain't going anywhere."

The guys are getting restless. They are beginning to wish that something —— anything would happen to get us out of here. But I have a hunch that when things do happen, we will wish we were back in our crowded but protecting cell.

We scratched our names with a nail on the wall of the dungeon. And underneath, we put:

We Are Kidnapped.

That's in case we don't come back and people try to trace us.

THE BRIEFING

Two days later

They let us out of the Cage at last. We marched down several corridors, escorted by the genial Captain Craig. He seemed to have no fear of us and carried no weapons.

We felt all dirty and crummy. Craig, however, had provided for "his good lads." He took us to a washroom where we could shower and gave us clean clothes. Then down another corridor to a fancy panelled room, ringed with armchairs, folding chairs and benches. Here, Craig told us, we would receive "a briefing."

We wondered if *Number One* would appear and reveal his identity. He didn't. The men who came in were Mr. Bartlow, Smeer, Vedemore, Klayborne, Eberle and Powell. Except for Bartlow, they were all lesser henchmen. And Bartlow, I was pretty sure, wasn't *It.* The

Mystery Boss was probably watching us on his closed circuit television.

Bartlow and Company had brought along several new guys who were armed and mean looking. More than enough to handle us, if we got any ideas. The Masters must have feared we might attack them or try to break loose. But they didn't have to worry. We were pretty helpless down here with no weapons and no way of breaking out. And we had the collars on. They hadn't used those on us yet.

Mr. Bartlow, however, was all smiles. "I believe we have here all twelve members of the Coyote youth gang. Sit down, boys."

We sat on the benches. The Masters sat in the armchairs. The guards sat in the folding chairs or leaned against the wall.

Mr. Bartlow remained standing. "I want to congratulate you boys. We have put you to the test and you have passed it. We are expecting great things from you."

We looked at each other in amazement. We were used to being told how rotten and worthless we were. Getting praised was totally unexpected.

"I won't say what you were in the beginning. But you have become a team. You have learned to live together, to work together. To face danger and hardship together . . .

"Of course, we were watching you all the time. We knew all about your little tricks. Your secret meetings, your stolen keys and your hidden tools. We had high hopes for Cameron, the Cat Burglar, and he did not disappoint us. Of course, we had you spotted all the time when you were out prowling and spying.

"We liked the way you stood up for each other and fought for Donald and Troy and Roger and Steve and Brandon. And how you rallied for Cameron. When you marched on the mansion, that, too, was a test. You did what we hoped you would do. You have courage and resourcefulness and we need that.

"As you can now surmise, Kaah Naghallah was not a reform school. We brought you here not for correction, but because we can use you and your special talents.

"We have an important mission for you. It's —— a kind of treasure hunt. It is a difficult mission, but also a glorious adventure. If you succeed, you will be well rewarded.

"Your tasks will be revealed to you, as you progress. You will be told everything you need to know, but no more. There are good reasons for this. But I can tell you in a general way it will involve stealing something; an activity in which most of you have had a good deal of practice. Is there a question? Yes, Robert?"

"What is this thing we are supposed to steal?" asked Bobby.

"You mean the name of it? It is —— quite unlike anything you have ever seen before. It is a Thing of great value, but only to those who know how to use it. Just call it *The Thing Without a Name*. Yes, Keith?"

"Am I right that we are not the first to go on this mission?"

"There have been several failures. But we have learned a great deal. You will have better equipment and be better prepared.

"We also think you are better fitted than the others. There is a barrier that must be crossed. More of a mental than a physical block. We think young boys in their formative years will be better able to get through than adults."

"What are our chances of getting back?" asked Keith.

"Very good." Mr. Bartlow had been prepared for that question. "We wouldn't go to all this trouble, if we didn't expect you to succeed."

"If we're working for you," asked Raymond, "how about getting these slave collars off us!"

Mr. Bartlow smiled. "Those aren't slave collars, Raymond. They are for your protection. Those collars are the only way of communicating with you, where you are going.

"Be thankful for your collar, boys. The collar is what will bring you safely back. Yes, Jaymie. You have a question?"

"It's about Karl Hasserman, sir. The man who owns this property. How does he fit in?"

Commander Barlow paused. It was something he would rather not talk about. Then he said, "We are all aware that Karl Hasserman is not among us. He was a very old man. Physically, he remained in excellent health, considering his years. But his mind deteriorated and he was no longer capable of handling his affairs."

Vedemore broke in: "He went quite mad. Completely paranoid. He accused everyone around him of plotting against him. Even trying to kill him."

Bartlow gave Vedemore a sharp glance, as if to shut him up. Vedemore had spoken too much.

"This thing we are supposed to steal, sir. Is it something that once belonged to Karl Hasserman?"

"Yes, Jaymie, How did you know?"

"Just a wild guess, sir." K.H. had disappeared and taken the *Thing* with him. It must be something of great power, and not just a valuable gem or any ordinary wealth.

"This *Thing*," said Vedemore, "did not belong to Karl Hasserman. He stole it himself."

Bartlow gave him a chilling look. "That is more than I intended to tell you. But sooner or later you had to know. It is something that in the wrong hands could be very dangerous.

"Karl Hasserman was last seen in this very room. He did not return to his home. We think he went the other way. Into the Labyrinth, as you will go. Of course, he had been there before. Karl Hasserman travelled in and back as a young man. That is how he first obtained the *Thing*.

"We don't know if he went of his own free will, or was taken by —— Unnatural Forces. He had the *Thing* with him."

Bartlow looked at his watch. "I'll give you one more question. Cameron?"

"I'll ask the big one, sir. What will happen if we refuse to go?"

Bartlow's friendly manner changed into something hard and ugly. "It is too late for *that*. There is no time to prepare anyone else."

If we went into the Labyrinth, we might not come back.

But if we didn't go, they weren't going to release us. We knew too much.

Some things were beginning to fall into place. Dr. Mehary was a weirdo, but he was sincere. He really believed in this nutty *behavior modification,* with *"training and treatment"* and *"adversive conditioning"* to "turn us juvenile hoods around." But Number One and his minions had just used the Doctor to collect a group of punks who wouldn't be missed. Except maybe me and Danny. And Bartlow, who was Father's boss, could handle the Larrabie family.

"They ran away from the school. They were a wild bunch, these twelve boys. Like a pack of wild animals. We couldn't find any trace of them. But don't give up hope. They may still be alive."

When the time came to send us on the crazy, dangerous journey, Dr. Mehary must have balked. Worse than balk, he may have threatened to blow the whistle on them. But at *Kaah Naghallah* they played for keeps. Mehary was expendable and they expended him.

Maybe we were a bunch of guttersnipes. But we were his boys and he died trying to protect us. It made us feel a little better about the old codger.

"I withdraw the question, sir," said Cameron. "The Coyotes accept the mission. We will go into the Labyrinth and bring back *The Thing Without a Name."*

"You have made a wise decision," said Mr. Bartlow.

He became friendly again, recognizing that volunteers fight better than forced conscripts. "You boys haven't asked yet about the reward you will get. Don't you want to know?"

"Yessir. What reward will we get?"

"One million dollars," said Mr. Bartlow. "That much I can promise you. It might be even more. Say one million dollars for *each* of you."

The guys couldn't imagine that kind of money. Most of them weren't even sure how many zeros there were in a million. They were concerned with the things they knew about.

Brandon asked, "When we come back, will we still be going to school at Kaah Naghallah?"

"I suppose so," said Mr. Bartlow. "For a while anyway."

"If we get the reward," said Troy, excitedly, "things will be different, won't they?"

"What do you mean?"

Everyone had a different idea. "Will we get the same food as the Masters?"

"Can we go swimming in K. H.'s lake?"

"Can we play ball on the lawn?"

"Can we ride the horses?"

"Can we go camping in the woods?"

"Can we have a radio? Can we have TV?"

"Can we go in to Mountainville to the movies?"

"Your demands are very modest," said Mr. Bartlow, smiling. "Why don't you ask for no school and no work?"

"We don't mind school or work, if we don't get too much of it."

"How about a private room and bath for each of you?"

"We don't need it. This dorm is okay. If the Masters leave us alone."

"How about a car for each of you?"

"Yeah! Hey, that would be great!"

"But you have to go through the Labyrinth first. Cross the Barrier and find Karl Hasserman's treasure. Then things will be very different, I promise you."

And with these cryptic words, he ended the briefing.

Bartlow signalled to Captain Craig, who spoke for the first time. "Karl Hasserman once told us about *The Others*. Trans-humans, he called them..."

The *Others* were neither Angels, nor Demons, nor Beasts; but *Something* in between.

"He said, '*When they once put their Mark on you, you cannot escape!*'"

"He was raving," said Bartlow. "Take the boys to their quarters."

THE MAD SCIENTIST

It was Vedemore who gave us our instructions. He was the one who had designed and built most of the machines and equipment in this weird place. We could thank *him*, I guess, for our collars.

Troy thought Vedemore looked like a mad scientist and he did in a way. With his two-prong beard and heavy dark glasses that concealed his eyes. He had a squeaky, nervous laugh and laughed at his own jokes, even if nobody else did.

Vedemore, however, must be real clever to have worked out all these gadgets. Without him, the Masters would be stymied. None of us liked Vedemore; probably because he had a low opinion of us. We were just another gadget, or rather twelve gadgets to be manipulated to further his schemes. He was hoping he could make us work right for him. If we didn't, we would be scrapped in short order.

Vedemore told us we would be going into a Maze. "But you won't have to walk; at least not for a good while." We would travel in a vehicle that could move on both land and water. There were canals in the maze. And a network of dry tunnels. Also, underground lakes and rivers. They knew that from the earlier people who had failed to return.

Our vehicle was easy to run. "You navigate it like a car or an electric boat." It moved real slow, just a few miles an hour. But we really didn't have very far to go. "Hasserman went in and out in less than two weeks and he travelled on foot. So he told us."

The amphibian was powered by special energy batteries. "Each one is good for a month and you have seven spares. If you have trouble coming back, it won't be for lack of power."

"I think we have several young gentlemen here who are quite experienced with stolen cars. *Hee hee hee!* Keith and Steven and Bobby and Raymond and Danny. *Hee hee hee!* And a stolen motorcycle, too. Right, Troy? *Hee hee hee!* Nothing like having experienced thieves around when you need them." Another giggle followed by a big laugh.

"Whenever the canal or the tunnel divides, you will check back to Headquarters and we will direct you which way to go."

"How can you tell us, sir?"

"With the collars. That's what we have the collars for."

"Do you have a map, sir?" asked practical Keith.

"Yes, we have one. But it will be quite useless to you. It is completely wrong." That was the crazy part of this maze. Every time you mapped it, it was different. The passageways never seemed to be in the same place. "But we know where the earlier people went wrong. And we'll try to keep you away from those places."

Troy held up his hand. "Yes, Troy?"

"I read a story about a labyrinth with a monster in it that ate everybody up."

"Really?"

"Yes. But this guy, Theseus, was a hero and killed the monster. And a Princess gave him a ball of twine. Then he could follow the twine back out again."

"We have thought of that too, Troy. But twine can be cut. Better than twine, the amphibian you ride will leave magnetic tracers. We did that on the last expedition. There was only one trouble." He paused and gave his squeaky, nervous laugh. "When we tried to follow the tracers, they stopped in the middle of *nothing.*"

Bobby Alliconda rubbed his shaved head dolefully. "Why do we need the collars, sir? Couldn't we communicate without them?"

"Perhaps," conceded Vedemore. "But we want to make sure you go where we tell you and do what we tell you. We have put a lot into this venture and don't want it to fail."

"May I ask, sir, why was it necessary to shave our hair off?"

"Yes, you may, Robert," Captain Vedemore broke into that squeaky laugh again. "There are things in the tunnel that get into your hair. You will be glad you haven't any."

None of us thought that was the real reason. More likely, it was a carry over from Dr. Mehary's *Behavior Modification.* The Samson effect in reverse. A youth with a large head of hair feels strong and powerful. Take away his hair and the guy feels weak and helpless. *And is easier to control.* They showed us our supplies. Compressed foods, first aid materials, an electric battery stove, tools and lanterns, a change of clothing, a directional compass and an earth altimeter. We must be a hundred feet below ground. But the altimeter registered nine hundred feet above sea level. *Kaah Naghallah* was located on high ground. To my surprise, I got my watch back. "You might need this."

We also received some minor weapons. Perhaps as a joke, they gave us back the very weapons we had carried when we marched on the mansion; five kitchen knives, two axes, a hammer, a crowbar, a machete and even the broomstick. But no gun.

"At some point, you may have to leave the amphibian and proceed on foot, leaving most of your supplies behind. But you will drive as far as you can." There were oxygen masks and liquid rations. "But you probably won't need them. The air and water in the Underground appear to be quite normal.

"We have not discovered any physical poisons. But there are — — *other things.*"

"What things, sir?"

Vedemore broke into that squeaky laugh again. "That's why we're sending you boys in there. So *you* can tell us."

TERROR AND GLORY

The amphibian was docked in a large hollow where several tunnels came together. It was like a huge canoe with the driving mechanism underneath and a transparent shield over the top. We wondered why we would need a shield here in the Underground. Vedemore said it was to protect us not from the rain and wind, but from things that came out of the wall of the Labyrinth.

Major Powell and a group of guards and Masters came to see us off. The guards carried clubs and side arms. I guess they didn't trust us and thought even at the last minute we might balk and refuse to go.

The men looked grim and worried. Only Captain Craig was cheerful and he was the only one to wish us luck. "Come back safe, lads.! Come back soon and bring home the prize." And as a farewell gift, he handed us a pair of field glasses.

Far back in the hollow, half hidden in the shadows, was another amphibian built something like our own, but much larger, and with a trailer attached. This one had far more equipment than we did. Among other things, there were machine guns and computer panels, and communication equipment designed to keep in contact with the surface world. We got no more than a fast look before they hustled us away.

I saw now what they were planning to do. We would go first. The Masters would follow, guided by the collars we were wearing. We were the expendable foot soldiers, the peasant infantry, breaking a hole for the Nobles in the enemy lines. We were the lightning rod that would draw a foe's hostile fire. If there were a trap, it would be sprung on *us.*

Or perhaps we were like the canaries in the mines, testing the air for poison. We would be stricken first, giving the others a chance to flee. We would be the shield behind which the Masters would move. If disaster befell us, they could withdraw. And if by some chance we should succeed and gain the prize, they could take it from us. Then we would no longer be of any value to them and they would have no reason for keeping us alive.

If they were too squeamish to waste us outright, they could just leave us in the labyrinth without supplies or ways to return. I didn't trust their promise of a reward. Nor did Cameron. We knew too much.

Of course, they didn't tell us what they were planning to do. They spoke again about a mysterious *screen* that adult humans could not penetrate. But we, "in the threshhold years between childhood and manhood," would be better fitted to break through. It was a screen of strange powers, less over the body than over the mind.

Perhaps that much was true. They needed us to get through the *Mindscreen,* whatever it was. Those earlier expeditions had tried and failed and met disaster.

The odds were heavily against us. There appeared to be no way that we could win. But we had little choice except to do their bidding. Those collars held us in the Masters' power. By the collars, they could know everything we did, perhaps even our thoughts. They could put down any rebellion before we even started it. We could be terminated any time we were no longer useful.

But the other guys didn't feel that way. They alternated between feelings of terror and the excitement of glorious adventure. As we went along, the glory of adventure submerged our fears.

BEYOND THE GATEWAY

Day One

"Attention, boys! You are about to cross the Gateway. When the buzzer sounds, turn up the knob of your collars and answer promptly. Let her roll!"

Cameron navigated the amphibian. He was in front with Jody and Roger. The others were in pairs; Stevie and Danny, Raymond and Bobby, Keith and Brandon, Troy and Jaymie. Donald sat alone at the back. He preferred to be by himself.

We moved across the Hollow to what at first seemed like a solid wall, marked by a dull red light. As we approached, the wall opened. A black gate was lifted upward, like the portcullis of a medieval castle. It closed again silently behind us.

We were entering a tunnel far beneath the ground. Everything should have been completely dark. But it wasn't. There was a faint, eerie glow that came from the walls and roof of the passageway.

The other side of the Gateway seemed new and built by human hands; perhaps by Hasserman's men in recent years. But these walls appeared the work of Nature, rough and irregular. An ancient structure from Long Ago. Dark purple stones on either side, with occasional streaks of silver, yellow and red. Everything gave the feeling of great age. Before the dawn of history, when men walked on all fours, when the mammoths and the mastodons roamed the earth, these stones were standing here.

"This is *It*, Brother Jaymie. *The Place of Evil Secrets*."

"Do you know what will happen, Don Don?"

"No." He put one hand on my shoulder and the other hand on Troy's. "Yes, I do. There is great danger. For all of us. But there is a way. Donald can find the way."

Nobody took Donald's words too seriously. But we were glad to hear him talking again, like a normal person.

Brandon asked, "Will we find it, Don Don? That *Thing-Without-a-Name?*"

"I do not know yet," said Donald. "But it has a name, that *Thing*. It is the sound of thunder — and fire — and lightning. It is called ——" He struggled to make his lips move —— "The V-r-r-o-o-o-h-n."

Troy jumped up and down excitedly. "Don Don has a name for Karl Hasserman's treasure. It is called *The Vrrroooohn.*"

We kept going. At once, there was a ringing sound in our collars next to the ear. We sat there looking at each other. Now there was a second ring, loud and angry. Then a buzzing noise and we all felt a sting in our necks.

Quickly, Cameron reached for the collar knob. "Westcott speaking. We're moving right along. Everything is okay."

"Give your readings, Westcott."

"Direction, West Northwest. Altitude 821, curving left and down."

"Any sign of a fork?"

"No, sir,"

"Call immediately if you come to a fork. And Westcott——"

"Yessir."

The Labyrinth of Bane N'Gai.

The Place of Evil Secrets.

"Answer more promptly next time." *Sign-off.*

We knew now. Those collars could burn and sting, if we didn't do what they ordered. "Slave collars," said Raymond, bitterly. "I told you!"

Could they listen to us when we talked to each other? Maybe, but we talked anyway. "That voice sounded like *Number One* again." Who was *Number One?* Keith figured it was Lammington. He was the only one of the Masters who stayed away from the briefing and never appeared since they locked us up. He wanted to remain aloof and mysterious. The better to inspire fear and command obedience.

Number One must be down here now. With his partners and henchmen tracking us in that second amphibian. With the perils of the Underworld before us and the ruthless Masters driving us on, the Naghallah boys were not a very good risk for life insurance. Unless that kid with the yellow eyes really had some great and hidden powers. But Donald had become once again the autistic, retarded youth, talking gibberish.

"Weather tomorrow fair and rainy, with eclipse of the sun and moon. The sky will be windy, with comets and meteors.

"Watch out for the Coyotes! Here come the flying Coyotes! How-woo- How-woo! How-woo! Woof! Woof! Woof!"

The guys all laughed except Jaymie. My hope for Donald's secret powers was an empty dream.

Two Hours Later

"The Naghallah boys reporting, sir. Cameron Westcott speaking. Altitude 734, going down. We have hit a fork. Tunnels West and North."

"Go North, boy!"

"The West tunnel looks more promising, sir. It is wider and lighter."

"*Go North!* That's an order!" Once again our collars buzzed and we felt that sharp twinge of pain.

Cameron said. "We will follow your orders, sir. You don't have to do that. You wanted a full report."

"Just report what you are asked to report!"

"Yessir. We will go north."

"Nice guy!" Stevie rubbed his neck with helpless anger. "That fucking collar started to burn!"

Cameron said, "We'll have to do what he tells us. Unless something turns up."

The passage way kept curving around, maybe in a spiral. All at once, the collars buzzed and stung. An angry voice yelled, "Why didn't you report, boys?"

"There was nothing to report, sir."

"You didn't pass a fork in the tunnel?"

"No, sir."

He didn't apologize. The tunnel we were in didn't conform to the Masters' map.

That last buzz made Donald go wild. He leaped up, tearing at his collar and started yelling. Donald once had been in an institution for the retarded, where they used shock rods on the helpless kids when they became "uncontrollable". That bad memory was coming back.

Keith said, "Cool it, Don Don! We'll find a way to get the collars off. We all got to wear them now."

What a strange kid Donald was! Now suddenly he began bawling.

"What are you, a Coyote or a mouse?"

"I'm a Coyote," said Don Don, wiping off his nose with his sleeve.

Another half hour down the winding tunnel. Then another fork. This one had three branches, North, Northwest and West. "Take the middle branch," ordered the Voice.

"Yessir." No sting in our collars this time.

"Good, boys. Do what you are told and there won't be any trouble." *Sign-off.*

"I wonder," said Bobby, "what would happen if we told them a lie."

"They'd get mad."

"How would they know it?"

"I ain't gonna try it," said Cameron, putting his hand to his neck. "These things could really hurt."

RIVER OF THE DEAD

We passed another eighteen forks and side tunnels. We kept getting lower, if you could believe the altimeter. The Masters did seem to have a plan for us. We were going mostly westward and northward. But the tunnels curved and twisted in every direction. There was no way to tell how far we were on a straight line from the Gateway.

North and West of *Kaah Naghallah* would bring you to a wild mountain region where Karl Hasserman's property ran into the Grey Mountains. If we were still on Earth at all.

Strange patterns were on the rocks. The distorted faces of men and beasts. Teeth without a mouth, arms and heads without a body, gigantic insects crawling from a collossal egg. As you watched them, the things seemed to be moving. Arms began reaching out, jaws opened up.

"Great place for a horror movie," said Brandon.

Keith and Jaymie each had a record book, trying to make a map. It might help us find our way back. *If* they let us come back. We marked off the forks and cross tunnels. *Left. Right. Up. Down.* So far we agreed.

"We've hit water, sir," reported Cameron. The tunnels had turned to canals and the amphibian moved along as a boat. The canal grew wider and entered an underground river. The roof of the cavern here was high and shimmering white. Stalactites of gleaming silver hung downward, like swords about to fall.

We crossed the river slowly. Everything was silent here, except for the soft purr of our vehicle and the occasional shouts of the twelve youths on board. We called out, hoping someone would answer. Perhaps the people lost on earlier missions would hear and call back. But no one did.

The water flowed sluggishly and had a reddish color. Troy remembered his Greek legends. "This looks like the river down in Hades. The River Styx."

"There ought to be ghosts here."

"We'll be ghosts ourselves in a couple of days," predicted Raymond.

The river wasn't too cold. "Hey, Cameron. Maybe we could go swimming."

"Swimming in the River Styx! That would be something!"

"Be careful! We don't know what's in the river."

"Dead things. They may pull us under."

"Why should they, if they're dead?"

"Maybe they want company."

"This ain't too bad a place to be dead in," reflected Bobby.

On the other side of the ghostly river was a low, flat rock. "There's a good place to spend the night. We can park the amphibian and eat."

Cameron turned the collar knob. "Westcott speaking. We have crossed the river. We're going to stop here, sir."

To our surprise, there came an angry buzz and painful sting. "You will *ask* permission when you want to stop, boy. That goes for *all* of you!"

Cameron cursed. He had been pushed about as far as he could take it. Another angry buzz. "What's the matter with you, boy? Answer, will you!"

Cameron cursed again and kicked the side of the amphibian. I turned my collar knob. "This is Jaymie Larrabie, sir. Altimeter reading 402 at river level. We are very tired, sir. We ask permission to stop for the night."

A pause. Then the Voice came. "You may stop. Permission granted."

"Thanks, Jaymie." Cameron put his hand to his collar. "I was about to blow my top and get blasted. I guess I got us all blasted. Sorry about that."

Raymond laughed. "You haven't learned yet to be a slave boy, Master Westcott."

The River Styx.

The Naghallah Boys couldn't resist taking a swim.
Even in the River of the Dead.

Cameron said he was sick of being Gangleader. "You want the job, Ray Ray? No? Anybody else want it?" Nobody did. "You got to navigate, Cameron."

"Anybody could do what I did today."

"Tomorrow may be tougher."

"A lot of you guys can do it as well as me." He drafted the Larrabie brothers. "Danny will drive. Jaymie report."

"I got to make the map," said Jaymie.

"I'll make the map, Gifted Child. You do the talking. *Yessir. Nosir. As you wish, sir. Certainly, sir.*"

We took a dip in the river, but stayed close to shore. Not deeper than our waist. The water felt slimy. Roger got out fast. He claimed there were ghosts in the river.

"What do you expect down in Hades? We're in ghost country now."

"We're in Hades? Not Hell?"

"We won't hit Hell till we get further down."

We dried off and ate. On a soft white rock, we carved our names. Bobby wrote: THE COYOTES WERE HERE and we made our mark, *The Shell and the Arrow.*

We decided to sleep in a circle with our heads together and our feet sticking out. Each guy kept a weapon close to his side.

The guys mostly fell asleep fast. Jaymie took a long time. There was no sign of anything. Nothing you could see or hear, man or animal, living or dead. Yet I had the feeling of being watched.

THE ROAD TO NOWHERE

Day Two

We were in the land of eternal twilight. Morning was just like night. The only way you could tell was you felt hungry and no longer sleepy.

We had lanterns, but didn't use them. Cameron said to save the power until it became really dark. Also, if there were people killers lurking in the tunnels, the lantern light would make us an easy target. Both Donald and the Cat Burglar could see with very little light. After a while, the rest of us would get that way, too.

We piled into the amphibian, me and Danny in front. Before I could check in, there was an angry buzz and a collar shock. "What's the matter with you boys? Why don't you report?"

"Sorry, sir. Jaymie Larrabie speaking. We're about to take off."

"Are you the Gangleader now. Larrabie? Have you taken over from Westcott?"

"No, sir. Cameron is our leader. He told me and Danny to navigate. Cameron is making maps."

"You can forget about the map making. *We'll* tell you where to go."

"Yessir," said Jaymie, sticking his tongue out. "I'll tell Cameron." *(Who, of course, was listening.)*

"What are your orders, sir? We can go up the river, down the river, or straight ahead into a dry tunnel?"

"Take the tunnel. Put your brother on."

"Yessir. Danny Larrabie speaking."

"You're the driver, Larrabie? Well, get moving will you! Shove it!" *Click, Sign-off.*

Danny muttered under his breath and made the *Fuck-you* sign.

We were speeding along at five miles an hour. That was as fast as Danny could make her go. "Another intersection, sir," reported Jaymie. "East and North."

"Go North," was the command, "What is your height reading?"

"Altimeter 213 and going down, sir." We must be at least a thousand feet below the mountains. There seemed to be no pattern to these tunnels. They curved and twisted in every direction, up and down, left and right.

Danny's face had that defiant, rebellious look he used to have at home, before *Kaah Naghallah.* "Lie to him, Jaymie. See if they can tell when we're lying. Come on, Jaymie. Don't be chicken! We got to know."

I took a deep breath. The passageway was straight and clear, but I reported. "We're at a fork, sir. Northeast and Southeast."

Almost immediately, there was a buzz and a collar shock. "I want an accurate report, Larrabie. Don't report tunnels when there aren't any." He didn't sound angry. Rather gleeful and gloating that he had caught us in a lie and put us in our place.

The creep gave everyone a nasty collar sting, not just me and Danny. But the guys weren't mad. "Nice try," said Bobby, "even if it didn't work."

Now we know for sure. We're slave boys and they have us in their power.

We passed another sixteen forks and cross-tunnels on the *Road to Nowhere.* Cameron compared maps with Keith. So far, full agreement. But we were running low on paper. "We'll have to make just one map, instead of duplicates. And write smaller."

Now the tunnel became wider and the roof higher. Little streams of water trickled down the walls. A pale green mould grew in patches on the rocks. "We're in a hollow, sir," reported Jaymie. "Altitude 98 feet. There are signs of life here. Request permission to stop and investigate."

"Are you telling the truth, Jaymie? Or is this another falsehood?"

"It's the truth, sir."

"Why did you tell a lie before?"

"To see if you would catch it, sir."

"Whose idea was that, Jaymie?"

"Mine, sir. I apologize."

A pause. Then, "Very well, Jaymie Larrabie. You may

stop and investigate."

The tunnel opened up into a chamber as big as a ball field. The stone walls gleamed with a pale, phantasmic light. In the light of the lantern, the stones had rainbow colors. Azurite blue. Malachite green. And streaks of gold, red, silver and orange. The floor, too, was studded with multi-colored rocks, rounded and heavy when you picked them up. A scene of wonder! The guys all stood there open-mouthed, staring at the weird and unbelievable beauty.

In the center of the hollow was a grove of pale green plants, with spiny leaves and twisted branches. They were like arms with many hands, reaching out in all directions in search of prey.

By the unearthly trees was a pool of water, blood red and having a sweet, unnatural scent. Roger touched it. "It feels cold and creepy."

"Keep away from it," Cameron warned.

Beyond the pool was a mound of stones, piled up carefully, as if by human hands. "Looks like a grave," said Brandon.

It was a grave. On a flat rock, someone had scratched a name:

DEAN HARLOW, R. I. P.

Perhaps one of the lost people from an earlier expedition. We stood before the mound in silence. *Rest in Peace, Dean Harlow. Whoever you are and Wherever you are now.*

Jaymie was standing close to one of the spiny trees. A branch reached out like a great claw and fastened on his shoulder. Jaymie gave a cry of pain. Danny broke me loose and pulled me away.

"Let's get out of here!"

We turned and ran back to the amphibian, fleeing the hollow of death.

Danny said, "They almost got you, Little Brudder. What do I get for saving you?"

"I'll give you half my reward for finding Hasserman's treasure."

Danny laughed. "That reward was a lot of bullshit, Jaymiebrudder. If we get out of here alive, that's all the reward I want."

"We found a grave, sir," reported Jaymie. "The grave of Dean Harlow."

"*Dean Harlow?*" That name meant something to the man at the other end. He spoke not to Jaymie, but to his companion. "Dean Harlow is dead. Then the others must be dead, too."

*   *   *   *   *   *   *

We passed another hollow. There were more grave markers here. But the killer trees were growing around them, so we didn't stop. Jaymie had a bleeding wound on his chest and shoulder. Keith had a bite on his arm. We spread our first aid stuff over the wounds and they healed in time.

"We'll give you guys a Purple Heart," announced Cameron. "In the name of the *Keekereekee.*" He was always making up medals and decorations. Cameron kept us laughing, no matter how rough things got.

We reported the wounds and the flesh-eating plants. The Masters wouldn't believe us, or said they didn't. In our vengeful hearts, we hoped they got bitten, too.

We hit a new kind of intersection. Two tunnels, both West Northwest, one going up the other down. "Take the down tunnel!"

That was when we began to hear the Voices. First there were whispers, calling our names. "*Go back! Go back! Go back!*" *Over and over and over again. . . . Then,* "*Going . . . Going . . . Gone! . . . Going . . . Going . . . Gone!*" Followed by wild, maniacal laughter. Then a scream of terror and agony, like the cry of a lost soul in Hell.

Again and again those voices came. Sometimes they seemed just in front of us, sometimes behind us. Sometimes above or below. The guys were getting jittery. Roger and Jody were shaking.

"It's only a noise," said Cameron. "A noise can't hurt you."

The kids kept trembling. Now Brandon and Troy were trembling, too. "Come on, guys," called Cameron. "Who's afraid of a noise? We can make a louder noise than that. Let's give a cheer for the Coyotes!"

We shouted, "C—O—Y—O—T—E—S! Coyotes! Coyotes! Coyotes! Y-a-a-a-a-y!!!"

Every time we heard that laugh and scream, we cheered and drowned it out.

GOBLINS' BREAD AND GHOSTLY VOICES

We found another hollow to spend the night in. This one was bare and lifeless. The ground was covered with reddish sand. Brandon prepared the supper from dehydrated concentrates. Pretty tasteless, but you couldn't blame the cook.

Our drinking water was going fast. Cameron said we'd have to ration it. No washing, just drinking. There was lots of water in the labyrinth, but it all seemed polluted. We didn't trust the Masters' purification tablets.

"Donald find water," he told Cameron.

"Go ahead, Don Don."

He began digging in the red sand. The lower sand was wet. Donald kept digging and ran into a flowing stream. "Drink!" Donald urged. "Water good."

"How do you know?"

He put his head against the sand. "It makes a good noise."

The guys were rather leery at first. Donald filled up his canteen and drank it and nothing happened to him.

Cameron put his arm on Donald's shoulder. "Great, Don Don! I hereby name you *Grand Water Wizard of the Coyotes*. In the name of the *Keekereekee*." Donald looked pleased.

The end of the hollow opened into passageways that narrowed until they became too small for any human to enter. But big enough for something to come out. There was a hissing and a whistling and a roaring, coming out of the holes in the rock. Then a whispering of words in an unknown tongue. Uncanny and terrifying, like some forgotten childhood nightmare.

The guys began to see things, too. Each guy saw something different. Bobby saw a pair of phantoms with faceless heads. Stevie beheld a mass of snakes. Danny perceived a demon with horns and many arms. Jody saw an ogre with ferocious jaws. There must be something working on our minds and made each of us see the things he feared.

Roger wandered around and came back yelling. He had seen *The Bogeyman.* So he said.

"Aw, go on," said Keith. "Do you believe in the Bogeyman?"

"No, but I seen him. And he chased me."

"What did he look like?"

"Nasty and ugly," declared Roger. "With a crazy face. Everything in the wrong place."

"Maybe you looked in a mirror," suggested Troy.

No matter how much the guys joked and wisecracked, we kept on feeling jittery. We would sleep in a circle, Cameron decreed. And we piled up loose rocks as a barricade around us. A two or three foot rockpile wouldn't stop anything, but it made us feel better.

Cameron decided to post guard. Two guards. "Roger and I will take the first watch."

Roger pleaded, "Don't make me guard, Cameron. Please don't make me! It's so dark here."

"You're a Coyote, ain't you? Coyotes are night creatures. They like the dark."

"Do they?" Roger looked troubled. "You mean I got to like the dark, even though I hate it?"

Cameron handed Roger the broomstick. "That's right, Roger. Get on guard. And if the Bogeyman comes, chase him away."

* * * * * * *

Jaymie and Donald guarded together, me with an axe, Don Don with a knife. After a few minutes, Donald took off and disappeared. I didn't dare go looking for him. I had to stay close to the circle of sleeping guys. All kinds of shadowy shapes were moving around us, but when I turned the lantern on them, they disappeared. And all the time, I could hear the voices whispering words that didn't make sense.

At last Donald came back, carrying something round and flat and white, like the top of a giant mushroom. Donald cut a slice. "Eat, Jaymie."

Those voices were whispering again. This time I could hear the words. *Don't take that, Jaymie. Don't even touch it. He is trying to poison you. Donald isn't human.*

I had lived with Donald for many months. Now he suddenly became different. As though he had been wearing a disguise that now was torn away. There was something about Donald's face that frightened me. Something I had not seen before.

All we knew of Donald before *Kaah Naghallah* was what the late Dr. Mehary had written. He was a victim of Kessler's disease. *Abnormal genes. Hopelessly defective.* "The victims of Kessler's disease live in a bizarre world and do not react as normal people do."

Donald was holding that slice of something in his hand. "Don't you want it?"

"I'm not hungry," said me.

Donald chewed and swallowed it himself. He had a name for it. *Goblins' Bread.* As if he could read my thoughts, he said. "It won't hurt you, Jaymie. I wouldn't give you anything to hurt you."

Five minutes later, Donald was walking around unpoisoned, vigorous and healthy, turning somersaults and walking on his hands. I had a feeling of shame for misjudging Don Don. There were mysterious and hostile forces here. They were trying to terrify us into total panic. Or, failing that, to turn us against each other.

Maybe that was how the earlier expeditions were destroyed. They began by suspecting each other. Then suspicion turned to violence and violence to death. *It must not, it shall not be that way with us.*

"Give me a slice of Goblins' Bread, please, Don Don. Thank you."

It didn't taste bad. A little like real bread and a little like a mushroom. Better than the Masters' food pills. Donald looked so pleased when I said I liked it. Like a happy puppy, wagging his tail — if Don Don had a tail to wag. How could I have thought so evil of him!

The guys all had a slice for breakfast and liked it well. If there was more Goblins' Bread in the Labyrinth, at least we wouldn't starve for food.

FLAMING CHARIOTS

Day Three

They woke us up again at 6:00 A.M. with a buzz and a collar sting. "Get moving! Shove it!" This time, Keith and Stevie navigated. By the distance recorder, we had covered about seventy miles from the Gateway.

Altimeter reading: *Dead Zero.* We were at sea level, at least a quarter mile below the surface world. Yet the air here seemed quite normal. There must be openings by which the air could get down into the tunnels. And if there were — then maybe the Naghallah boys could get back up.

They wouldn't let us go back the way we came. Not without that Thing Donald called *The Vrrooohn.* And if by some stretch of luck we found it, they would take it away from us.

As we rode along, we suddenly heard a series of gun shots. "Get down!" yelled Cameron, closing down the protective shield of the amphibian. We threw ourselves flat, hoping that shield could stop a bullet. Stevie kept going full speed ahead, trying to get out of the line of fire. But there was no way to tell if the attackers were ahead or behind us.

For a few minutes, we lay there helpless. Gradually, the shots receded and then died out. Were there other humans down here with guns, ready to shoot anyone who invaded their territory?

Keith had another idea. The Masters were following us and *they* had guns. "I think *they* are the ones who were doing the shooting."

"Why should they shoot at us when we're doing what they want us to do?"

"They weren't shooting at *us*. They were shooting at something else."

The tunnels of the Labyrinth kept twisting and curving. More like the web of some collossal spider than the roads on earth. The Masters might be following thirty miles behind us, yet actually be but a fraction of a mile away. And the way sound carried in this fantastic place, a faraway noise might echo through the tunnels until it seemed right behind us.

"If the Masters are shooting, they may be in trouble," reflected Bobby. "Something may be attacking them."

We were supposed to be their protective shield. If there was danger, it would hit *us* and give them a chance to get away. That's the way grown-ups thought. Dangers would stay in one place. Kids knew that dangerous things can move. They can come at you not only from the front, but from the sides and from behind you.

Keith reported. "We have reached a fork, sir. *West* and *South*." There was a long pause before the answer came. "Go West, Caldwell. What is your altitude?"

"Still zero, sir. We heard gun fire. Is everything all right?"

We weren't supposed to know the Masters were in the Labyrinth and following us. The Voice came back somewhat irritated. "Of course. Keep going!" Maybe the Masters just got panicky and were shooting at *Nothing*.

The walls of the tunnel changed color and became a lurid red. The tunnel widened, then plunged sharply downward. Stevie had to apply the brakes with all his power.

We came into an enormous cavity, an underground hall all red and strangely bright. Blood-colored moss grew on the crimson rocks. Red pebbles covered the floor, gleaming like rubies. In the center, flowed a stream of rusty water. The red canal was hot and dirty. But the Naghallah boys could not resist taking a swim in it. Red smoke or mist came out of the ground and covered the roof of the cavern with scarlet clouds.

"Request permission to stop for the night, sir."

"Permission granted." For the first time, the Voice seemed a bit weary. We were 110 miles in and had found *nothing*.

"There are dead things here," said Raymond. "I can feel them."

Ghosts of the departed? Why should we fear the dead who in life had been people like us? Perhaps friends and loved ones. I remembered Grandfather with his meerschaum pipe and merry laugh. I called to him and tried to feel his presence. But there was no sign here of grandfather or any other human dead. What I felt instead was something utterly alien and menacing.

We made camp, sleeping in a circle, facing outward. Everything was silent. There were no voices here, nor any sign of life except the crimson moss. We were too weary to post guard. Besides, it wouldn't help any. "If something comes at us, we got no place to run."

Now we saw the apparition for the first time. Far above us, moving silently. A flaming chariot, surrounded by a halo of golden light.

Who would ride in such things? Perhaps the Rulers of the Underworld, inspecting their realm. Or whatever gods there be in this haunted place.

For a moment, the vehicle hovered over us. Then dipped and circled and vanished as suddenly as it had come. They must have seen us. Either we were unworthy of their attention. Or else, they had us in their power and could get us any time they wanted.

Defiantly, we made our mark on the rocks. The Shell and the Arrow. And *The Coyotes were here.*

THE SILENT SCREAM

Day Four

We were awakened once again at six by a collar sting, unnecessarily sharp and prolonged; bringing curses and yells of pain. If we had become prisoners of those Beings in the shining chariots, they might treat us better than the Masters did.

"Come on, get moving, boys! Follow the red canal. *Northwest and down.* Who is reporting today?"

"I am, sir. Bobby Alliconda. And Raymond is navigating."

"Well, report then. Why are you boys always so late in getting started?"

"Altimeter reading *zero,* sir."

"Impossible!" It was stuck right on *zero.* That got the Master at the other end mad. He buzzed us angrily.

"That's the truth, sir. What is it supposed to be?"

He didn't say. "You are 110 miles in. You should have hit the Barrier by now."

"Is there just one barrier, sir? Or more?"

"You'll find out after you get through the first one."

We took off. The canal flowed peacefully through high walls of red marble, growing broader, fed by underground streams.

"Our fourth day," said Brandon. "And we're still alive."

"Maybe we ain't," declared Keith. "Maybe that really was the River of the Dead we crossed. Now, we're down in Purgatory, doomed to wander forever for our sins."

Stevie thought it was a pretty creampuff Purgatory. "I wouldn't mind wandering like this forever. As long as we're all together and get food and water."

The other guys didn't mind it either. If we could get rid of our hated collars.

We followed the canal until it split into two branches. We were ordered to take the left branch, narrow, dark and gloomy. It was hard to see here. A heavy fog hung over the canal. We put our lights on.

We rounded a corner and ran into a deadly trap. A huge blotch of darkness stretched across the canal, like an enormous ink blot. And we were headed straight into the middle of it. It swelled and pulsated like a living thing. Raymond slammed on the brakes.

"Go back!" yelled Cameron. "Reverse engine!"

But we had reckoned without our slavemasters. "What are you doing? What's the matter with you?"

"We've run into smoke and fumes, sir." Bobby didn't know what to call that great Blob. "Request permission to backtrack and go another way."

"Keep going, dammit! This is the only way. Don't ever backtrack! Put your masks on!" This was followed by a painful sting in our collars.

Still, Raymond tried to reverse. But we kept going forward. Maybe the Masters could move us by remote control. Or else the Horror was drawing us into itself. Cameron yelled. "Go forward, Ray Ray! Give it all the power you can!"

We grabbed for our masks. Donald didn't want to put his mask on. I stuck it over his head. Donald tore it off again and gave a wild yell. It sounded like a battle cry rather than a cry of fear. The other guys lay flat and closed their eyes.

We lurched forward. The amphibian trembled violently, like a battle horse driven into cannon fire. The black blot closed around us and we were swallowed up in the belly of the *Unthing*.

We were in total darkness. The night that had no day. For an endless moment, we could not breathe nor think. Time stood still. There was no future and no past. There was nothing but the silent scream of the *Blob* and the smell of terror, decay and death. Then the amphibian leaped forward and we were out of it. The madness of the *Unthing* gradually cleared from our minds.

The buzzer sounded. The voice of Number One. "Report! What happened?"

"We got through the Blob," said Bobby. "We're still alive, no thanks to you."

Such insolence would ordinarily have aroused the Master's anger. This time, he said, "Nice going, boys."

For a few moments the guys sat there in terrified silence. That's the way it usually happens. You don't really start feeling fear until it's over. Then Cameron said. "Is everyone okay?"

"I'm dead," said Troy.

"Brother Troy is dead. We'll have to dump him in the canal to resurrect him."

"No, don't!" cried Troy. "I can resurrect myself."

TRIAL BY FIRE

Day Four

We went on. Once again, we heard that wild laughter. And those moaning voices. Both very far away. Then we left the canal and climbed into a tunnel of solid rock.

The tunnel grew wider and brighter. The other tunnels had been winding and twisting sidewards. This one went up and down like a roller coaster. With each rise, the light grew stronger.

Now we came to a high point. Down below was a *Wall of fire*. The entire tunnel seemed ablaze. Raymond threw on the brakes with all his strength and the amphibian ground to a shaky halt.

"Back up, Ray Ray! Can you put the reverse on?" Raymond was trying.

Again that collar sting and the Slavemaster's furious voice. "Don't stop! Keep going, Ridgeway! What in Hell are you trying to do?"

"Fire!" cried Raymond. "We have to go back and go around it."

"You can't go around. All other ways are blocked. This is the only way you can make it!"

"We can't!" pleaded Bobby. "The fire ——"

"There is no fire," cried the Voice. "Put your shield down. Follow your orders. Go through, dammit!" And this time a really nasty collar burn, the worst one yet.

The brakes were not holding. We were beginning to slip. Cameron yelled, "Down, everybody! Go fast, Ray Ray!"

We hit the floor and covered up our eyes. A shower of sparks and flaming embers was swirling around us. We tore down the incline and went crashing into the fire. For an awful instant, we were paralyzed with shock and terror. Then we were out of it.

There were no burn marks on our clothes or bodies and no fire scars on the vehicle that carried us. We raced down hill at a furious pace, then swung up again, leaving the firewall behind.

Was it a real fire or the false image of one? A cold flame that didn't burn? Or was there something working on our minds to give us a collective hallucination?

Anyway, as Troy yelled, *We made it!* The guys cheered. "Nothing can stop the Coyotes!" Twelve glorious heroes of *Bane N'Gai.*

No wonder they chose us for this mission. Any grown-up would have balked on that one. Or panicked and blown their top. "Stupid boys," they must be saying. "They'll do anything, if you put the pressure on them."

"We are through the fire, sir," reported Bobby. "We are going to stop for the night."

Our Slavemaster appeared satisfied. "You have done well today, boys. Permission is given to stop."

We halted in a sandy hollow where the red moss grew and silver beetles scurried in and out of small holes in the rocks. Once again, Donald found us Goblins' Bread and clean water.

THE ABYSS

Day Five

Troy and Brandon had been eager to navigate the amphibian. But after yesterday they didn't want to. That left only Roger, Donald and Jody who hadn't had a turn to drive or report. Cameron didn't think they could handle it. So, on this fifth day, he decided to take over again himself.

It was Donald who protested. "My turn today!"

"You don't know how to drive, Don Don."

"Yes, I do. Donald can see things."

Cameron didn't want to hurt his feelings. "I tell you what, Don Don. I'll drive and you sit next to me and direct me. Okay?"

Donald remained unhappy. "I can see things, Cameron. None of the others can. Donald will help brothers. Donald has power."

"I know, Don Don. We need you and we're counting on you. But driving this thing is awful tricky."

Disappointed, but without rancor, Donald accepted Cameron's decision.

We travelled through branching tunnels. The altimeter was still stuck on zero, but we seemed to be climbing. The tunnels grew wider. There was life here. Green mold on the rocks, yellow barnacles and abundant Goblins' Bread.

"We're stopping to gather food, sir." No objection from our Slavemaster.

The rocks here had weird shapes, like the heads and bodies of some mythical beast. A winged lion, a horned bird and a three-headed snake. The hollow shone with an eerie silver light. The floor was covered with golden sand and red clay. There were footprints in it, the footprints of a large creature with cloven hoofs. There was also a set of human footprints. They led into a cave and didn't come out.

"It's spooky here," said Roger.

"The whole fuckin labyrinth is spooky," declared brother Danny.

We started to explore the cave. The entrance was

covered with strange markings that might be the runes of some ancient language. Keith pretended to read them. "It says *Keep Out.*" Once again, we could smell the weird odor of decay and death.

Troy went in first and came out shouting. There were bones here and the skeletons of animals. There was a pair of discarded boots, a blackened sleeping bag and the grey ashes of a bonfire. Propped up in a corner on an iron pike was a human skull with several teeth missing. The mouth was opened as if about to speak.

Stevie said, "Whoever it is, we better bury him. Otherwise, his ghost may haunt us."

We buried the skull in sand and clay and marked beside it, *Rest in Peace,* instead of our usual *The Coyotes Were Here.* Once again, we had the feeling someone or something was watching us. We hurried back to the amphibian and drove away, leaving the cave of death behind.

We kept climbing. The tunnel opened up, wide and high. The ceiling now was far overhead, covered with gleaming yellow stalactites. The side walls glistened with many colored radiant stones. But in this strange place, rare beauty was often a sign of danger.

All at once the road stopped and we hit the abyss — a big black hole of *Nothing.* Below us was a tremendous drop into utter darkness. Before us was a bottomless pit, bounded on each side by a giant precipice of sheer rock. The road on which we travelled ran directly into the Pit. There was no way to turn away or turn back. *We were moving headlong into the abyss. There was nothing to stop us.*

Cameron struggled with the brakes, trying to check our drop into oblivion. The brakes weren't holding and he tried to go backwards. We reached out and grabbed onto rocks outside, trying to hold. We ignored the buzzing in our collars and the frantic voice of the Slavemaster. "Don't stop now! Keep going!"

"We'll crash, sir," cried Cameron. "We're right on the edge of a cliff!"

A series of violent stings. "Keep going, I tell you!"

"There's a terrible drop, sir. We can't even see the bottom. Let us go back!"

"I tell you there is no drop. You're a bunch of cowardly punks. Keep going, I tell you. Go!"

Another series of violent stings. We were like cattle being driven with shock rods into the slaughter house. "Go, damn you! Go!"

Cameron sat there helplessly. His hands were shaking. Then Donald by his side said, "Go, Cameron. Go straight ahead."

In desperation, Cameron pushed the accelerator forward. The amphibian moved to the very edge of the abyss. Then, to our amazement, the road on which we travelled was extended, like a bridge built into thin air. Each time we seemed to reach the edge, the bridge over the abyss grew longer. Now we passed the middle of the Great Gulf and were approaching the other side. Three hundred . . . . Two hundred . . . . One hundred yards away.

With a combination of hope and terror, we watched the gap narrow. At length, the amphibian crossed the gulf and landed safely on the other side. For a moment, we could see the bridge behind us. Then the bridge vanished and there was only the terrible emptiness of the abyss.

There was no cheering this time. Just unimaginable relief. That invisible bridge across the gulf was what Keith called an *anti-mirage*. That is when you *can't* see things that *are* there.

"Did you see the bridge, Don Don?"

He wouldn't tell us. He just smiled.

"You want to drive, Don Don? You can if you want to."

"Cameron drive. I will report," decided Donald. He pushed the communicator. "This is Donald Turrentine, the cowardly punk. We're over the pit, Slavemaster. Foo! Foo! Foo! We made it!" Followed by a series of bird and animal noises.

The buzzer sounded. The Voice of *Number One:* "Was that the dummy? Don't let the dummy report. Put someone else on, will you."

"That dummy," said Cameron, "is the one who got us across the abyss. We can thank Donald that we're here."

THE CLIFF GIGANTIC AND
THE HEIGHTS UNBOUNDED

Day Five

We would like to have stopped now and rested. But the Slavemaster wouldn't let us. We had crossed the Barrier now — three of them. The Blob, the Wall of Fire and now the Abyss. In this mad treasure hunt, we must be getting hot. We were closing in on Karl Hasserman's Thing. The *Vrroooohn* could not be far away.

We rode on through the eternal twilight. The road turned steeply upward and we began to hope we might be returning to the surface world. But that hope was short-lived. We turned downward again, zigzagging around sharp turns.

The amphibian was racing like a toboggan. The guys had overcome their fear and gloom. They cheered and urged Cameron to go even faster.

Only Donald yelled. "Slow, Cameron! Watch for the wall!" We could see nothing ahead.

"Anmir!" shouted Don Don. "Anmir! Brakes! Stop! Quick!"

Cameron slowed to half, then half again. I thought Don Don was kidding around. The tunnel ended abruptly in a dead end. The nose of the amphibian crashed into solid rock. Had we been going full speed, we might have smashed up completely. As it was, we were just shaken up a bit. That high rock that blocked the tunnel was another anti-mirage; or what Donald called *Anmir*. You couldn't see it until you were right on top of it.

A collar buzz and the Slavemaster's voice. "What happened?"

"The tunnel is a dead end. We ran into a cliff."

The Slavemaster cursed us for being stupid punks and worthless trash, with the brains of a bullfrog. "Is the machine damaged?"

"No, sir."

"Then keep going. Put on the climbing gear."

"We can't, sir. The cliff is almost perpendicular and awful high. May we have your permission to go back?"

"No, you may *not* have permission to go back. You never go back! Go on by foot, you defective whelps! Carry what you can and check in every hour on the hour."

"It is very late sir. Request permission to rest here and climb the cliff tomorrow."

"Permission denied. You can rest when you reach the top." Then more abuse and the usual collar sting to show us who the boss was.

It looked to me like an impossible climb. Cameron thought we could make it. The Cat Burglar would go first. Donald would go last, the anchor man on the rope that would be tied around all of us. We all filled up our knapsacks. We had to leave most of our supplies behind. We were sorry to leave the amphibian. It had been a good friend. Almost like a living thing.

Cameron didn't try to climb straight up. He circled around, zigzagging back and forth, finding a series of footholds, crevasses and projections; each one rising a little higher than the one before.

Cameron was a truly great climber. He went up like a mountain goat, breaking a track for all of us. But Donald was perhaps even better. He went up like a squirrel on all fours, taking Roger with him. Cameron went real slow, making sure everyone was okay before he took the next step. Anyway, we finally made it.

Jaymie was about the worst climber of the twelve. I almost slipped once, but Brother Danny grabbed me. "Hey, Jaymie brudder, what do I get for saving your life on that climb?"

"I'll give you the rest of my reward for finding Karl Hasserman's treasure."

"You know what we're gonna get, Jaymiebrudder? Zero. A big fuckin goose egg."

Danny didn't make the obvious wisecrack. "That's about what you're worth, Gifted Child." Instead, he got sentimental. "I promised to watch over you, Little Brudder, and I'm gonna do it. I sure would miss you, if you weren't around."

"We have climbed the cliff, sir." Cameron reported.

"We're on the top now."

The Voice came back, "Congratulations, Westcott. Tell the boys that I am proud of them. I may seem like a hard taskmaster, but that is because I expect a lot from you. You may rest now." *Sign-off.*

THE PURPLE HORRORS

Day Six

We camped on a high plateau beyond the cliff and slept in a circle with our boots on. That's the way we slept every night.

We were awakened again at six by a collar sting. Our accomplishments of yesterday didn't win us any favors or change our condition. We were still slaves. "Come on, you lazy punks. Get going!"

There were no tunnels here like there were below. The roof of the labyrinth was far above us, so high it appeared almost like a gray sky. Ahead were mountains, cliffs and crags, with canyons and passes running between them. Very rarely did we find a smooth passageway. Often, we had to climb up over high rocks or descend through narrow holes. Up here, the amphibian would have been quite useless.

There was no orderly pattern of roads and crossings. "Use the compass then." ordered the Slavemaster, "Go *West Northwest.* Report every time you hit a hollow or change direction. Check in at least every hour. Do you understand, boys?"

"Yessir," said Cameron, silently making a face.

"Who wants to report?"

Brandon shyly put his hand half way up, then pulled it down and shook his head negatively.

"Brother Brandon," said Cameron, "I seen you the first time. You are drafted to report and I'll navigate."

"Form column of twos," Cameron ordered. He walked first, followed by Brandon and Jaymie, Stevie and Danny, Jody and Roger, Keith and Troy, Bobby and Raymond. Don Don walked alone at the end. "Donald guard rear," he announced.

We marched in formation down the Northwest passageway. There was plant life here. Silver vines, growing on the rocks, small red mushrooms and some leafless trees with petrified trunks, more stone than wood. At length, we hit another steep cliff, this one going down. We had hardly reached the bottom when our collars stung again. "Why didn't you report?"

"Brandon Zuchtig reporting, sir. The hour wasn't up yet."

"I said to report if you changed direction."

"We just went down a cliff, sir."

"That's changing direction, isn't it?"

"Yessir. Yessir," said Brandon.

"Are you in charge of the group now, Brandon Zuchtig?"

"No sir. Cameron's in charge."

"You boys have the stupidest system I have ever seen. Select *one* person to report and *stick* to him."

"Yessir," Brandon stuck out his tongue and made a *Fuck-you* sign. Fortunately, our Slavemaster could only hear and not see us.

We went on. The Labyrinth was changing. The roof seemed higher and became blue instead of grey. There were faint lights up there that almost looked like distant stars. The ground had become a vast and stony plateau that looked the same in all directions.

There was no way of mapping this territory. The maps Keith and I had so painstakingly made were now quite useless. Anyway, we had run out of paper. We hid our maps in the hollow of a petrified stone tree and scratched on it the mark of the Coyotes, *The Shell and the Arrow*. If we ever returned to Earth again, it wouldn't be the way we came.

We began to see trees now that had leaves on them. Unlike the surface world, these leaves were pale yellow or silver white. There were signs of animal life, too. Small creatures in snail-like shells scurried over the rocks and sand. Other creatures that looked like yellow bats were roosting in the silver trees and took off as we came near.

There were pools of water with turtle-like creatures hopping around, then leaping and diving under the surface. Some of the guys wondered if the little animals might be good to eat. Cameron said, "Let's not kill anything here, unless we have to. I have a hunch if we start hunting, *Something* is gonna come along and hunt *us.*"

We decided the snails, bats and turtles, or whatever they were, weren't bothering us. So let's not bother them. Passed by a 12 to 0 vote and made into a Boylaw. *We'll leave alone all creatures that leave us alone.* (Boylaw Number 14, if anyone is counting)

We came to an open space where there was soft moss and clear water cascaded over sparkling white stones. A good place to stop. Some yards away was a strange forest of purple stalks with twisting arms attached. They were weird, those arms. More like the tentacles of a squid than a tree branch. A few were swollen at the end with eyes in them, like the head of a snake. The purple things were rigid and motionless, if you looked straight at them. But if you looked at them again, they seemed to have moved.

Wearily, Cameron reported, hoping the Slavemaster was in a good mood. Maybe he would let us rest, although by earth time it was but mid-afternoon.

We received a pleasant surprise. Instead of the Slavemaster, came the cheery voice of Captain Craig. "How are you lads? Good? Good! Sure you can rest, lads. You have food and water? Good! Good luck to you."

We ate and were relaxing when we got a buzz and collar sting. The Slavemaster had returned. "Why didn't you report?"

"We did, sir. Captain Craig gave us permission to stop."

"Captain Craig is not running things. *I am.* It's much too early to stop."

"We're really beat, sir."

"You covered very little ground today."

"It was tough going, sir. Our feet ache. We're sore all over. We made camp for the night, sir. Our legs ——"

"I don't want to hear any more about your ailments." We were a bunch of whining crybabies. Lazy, rotten, miserable urchins. Useless bums and shirkers. But since Captain Craig had given permission, we could stay here now. "Tomorrow, I want a full day out of you.! No whimpering and no stalling!"

"Yessir."

The Slavemaster appeared worried. Things were not turning out as he had expected. Karl Hasserman had gone in and out of the Labyrinth in two weeks or less. With the amphibian, the time should have been shorter. But tomorrow was the seventh day and there was no sign we were anywhere near the end of our journey. Except for Don Don, we would be getting low on food and water. The Masters had more stuff than we did. But each day their supplies were less.

When we first arrived here, those purple stalks with their tentacles and snake-like off-shoots must have been at least two hundred feet away. Now they seemed much closer, only half as far, although nobody had seen them move. Furthermore, they had been bunched up to the East of us. Now they were spread around us in a semi-circle, from North to South.

I told Cameron. He said, "You're seeing things, Jaymie. You and Roger. He sees the Bogeyman every place we go. You see trees that move."

"Okay," said me. "Let's pace them and make sure they don't come any nearer."

43 paces. As I came close to those purple stalks, those tentacle branches seemed to reach out and grab for me. I didn't tell that to Cameron. He would think I was completely looney.

"Let's turn in," said Cameron. "We'll post a guard though. To watch those purple stalks. You take the first watch, Jaymie.

"Roger, you stand guard with Jaymie. And call me, Roger, if the Bogeyman comes."

"I don't see him every night," protested Roger. "Maybe I won't see him here."

The other guys lay down in a circle. Me and Roger stayed on our feet. Roger looked at me dubiously, wishing he had one of the big boys as a guarding partner. If the Boog came to snatch him, I wouldn't be much protection.

I paced the purple stalks again. *34 paces!* Furthermore they were now surrounding us on three sides, forming two-thirds of a circle.

I woke Cameron up. He said, "You must have made a mistake, Jaymie. Pace them again." I did. *29 paces!* Three quarters of a circle around us. Still they didn't seem to move.

Roger yelled and pointed to the ground. The purple things didn't move. But new ones were coming out of the ground all the time.

They were coming at *us*. Closer. Faster. *20 paces* now, or less. Around us in seven-eighths of a circle. The escape opening was getting narrower. You could see it closing. Those snake-like tentacles had become alive. They were reaching out to grab us, making a hissing sound.

Cameron gave the Coyote danger howl. "Up, everybody! Grab your stuff and follow me! Fast!"

We were quick, but not quick enough. Even as we reached the circle, the gap closed. Cameron and Stevie swung the axes. The other guys cut with their knives at the grasping tentacles, kicked with their boots or struck with make-shift weapons.

Troy fell down and the tentacles closed around him. We struck at them fiercely, with all our might and broke Troy loose.

More purple stalks were arising in front of us. "Run!" shouted Cameron. Fortunately, we had trained ourselves to run in formation. Had we panicked and split up, we might never have found each other again.

We kept running. Every time we stopped, new purple stalks began to rise out of the ground. At length, we reached a pile of boulders. "Follow me!" yelled Cameron. We climbed the rocks. The purple things couldn't follow us

Troy was trapped by the Purple Horrors.
The Naghallah Boys struck furiously to rescue him.

up here. They had to have soil in which to plant their roots.

After a hundred foot climb, we reached a cave and went inside, Nothing was coming after us now.

THE CAVE OF THE GIANT RATS

Exhausted, we threw ourselves on the floor of the cave. Cameron counted us. *Troy... Roger... Stevie... Keith... Raymond... Bobby... Brandon... Donald... Jody... Danny... Jaymie...* and *Cameron.* All here. The guys cheered.

It was a real snug cave with an abundance of drinking water and Goblins' bread. The only trouble was we weren't alone. Something was moving in the shadows at the back of the cavern. Not one, but many things, with shining red eyes. They were coming nearer.

"Goblins!" cried Jody.

I always thought Goblins looked like people, only they were small and had big heads. There creatures didn't look like people at all. They had long, stringy tails and were covered all over with fur. They had snouts and sharp teeth. About two feet long and walking on four legs. They resembled — yes, they were — *giant rats!*

The creatures didn't like us. We were invading their cave. They were making growling noises and bared their teeth. We grabbed our weapons. They kept coming closer. We shouted at them and started throwing things. That seemed to frighten them off and they went away.

After a while, the giant rats came back. This time, they stayed at a distance. If we went to sleep, the creatures would attack us. Between the Purple Horrors outside and the giant rats here, things looked really rough.

The creatures now were squeaking and squealing, with grunts and growls mixed in. Donald crawled over toward them and began making noises, too. From the sounds he was making, Donald could have been a rat himself. When the rats screeched, Donald screeched. They chirped and squawked and so did Donald. After a while, the rat noises were softer and less angry. Finally, to our surprise, the creatures went away and left us.

Donald claimed he had been talking to the rats. He promised we wouldn't hurt them or take their cave away. We were just here for the night. We wouldn't take all their Goblins' bread. Just a little of it and the rest would grow back. We had been attacked by the Purple Things. The rats didn't like those Purple Things either.

That's what Donald claimed he told the giant rats and they told him. Anyway, the creatures left us alone for the rest of the night.

REVOLT OF THE SLAVE BOYS

Night Six and Day Seven

There was a light in the back of the cave. It was coming through a hole in the ceiling. We climbed up through the hole and found there was another cave on top of the first one. A marvelous and amazing cave!

The walls appeared to be made of fire. A cold fire that didn't burn. The stones glowed and glittered as if they had a moonbeam locked inside. Some were embedded in the walls. Some were implanted in the cavern floor. And other pieces hung down from the ceiling. They hung like icicles, very thin and razor sharp. For several moments, the Naghallah boys stood there in silence, enchanted by their beauty.

"They look like diamonds," said Bobby.

"Hey, maybe they *are* diamonds," said Steve. "Just think, if we had these things on earth, we'd be rich."

"Well, they ain't any good to us down here."

"Maybe they might," said Cameron. "A diamond is the hardest substance known. Maybe — just maybe — they might cut through our slave collars."

We tried to break off one of the hanging shards. That stuff was really hard. The axe didn't make a mark on it. We couldn't have broken off any of the shards, except one was loose and about ready to fall off anyway. We used that shard to cut off another.

Now to try it on our collars. "Let's start with Brother Brandon first. He was the first guy to get collared. Maybe he'll be the first guy to go free."

Cameron put one diamond shard inside the collar to protect Brandon's neck and started cutting with the other. Whatever we did aroused the Slavemaster. There was an angry buzz and sting. "What in Hell are you idiots doing?"

"We were attacked, sir. We had to run. We're in a cave, sir."

"Who attacked you?"

"Some purple trees with tentacles, sir. And giant rats."

"Oh, come off it, Westcott. Don't give me any fairy stories."

"It's the truth, sir. There are life forms here that don't exist on earth."

A growl of disgust. "Report in the morning." *(Sign-off.)*

It was now ten P.M. earth time, by Jaymie's watch. Cameron didn't touch the collar again until midnight. Even Slavemasters have to sleep. The diamond shard cut slowly. But cut it did. The collar had to be cut in two places. Then "the urchin bold with hair of gold" (or whose hair was gold before it was shaved off) was able to get his neck out of the hated collar.

Brother Troy was next. Meanwhile, the other guys had managed to break off several more shards. Danny and Stevie freed each other. So did Donald and Jaymie. So did Bobby and Raymond. Raymond jumped with joy and turned cartwheels. "A slave boy no more! I'm free again!"

In a few hours, we were all free. Cameron, our gallant captain, was the last. We kept expecting the dreaded buzz and collar sting. But this Slavemaster was sleeping, while the slaves broke loose.

We resisted the temptation to sass our Keepers. It would be better just to fade away and disappear. That to the Masters would be more terrifying. Something must have got us and that *Something* might get them, too.

We left the remnants of our slave collars discarded on the cavern floor. At three in the morning earth time, we climbed out of the Cave of the Giant Rats.

A few hours later, the collars buzzed angrily and vainly. The Slavemaster shouted frantically at the now vanished boys. He cursed and threatened and threw the sting on to full power. Finally, he pleaded. "Answer, boys! Answer, will you!"

No answer came, except the distant squealing and grunting of the giant rats.

THE GREAT COYOTE

Day Seven

We stuck the diamond shards in our belts. The guys cut off extra shards so we each had one. Back on Earth, these things must be worth a fortune. But the Naghallah boys now weren't worried about becoming rich. Just about staying alive.

The diamond shards would make good weapons. Also, if we met any other humans or any intelligent life forms, we could trade them for information on how to get out of the Labyrinth.

We climbed down the rocks in a different spot. There were purple stalks here, but they didn't move or spread. Those purple horrors were relentless and deadly hunters. But, fortunately, they were slow in getting started. They couldn't follow us over rocks or across water. We hoped.

We put a lot of distance between them and us. *West Northwest* by the compass. That was the way the Masters had told us to go. That must be the way to Karl Hasserman and his treasure: the *Vrrooohn,* Donald called it. That *Vrrooohn* must be a power thing. Finding it might be the only way to get out of the Labyrinth.

We waded across a river, crossed a range of rocky hills, then over another, deeper river. At last, we found a spot where we could safely rest in peace. We hoped.

There were trees here that looked like earth trees. Hemlock, oak and pine, growing tall and straight. Only their leaves were silver and yellow, instead of green. Nearly all plant life here appeared to be silver and yellow.

In our flight from the purple horrors, we had lost a lot of stuff. Nearly all our extra food and clothing. From here on, we'd have to live off the country.

Here, at least, we were better off than the Masters. We had Donald. Once again, he found us water. He also found us some bluish plants with heart-shaped leaves. *"Gai-nabs"*. Donald's fingers dug in the soft ground beneath them. After a while, he pulled out something that looked and tasted like a giant potato. We dug up a dozen of them, one for each guy. *Gai-nabs* might be better roasted, but we ate them raw.

How did Donald know about *Gai-nabs?* He wouldn't say. He just laughed.

We flopped down in a circle, too weary to post guards. Nobody slept last night, not even Keith who could sleep standing up. It was barely noon earth time, but that didn't mean anything here. The light was always the same, something between twilight and the light of a full moon.

What a strange labyrinth this was! The roof was miles away and beginning to look like a real sky. There was even something up there that looked like a moon. Not just one moon. There were three of them. The middle one a little bigger than the others. The silver woods were peaceful and beautiful. The tree tops swayed and rustled in a gentle wind. This place seemed too unreal to be true. But if it was a dream, it was a good dream.

We lay there on the edge of sleep. All at once, we could hear the howling of a forest animal. First it was far away, then it grew nearer. Now something was moving in the underbrush. A huge grey beast with gleaming teeth.

"A wolf!" cried Troy in alarm. "Look how big he is!"

Cameron said, "That's no wolf. That's a coyote. Maybe the Great Coyote, the *Keekereekee* himself."

"What will we do?"

"Howl at him," urged Camreron. "Show him we're Coyotes, too."

Twelve boys howled and the creature howled back and we howled some more. The creature looked at us and howled again, then turned around and went back into the forest.

"Now we can sleep," said Cameron. "The Great Coyote is watching over us. Nothing can hurt us here."

We slept the rest of the day and a full night.

The Great Coyote

THE SILVER FOREST AND BEYOND

Day Eight

Our bodies and clothes were wet when we woke up. The sky or roof was covered with silver clouds and rain was falling. It was a hot, tropical rain that washed us off and it felt good. You wouldn't expect clouds or rain in a hollow underneath the earth. But nothing happened in this strange place like you expected it. *Bane N'Gai* seemed less and less like an underground region on earth and more like an alien and totally different world.

We ate more *Gai-nabs* and marched through the forest. *West Northwest* by the compass. Everything was silver here or golden yellow. There were huge ferns and mushrooms higher than a house and trees whose top extended up into the clouds.

The raindrops glistened on the leaves like silver lanterns. The ground was covered with a carpet of golden moss. Heavy vines grew on the trees, bearing exquisite silver-blue flowers. They had a fragrant perfume. But you learned not to get too close to them. They stung like nettles, if you touched them. Roger said a flower bit his nose.

Small silver creatures scuttled between the vines. You could see them only in flashes. They were shy and kept in hiding.

The vines grew thicker, forming heavy nets between the trees, blocking all paths. We had to use the diamond shards to cut our way through. The vines seemed to close again behind us. We walked single file, holding on to each other. It would be easy to lose a guy here and never find him.

At times, the ground began to tremble and shake, like we were walking on jelly. We were glad to get out of those woods, one of the loveliest and scariest places I have ever seen.

We crossed a silver meadow and hit a fen. At least that's what Cameron called it. A cluster of swamps with dry islands in between them. Cameron decided to cut across the fen. It might take days to go around it.

The ground looked treacherous. "Watch out for quicksand!" Once again, we tied the rope around our bodies. Donald balked and wouldn't put the rope on. He hated being tied. "I can find my way."

"That ain't the idea, Don Don. The other kids may get stuck. If you're roped, you can pull them out.

"Come on, Don Don. Don't you want to help your brothers? We're a team, Don Don. Play on the team!" Donald grumbled, but he let himself be tied.

We stumbled and staggered and splashed across the fen. The surface here was covered with weird vegetation. Giant water lillies, huge floating cabbages and shoots that rose into the air like Jack's beanstalk.

The water was getting real deep here, almost up to Roger's chin. About a hundred feet away, a gigantic creature with a long neck lifted up its head.

"Hey, look at that!" It's body was longer than a tennis court.

Cameron said, "I seen that thing in a museum. What is it, Gifted Child?"

"Looks like a brontosaurus," said Jaymie. A real dinosaur, extinct on earth but not here.

"Does it eat people?"

"The earth ones just ate plants," said Keith. This creature didn't look at all dangerous or even interested in us. It was taking a peaceful mud bath. Troy thought it was a lady brontosaurus.

On one of the islands in the fen, we found a muddy hole with six eggs in it, each larger than a football. "These must be dinosaur eggs!"

"Hey, if we could bring these eggs back to earth, we could hatch them and raise brontosauruses," suggested Bobby.

"We got to get *ourselves* back to earth," reminded Cameron.

We left the eggs untouched and kept going.

THE WHIRLPOOL

It took the rest of the day to cross the fen. The water got real high. In some places, we had to swim. While swimming, we saw something that looked like a log. It turned out to be a crocodile. We got to the next island awful quick. Fortunately, the creature wasn't hungry.

Some little things we couldn't see got underneath our clothes. They bit and pinched and stung us. They hurt, but did no permanent damage. We sure were glad when we reached a long sand bar and could walk on dry land.

The sand changed to rocks. We kept going, looking for Goblins' Bread and finally found some. We climbed over a crest of rocks and came to a level spot on the edge of a large, round lagoon. Waves of white foam and blue water cascaded against the shore. The guys took turns trying to throw a stone across it. The other side didn't look too far, but somehow the stones always fell short.

The center of the lagoon was churning around. Too rough to swim in. We coiled the rope and stretched out on the rocks. There was now no slavemaster to drive us.

The water in the pool below was swirling and twisting around. The lagoon had become a whirlpool, throwing fountains of white spray into the air. There were rainbows in the foaming spray. The whole lagoon seemed to be alive with rainbows and the blue water whirled beneath them. Somebody threw a piece of wood in and the whirlpool sucked it down.

Fascinated, little Jody crept to the edge of the whirling lake. Too late, Cameron yelled at him to get back. A tremendous wave swept around Jody and pulled him into the water. It happened so quickly, he could only give a muffled scream.

We stood there frozen with horror, while the whirlpool sucked Jody down. Danger strikes when you least expect it. When your guard is down. We were paralyzed, unable to move. All of us, that is, excepting Don Don. He took a flying leap and dove right into the center of the whirlpool.

For a moment, I had a horrible feeling we had lost both of them. There were only ten of us now. As the days passed, we would be fewer and fewer. Until, like the other wanderers in the Labyrinth, we would all be wasted.

Then Don Don reappeared out of the whirlpool. His legs kicked and his right arm was moving furiously. Donald's left arm was clutching Jody's body. He struggled over to the rocks and we lifted both of them onto the shore.

Cameron threw himself on Jody's body and started mouth to mouth resuscitation. In a few minutes, the kid began to breathe in little gasps. Life-saving, Cameron told us later, was the only useful thing he learned in military school, before he got kicked out. Gradually, the almost drowned youth returned to life.

"We almost lost you, brother Jody."

"Thanks," said Jody.

"You have to thank Brother Donald here."

"Thanks, Don Don."

Donald stood there very pleased with himself, looking for all the world like a puppy that has retrieved a ball and expects to be patted on the head.

"Donald save brother. I told you. Donald has power."

"You sure do, Don Don. You're a hero."

"Donald hero," said Donald. He repeated it several times.

"Come on," yelled Cameron. "Grab our stuff and let's get out of here!"

Steve and Danny crossed their arms to carry Jody.

"I can walk," said Jody. He was okay, but very scared. We slept that night with Jody in the middle and the rest of us in a protecting circle around him.

Day Nine

The next day, we continued going over flat, rocky ground. We found more *gai-nabs* and a thorny bramble patch, containing something like blueberries. We ate well.

Toward the end of the day, we hit another fen. An endless swampland, spreading out as far as the eye could see; even deeper and nastier than the last one. Everyone started cursing and grumbling. Cameron said, "Okay, I ain't your slavemaster. If you don't want to cross it, we'll go around it. Even if it means backtracking for a while."

The guys still grumbled, saying they were tired. So we stopped and made camp.

That night, we saw them again, those flaming chariots. There were three of them in the distant sky. They paused in mid-air, hovered for a moment and then passed suddenly out of sight.

Were these *The Others?* Trans-humans, Hasserman had called them. *"They are neither Angels, nor Beasts, nor Demons, but something in between.*

"When they once put their mark on you, you cannot escape."

THE GARDEN OF EDEN

Day Ten

We skirted the fen, going south and east, crossing meadow and marsh. Through heavy grass and tall reeds, silver and yellow like the leaves of the forest. There was life now here. Clusters of shrubs with bright, silver flowers. Turtles and frogs and flying things that looked like dragonflies, all of them real big. Snail-like creatures and furry little brown things were splashing in the shallow water. Flocks of yellow birds flew low over the fen, making loud noises.

On the other side, was a plain of yellow grass and beyond it a forest of those silver trees. The plain grew wider and replete with multi-colored flowers. We kept marching. Startled rabbits and ground birds raced out of our way. There were butterflies here as big as crows.

We reached a hill and rested. Donald crossed the hill and cried out, not in fear or in amazement, but in sheer delight. Here, animals with a silver mane were racing and jumping and leaping about. They had golden hoofs and a single golden horn in the middle of their forehead.

"A unicorn!" cried Keith.

Bobby stared with his mouth open. "I thought these things were just a myth."

"Everything down here is a myth."

"If you're pure in heart and free of sin," declared Cameron, "a unicorn will come over and stick its head in your lap."

"They're looking at us. But none of them are coming over."

"Don't we have one pure guy here?"

They made some suggestions. "How about Jodyboy? How about Roger? How about the Gifted Child?"

We hastened to insist that we were thieves, liars,

trouble-makers and juvenile delinquents, thus eminently qualified to be a member of the Coyote youth gang and unqualified to receive the attention of a unicorn.

They stared at us briefly and then went on with their frolic. What beautiful creatures they were! I wished we had a movie camera. If we ever get out of this place alive and return to Earth, no one will ever believe what we have seen here.

There were deer here, too, with silver, branching horns. And three-horned goats and golden-haired llamas. Nothing was afraid of us. I was glad we didn't have a gun. Somebody might have been tempted to shoot. The guys agreed if we didn't hurt anything in *Bane N'Gai*, there was a better chance that nothing would hurt us.

A broad creek flowed into the Fen. We followed it upstream and came upon a warm water lake. It looked great for swimming. About six feet deep and two hundred yards roughly square; with a laurel-covered island in the middle. No whirlpool here. No Purple Horrors. There were some frogs and turtles and snail-like creatures and water birds. But we didn't bother each other.

A spring of clear water gushed from a silver rock. Such tasty, refreshing water! The unicorns and other creatures of the plain came here to drink.

Beyond the pool, was a grove of trees and shrubs, a truly Heavenly garden. Magnolia, mimosa and dogwood in full blossom. Giant-size azaleas and rhododendrons. Cherry trees bearing both flowers and fruit.

And there were strange varieties unknown on Earth. We gave them names. Many-colored Rainbow trees. Shining Star-trees. Mirror trees, Heart-trees and Trees of Lace.

There were many fruits here, something like Earth's but generally larger. Silver pears and red oranges, melons shaped like a football and sweeter than honey. Delicious apples and peaches growing long like a banana. There were nuts here, too. Large walnuts and still bigger nuts that contained a creamy jelly.

There were *Gai-nabs* here, wild carrots and great stalks bearing many ears of sweet corn. Goblins' Bread and giant blueberries grew in abundance. And from the silver maples there flowed a syrup, thick and sweet.

We brought each new thing to Donald, who tested it. By now, we had learned to trust him. In this Garden of Eden, everything was good and, no matter how much we ate, there was always more.

There were tall reeds here that you could weave when they dried. Enough to make a loin cloth, which was all the clothes you seemed to need in this warm place.

Around the Garden were nearly all the creatures we had seen before and some new ones. Silver-feathered owls and song birds in the high trees, along with squirrels and climbing lizards. A great oak sheltered a colony of silver bats. One gigantic pine had a trunk as wide as a truck. There was a hollow in it big enough to shelter the Naghallah boys. Brother Danny started to climb inside. He ran into a family of raccoons who spit and snapped at him. "Okay! Okay!" said Danny. "You got the fuckin hollow first. You can keep it." After a while in the Garden of Eden, we got to talking to the animals like they were people.

There were snakes, too, in this Paradise. Real cute. About two feet long, with horns and a double tail. The other animals gave them no heed and we didn't either. No poison fangs on them. They liked to crawl on top of you. Sometimes, a guy would have three or four snakes on him, when he woke up. But they never hurt us. We had to be careful not to step on them.

There were silver moles that burrowed in the ground and silver monkeys that threw nuts at us. We threw them back and had a nut fight. That was great fun for everyone. I think the monkeys got the best of it.

There were brightly colored lady bugs and noisy grasshoppers and nesting birds, red, yellow and blue; fragrant herbs, spicy roots and arbors of the sweetest grapes you ever tasted.

One plant gave forth a chocolatey gum; another, a delightful milk. Everything you picked would grow back almost overnight.

PARADISE II

Days Eleven to Fifteen

We decided to stay around for a while. And why not? We were free kids now and could do what we liked. Keith was a great mimic. Each morning, he would impersonate our abusive ex-Slavemaster. "Get up, you lazy, good-for-nothing, putrid punks! Move your asses!"

The guys would yell back, "Fuck you, Slavemaster! Go jump in the sewer!" And then turn over and go to sleep again. Said Troy, "I get a kick out of telling him off, even though I know it ain't really *him.*"

We swam, climbed trees, played football with a melon as a ball, ring-a-levio and prisoners' base. We had nut fights with the monkeys and with each other and loafed around. The unicorns watched us. They liked to have us scratch their heads and necks, but wouldn't let us ride them.

We explored the Garden and the surrounding meadows and forest. Each day, we discovered something new and exciting. A beaver dam, a flock of flying peacocks, gigantic snails that made musical sounds, like the strains of a violin. Fireflies that glowed as bright as a candle and huge green crickets that called to each other with almost human voices.

We found a grotto piled with round red stones that looked like rubies. We divided them up and shot marbles with them. Raymond won himself the biggest pile. Then, while we slept, the monkeys came and stole them. Cleverly, we yelled insults at the monkeys and they threw the rubies back at us, instead of nuts. Great fun!

Then, we found a block of translucent marble, covered with strange markings that we couldn't read. That block was warm and quivered like it was alive. Each night, it moved a little.

Exploring the plain, we came upon a herd of small horses, about the size of a large dog. They each had silver wings, like in a fairy tale. The winged horses let us get real close to them. But when we tried to touch them, they unfurled their wings and took off.

The velvet sky now had three silver moons and star clusters unlike anything ever seen on Earth. The stars were brighter than the Earth stars and there were more of them. There were other celestial bodies that were planet-like; one red, one blue, one golden. And almost every night, one of those flaming chariots moved in majesty across the sky; more like a heavenly body than like anything made by a mortal. How beautiful they were! I could not believe there was evil in them.

"They must have made a mistake," said Keith.

"Who?"

"Whoever put us here. There can't be a real place like this. It isn't possible. Therefore ——"

We had had that idea before. Ever since that first night, when we crossed the River Styx. We weren't alive any more. Somewhere along the line, we got wasted. Maybe in the fire, in the Pit, at the Cliff or by the Purple Horrors. Maybe the Whirlpool got all of us, not just Jody.

We were supposed to be stuck in Hell and tormented for our sins. It was part of our torment not to know if we were alive or not.

"If we're being tormented down in Hell," said Steve, "all I can say is it's a pretty creampuff torture. It beats being alive."

"Could you take it forever?"

"If the twelve of us are together and in good shape like we are now, yes, I could take it forever."

"That's what I mean," declared Keith. "Somebody goofed." Maybe one of the Beings who rode around in the flaming chariots. "They stuck us in Paradise, instead of Hell."

Cameron didn't feel our Garden of Eden was quite Paradise. He would have liked a couple of girls around. "I'd give one of my ribs for a girl."

"If we all gave a rib, we could each have one."

But even without girls, this place was as close to Paradise as we sinners could expect. We decided to stay here forever. In fact, we voted it. 11 to 0. *We, the twelve boys of the Coyote youth gang, shall live in the Garden of Eden forever.* Donald didn't vote. He just laughed.

The Garden of Eden

NIGHTMARE

The Sixteenth Day

There was something wrong. There were no snakes on us when we woke up, or anywhere around. The snails and turtles and frogs were gone from the pool and garden. There were no butterflies among the blossoms and no birds chirped or sang.

There were still some unicorns and other hoofed animals upon the yellow plain, but they no longer raced or frolicked. The creatures stood around despondently, as if awaiting some unnatural disaster. That marble block with its ancient runes was trembling and shaking violently. Somewhere in the distant tree tops a monkey screamed. Then there was silence. We shivered and felt cold.

Now we heard a bone-chilling sound. Something like the clinking of a glass and something like the tearing of a piece of cloth. Only far louder and constantly repeated. Then there was a second ugly sound, like the squeal of a machine that needs oiling.

The weird cries came from the direction of the fen. Something was happening there. Cameron watched with the field glasses. A cloud of mist rose out of the marshes and drew together in a whirling mass. An island of rock and mud exploded and the mud and mist appeared to form itself into a gigantic animal. A huge hunk of matter moved across the fen.

Now we could smell a hideous odor. Not the clean stench of feces or rotten eggs, but of something poisonous and paralyzing.

The creatures of the plain saw and heard the Thing and stiffened in alarm. Then, with a cry of terror, they made a frantic run for the safety of the forest.

The fen monster was moving in our direction. A swelling mis-shapen mass, now larger than a trailer truck, was crawling on a hundred legs.

The nightmare thing had reached the brook. Cameron yelled to grab the rope and weapons. "Run into the woods!" And we followed the unicorns, deer and llamas.

The fen monster appeared to have no head or eyes. It looked like an enormous ink blot, with wires sticking out above and below. But the Thing had a brain. It had spotted the Naghallah boys and it was going for us.

Jaymie and Jody were the last to reach the woods. We just made it. It was amazing how fast that ink blot thing could move. The huge trees here were only a few feet apart. You could see now why the animals had taken refuge here. The fen monster, some twenty feet across, was unable to break through so narrow a gap. We were like a man who has taken refuge in a tiger cage, while the hunting tiger waits for him outside the bars.

We feared that this unnatural creature, becoming soft and jelly-like, might change shape and crawl between the tree trunks. But the fen monster had a hard, solid body. The great trees barred it.

However, our relief was short-lived. The monstrosity had no visible mouth. But every part of the Thing was mouth. Its wires were a kind of tooth that began chewing up the trees that blocked the creature's path. And all the while it was gurgling and hissing and making those horrible shrieking noises. Truly a Hellish creature and a fitting denizen of Hell — if that's where we were now.

Two great trees splintered and the Nightmare broke through. A hundred arms or tentacles were reaching for a victim. We fell back to another barrier of trees, which splintered likewise when the monster attacked.

We retreated again, this time over a heap of rocks to higher ground. Sooner or later, the monster would get us. Our weapons were puny and futile. Knives, axes and the diamond daggers were useless against *The Nightmare*. If it had had a heart or some vital spot, we might have had a chance against it.

It was climbing up to get us. We hurled stones and rolled down rocks. These seemed only to enrage *The Nightmare*. Stevie and Danny pushed down a huge boulder. It struck the crawling Horror and knocked the Thing backwards.

The monster appeared stunned for a moment, then started crawling up again. There were no more loose

The Attack of the Fen Monster.

boulders. Cameron ordered us to tie our rope around the top of a fallen tree. "Now pull it up!"

Nine guys strained and pulled the huge silver oak into upright position. The other three kept chucking rocks. The crawling horror gave forth the foulest odor, the smell of sulphur and of burning rubber, mingled with the stench of death.

The Thing crawled higher and its wire arms stretched out. As the *Nightmare* almost reached the top of the rocks, Cameron yelled, "Let go the rope!"

The great oak crashed down. It struck the fen monster with deadly force. With a horrible cry, the creature slipped and toppled backwards. A stream of dark liquid dribbled from its side. Badly wounded, but still not dead, it began to crawl away in the direction of the fen, leaving a tarry stream of monster blood to mark its track.

Thus perhaps did our primitive ancestors, the first humans, fight the Tyrannosaurus Rex. But there were no cheers of victory. We were too stunned and exhausted.

We were the first to leave the forest. The frightened animals remained in hiding. Cautiously, we followed the trail of the bleeding monster. We had destroyed *The Nightmare*. At the edge of the Fen, lay the remnants of the Thing, gradually dissolving into the slime.

We returned to our homestead. It was a melancholy scene. The mimosa and magnolia were withered, the pear tree shrivelled, the great maple and rainbow trees uprooted. The beaver dam was smashed. The marble with its ancient runes was shattered and destroyed.

The garden flowers were drooped and wilted. The delicate Heart tree and the Tree of Lace were blackened stumps. Our crystal lake was covered with muck and scum. A single glorious Star Tree had survived. The rest were wasted and gone.

Around us lay the bodies of several dozen animals that didn't get away. Frog, turtle and goat; chipmunk, owl and snail; monkey, snake and rabbit. There were no raccoons in the tree hollow. We hoped they escaped in time.

The Lord Jehovah did not give us dominion over this

Garden of Eden. Neither did anyone else. But as the only humans, we felt somewhat responsible. We buried the dead creatures around the Star Tree.

We knew not what we had done wrong. But we had destroyed our Paradise as surely as Adam and Eve destroyed theirs. In some way, we had aroused that sleeping Evil and by our presence drawn *The Nightmare* out of the Horror-realm beneath the Fen. We had summoned up this ghastly Thing and released it into this world of gentle beauty.

We were the first target. *If we remain here, there will be another Nightmare, or something worse. If we leave, the Garden will become again as it used to be.*

We decided to go. An inner voice said, "Ye cannot stop. Ye shall find no rest, neither in forest nor field, in valley nor mountain. Ye are doomed to wander unendingly in search of the *Vrrooohn* on the *Road to Nowhere.*"

We took corn and *Gai-nabs* and drinking water and left the rubies behind. Let the monkeys have them. We managed to recover most of our tools and stuff.

"Form column of twos," said Cameron.

"Which way are we going?"

"South and East like before. Along the plain. Unless you guys want to cross the fen?"

Nobody did.

"We'll keep going around it then."

Paradise, farewell.

MEMOIRS OF A SLAVEMASTER

The Seventeenth Day

It seems we are getting around the fen. We are going Southwest now, instead of Southeast. Last night, we camped out on the plain. Today, we camped by a lake. We stopped early and went swimming.

There were many waterbirds here. Swans, geese and ducks; magnificent flamingoes and silver gulls. Red-breasted robins and crimson cardinals were swimming around, birds that on earth would have shunned the water.

While we were swimming, some silver bears raided us and grabbed most of our food before we could chase them. It was lucky for us they ran away when we came. If the bears had turned around, *we* would have done the running.

But we didn't go hungry. There was plenty of food, only you had to climb for it or dig for it. *Gai-nabs,* nuts, sugar beets and beanstalk corn.

Something was happening out in the fen. There were flashing lights. Cameron didn't know if this was a natural occurrence or if it signalled something dangerous. He decided to post a guard while we slept. One hour each for all the guys, excepting Jody and Roger.

Surprisingly, the little kids complained. "We want a watch!"

"Okay," said Cameron, "you can have a watch. But with a partner, not alone."

Jody took the first watch with Donald. Donald promptly disappeared and was gone for the rest of the night.

We worried about Don Don. Cameron yelled at him when he returned. "You're on a team, Don Don! Stick with team! Don't let the other guys down!" Etc. Cameron bawled you out like a football coach. You could almost predict what he would say.

Donald just stood there with a stupid, blank face, as if he couldn't understand what Cameron was talking about. Then he said, "Donald go scouting."

"Did you find anything?"

Donald handed him a hard cover notebook. On the flyleaf was the inscription: *Memoirs of Stanley Vedemore* "Stanley Vedemore!"

"Captain Vedemore? You mean the Masters have been here in this territory?"

Donald pointed south along the rim of the never-ending fen.

"Are they there now?"

"Gone," said Donald.

Cameron read the book aloud. Unfortunately, it was water-logged. The ink had run and most of the writing was illegible:

. . . we have heard nothing from the boys. We don't know what went wrong. They are poorly equipped and have little skill or intelligence. They can hardly survive for very long on their own. I fear the boys have been expended with very little profit to ourselves . . .

Great hunting! Eberle and I hunted together. We shot . . . .

The fabulous unicorn exists! . . . . with golden hoofs and horns. Is the horn really . . . . ? . . . . very valuable . . . . . . A magnificent specimen. We fired point blank. It seemed impossible to miss, but both our guns misfired . . . . The unicorn herd stampeded . . . . Eberle was determined to bag a unicorn. He tracked the herd . . . . Eberle did not return. After a cursory search, Lammington decided to go on without him . . . . I thought his decision rather callous.

. . . . Bad luck continues to plague our expedition . . . . Leon is gone. We found his body in a ditch outside the compound. Lammington said he had a heart attack, but I think he died of fright . . . . . Eberle, then Leon. Who is next?

We are in the hands of a madman . . . . . *He will not turn back. Each day, we go closer to oblivion* . . . .

————————————

. . . . *poison* . . . . *I can no longer write. The cramps in my stomach are getting worse* . . . . *My hand can hardly hold a pen* . . . .

Cameron closed up the notebook. "That's the last entry. There isn't any more."

We were all silent. Then Keith asked, "Did you find anything else of Vedemore's, beside the Memoirs?"

"His grave," said Donald.

RAYMOND'S REVENGE

Day Eighteen

"Is the compass still working?"

"It's pointing to *something*. It's the only guide we got."

The watch was still working, too. Though here day and night didn't mean much. It was sort of between a very dark day and a moon-bright night. We counted the days by a sleep and a wake-up.

We marched south by the compass. After a while, it began to rain heavily. There was no shelter here. We all got soaked and chilled.

We stood around shivering. "Come on, guys," said Cameron. "We'll be less cold, if we keep moving."

A fierce wind blasted against us. Troy's lips were blue. "We ain't in Heaven, that's for sure," said Troy. "We're either in a real place or in Hell."

"How many days have we been in the Labyrinth?"

"Eighteen," counted Keith.

"Forever in Hell, less eighteen days," said Bobby. "How much time do we still have to do?"

"Let's hope the rest of *Forever* is no worse than this."

After about an hour, the rain stopped. Still cold and soggy, we marched across the rock-strewn moor. Jaymie broke formation. There was a heap here of black and grey quartz rocks.

Cameron yelled at me. "Come on, Jaymie! Quit fooling around! Get back in line!"

Something registered. Back in the early days of the Gifted Child class, we were a Stone-age tribe. We were always discovering or inventing wonderful things. At least the teacher did it for us. We discovered the sun dial, corn growing, clay pottery, the alphabet and numbers. And how to make fire like a cave man. With *flint*. That's what those quartz rocks were.

Back at *Kaah Naghallah*, we were dangerous juveniles and not allowed to have matches or lighters. We didn't have any on this trip. We had a battery stove, but left it in the amphibian.

We were wild boys now and getting used to eating things raw. But there were other reasons for a fire beside cooking. To keep warm. To get hot water. To keep people-eating monsters away.

We had tried to start a fire rubbing two sticks together, but it didn't work. I hoped the flint would work. It never seemed to work in school. We sliced up some twigs into dry slivers. The flint struck sparks against our steel knives. After about ninety tries, we got a fire.

Danny said, "Gee, Jaymie! At least you learned *one* useful thing in that Gifted Child class."

Cameron gave me the title, *Grand Shaman and Fire Wizard of the Coyote Tribe.* And he entrusted to me the "twelve sacred rocks", which were pieces of flint. "Give thanks, ye punks! To Jaymie the Fire-giver and to the *Keekereekee.*"

We had rounded the fen. From here, the shore curved northward. We could go *West Northwest* again. If that compass reading meant anything.

It was early afternoon, but we decided to stop. We had covered very little ground today, but who cared? The devils, or whoever was driving us, didn't put the pressure on. They appeared satisfied as long as we kept moving.

Now that we could make a fire, we no longer needed one. In *Bane N'Gai,* the climate and terrain change fast. The ponds and streams here were all warm, the rocks hot, the air torrid. A geyser of steam was spraying out of the Underground. If we were anywhere on Earth, there must be geothermal springs here. If we were in Hell — what else could you expect?

"Maybe the Devil ain't really bad," reflected Bobby. "He just likes to play tricks on people."

In the sky above now, we could see a flaming chariot crossing the fen. "That's probably *him,* " said Keith. "Flying around, looking things over."

"Let's be careful not to make him mad."

Now in the distance we could hear an agonizing cry. A tragic, helpless yell of pain and anguish. Then silence.

"What was that?"

"Was it a bird or beast?"

"It sounded like a man," declared Raymond. "It came from the fen."

Raymond gazed out with the field glasses. The fen was a sea of mud and sand, with islands of some purple weeds and pools of yellow water. The whole area was treacherous. What looked like solid ground would collapse under your feet. And underneath was a lake of man-swallowing quick sand.

Those purple weeds were moving. No, it wasn't the weeds that moved. In them were some worm-like creatures that seemed to have a head at each end. Another impossible life form.

There was no true shore line here. Strips of mud and mire projected out like fingers in between layers of solid rock. In the fen, stood a blackened tree trunk and there was a dark shape clinging to it desperately. "It's a man," said Raymond. "It's — *one of the Masters.* "

"Which one?"

"It's Smeer," said Raymond. "And he's going down."

"Our old schoolmaster? The guy who clobbered Roger, the Denominator Kid?"

He was a fucking bastard. Still, he was a human being. Raymond said, "Tie a rope on me, I'll see if I can pull him out." That was a risky business. The rescuer might get caught in quicksand himself.

Smeer had punched Raymond in the face and called him some nasty names. Among other things, he had called Raymond *a Junglepunk* and for some reason the name rankled. You couldn't blame Raymond too much if he failed to risk his life for the S.O.B. Raymond, however, was planning a strange but satisfying revenge. Save the old creep and then tell him, "How do you like being rescued by a *Junglepunk,* muckler?"

The other guys weren't too keen about the rescue. Stevie said, "If one of us were stuck out there, the Masters wouldn't do a fucking thing for us."

"Fifty Masters ain't worth one Coyote kid!" Still, we wouldn't feel right unless we tried.

Cameron said, "You can't do it alone, Ray Ray. We'll form a human chain. Walk on the rocks, everybody. We'll get as close as we can."

We yelled to Smeer, "Hold on! We're coming!" He didn't seem to hear us. The rising mire had almost reached his neck.

We tied the rope around ourselves and bound one end to a heavy boulder. The guys formed the human chain, with Roger and Jody bracing the rope. Raymond was the end man. He was just able to reach the sinking Master.

Raymond held Danny's wrist with his left hand and with his right hand was able to pull the Master loose. But Raymond missed out on his vengeance. The Master was so terrified and grateful, you couldn't help feeling sorry for him.

Smeer groaned in pain. There were three puncture wounds on his upper legs. The skin around the wounds was blue, a sign of poisoning. Cameron cauterized the knives and thrust one into each wound to make it bleed and draw out the venom. Only then did Raymond reveal that he, too, had been bitten. Maybe by one of those two-headed sand worms. They looked like they had fangs on them.

Smeer's three bites and Raymond's one were beginning

to swell. Stevie sucked out Raymond's wound and we took turns on the Master's.

Among the few things we still carried with us was the First Aid kit, which has some anti-venom. It was intended for poison earth snakes. We didn't know if it would work with the two-headed fen worms of *Bane N'Gai,* but we tried it.

We made Raymond lie down and keep his leg low. Brandon prepared some hot soup for him. We made a fire to keep any other poisonous things away. Smeer kept moaning and shaking. We had no painkiller. Smeer had a flask of brandy and asked us to pour it into his mouth. Then he said he felt better. The swellings had stopped and were going down a bit.

Smeer took some more brandy. Then he said, "Thank you, boys. I owe my life to you. If I live ——"

"You will," said Keith. "You'll be all right."

Smeer took still another slug and then began to babble. It was hard to follow him as he skipped around and mentioned names and things we had never heard of.

As we expected, Lammington and his men had followed us into the labyrinth, hoping to use us to break the way for them. Nine men had started out. Seven were those we had been taught to call *Captain* and respect as *Masters.* Two were armed guards, highly trained in the martial arts. From the beginning, there had been angry arguments.

The Masters' amphibian had gone through the Blob and the Firewall. Lammington shamed them into it, saying the kids had gone through. But when they reached the *Abyss,* the men refused to cross it. Jack Eberle held a pistol to Lammington's head and made him turn around.

The Masters clung to their amphibian and would not go by foot. They went around in circles, backtracking and zigzagging. Lammington and Striker refused to turn back. Each day, they pleaded for one day more. Jack Eberle perished. So did Leon, one of the guards. So did Vedemore, the engineer. "When I go, there will be but five survivors."

Smeer became separated from the group when something attacked them. A Horror that came out of the earth. He couldn't describe it. The others fled in the amphibian, leaving him behind. He thought they would return for him, but they did not. The Masters abandoned Smeer, just as they did Jack Eberle. Smeer had been travelling on foot and strayed too far out into the fen. The ground collapsed around him and Smeer was trapped in the mire.

"But you are all here, boys. All twelve of you. Without your control collars. I thought at first they had sent you for me. But you came on your own.

"You were good boys. You were good to Old Smeer. I was your teacher. I didn't teach you very well. Sometimes you wish you had another chance, but you never get one ——"

"Let me tell you something, boys. That reward they promised you. *That was a lie!* They don't intend to let you come back from *Bane N'Gai.* After you get that Thing from Karl Hasserman — if you do — they are going to take it away from you. They are going to leave you down here." He gasped for breath.

"I want you to know — We didn't all feel that way. Craig and I —— I said 'Let's find the boys and then get out of here. Take them back to the school. And seal off the Gateway so that no one else can ever enter this Hellish place. . . .'"

"Captain Smeer," asked Keith. "What is this thing we are looking for? Karl Hasserman's treasure?"

He didn't seem to understand.

"The *Vrrooohn?*" asked Jaymie, using Donald's word.

"The *Vrrooohn?* It is an evil thing. It brings only torment and grief. Karl Hasserman used it to gain a great fortune. But he lost everything else. He lived his last years crazed and maddened, plagued by a hundred demons. The curse of the *Vrrooohn* fell on all around him. —— But not yet on you."

He looked up in alarm. "It's there again! That thing in the sky . . . " It was another flaming chariot. "I saw one after Leon died. And after Vedemore . . . . They hang like vultures feasting on the dead . . . . A demon ship, waiting to carry your soul away . . ."

His head drooped back. Smeer was unconscious. His heart and pulse were racing furiously.

"Let him sleep," said Cameron. "That's all we can do."

"How are you feeling, Ray Ray?"

"Better. But gimme some brandy."

There wasn't much left, but it helped put Raymond to sleep.

*   *   *   *   *   *   *

The light in *Bane N'Gai* is always the same. Except for the wrist watch, you couldn't tell when morning came. We looked anxiously at Raymond. He was lying on his belly. We turned him over. Ray Ray woke up cursing.

"I was having a real sweet dream. You mucklers woke me up!"

"You scared us. You were lying there so quiet."

"I ain't wasted, if that's what you mean. Help me up. I'm stiff." Raymond's legs looked quite normal.

"How about Smeer?" The Master was turned over on his back. "He's awful still," said Brandon. "He isn't breathing." Brandon looked again. "I think he's dead."

We got Raymond just in time. But for Smeer it was too late.

Twelve juvenile hoods knelt down beside the body of their former teacher. A few weeks ago, we all hated Smeer. Now, we wept.

Death of a Schoolmaster.
A few weeks ago we all hated Smeer. Now, we wept.

THE DESERTED CAMP

The Nineteenth Day

We buried the Master under a pile of rocks. We mumbled a prayer and sang a couple of hymns.

Smeer might have had some stuff on him that we could use. But his pack and gear were lost and his gun holster was empty. Cameron did take Smeer's boots and put his own, which had holes on them, on the Master's feet. Stevie took Smeer's watch and Keith his fancy knife. They weren't any good to him now.

We marched single file, West Northwest by the compass, through a grove of giant silver ferns, as high as a telephone pole and very thick. Donald had been at the end of the line and when we came out of the fernwood, he was missing. We waited and yelled at him when he finally showed.

Cameron was mad and cursed at Don Don. Donald claimed he had heard voices calling to him. Donald often heard voices, even before he came to *Kaah Naghallah*. But only now could he talk well enough to tell about them.

Cameron kicked his ass and made him walk in front between Stevie and Danny. "We hear all kinds of noises in this weird place. If you hear a voice, just ignore it."

One thing about Don Don. He never gets mad, at least not at any of the Naghallah boys. Donald walked along meekly, just as Cameron had commanded. His yellow eyes looked appealingly at Cameron, as if asking forgiveness.

"Ugh!" said Donald, pointing.

He led us to the charred remnants of a campfire. Perhaps this was where the Masters camped before they abandoned Smeer. There were no spoils here worth taking except some food tablets and a canteen. Jody took the canteen to replace the one he had lost in the Whirlpool.

We looked around anxiously. Perhaps whatever had caused the Masters to flee in panic was still lurking in the vicinity. But there was nothing more formidable than a flock of speckled butterflies and some horned, snail-like creatures. A meadowbird gave a mournful cry.

Now, Brandon came running in, yelling excitedly. He had found a holster with a loaded revolver hanging in the thicket. Brandon waved the gun around.

"Give me that," said Cameron, "before you shoot your foot off."

"The safety catch is on," retorted Brandon. "I know how to handle it."

"Anyway, we only got one gun and the Gangleader ought to carry it." Brandon demurred. He didn't want anyone to go shooting animals. "I ain't gonna hunt with it," Cameron agreed. We would never use the gun to hunt and kill our fellow creatures. Only to defend ourselves if our lives were in danger. "I promise. Okay, Bran?"

"We voted that already," reminded Jaymie. "*Boylaw Number 14.*"

"Stevie laughed. "I'll bet nobody remembers what the other thirteen Boylaws were."

"I'll bet the kid brother does," declared Danny. "What's Number four, Gifted Child?"

"No snitching," remembered Jaymie.

"See! And Boylaw Number Thirteen?"

"That's the one about not going through the metal door in the Under-sub-basement."

"We all broke *that* Boylaw," said Stevie. "And now we're fucked!"

Anyway, we voted that last law over again, 12 to 0. *No killing or hurting anything, unless it attacks us.* Then Brandon gave Cameron the gun.

"Thanks. Hey, Bran, your hair is growing back! You're going to be *the urchin bold with hair of gold* again."

THE RAVINE

The Twentieth Day

We crossed a shallow river and came upon a solid wall of sheer rock that seemed to have no top to it. Even the Cat Burglar found it too tough to climb, so we travelled north to find a break in it. After a couple of miles, we came upon a canyon that wound its way between the towering cliffs. A gateway to Something.

An inner voice told me not to go there. In another life, I had travelled this way with my companions and a frightful thing had happened. I couldn't remember what or when.

This time, Cameron kicked *my* ass. "Not *you.* Jaymie! Don't tell me you are hearing voices, too. Don't be a jerk!" There was no other way to go.

We entered the ravine. It was steep and stony. The grey crags on either side were bare and barren of vegetation. The cliffs seemed endless and cast gloomy shadows that grew deeper and darker as we went along. A melancholy place.

We walked in silence through the dreary chasm. Our footsteps made no sound as we marched. Bobby said, "If we ain't in Hell yet, maybe this is the way in."

We halted. Somewhere in the distance you could hear the sound of a woman crying. Sobbing as if her heart would break. We searched, trying to find the sorrowing lady. But the voices seemed to come right out of the walls of the ravine.

Again and again, we called out to her. But there was no answer. A moment of silence. Then those heart-rending sounds would begin again. Sometimes the voice came from the cliffs above. Sometimes from the ground underneath our feet. Ahead of us. Behind us. Always that sobbing voice that never answered.

At length, Cameron said, "Something is trying to stop us going this way. They're trying to break our nerves. Let's show them. *You can't break the Coyotes!*"

The guys were getting jittery and jumpy. Cameron ordered us to sing. We shouted out Captain Craig's old school song:

We are the Kaah Naghallah boys,
A rough and ready crew.
We get the best of everything,
In anything we do . . . .
When we are challenged,
And they put us to the test,
You can hear them saying,
"The kids of Kaah Naghallah are the best."

After we sang our song about fifty times, the voices stopped.

Now we began to see sparks of light dancing in the air around us. Rising and falling, like snowflakes in a high wind. The ground was shaking and trembling under our feet.

"Put the rope on!" shouted Cameron. "Tie it under your arms!"

"Why?" asked Stevie.

"The ground might open up and somebody might fall in. Do it, will you! Everybody!"

Stevie is a rebel. Cameron is probably the only guy in the world he would obey. He put the rope on. We all did. And a good thing, too. The ground did open up, just as Cameron feared. Keith was almost lost. The rope held him.

All twelve Coyotes were still together. Troy . . . Jody . . . Jaymie . . . Raymond . . . and now Keith. Each was rescued. Each of us could have gone to — wherever bad boys go after they have been wasted. Unless the twelve of us were there already.

The ground was heaving and swaying now, almost like the waves of the sea. Still, we kept going. Nothing can stop the Coyotes! Sometimes we had to grope our way along the cliffs, clinging on with all our strength to keep from falling.

Sometimes we had to crawl over the rocks on all fours, with bleeding knees. But we kept on going. *Forward! Ever forward!* Through the dismal pass and out at last into a wide hollow.

Everyone was mighty weary, so we flopped down for the night. No Goblins' Bread or *Gai-nabs*. We ate the condensed food tablets. We sure could use some new clothes, or at least a chance to wash our old ones.

We lay down in a circle, head in, feet out. Cameron said, "We're all here together, all twelve of us. Whoever is in charge of us now, be it God or the Devil, *Thanks for that!*"

THE DARK WONDERLAND

The Twenty-First Day

The twenty-first day in *Bane N'Gai* was another day of marching and climbing over bare rocks, through ravines and canyons in these Underworld mountains. Ever since we reached the fen, the cavern roof had become an open sky, studded with planets, stars and moons. The pattern kept changing and was utterly unlike anything seen from Earth. But one thing was constant. There were three silver moons, more or less in a row. It never got bright or totally dark. The sky gleamed with a golden glow, like the first break of dawn, before the sun appears. Our eyes had grown sharper and we could see with very little light.

The ravine broadened and became level. We noticed now there were signs of life again. Flying creatures, like lizards, with broad, scaley wings. One of them, bigger than an eagle, was perched on a nearby rock, looking us over.

"Hey, what are these?" asked Steve. "I seen one like this in a biology book."

"You read a book?" asked Bobby.

"I looked at the pictures," said Stevie.

"What are they, Gifted Child?"

They looked rather like pterodactyls, the first birds. They were supposed to be extinct.

"Not down here, they ain't. They still got a lot of them."

"They got everything down here," said Raymond.

"Except human people."

"We're human people, ain't we?"

"That's a matter of opinion. Not everybody thinks so."

There seemed to be hundreds of the pterodactyl-like creatures living up on the high ledges. "There must be lots of nests up there. I wonder if pterodactyl eggs are good eating."

We just wondered. We didn't try it. Bothering those nests would be a good way to get chewed up. We let the pterodactyls alone and they let us alone. What magnificent creatures they were! And how gracefully they flew! Some of them had a wing span almost as big as a plane.

What a strange place *Bane N'Gai* was! A scene of horror side by side with wonder and beauty!

The ravine halted in a dead end. But the cliffs here weren't too high and had many footholds. We climbed them with a rope and reached a wide plateau. There were small, stunted growths here of yellow spiny trees, blue moss and bloated mushrooms that Donald said not to eat. The plateau was covered with loose rocks, round in shape, like gigantic bowling balls.

At the end of the plateau, the sides dropped away. It was too dark to see what was below. All you could make out was a vast, black hole, a sea of nothing.

We rolled one of the stone balls off the edge. It bounded downward and made no sound when it hit the bottom. *If* it hit the bottom. Maybe this hole didn't have a bottom.

A rock stuck out like a peninsula into the great yawning Pit below. Some weird fascination drew me onto the projecting rock. I felt the wind blowing through me, though there was no wind. All at once, I could hear music. It was the saddest and the sweetest music I have ever heard.

Somewhere out of the night around me, a voice kept calling. And the voice I heard was my own:

Leap, Jaymie! Come into the Dark Wonderland. The well of the Nothing that is Everything.

For a moment, I stood there spellbound. Then I shuddered and pulled myself away. Back onto the plateau.

A bit sheepishly, I told Cameron and the others about the Voice from the deep that called you to destruction. "Don't let anyone else go out there!"

Cameron wanted to go himself. But he agreed to have the rope tied on him, just in case the deadly call of the Pit overcame his reason. He came back pale and trembling. "I see what you mean, Jaymie. I heard the call, too. And the voice I heard was my own."

After Cameron, Raymond and a couple of other guys tried it. They all came back real shaky. I wondered how many others might have stood upon the death rock, heard the fatal call and leaped.

Was this a conscious intelligence trying to destroy us? Or was it some mindless thing left over from the chaos before the world was made, seeking to make everything mindless like itself.

"Come on," called Cameron. "Let's get out of here!"

We found a good spot to spend the night, about a quarter of a mile inland, in a circle of protecting stones. There was water here and Goblins' Bread again. We slept as usual in a twelve-boy circle. Roger was on one side of me and Danny on the other.

I woke up suddenly during the night. I felt chilly all over. Roger was turned over on his belly. Danny wasn't there. Nor was he anywhere in the stone circle. I called to Danny, but he didn't answer.

Had he heard the mad call of the Dark Wonderland, the summons of Death? That night back in our parents' house, Danny had stood on a chair with a belt around his neck. *"Kick away the chair, Jaymie! Do this one thing for me, will you!"* Could he resist the death impulse now?

I ran toward the precipice. There, in the eerie light of the three moons, I saw Danny. He was standing out on the peninsula. The call of Destruction had him in its thrall. He was drawing nearer to the edge. There was no time to reach Danny. And even if I did, I couldn't stop him.

"Danny!" I shouted. "Help me! Help me! It's Jaymie. Please help me!"

I kept yelling, "Danny, help me!" Danny turned. He was drawing back.

I rolled one of the boulders over my leg. Now he came over and stood beside me. "What's wrong with you?"

"The rock — on my leg — It's crushing me!"

Danny rolled the rock off.

Danny took my boot off. "Move your toes. You can move them. Nothing's wrong. Okay, Little Brudder? Feel better?"

I nodded.

Danny put my boot back on. "Hey, fucking Jaymie. How did you get that rock on you?" Then he caught on. In some ways, Danny is sharp. "I wasn't going to leap, Little Brudder. I was just looking."

Danny put his arm around me and walked me back to the circle of stones. "That's twice you saved me, Jaymie brudder. I saved you once on the cliff. You're one up on me."

We counted the guys in the circle: *Roger . . . Stevie . . . Raymond . . . Cameron . . . Jody . . . Bobby . . . Donald . . . Keith . . . Brandon . . . Jody . . .* All there. But me and Danny didn't sleep the rest of the night. We kept watch, in case someone else should hear the death call of the Dark Wonderland.

A PLACE OF DELIGHT AND DREAD

The Twenty-second Day

We went north to avoid the Pit and then cut west. By the compass, that is. But we began to wonder if the compass meant anything. Patterns in *Bane N'Gai* seemed to be repeated. The Pit of the *Dark Wonderland* was like the *Abyss* we had crossed in the amphibian seventeen days ago. Now we came again upon a silver forest and a rolling plain with grazing horned animals. There were unicorns, goats, deer and llamas and jumping animals resembling a kangeroo. There were woolly sheep, wild horses with a silver mane, buffaloes and frolicking calves. The plain was silver and studded with wildflowers of every shape and color. Magnificent roses climbed over shining white rocks.

We stopped in a grove of fruit trees. There was a warm water pond here where we could swim and wash our clothes. No fen around and, hopefully, no monsters.

"Here we go again," said Keith. "From Hell to Paradise."

"And back again tomorrow."

There were many birds here with bright, colorful plumage. A group of large, white-feathered birds were gathered by the pond, stretching and flapping their wings.

Young Roger stared at the big birds curiously. "What are them?"

"Storks," said Bobby. "Those are the birds that bring the babies. One of them brought *you* around."

"Gowan!" said Roger. "I know how babies are made."

"The stork brought Baby Roger," insisted Troy. "The rest of us were made by fucking."

One of the big birds stared at Roger. "See Rodge! He's looking at you. That's the one who brought you. He's figuring to bring you back where you came from."

"Maybe the storks could bring us a couple of girls," said Cameron, wistfully.

None of the creatures acted like they had ever seen humans before and didn't know enough to be afraid of us.

Some of them would come right in and grab our stuff, if we didn't watch it.

One crow-like bird made off with Stevie's boot. He tried to carry it up into a tree, but it was too heavy and he dropped it. Lucky for Stevie who had no other shoes.

Danny and Raymond tried to ride the wild horses, but they bucked and threw the guys off.

We made camp at the edge of the silver forest and put the Coyote mark on a rock. Some of the trees were huge, branching and rebranching in every direction. We tried climbing them, but no matter how high a guy climbed, there always seemed to be still more branches.

The woods and plain looked friendly and peaceful. But in this strange country, things could change suddenly, without warning. Cameron slept with the gun by his side. "We got four shots in it. I hope we never have to use them."

* * * * * * *

Day Twenty-three

The next morning, Donald was gone. Jody thought he heard Donald talking to someone or something during the night. But it wasn't to any of us. We called and searched in ever larger circles. To no avail.

The hours passed with no sign of Donald. The guys were growing edgy. The pond, the trees, the lovely meadow were no longer pleasant. We had met many perils, but we had always faced them together. We never expected that one of us would be snatched away in the night like this. Our field of *Delight* had been turned into a place of *Dread.*

We widened the search. Cameron warned us to stay together. The sinister force that might have taken Donald could snatch us, too, if we were alone.

THE SEARCH FOR DONALD

It was late afternoon now. At a wet spot in the woods, we found some muddy boot prints. They might be Donald's. Crossing a brook, we found a trail. More boot marks, four left and three right. Then they stopped. And besides them, a second footprint. Of enormous size. And of a shape that wasn't human . . . Nothing more.

We went back to camp with a feeble hope that Donald had returned. He wasn't there. But now we noticed something we hadn't seen before. A Coyote mark. And an arrow pointing down the trail.

Had Donald left voluntarily and left this mark for us to follow? Or was some sinister power leading us on in order to entrap us?

"We'll go down the trail," Cameron decided, "if Donald isn't back by morning." There was no use waiting around any longer.

Day Twenty-four

The next morning, we started down the trail. We moved slowly, leaving marks for Donald to follow. If he should return to camp and was able to follow us.

There were no further footprints, either of Donald or of that other Thing or Being. The leaves of silver gradually turned to green and the woods became more like an earth forest. Groves of laurel and rhododendron grew here, along with giant ferns and huge red mushrooms. In the beginning, we saw many forest animals. Possums and porcupines, woodchucks and chipmunks, an elk and small red foxes. None of them fled when they saw us. There was no fear here. Quails and pheasants greeted us with loud outcries. A pair of plated armadillos watched us curiously from their burrow in the moss-covered ground.

The animals grew fewer as we went along. The birds were silent. Finally, we didn't see any creatures at all. The trees grew stunted and further apart. Then the woods opened up and we came onto a barren field.

At the end of the field, there was a curtain of mist. Unlike earth fog, this thing seemed to have a solid boundary, like the curtain of a theater. There was something rather frightening about this curtain that concealed whatever lay on the other side. Something we did not want to see.

Cameron had heard the Masters talk about a mysterious *Shield* that could turn the minds of adult men to madness. But the undeveloped brains of juveniles like us could somehow penetrate the *Shield* unscathed. So they believed or at least hoped. Was this *It?* This Veil of mist? This curtain of Mystery?

We decided to camp here in front of the *Veil* on a long chance that Donald might be following our path. "Give him one more night to find us." That was a cop-out. We didn't really expect Donald to come. Somehow, we wanted to put off going through the *Veil* as long as possible.

BEYOND THE VEIL

The Twenty Fifth Day

Donald did not come back. I feared we would have to accept that he was gone. Donald had been off scouting by himself, though Cameron had warned him against it. Something had pounced on Donald and done away with him.

We would always remember those shining, yellow eyes, that straw-colored hair and that too-white face that never seemed to get sunburned. The grown-ups had deemed him retarded and defective, the victim of some obscure genetic disease. But we, Donald's friends and companions, were just beginning to realize his hidden powers.

Goodbye, Donald. Farewell, our friend and brother.

"Come on, guys!" called Cameron. "Let's go through the *Veil.* Form column of twos and follow me!"

Me and Troy were at the end of the line. The others,

when they hit the curtain of mist, just disappeared. Then me and Troy hit it. We were holding on to each other. My hand slipped and Troy disappeared, too.

A wild madness swept over my brain. Everything became a big shapeless void that exploded into a billion pieces. One of the pieces became a blur. It closed around me, spreading out in all directions. All the senses became one. The thing was loud and shrill and blue and hot and sour and acrid. Then the Blur exploded and there was *Nothing*. A big long *Nothing* that swelled up and exploded, too.

Now, I could hear a babble of voices. A lot of weird, distorted creatures were shouting at me. Then they vanished.

Flashing memories came to me of things from the forgotten past. Yet they seemed to be happening now . . . I was in a baby carriage and I was frightened and yelling. Miss Ferris, my old nurse, picked me up and carried me into the house . . .

I was riding now on a carousel. On a high hobby horse that was bobbing up and down. I slipped and was starting to fall. I yelled and my mother came and held me . . .

Now I was in a sand box building a sand castle. There was a bigger kid here, with yellow hair. He began throwing sand at me. Some of it went down my neck. Then that big kid socked me and I started to bawl.

Now I was standing in a desert and there was sand all around me. That boy threw sand at me again. I saw now it was my brother, Danny. He had grown much bigger than in the sand box.

My big brother punched me. I began to yell and then stopped. For I was a teenager now and so was he.

That punch woke me up and I remembered. Anxiously, I looked around and counted: *Brandon . . . Roger . . . Raymond . . . Keith . . . Stevie . . . Bobby . . . Jody . . . Cameron . . . Troy . . . And Danny.* All eleven of us had crossed the Barrier.

"That Fog Thing really blows your mind out," said Danny. "But we all came through." Jaymie was the last one to come out of it.

We were in a desert that stretched endlessly in all directions. Barren and bare, with no trees or vegetation. The Curtain of Mist behind us had disappeared.

We marched across a series of dunes, each higher than the one before. In the distance, there was a shining light. Now we reached the highest dune and stood there, gazing in wonder. Across the desert sands was a white, gleaming structure. A golden radiance of shimmering beauty, brighter than anything we had seen since entering the Netherworld.

"The Gates of Heaven!" exclaimed Bobby.

The structure rose up grandly like a storybook palace, unearthly and unbelievable. We started toward it and though we walked for hours, the shining structure never seemed to get any nearer.

"It must be a mirage," said Keith.

We had just about decided the thing wasn't real when all of a sudden it appeared right before us. A colossal temple from ancient days, now falling into ruins and partly buried in the orange sand. The temple had a gold-leaf roof and walls and pillars made of marble, jade and alabaster. Now all had crumbled. Still standing was the high altar, constructed of a strange material that glowed with a light of its own.

Behind the altar, were a group of statues, of enormous size and fashioned so skillfully they almost seemed to be alive.

They represented legendary monsters, or perhaps Devils from a forgotten age. Six were bestial. Six scaley horrors with extra heads and feet and eyes. And cruel mouths and deadly tentacles. The seventh, the middle figure, was of humanoid shape; the largest and most terrifying. With huge, ferocious jaws and six grasping arms ending in claw-like fingers stretched out murderously to rend and destroy. Two cruel spikes protruded from its chest and back. A ghoul . . . An ogre . . . A demon from Hell . . . Perhaps the very god of Death and Madness in some primeval belief.

As we stood there, the temple lights dimmed. Dark shadows covered the altar, though there was nothing to throw a shadow. The whole place reeked of evil and decay.

Now we could see it . . . Piled on the altar were the bones and skulls of men and animals. Traces of skin and hair and the remains of corpses. A place of human sacrifice and ritual horror, where victims were offered up to the seven stone devilgods. There were marks here of dried up blood, as if the death orgies had taken place not long ago.

Cameron said, "Let's get out of here. As fast as possible!"

Then Brandon gave a yell. "It moved!"

"What moved?"

"The Thing in the middle. The Ogre. The arms moved and the teeth moved."

"It can't move! It ain't alive."

But the Demon-thing now was different. The jaws had opened wider and the arms were reaching out further.

We left that place in a hurry. Our hearts were beating wildly. Each of us felt the chill of terror. There was an impulse to panic and flee in mindless fear in every direction. But by now, the juvenile delinquents of *Kaah Naghallah*, defiers of authority, lawbreakers and rebels against adult society, had developed their own kind of discipline. That saved us again and again.

Now, to our horror, the Thing did start to move . . . A step . . . Then another step . . . Closer and closer.

"Form column of twos!" yelled Cameron. "Follow me! On the double! Stevie and Danny watch the rear."

We jogged across the empty desert. Cameron turned from time to time, slowing his pace and looking backwards, making sure nobody was left behind. We didn't stop until we had left the stone images miles away.

HUNTED

Shards of fog moved slowly through the air. Unlike earth fog, these mist fragments were drawn together in a body. With a sharp boundary, almost like a living thing.

The fog things took weird shapes, like bacteria seen under the microscope. Big round balls, or floating cylinders or spiral shapes, like a cork-screw. They multiplied like bacteria, too, splitting apart and each part forming a new fog body. They danced around madly, like pale, demented phantoms. We tried to touch them, but they were always just out of reach.

The fog bodies were the only sign of life. The endless dunes were as barren as the surface of the moon. Like something out of a crazy dream.

After an hour of jogging, Cameron slowed down to a rapid walk. The pace was too fast for weaklings like Roger and Jody. And Jaymie. Now in the distance we could glimpse the white cliffs of a mountain range. Cameron wanted to make it by night fall. Of course, there was no night in this eternal twilight. We measured time only by our earth watches and the weariness of our bodies. We appeared to be the only living creatures in this lonely country. Yet somehow we had a feeling of being followed. *Hunted.* I had a creepy sensation at the back of my neck, like when I was a little kid going upstairs in the dark.

Now, over the mountain cliffs, we could see a black speck. It came nearer until it was right above us, throwing a huge, dark shadow across the landscape. It was a bird! The biggest bird we had ever seen, like the roc in the legends of the East. Not quite as big as a house, but surely as big as a large truck.

The giant bird circled around. We drew close together, fearing it might swoop down and carry one of us away. Cameron drew out his gun. The rest of us readied our weapons. But the roc made no move to attack us. It darted in and out of the cloud bodies, then circled us again and soared away back to the mountains. Maybe it was just watching us. Or maybe it decided we weren't worth hunting. Anyway, it was gone.

"If there are more things like that in the mountains," said Brandon, "perhaps we ought to go the other way."

"Back to the temple and those idols? No thanks!"

Cameron said, "Those mountains are Northwest. We have to cross them, if we're going to get — where we're trying to go."

To find Karl Hasserman and his treasure? I wondered if there ever was such a person. By now, everything that had happened before we entered *Bane N'Gai* seemed like a distant dream.

We marched on toward the mountains. And once again came that weird feeling of being hunted. Those mountains didn't seem to be getting any nearer. They were hard to see now, covered up by innumerable fog bodies.

We came upon a rocky hill. There were boulders here, piled in a protecting heap and behind them, a small cave. The kind the poets call a grotto. It looked like a good place to camp.

There was a steady trickle of water in the grotto. Enough to fill our empty canteens. That heap of rocks that covered the mouth of the grotto was a good protection against marauders. No Goblins' Bread or fruit or nuts. But we still had compressed food tablets.

We talked about making a fire and decided against it. If anything were hunting us, a fire would draw their attention.

That great black bird, the roc, was in the sky again; or what looked like the sky down here. The fog bodies came low and clustered together. You could touch them now.

"They feel like a ghost," said Troy.

"What does a ghost feel like?"

"A big, wet, slimy hole."

We ate and decided to post a guard. Two guys at a time. The grotto was about as safe a place as we could find, protected on all sides. But we could be trapped in it. We kept feeling jittery and uneasy.

Brandon wished we were back in *Kaah Naghallah*. No matter how mean the Masters were or how boring it was.

"I miss Don Don."

"We all do. But let's not think about that now."

Troy and Keith took the first watch outside the grotto. They were out barely fifteen minutes, when they started yelling. "The Thing! It's coming!"

The Evil Thing! That horrible six-armed idol! The Demon-god of Death, with the ferocious jaws and claws that rend and cruel spikes!

It came. A ghastly parody of a human being, three times the size of any ordinary man. A golem, made of something that was neither stone, nor flesh, nor metal, but of something in between.

It moved jerkily, like a mechanical toy. Perhaps it could not see or hear too well and would pass us by. On Cameron's signal, we crouched on the ground in silence.

The Terror-idol had passed the grotto. A few more steps . . . and then *it stopped.* Now it turned in our direction. The Horror was hunting something. It was hunting *us!* There was a snarl of triumph and excitement. Those spikes began to pulsate with a reddish glow.

We could make a run for it. But the Ogre would get at least one of us. Those huge legs could easily overtake us on the open plain.

We drew back behind the heap of rocks into the cave. Like mice who flee from a cat into their hole. That was the advantage of being small. The Idol was too big to come in after us. But those terrible arms could reach a long way.

Cameron drew the gun and stood in front of the cave. He was pale and sweating. The heap of boulders proved only a momentary protection. The Golem-Ogre pulled the heap apart, with the colossal power of a wrecking machine. Now the mouth of the cave was bared.

Fumes came from the Horror's mouth. A poisonous vapor. The stench of sulphur and burning plastic and corrosive acid. And a fourth thing, perhaps the smell of Death.

The Golem-Ogre was reaching down. Cameron pointed the gun and pulled the trigger. There was a wild explosion and a great roar. The Thing was hit and drew back. A pale liquid was oozing down its neck. Enough to madden the Demon-Creature, but not enough to stop it.

The Golem-Ogre came again. Its six arms were spreading out, ready to pounce. Its teeth were like the teeth of a rip saw, its tongue like the tongue of a viper. It slashed at Cameron, who leaped back just in time, then blasted it right in the neck. There was a roar and a shriek and a bellow of rage. The head sagged to one side. The arms reached up and pulled the head back into position. The tongue lashed at Cameron and the claws struck at him from both sides, but missed again.

Cameron shot and shot again. Into the gaping mouth and at the Monster's neck. But nothing seemed to stop the Thing.

Cameron took his last shot at the Terror's sagging neck. It bounced off futilely. All six claws slashed at Cameron and one of them got him. The blood flowed from Cameron's chest and shoulders.

The Coyotes' outer defenses had been shattered. We fell back into the cave, drawing our knives and axes. The Horror was moving in for the kill. The lethal arms were reaching in. The poison breath was suffocating.

Stevie smashed at the reaching arm with his diamond knife. The claws ripped his chest and back. Bobby, too, had been ripped and was lying on the ground. Keith was still on his feet, but bleeding badly.

The smell of blood excited the Ogre. The arms jerked violently. The breath grew hot. Danny and Raymond slashed at the furthest arm. The cut was deep. The claw hung loose and useless. That pale liquid that was the Terror's blood flowed forth. Injured, the Thing drew back.

It was at least a defensive victory. Long as those arms were, they weren't quite long enough to get us. But sooner or later the Monster *would* get us. The cave was too shallow. There was no place to retreat. The Thing was starting now on a new attack. To tear apart the sides of the cave. We would be helpless and an easy prey.

We rallied for a final stand. Four of our best fighters, Cameron, Keith, Bobby and Stevie, were wounded and weakened. The Demon-Idol had five claws left.

But now a curious thing happened. There was a loud screaming cry, a cry of battle. It didn't come from the Ogre nor from any of us. The Monster-Thing suddenly drew away and turned to meet a new enemy.

Some of us crawled to the mouth of the grotto to see what was happening. *The Great Roc was attacking!* The huge black bird swooped down like a dive bomber, striking at the Monster's head. The Ogre struck back with his five remaining claws. But the giant bird moved too fast and maneuvered too skillfully, hitting hard with beak and claw. We watched with fear and fascination the battle of the Titans, hoping desperately that the Roc would win.

The huge bird looped like a plane and seemed to pick up a mist cloud as it dove. The great bird dove again and the mist swirled around the combatants. It was a fight to the death. The Idol's arms were flailing wildly and I saw now that the spike in his back was hanging loose.

The cloud had now completely enveloped the Great Roc, like a protecting armor. Somewhere in the middle, you could see a pair of yellow, shining eyes. The yellow-eyed body rose up slowly, and then dove down like a landslide. The Idol's front spike was severed from its chest. The Ogre gave a strangled cry, then staggered and fell backwards. It smashed and shattered on the ground. The grisly head roll-ed loose.

The guys cheered and started to run out. But Cameron said, *"Wait!"* We weren't sure what the Roc would do. "Stay close to the cave, so we can dive in again."

The Roc had landed on a large boulder. It spread its wings and gave a cry of triumph, looking rather like a gigantic crow. Now the fog came and covered it up. All you could see was two yellow eyes, shining through the mist.

Raymond was putting wound stuff on Bobby. Danny put it on Stevie. Keith and Cameron treated each other and belittled their injuries, although both were still bleeding. We examined the smashed Golem. It looked like a shat-tered idol now, headless and demolished. There was no sign it had ever been alive.

The Great Roc was attacking!

The mist that had enveloped the Roc was coming nearer. It moved forward as if it were walking on legs. The mist became a shadow and the shadow gradually took a manlike shape. Two arms, two legs and a head, with shining yellow eyes.

Now a face formed. It was a face we had seen before. We stared in awe at our Deliverer, as if he were a supernatural Being, descended from the sky. All at once, the figure broke into a laugh. It was the same laugh that had once caused a riot in the mess hall back at *Kaah Naghallah*.

Jody was the first to speak. "Hi, Don Don."

Nobody could quite believe it. Cameron addressed the Shape that had become a human boy. "Are you Donald Turrentine?"

"Don't you know me, Tony?"

Tony! In a moment of weakness, Cam had revealed that his birth name was *Anthony Cameron Westcott.* He didn't like that first name and dropped it. We used to call him that sometimes to tease him.

Now Brandon came forward and touched Donald on his arms and legs and body.

"What are you doing that for?"

"Just want to see if you are real."

Then everyone came forward to touch Don Don. They socked him and threw their arms around him, "to make sure you're not a ghost or a mirage."

"I ain't a mirage," said Donald, emphatically.

It was only afterwards that we found out what had happened. No, Donald was not a shape-changer and he didn't change himself into a roc. Though what he did was almost as remarkable.

Donald was able to ride on the roc's back and was concealed under the great bird's feathers. These giant birds, it seemed, have a kangeroo-like pouch.

Donald is better at doing things than telling about them. We gathered that he had rescued the roc's chick and by his strange power with animals, Donald was able to communicate with the mother bird. In gratitude, she agreed to help him find and protect his brothers.

On the night that Donald left us, he was exploring the woods and met the *Octocorn*, a furry creature with eight horns and enormous feet. The *Octocorn* led Donald to *The Lady of the Forest*. She warned him that we were in great danger.

The Forest Lady told Donald what path to follow, but the path led into the mountains, instead of back to our campsite. Here, Donald found the roc's chick that had fallen into a crevasse.

The life of the Demon-Idol lay not in its heart nor in its head, but in its spikes that vibrated in its front and back. Donald rode the giant bird as a war horse and slashed them off.

"What happened to the mother roc?"

"She flew back to her nest," said Donald. After having dropped Donald off to join his friends.

"You came just in time, Don Don. A few more minutes and that Thing would have pulled the cave apart and ripped us to pieces."

Donald was sorry he took so long. But the roc required some persuasion to join the battle. He warned her the Ogre would attack her chicks, after he had wasted Donald's brothers.

"You got there in time. That's all that counts."

"I told you. Donald has power. Donald will save brothers."

"You got the power, Don Don. Can you get us out of here?" asked Danny.

"Return to Earth? Yes. But the way is hard."

We were no longer in any underground labyrinth and could not just retrace our steps. Somewhere, in some way, we had crossed over into another world.

Cameron said, "Look, Don Don. We can only have *one* leader. And down here it's got to be *you*. Want to be Gangleader of the Coyotes?"

Donald looked shocked. "No. Tony Gangleader!"

"I'll be your assistant. I'll help. But Don Don will lead." He looked around. "How many of you guys want Don Don to be Gangleader of the Coyotes?"

Cameron held his hand up. I put mine up, too, knowing that was what Cameron wanted. Then Stevie and Danny held their hands up. And Raymond did. In a few seconds, all eleven hands were up.

"They voted you in, Don Don. We all want you. It's unanimous."

No matter how weird a situation was, the Naghallah boys had to make a joke of it. "Kneel down, Donald Turrentine," ordered Cameron. Donald kneeled. Cameron tapped him on the shoulder. "I hereby declare you to be *Gangleader of the Coyotes* in the name of the *Keekereekee.*"

"Do you solemnly swear — what's he supposed to swear to?"

"To lead my brudders with all my power," said Don Don.

"And if you're our captain, you got to stay with your men. You can't go off and leave us."

"Won't," promised Donald. He had a happy smile on him. *Gangleader of the Coyotes!* If Donald's title had been *Emperor of the World,* he could hardly have been more pleased.

Danny said, "We ought to go back to that temple place, wreck that altar and destroy the rest of those horrors."

"None of the other things looked alive. They were just statues."

"You can't be sure."

"Look," said Cameron. "This isn't our country. Let's not get mixed up into things. Let's leave things alone, if they leave us alone. You can't always tell the good guys from the bad guys. I almost took a shot at that roc.

"Right, Gangleader?"

Donald nodded. He didn't seem to know what to do in his new post.

"Command us, Don Don. Give us some orders."

"Okay," said Donald, imitating Cameron in voice and gesture. "Form column of twos. Stevie and Danny! Keith and Raymond! Bobby and Brandon! Roger and Jody! Jaymie and Troy! Cameron take and watch the rear!"

Bobby called, "Where are we going, Don Don?"

"To get the *Vrrooohn.* We are going to the *Vrrooohn.*"

"Why don't we just get out of here, Don Don?"

"We must find the *Vrrooohn* first. Then we will have the power to get out." That's what the *Lady of the Forest* had told him.

"Follow me, now. Forward march!"

We were no longer weary. Our bodies were filled with new energy. We marched forward, shouting. "Y-a-a-a-y, Don Don! Lead us, Don Don! On to the *Vrrooohn!*"

About an hour later and closer to the mountains, we hit another grotto. This one had water and Goblin's Bread in abundance. "Get in the cave." ordered the Gangleader. "And everyone sleep. I'll watch tonight. Tomorrow, we'll take a rest day before we cross the mountains."

There were more perils ahead, Donald knew. But we didn't have to think about them now.

"What was the *Lady of the Forest* like?" asked Troy. "Was she human?"

"Well ——" Donald used sign language. *So high.* Smaller than any of us. *Real Shapely.* Donald put two fingers to his head and wiggled them. *She must have horns or antennae. All silver, including her clothes.*

The Octocorn was a fierce-looking but gentle beast. Six-legged. Big enough to carry all of us.

"Will we meet the *Lady* again?" asked Roger.

"Hope so," said Donald. "She was nice."

In a few minutes, we were all asleep. Donald leaned against a rock at the mouth of the grotto. Soon, he was asleep, too.

THE CAVERN OF THE FALLING WATER

Days Twenty-six to Twenty-eight
The next day, we stayed in the cave. We all felt weak and exhausted, especially the wounded guys. Besides, it was raining. The rain poured down like in the days of Noah's Ark and didn't let up.

We shared the cave with bats and lizards, bright moths and squeaking mice. Also, there were glow worms, hop toads, gophers, eels and tunnel-digging moles. None of us bothered each other.

In the back of the cave was a pool and an underground waterfall. The water was warm, clear and full of minerals. Of all the denizens of the cavern, only the eels and human boys went swimming.

Behind the waterfall, we found a curious, pinkish mud. Donald said it was healing and put it on the wounds of the injured.

The second day, the rain lessened and we explored the neighborhood. We were out of the desert and in an area rich in strange vegetation and animal life. There was a grove of stalks like uncooked spaghetti, but enormous; taller than a telephone pole. Inside the stalks, was a brown, milky liquid and it was good. We filled our canteens with it.

Orange lillies grew on huge silver trees that sheltered innumerable birds. On a high crag, there was a nest of squawking pterodactyls. And Donald showed us a wild octocorn, grazing on the plain. A strange creature with a dinosaur-like body, eight horns and six elephantile legs. It would be great to have an octocorn to carry us. But this thing roared and bellowed. Nobody dared to get too close to it. Donald said it was a female and she was going to have cubs.

There were vines bearing corn and spiny shrubs that oozed with a glue-like substance. And gigantic lettuce-leaf plants with silver, rubbery leaves. Not good to eat; but we put them over the holes and rips in our clothes, and stuck the rubbery lettuce leaves on with the glue-like sap. If you put on several layers and dried them over a fire, they stayed on pretty well. It looked funny to have silver lettuce leaves all over our worn-out pants and torn shirts, but it kept our clothes from falling apart.

Donald had lost his boots in the battle with the Terror-Idol. Or took them off when he rode the roc. But he made a pretty good pair of sandals from the leaves. We all put leaves over our shoes, too, and covered up the holes. We had leaves all over us. From the distance, we must have looked like a walking vegetable garden.

"The Lettuce Leaf Kids," said Roger, giggling.

The guys liked our home here in *The Cavern of the Falling Water*. Some of them wanted to stay here.

"You mean *forever?*"

"It don't have to be forever," said Bobby. "Maybe the seasons will change and it'll get cold. Or maybe some other nasty thing will come along and drive us out. But let's not move until we have to."

Cameron thought we should keep going. If we wait too long, we may be trapped here and not be able to get out.

The Coyote youth gang is a free republic. Under the Boylaw, the Gangleader commands in battle or on the march. But in planning or deciding what action to take, we have to hold a gang meeting. One boy, one vote. Majority rules. If there's a tie, the Gangleader decides. And so we voted: *To Stay in the Grotto:* Bobby, Raymond, Troy, Roger and Brandon. *Five. To Go On:* Cameron, Danny, Stevie, Keith and Jaymie. *Five. Not Voting:* Jody, who really wanted to stay, but didn't want to vote against Cameron.

That left it up to the Gangleader, Donald.

"We go," said Don Don. "We must find the *Vrrooohn.* When we find the *Vrrooohn,* we will be safe."

More than safe. We would, "have power." Perhaps more power than any human beings ought to have.

Then, Bobby, Raymond, Troy, Brandon and Roger all changed over and made it unanimous. For one thing we were absolutely agreed on. Whatever happened, we would stick together, come what may.

THE COLOSSUS

Day Twenty-nine

After three days in our cavern home, we started for the mountains. We felt a bit sad about leaving. It had been a healing place. We had good times there.

After a two-hour march, we hit the white cliffs of the mountains. But now, we came upon a most curious structure. The huge cliffs, rising up over a hundred feet, were sheer with no footholds. Further, the top of the cliff projected outward in a wide overhang. That meant a climber would have to hang on from underneath, almost like walking on the ceiling. Not even the Cat Burglar could climb upside down.

It seemed that Nature had built an impassible barrier around these mountains. Donald said we'd follow the cliff and try to find a break in it. We did for over an hour. But, if anything, the cliff became higher and slanted out more.

After another hour, we came upon some vines. Huge vines like Jack's *Beanstalk*. Only, they didn't rise out of the ground, going *up*. Their roots were on the top of the cliff and they grew *down*. Most of the vines came down just half way or less. There was, however, one very thick and heavy vine that had grown all the way down to the ground.

That looked like the break we had been hoping for. There was just one trouble. About thirty feet up, there was a structure that looked like a huge spider web, with heavy, purple strands. More like wires than a spider's gossamer. None of us liked the looks of it. But there was no other place where the vines came down to the ground and that rock wall seemed to go on and on forever.

"We'll climb here," Donald decided. "Everyone put the rope on." Cameron first, Donald last.

One by one, we climbed off the ground, up the gigantic vine, across the wire-like web. It was enormous, that web, going almost to the top. We climbed up carefully, trying not to damage the Web. That might arouse the Webmaker. *He* — or *She* — or *It* must be enormous, too. However, there was no sign of the Webmaker now.

That Web was a beautiful thing, fashioned like a lace curtain and gleaming like tinsel on a Christmas tree. But it was a cruel trap that snagged its victims like fly paper or a hunter's net. Two silver birds, something like seagulls, were caught in it. They struggled desperately with losing force, becoming weaker and feebler. Cameron cut them loose. The two gulls fluttered to the ground. Then, gaining strength, they took off. Maybe that triggered an alarm.

We thought the Spider-creature, if it attacked, would come from above, where the roots of the vines were. We were prepared to slide down these vines in a hurry, the way Jack did down the beanstalk. But this creature came from below and cut off our retreat.

It wasn't exactly a spider. The Colossus had at least twelve legs and was bigger than a moving van. Covered with streaks of white and purple and spiny bristles on its back. With huge red mandibles.

The giant creature moved slowly. We should have been able to climb up the vine and get away. That web was something like fly paper. It stuck to you and could trap a bird or small animal. But it wasn't strong enough to hold tough kids like the Coyotes. Especially if we kept moving.

However, this Giant Spider had a nasty and unexpected weapon. It could throw out long threads of its deadly net and wind them around its victims. Not just a few but more and more, building up many layers of web around its prey. No matter how strong the prey was in the beginning, sooner or later there would be enough threads to crush him and hold him helpless, while the Colossus came in for the kill.

We were about half way up when the Giant Spider hit. The Colossus started up the vine and threw forth its deadly net. Donald was lowest on the vine and got it first. The Spider's cords struck Donald and wrapped around him like a thousand encircling snakes.

Brandon, next in line, turned back to help Donald. The Spider's cords whipped around Brandon, cut into his skin and bound him helpless.

Donald and Brandon were struggling now like the two silver birds. Danny came back, slashing at the Spider's death net. As the Thing advanced, Danny hurled his knife. It struck deep into the Monster's neck and stayed there. The Thing gave a loud shrieking sound and turned on Danny. A hundred, two hundred lashes seemed to wrap themselves around Danny's body, like thongs of steel. Donald, Brandon and Danny were smothered in the Spidermonster's grasp.

The Thing was climbing up now to capture and feast upon its prey. Donald, Bran and Danny were helpless in the lethal grip of the flesh-eating Colossus.

But now, the whole Coyote pack came down with fighting fury. Stevie struck with his diamond dagger, Keith with his knife. Bobby and Troy struck with their feet. Raymond was bleeding badly, but he drove his axe into the monster's head. Jody, Roger and Jaymie slashed the spidercords apart and let Brandon and Danny get loose. We had to do all this with one hand, clinging to the vine with the other.

Donald was in danger. The spider's cords were wrapped around him like a death shroud. Those terrible jaws were about to close on Donald. Cameron drove his knife into the monster's brain. The Thing released Donald and slid back to the ground.

We started up the vine again. But that creature wasn't dead. Not even with three knives and an axe in him. The Spider-giant started up the vine again, higher and higher. We were climbing, too, but not fast enough.

The Colossus was still throwing out his cords. However, his power was running out. He threw forth only a dozen strands now instead of a hundred. His net was no longer strong enough to hold us. The Coyotes could break loose.

Donald turned to face the climbing Spider. His face and body were covered with blood. But he readied his diamond sword, the same sword with which he had slain the Terror-Idol. The Colossus drew back. It had no stomach for an open battle unless it could paralyze its victims first.

Cameron had reached the top. He climbed over the ledge.

The Spidermonster
We fought desperately to save Donald.

One by one, the others followed him. When we were all up, Donald readied his sword and, in the manner of Jack of the Beanstalk, slashed off the vines.

The Web collapsed around the Giant Spider. The Colossus slipped and fell backwards and landed in a heap below. We watched the Thing squirming at the bottom of the heap and counted our numbers. The twelve of us were still alive.

That Spidermonster was pretty badly battered. We could have heaved rocks down and finished the Thing off. But, after all, the Coyotes started the war by invading the creature's web. Unlike the Terror-Idol and the Nightmare that had hunted the Naghallah kids for sport or to be nasty, the Colossus was defending its home territory.

The Great Spirit, or Whoever was in charge here, had spared us, so let us be merciful, too. That Colossal Spider might be the only life form of its kind, the biggest insect in the Universe. So we let it alone and after a while the Creature went limping and crawling away.

Cameron put his arm on Donald's shoulder. "We almost lost you there, Gangleader."

Donald no longer spoke in sentences. He had reverted to his earlier way of speech. He gave a grunt that sounded like *Don brud yak wook brud.* Translated, that meant *Last time, Donald save brothers. This time, brothers save Donald.* We called these things *Donnie-words.* After a while, you get to understand them.

West Northwest. Onward and Upward! Across the mountains. *On to the Vrrooohn!* The Coyote youth gang was moving again, bloodied but unbowed. The compass was smashed and nearly all our diamonds had been lost. But we could get on without them. Those three silver moons, roughly in a straight line, appeared fixed in the sky. *West Northwest* was roughly perpendicular to the moonline. Maybe a little to the left. That was where the *Vrrooohn* was supposed to be.

Old Mehary, with his behavior modification and his corrective, adversive conditioning, had trained us well; though

despised and pushed around, we had drawn together and
formed into a rugged team. We would fight for each other,
shed blood for each other and would stand up to *Anything.*
None of us would turn tail and run when a brother was in
peril, nor ever abandon a comrade.

The Masters of Naghallah, who averaged more than
twice our size and years and power, were shattered. And
we, the lowly reform school inmates, endured.

THE CAVE OF THE SILVER BEARS

We kept moving. The wounds of battle began to take
their toll. Raymond kept bleeding. Danny was unable to
move his injured arm. That web stuff must contain a slowly paralyzing poison. Brandon's legs became blue and
swollen. After a while, we had to carry him. A nasty red
rash formed on Troy and Stevie.

Donald, who had been most exposed to the web poison,
was curiously immune. There was blood on his face that
covered up his eye. But no rash or swelling on his body.

Donald led us across a rocky plateau covered with moss
and lichens and stubby, twisting bushes, bearing clumps
of yellow berries. The white peaks of the mountains rose
upward like the spires of a cathedral, gleaming in the unen-
ding starlight. A flock of silver birds circled above us. It
was a scene of rare beauty, but we were in no position to
enjoy it.

The Coyotes were in a bad way. Danny was just able to
drag his feet. Jody felt dizzy and held on to me. Bobby and
Keith were both limping now. Roger's face was turning
blue. And that rash was beginning to form on all of us. I
could feel my own right arm becoming numb. I didn't
think we could make it across the mountains.

Donald didn't try. He reached a ravine and followed it
downward. Here, there were several caves. Donald looked
in each and selected the last one, motioning for us to
follow.

The back of the cave was lined with that material we call- ed "pink mud", or perhaps rather soft, creamy pink clay. Donald stripped off his clothes and beckoned to us to do likewise. He rubbed the "pink mud" over himself, then on Raymond and Danny. We laid Brandon in the pink mud and covered him up completely. Then, one by one, we covered up each other.

That was potent stuff, that *pink mud.* It seemed to draw the poison right out of you and left you feeling warm and comfortable. By the next morning, our rash had largely faded and the paralyzed limbs began to move again. The swellings were down. Our body wounds were healing. One of the other caves had water and Goblin's Bread. We lay around and rested.

We didn't have the caves all to ourselves. There were not only bats and lizards, but a couple of silver bears. The bears were sleeping when we came in, but woke up growl- ing. Donald talked to them, making animal noises. After a while, the bears went back to sleep again.

"Don Don," said Jody, "can talk to any animal."

"Donald didn't talk to that spider" said Raymond, rub- bing on another dose of the *pink mud.*

"If he did," said Bobby, "he sure said the wrong thing."

Day Thirty

There were some strange animals here. Some that looked like logs with feet; snake-like creatures with horns and many legs; rock frogs and golden eagles and giant snails with many eyes.

We wondered what all these animals eat. Besides each other. The cave animals eat mostly Goblins' Bread. It grows back fast, almost overnight. Everything grows back fast here, in this exotic realm where there is no sun and no winter.

The Great Roc, Donald says, eats whole trees and cer- tain kinds of clay. He doesn't think rocs eat people, but you can't be sure what they would do if they had no trees or clay around.

If we could bring some of these strange things back to earth, we would be famous. *If* we ever get back to earth, which seems more and more unlikely.

Today was our thirtieth day in *Bane N'Bai*. Nobody cared, except Jaymie. Everyone else lived for a day at a time. The "Gifted Child" still tried to keep a record of things, though all our notebooks and writing stuff had been lost.

Each day, I made another notch in my belt. "Hey, Jaymiebrudder," said Danny. "You'll have your whole fucking belt chopped up and your pants will fall down, long before we get out of here."

My pants were falling down already. I had to put three new holes in my belt. I used to be a bit on the chubby side. Now, I was as thin as Brandon.

THE DOOR OF DARKNESS

Day Thirty-one

After a day of rest, we crossed the mountains. There seemed to be no end to them. Peak after peak. Gulley after gulley.

Gradually, the bare rock gave way to wooded hills. The scene was rich in plant and animal life. Most of the plants were green and earth-like. Others were silver, red and blue.

There were vast groves of laurels with fragrant pink blossoms and rich blueberry patches extending in every direction. The silver birds were gobbling up the berries. They seemed free of fear and made no move to fly away when we came near.

Deer and rabbits watched us curiously. There were many insects here, too. Swarms of red lady bugs and multi-colored butterflies and silverish katy-dids. Centipedes that burrowed in the ground and snails on trees.

Those three silver moons were our compass now. We followed the moonline. Perpendicular, a little to the left.

There were many other celestial bodies in the velvet sky now. But only the moons never changed.

We were going down hill now and came to a ravine between two towering mountains. Their crowns were white with something that could be ice or snow. But it was warm here, like an August day on earth. A thousand feet below us was a large lake that seemed to go on for miles.

This was a world of open land, plenty of water, clean air and good food, if you hustled for it. Except for the Monsters and assorted Horrors, *Bane N'Gai* wasn't a bad place to live.

How could we possibly have come here? And how do we get out?

"We won't," said Brother Danny. "We can't get out." He believed that somewhere along the line we had been wasted and were now in the Hereafter.

"You fought for your life — against the Terror-Idol and the Spider-Monster. Why fight, if we're dead already?"

Danny wasn't sure. "Maybe you die a lot of times. Not just once. Maybe the next Horror will get us. Maybe the next Hereafter will be lousier than this one.

"I knew I'd never make Heaven, but this place ain't bad enough to be Hell. It's a creampuff Purgatory. I'll settle for *this* right now."

Keith was the only one, beside Jaymie, who ever read books. He read Science Fiction. In some way, we had entered an Alternate Universe or Parallel World.

"Can we get back?" asked Troy.

"Only by dumb luck. Probably not."

"Karl Hasserman got back," said Bobby, hopefully.

"He was the only one. None of us have ever seen Karl Hasserman. We don't even know if he existed."

Raymond had another idea. He thought we were still on Earth but in a Hollow. A strange place that got cut off from the World above.

"It must be an awful big Hollow. We've gone hundreds of miles."

"If we went straight. But maybe we've been going around and up and down like a corkscrew."

We looked at Donald. He was smiling."Where are we Don Don? Do you know?"

Maybe. But Donald wouldn't say. He just laughed.

We sat around and talked and ate blueberies and wild grapes and *Gai-nabs*. All the poison and fever had left us and our wounds were healed. Tomorrow, some Monster might get us. But today was a day of joy.

Day Thirty-two

We slept in a circle, like we usually did. The next day, Donald led us down the ravine. The sides of the chasm grew higher and the light dimmer. We were strung out in a slovenly line, ill prepared against any sudden danger. "Form column of twos," Donald ordered. "Cameron guard rear."

We met no danger, but encountered some of the weirdest life forms we had yet seen in *Bane N'Gai*. The ravine was illuminated now by a bluish glow that came not from the sky but from gigantic fireflies, the size of a sparrow. They hung like floating lanterns in the air above us. Then suddenly they went out and disappeared.

There were small, flat stones that gathered in clusters. They shone in the dark like an illuminated wrist watch. I stooped to pick one up. Suddenly, the whole cluster flew apart. Each seeming rock rushed away on a dozen small feet.

There was a large boulder that blocked our path. As soon as we touched it, the thing moved away and climbed up the side of the ravine. And there was what looked like a human arm, crawling on seven fingers. They pinched and scratched at you, if you touched them.

There were red bats here, too, with enormous wings. And flying toads. And seal-like creatures that frolicked in an icy pool.

As we kept going down, the life forms grew fewer, until there were only the bare cliffs, silent and barren. The ravine grew narrower. We had to walk single file. All at once, the ravine halted. There was nothing ahead but a wall of stone. The guys started cursing, thinking we would have to go all the way back again. But right in that rock wall, amazingly, was a hinged door that appeared to be made of metal.

The door was covered with strange markings in an unknown tongue; ancient runes from a time long gone by. "What does it say, Gifted Child?" Being a "Gifted Child", I was supposed to know everything.

"This is the Gate to Hell.
Abandon Hope all ye who enter here."

Some of the guys believed me. Stevie and Bobby got a bit pale. In *Bane N'Gai,* you get to believe anything, because almost anything can happen.

"No, wait!" said me. "What it really says here is:
"Dare ye enter this enchanted passageway?"
Once again the guys believed me. "Do we dare to enter? Sure we dare. Come on, let's go in!"

I ought to tell them I had no idea what these markings were. They were like Chinese characters to me.

Danny, however, saved me the trouble. "Jaymie can't read that stuff. He's just bullshitting. I know the kid brudder."

The door was locked. But it was a weak lock, easily broken. Behind the door was a stone step, leading downward. It was real dark inside with a stale, musty odor. *The Door of Darkness.* Was that what the cuneiforms said? The words flashed into my mind, along with a feeling of fear. This door, perhaps, had been fashioned by the same people who made the Terror-Idol and the altar of bones and skulls.

We had trained ourselves to see in very little light. But here there was no light at all. We wished we still had one of our battery lamps. All that stuff was long since lost or thrown away.

Donald said he would go first. His shining yellow eyes could see in almost total darkness. Those glowing eyes were the only thing the rest of us could see now.

"Rope!" ordered Don Don. "Hold onto the guy in front."

We put the rope on. I was second in line, with my hands on Donald's shoulder. Donald was talking in sentences now most of the time. But sometimes he left words out, which made him hard to understand. "Down steps! Slow! Watch trap!"

The steps went on and on for what seemed a mile. I couldn't see a thing. At last we came to a ramp, level at first, then curving downward. Then more long steps and a second ramp.

We walked in silence, save for the sound of our feet. But occasionally we heard a faint growling or rumbling sound and a distant humming. It would grow louder and nearer, then stopped abruptly. That noise gave me the creeps.

Now the passageway split. One way was high and wide. 'Xi!" said Donald. *Xi*, we learned, was a Donnieword that meant something to be avoided. Instead, he led us down a low, narrow tunnel. We had to crawl through on our hands and knees. Jody bumped his head and yowled. Danny bumped his head and cursed. At last, the crawlway opened up and we were able to walk again. Only Donald's eyes gave us light.

At intervals, the passageway broke into forks. Donald chose sometimes the left fork, sometimes the right. There was no apparent pattern to his choice. Donald, however, still possessed the animal sense of smell that civilized humans have lost. He paused at each fork and pointed with his nostrils like a hunting dog. His sense of smell warned him to stay clear of one or the other of the pathways.

"What would happen, Don Don, if we went the other way?" the guys kept asking.

"Trap!" said Don Don. "*Xi!* Never get out." Or "*Nada Coy*", which was a Donnie word for "No more Coyote Brothers. We would be wasted."

Only once did we witness the trap that we avoided. There were three forks and Donald took the middle instead of the left. Suddenly, he halted. "Back!" he shouted. "*Xi!*" Right before us was a yawning hole, a deadly drop into *Nada*, as Donald called it.

That was Donald's one mistake and he caught it just in time. Without him, we would all have stumbled into oblivion.

It looked as if these passageways had been built by men and all the traps had been made to destroy intruders. Only the initiate, who knew the true path, could get through safely. There must be some clue that revealed the danger spots. Donald had found the clue, but couldn't explain it. Who were the people who had built these tunnels and who were the enemies they feared so much?

What strange powers he had, this boy they had called retarded. And how wise Cameron was to let him lead us. Since becoming Gangleader, Donald had never left us. He insisted on watching over us at night, while the rest of us slept.

Donald could see with his eyes closed. He was the only guy I ever heard of who could sleep and do guard duty at the same time.

THE PHANTOM RIVER

"Light!" said Don Don, pointing forward. But we walked another fifteen minutes before the rest of us spotted any light.

The tunnel opened into a wide hollow. There was no longer any sky above us. The light came from the glow of the white rocks that lined the sides of the hollow.

The hollow sloped downward to a river bank. The rocks here had strange markings on them, like the distorted faces of men and beasts. The river flowed sluggishly and had a dark reddish hue. The place had a foul odor, the smell of decay and death. The scene was oddly familiar.

"The River Styx!" shouted Troy. "The place we hit the first night in the amphibian!"

Brandon cried out in horror. "You mean we've gone around in a circle?"

"Maybe not," said Bobby. "it could be the same river but in a different spot."

A long, white rock protruded out into the water. There were markings on the rock. I could guess what they would be without reading them:

THE COYOTES WERE HERE

Steve... Keith... Bobby... Danny... Cameron... Troy... Raymond... Jamie... Brandon... Jody... Roger... Donald...

We looked at each other in bewilderment. "We're right back where we started!"

Somebody or Something was trying to make us think so. But it wasn't quite the same. They left the *"y"* out of *Jaymie.* And Donald never writes his full name. Just *Don.* It was a trick.

Some invisible foe was trying to break our spirit and destroy our hopes.

The guys felt low. I cheered them up a little. But mostly they remained unconvinced. "Just 'cause your name ain't spelled right, that don't prove nothin," said Danny.

"There's a tunnel on the other side of the river, just like last time. If we follow it, we'll go right around in a circle again. Only this time we won't make it."

It did look like the same tunnel we had crossed in the amphibian thirty-one days ago. We decided to keep out of it. Cameron, for once, seemed as lost as anybody. He looked at Donald helplessly. "What do we do now, Gangleader?"

"Eat," said Donald.

There was no sign of life here. No Goblins' Bread or anything else that could serve as food. We still had some food tablets left. Raymond, our Quartermaster, counted them out. He puzzled on how to divide 25 tablets among twelve guys. Then, he gave each guy *two* and the extra one to the Gangleader.

Donald didn't want it. He passed it on to Cameron. Cameron laid the tablet on the rock. "Our sacrifice to the Demons of the Underworld."

"We ain't giving them much."

There was a narrow, winding trail along the riverbank. Donald pointed downstream. "Rope!" he ordered. "Follow me." The trail rose up and then cut narrowly into the white, ghostly cliffs that lined the Phantom River. We marched single file, braced by the rope.

Donald was expecting trouble. He called out the order of the marchers, scattering the younger kids among the big guys. The Masters would have been amazed to see how everyone did what Donald told them.

Wearily, we followed the river, hoping to find food and drink. But there was nothing in this dead, dark world. Everything was silent, except for the occasional outcries of the Naghallah boys and the crunch of our feet on the stony trail.

Sometimes, out of the corner of my eye, I thought I saw a human figure. But it vanished when you turned your head. Sometimes a human arm or head rose out of the waves. But when you looked again, it turned into a patch of mist.

Now we could see something — a shining silver object, floating on the river. "A boat! A boat!" cried Roger.

It was a phantom ship, a mirage. When we climbed down to the water's edge, it disappeared.

Another mile downstream, we saw it again, gleaming in the eerie light of the Hollow. Once again, it vanished when we reached the river. Another mirage! The Coyote brothers groaned.

This time, I had an idea. I waded into the river where the boat had been. *It was there!* You could feel it when you touched the boat, though you couldn't see it.

As more guys waded into the river, the thing became clear. Not a mirage, this boat, but an anti-mirage. *An-Mir.* A thing you couldn't see that *was* there.

It wasn't our amphibian. This boat was larger and different, with an elaborate instrument panel. Maybe it was the boat of the Masters. The guys climbed in eagerly. Only Donald held back. He was suspicious. Or else was being very careful.

"Hey, Don Don," pleaded Bobby. "Let's take the boat. I'm tired of walking." We all were.

There were supplies here. Food tablets and bottled juices. Donald examined them carefully. "Cantake!" The stuff was okay to eat and drink. The guys cheered.

No one could figure out how to work the instrument panel or turn the power on. But steering was just like our old amphibian. We were going downstream anyway.

"Cam nav," said Don Don. Cameron navigated and the rest of us stretched out on the floor of the boat. It was kind of crowded, but we were tired enough to sleep sitting on a tack.

After an hour of navigating, Cameron woke up Danny who, after another hour, woke up Stevie. Who woke up Bobby, who woke up Raymond, who woke up Keith, who woke up Jaymie, who woke up Brandon. Nobody woke up Don Don. He deserved to have a night of real sleep.

All the while, the boat kept floating downstream at two or three miles and hour. We must have covered over twenty miles during the night. It was a lot easier than walking.

THE SILENT CITY

Day Thirty-three

When I woke up, Troy was steering the boat down the river we called *The Styx.* Jody and Roger were clamoring for a turn. They chose, odds and evens. Roger won and took over.

The country side had changed. We were no longer in an underground hollow. There were fields on both sides, with silver shrubs and grass. There was sky again, but you couldn't tell if it was the same sky. Those three moons that had guided us were now in a triangle and were larger and redder than before. The one thing you can expect in *Bane N'Gai* is that things are never like you expected.

I wondered where the River Styx would flow. Would it reach some distant ocean? Or would it go around in a big circle like most things in the weird world?

There was a haze over the landscape. We couldn't see too far. But what we did see was astounding. There was a huge silver rock, with windows, surrounded by flowering plants. We passed a series of them, at more or less regular intervals; each in the middle of a garden. Large structures, bigger than any ordinary house.

That's what they probably were. Houses, if not of humans, at least of some intelligent Beings.

There were many different structures, mostly spheres and cylinders, surrounded by growing plants and trees. Some appeared to be made of metal, others of glass, still others of a delicate gossamer fabric, mostly silver, but in many different colors and patterns.

Each dwelling had a soft glow that seemed to come from the walls of the structure itself.

Now Jody shouted and pointed with wonder. On an island in the center of the river, was an edifice with marble columns, a golden dome and a curving roof covered with glittering stones. Like an ancient temple, at least the way they look in the movies.

There were more earth-like buildings now, each one a landmark. A medieval cathedral, a stone castle, a silver skyscraper whose summit was lost in the clouds and an array of golden towers.

We were moving toward the center of a great city. The buildings were still far apart, by the standards of our crowded earth; each surrounded by woods and gardens. There was every kind of structure here. Marble, metal and mahogany; alabaster, jade and rainbow crystal; pink coral, white pearl and blue chalcedony; moonstone, topaz and jasper; onyx and azurite; silver and gold. And there were structures that appeared to be tremendous living trees with green and scarlet leaves. A storybook city!

But everything here was silent. There were broad streets, but no vehicles moved on them. Nor did any other boats pass us on the river. The city seemed empty and abandoned, as if all the people and even the birds and beasts had fled from it.

We turned off the river into a canal, lined by stately and magnificent dream buildings. The canal ended in a series of empty piers. This was as good a place to stop as any. We secured the boat by rope and went ashore.

Could this be the place we had been searching for? Where the *Vrrooohn* is? Or had some power drawn us here to trap us? Was this the beginning of a nightmare horror or a glorious adventure?

"What'll we do, Don Don?"

"Form column of twos," said Donald. "Cam guard rear. Follow me!" He didn't have to tell us to stay close together.

We wandered through the silent streets. It was a fantastic scene of unforgettable beauty. Broad boulevards were lined with silver-leaf trees and a few that were red and green and some that were orange and golden. There were wide open spaces between the buildings, with gardens and lawns of silver grass. There were flowers here of many colors. Some like Earth, resembling roses and lillies and some with exotic shapes and colors we had never seen before. Here were fragrant ferns, and spiral vines, bearing blossoms and berries, grew upward to astounding heights. Ponds and small lakes abounded.

The buildings were even grander and stranger than along the river bank. A medley of domes, towers and spires. Here was a giant pyramid, built from stained, translucent glass and a golden structure, resembling an enormous pinwheel. They floated in the air with no apparent foundation.

There were cross streets, each marked with a picture instead of a sign, celebrating some bird or beast or thing of nature. The unicorn and the pterodactyl, the brontosaurus and the roc. But also the cow, the rabbit and the goose, the mouse, the chicken and the snail.

Along the route were cascading fountains and marble statues. A few looked human, but most were mythological creatures that did not exist on earth. Winged creatures, goblins and storybook fairies, animals with human faces or people with animal bodies; and gigantic figures that looked like primitive gods. All formed with great skill and beauty. Every few blocks, there was an open area, apparently a park. There were benches here, of human size. But no one was there. Most curious of all was a range of mountains, with white, gleaming peaks that cut across the city. They looked man made. Too regular to be natural.

A miraculous city! But why was it empty and deserted? What catastrophe had caused these glorious streets to be abandoned? Yet once in a while we were conscious of moving shadows. Was *Anything* watching us?

"Let's try one of the houses," urged Bobby.

"People might get mad if we bust in."

"It don't look like there's anyone around."

We tried some of the more earth-like houses. Strangely, there didn't seem to be any door to enter. No bell or knocker or signal light. Nothing but walls.

The city was big. By now, we must have walked a couple of miles. At length we came to a street marker that looked like a wolf.

"A Coyote!" cried Brandon, happily. "That's our street. *Coyote Road!*"

A few blocks down "Coyote Road" was a building constructed of blue quartz and with a crystal roof. There was an archway here that opened into a courtyard. Donald led us in. I had a feeling we were being guided where to go. We weren't making up our own mind.

Inside the courtyard, was a grove of palm trees, surrounding a lotus-covered pool. The building was a quadrangle, with four doors, each of blue crystal. It looked like a palace or at least a great mansion. All the buildings did. There were no slums or shanties in this silent city.

We tried each door. There was no answer when we called and knocked. Just one door opened. Inside, was an elegant chamber that looked like the foyer of an expensive apartment house. Rich carpets, and elaborate furnishings, immaculately clean except for the dirt tracked in by our muddied boots. All at once, we felt crummy and out of place.

We discovered a spiral ramp and followed it upwards. The ramp ended in another blue crystal door. We knocked and called, not expecting anyone to answer, then pushed inside. The blue door closed behind us.

We counted our numbers. All twelve Naghallah boys were here. Cameron said, "Let us give thanks, brothers."

"To who?"

"To the Powers that be. Whoever runs this place."

The guys mumbled something. Troy, however, cried out in shock and fright. There was no longer any door behind us. Where the door had been, there was now a solid wall.

PRISONERS

We looked around. The room we entered was even fancier than the foyer. Like the throne room of an emperor. Two stories high, with delicate chandeliers, royal carpeting and furniture that belonged in a museum. There was even a carved and gilded chair that resembled a throne. We took our shoes off so as not to soil the rug.

Live flowering plants grew along the walls up to the ceiling. And lace-like leaves gave forth a gentle incense, like pine or new-mown hay.

There were windows here. We didn't remember seeing any from the outside. These windows, however, didn't look out either on the courtyard or on the city. One viewed a forest glade; another, the sea; another, a snow-capped mountain range; a fourth looked out on the open sky, with the three silver moons. Even as we watched, the scene changed. The sea became a river and the woodland glade a ravine.

"It ain't real," said Keith. "It must be some kind of a hologram. There really ain't any windows. We're locked in."

We were prisoners and had walked into a trap. But what a strange place to lock up twelve dirty, messed up gamins.

Earth prisons were never like this!

We had a moment of anger, fear and consternation. Stevie kicked wildly at the wall where the door had been. Then Bobby yelled, "There's food in the next room!"

And so there was. A real feast! Baked loaves of Earth style bread, rich butter, cheese and fruit. Dumplings, salads, puddings and pies. Tarts and fritters and a sweet drink that tasted like something out of Heaven. Whoever had taken us prisoner at least did not intend to starve us.

Hungry and thirsty though we were, we touched nothing until Donald had examined each food and declared it eatable.

For me and Danny, it was the best meal since we got shipped to *Kaah Naghallah*. Bobby and Raymond said it was the best meal they *ever* had. Maybe we were prisoners. But our captors couldn't be too mad at us. They could have terminated us without going to all this trouble.

Cameron said, "Thanks for the meal, Warden. But is there any place where we could wash?"

As if in answer, we saw another blue door that opened. Beyond it was a large bathroom with warm water and showers. And even structures like Earth sinks and toilets. And a cleansing, soap-like salve. We stripped off our clothes, patched with those cabbage-leaf plants and bathed.

There was also a chamber with nothing in it. But when you turned a silver knob, you could feel a warm radiance flowing through your body. It took away your aches and pains and gave you a wonderful feeling of strength and vitality. Must be some kind of rays.

The guys all thought it was great. "Good for whatever ails you." "Here's something they haven't invented on Earth yet."

Was there a bedroom? Yes, a real big one. With eight giant-size beds. There were sheets and pillows, too, like we never had at *Kaah Naghallah*.

We lay on our enormous beds with no clothes on. Maybe our captors would give us clothes . . . Sure enough, they did. First, our old clothes vanished. Then our new clothes suddenly appeared. Blue pants, socks and shirts, not quite the right size. Too big for Roger and Jody. A bit too small for the big boys. Our boots also disappeared and were returned later. They looked like the same boots, repaired and polished.

In the same way, our next meal came. It just appeared. We didn't see anybody bring it.

"Being locked in," said Bran, "makes me think we're back at the Institute."

"Yeah," said Keith, "but *Kaah Naghallah* was never like this." We ate waffles and melon and muffins and jam and a cocoa-like drink.

"What do we do now? Try to break out of here?"

"Why?" asked Cameron. "Let's just rest and eat. If we did break out, where would we go?"

Indeed, there was more to our quarters than we first thought. Beyond the bedroom was a disguised door that opened into the handsome chamber. All blue and gold, with a dozen arm chairs. Here, there were a number of cabinets containing strange machines and shelves piled with silver boxes bearing red markings. At the end of the room, was a sort of stage with a huge white screen. We guessed these machines must be some kind of movie projectors or record players. But we were too stupid to figure out how they worked.

It was like giving a computer to a two-year old. All we could do was make them whirl sideways and up and down. We turned them off. We didn't want to get our keepers mad by breaking them.

Roger and Jody kept exploring. They found another chamber, beyond the Blue and Gold room. It looked like something in a botanical garden. A huge place, filled with trees and shrubs and vines, fragrant herbs and growing plants.

There were fruit and nut trees and gigantic ferns and a vast array of flowers, seeds and berries. There was a flowing stream and a man-made grotto, with Goblins' Bread growing on the rocks. In the center, was a tremendous, spreading tree with heart-shaped, many-colored leaves, whose branches reached the high ceiling.

For the first time in the city, we saw animal life. Red and yellow birds and birds of blue and green, hiding shyly in the multi-colored leaves. There was also a pair of orange squirrels and a pair of red squirrels, three on a branch and another that ducked into a hollow.

In *Bane N'Gai,* the vegetation was remarkably fertile, yielding a new crop soon after the old crop was picked. There must be abundant food for these creatures right in the garden. But we brought them the left-overs of our feast.

It took some time until they came to us. The squirrels came first, grabbing a morsel and then racing away fast. Most of the birds came only to Donald, but the red birds were bolder and would grab food from all of us.

We were growing tired and returned to the bedroom. Here, eight Emperor-size beds with blue and gold covers were lined up in a double row.

For some reason, I started feeling scared, like when I was a little kid and couldn't sleep alone. The other guys felt that way, too. Not just Roger and Jody, but even Cameron and Stevie. Like something in the night would grab you, if you were alone. So we teamed up: Cameron and Roger, Donald and Jody, Bobby and Raymond, Keith and Stevie, Danny and Jaymie, Troy and Brandon. We left the two end beds empty.

Danny was in a mood for talking. "Hey, Jaymiebrudder!"

"Yeah, Dannybrudder."

"I hope they don't forget to feed us tomorrow."

"I hope so, too," said me, sleepily.

"If they do," continued Danny, "we can eat Goblins' Bread. That ain't bad, is it, Jaymie?"

"No, it's okay," said me, yawning.

"Hey, Jaymiebrudder. We seen a lot of Goblins' Bread. But you and me never seen a Goblin."

"Not yet," I agreed.

"We may see a Goblin soon, though. Maybe it's the Goblins that got us."

"I don't think it's the Goblins. They wouldn't have big beds like this."

"Goblins don't have to be small. They could be real big," declared Danny.

No answer.

"Hey, Jaymiebrudder! Don't go to sleep on me! I got to ask you a question. *Do you think we'll ever get home again?* You *want* to go back, don't you?"

"Not unless we all go back together."

"I'll stick right here," said Danny, "if things never get any worse than this."

THE GOLDEN PRISON

Day Thirty-four

An easy day in our golden prison. Great food and no labor. We might as well enjoy it and not worry about the future.

We kept exploring to find hidden cupboards and closets. We tapped the walls to see if they sounded hollow and did find a few hidden places. There was a sliding panel in the bedroom. Inside were towels, blankets, sheets and more earth-style clothing. All blue, even the sneakers. Enough for a couple of changes.

Troy discovered a hidden closet in the second room. There were lots of gadgets here. Most of them looked like some kind of games, but we couldn't figure them out. Maybe some alien psychologist was giving us an Intelligence Test. If so, we flunked.

There was a silver box with marking that we couldn't read. Maybe it said *Earth Toys for Infants.* In it were rattles, marbles, building blocks, clay and balloons.

We played marbles. We blew some balloons up and played balloon baseball. And we threw the clay at each other. Great fun! Later, we cleaned the clay up. That way, the alien shrink wouldn't figure us for idiots. Just imbeciles.

Day Thirty-Five

Another carefree day with nothing to do but goof around. Our food kept coming. The plants and creatures in the greenhouse make us feel like we were back in the Garden of Eden. Friendly and beautiful.

We found a hidden closet beyond the other closet. Inside was a silver tool chest. Some of the gadgets were weird. None of us could figure out any use for them. But some were the kind you would find in any American tool box. Hammers, pliers, wrenches, cutters... Useful if we wanted to break out of here. But nobody was in any hurry to try it.

We knotted up a towel and played our own form of football. That was a game we made up back at the Institute. Sooner or later, the Masters of *Kaah Naghallah* would break in and yell at us for being noisy. We'd end up having to do push-ups and bendovers. "Maybe *this* will tire you out and keep you quiet!" Nobody bothered us now.

The food was great! They were treating us well. We gave a cheer for our keepers. There was no reply. Donald, however, pointed to the wall. That wall had been heavy and solid before. Now it was somewhat transparent. You could see vague shapes moving on the other side.

"I guess we're sort of like animals in the zoo," said Keith. "They stick us in a fancy cage and watch us to see what makes us tick."

Or maybe they were trying to decide if we were dangerous.

THE SECRET ROOM

Day Thirty-Six

We talked about escaping and decided not to. "Let's enjoy our *Now*," urged Cameron. "Can you imagine a better set up than this?"

We tried to figure how our food got in and how our garbage got out. There must be secret passages somewhere. We searched, but didn't find them.

Troy, however, found when you rolled back the carpet in our bedroom, there was a trap door underneath. A folding ladder led downward. Was this a way to get out?

No. The ladder led down to a windowless room. The walls were covered with a rich brown wooden panelling. No sign of a door. But when we tapped, one wall was hollow. There was another hidden closet behind the panelling.

Something was moving inside the closet. Rats or mice. Their small eyes stared at us in surprise. Then they scurried out of sight. Where did they go?

The closet was empty except for a huge, bulky box. For some reason, I thought it was a coffin. I expected to find a dead body in it. I didn't know why or who.

Troy thought it was a pirates' treasure chest. "It must be filled with gold nuggets and pieces of eight."

As we looked closely, it turned into an old-fashioned steamer trunk. Locked up and bound by heavy wire. That trunk was awful heavy, like there were rocks in it. It took six of us to move it.

Taped on the top was a large, brown envelope. We opened it eagerly, only to find inside another brown envelope. Then still another envelope inside that. All blank. Must be somebody's idea of a joke.

That last envelope was still quite large and thick. We expected to find still more envelopes inside. Like the trick Marjorie Meyer and her sister played on Brother Danny on Valentine's Day. Nine different envelopes inside each other, all blank. Those girls must like Danny a lot to go to all that trouble.

But we could see markings on that third envelope that shaped into printed letters:

Karl Hasserman
Last Will and Testament

"Karl Hasserman!" Raymond whistled.

To Whom It May Concern:
I give the contents of this trunk to whoever shall bring these papers back to Earth and shall deliver them to the proper authorities.

Karl Hasserman was a multi-billionaire. So they said. Unless they had embezzled all his money. We wondered what kind of a will a billionaire would leave.

It was hand-writen, each letter carefully shaped. Although in English, some of the letters were in the German script. Like the number seven always had a line through it.

$$7$$

Karl Hasserman revoked all previous wills and made some bank his executor. Not Bartlow, his money man, nor Lammington, his Director-in-Chief nor any of the Masters of Naghallah. They weren't mentioned in the Will at all.

There followed a list of seventy people and organizations, each of which was to receive Seven hundred thousand ($700,000.00) dollars. Johanna the Cook and her sister, Minnie were on the list. So was Old George, the Gardener and Lyandra, the Nurse. Goose egg for Bartlow, Lammington, Striker, Klayborne, Powell and Company.

The Kaah Naghallah mansion and grounds and all the rest of his property were given to *The Karl Hasserman Foundation* to establish *The Karl Hasserman Museum* and *The Karl Hasserman Park and Nature Conservatory.*

That whole crowd of creeps we called *The Masters of*

Naghallah weren't going to like this Will at all!

Karl Hasserman's name was signed in flowing script, with elaborate curves and swiggles. And his seal was added. Dated about a year ago. There were three witnesses: Dean Harlow, Alice Harlow and Jerry Golding.

"Dean Harlow!" cried Jaymie. "That's the guy whose grave we found!"

"He's dead," said Raymond.

Bobby said, "Maybe we're dead, too."

"I don't feel dead," declared Troy.

"Who knows what it's like to be dead?" said Keith. "Maybe you die a whole lot of times and wake up in a different life."

"You're still the same guy?" asked Roger.

"We're all still like we was back on Earth, ain't we?"

"Is Karl Hasserman dead?" asked Stevie.

"Probably. If he's down here," reflected Cameron. "We can't be sure."

"If he's dead," asked Brandon, "what happened to the *Vrrooohn?*"

"Maybe it's in the trunk," said Danny, hopefully.

It was a tough job getting into the trunk. Nothing would cut those binding wires. But we managed to file them down until they broke. It was even harder to force the lock.

"Here goes!" cried Cameron.

He threw open the lid and yelled. We all yelled. For inside there was a host of hissing scorpions that flew out in all directions. I swear I felt a dozen of them land on me.

The people of *Bane N'Gai.* have the power to play tricks on your mind. When we looked again, there were no scorpions. The whole thing was a hallucination. The trunk was empty.

"It can't be empty!" cried Raymond in dismay. "That trunk was heavy!"

We looked again for the third time. Now, the trunk was full. Piled high with — with the most magnificent jewels we had ever seen or imagined. Something out of Aladdin's cave. Or the crown jewels in an emperor's strong box. Shining with unbelievable brilliance. Diamonds the size of an egg, bright red rubies, blue star sapphires, green emeralds and other stones of exotic colors and patterns, gleaming and glowing like a piece of the sun.

I shut my eyes again, expecting the jewels to disappear. They didn't. They were still there. The guys put their hands into the trunk to make sure the jewels were real. Each kid grabbed a fistful. We started to throw them at each other, like they were snowballs.

"Hold it!" cried Cameron. "Don't throw this stuff around. If we ever get back to Earth, these things are worth millions!"

"They got to be phony," Bobby insisted. "They can't be real."

"They're real if they come from Karl Hasserman."

"It's a set-up," said Keith. "This whole thing. They're watching us, whoever they are. They put this Hasserman stuff here to see what we would do."

"If they're watching us," said Cameron, "let's not act like a bunch of fucking assholes. Let's have a pillow fight or a shoe fight. But put the jewels back. Right, Gangleader?"

"Right," agreed Gangleader Don Don, a bit out of his element now that we were back in civilization. Donald had a fist full of jewels that he dropped reluctantly back into the trunk and the rest of us followed.

We gathered up the scattered jewels and closed up the trunk and the secret door. Then we went upstairs and had a shoe fight and a pillow fight and a water fight. We broke one pillow and the stuffings went all over the place. If that alien psychologist had marked us down before as half-wits, we must be rated nit-wits now.

The Meyer Family.

WHAT EVER HAPPENED TO THE KAAH NAGHALLAH SCHOOL?

Back on Earth, a new red station wagon drove down the long road from Mountainville to *Kaah Naghallah*. In it were Mr. and Mrs. Conrad Meyer and their daughters, Marjorie and Joyce. They were halted by a barrier at the entrance.

The party continued on foot and encountered a tall man in a brown uniform. The guard viewed them with suspicion. "This is private property."

"We came to see the boys, Daniel and Jaymie Larrabie. They're at the school here."

The guard told them no visitors were permitted.

"We came all the way from Greenwood to see the boys," pleaded Hilda Meyer. "We're friends and neighbors."

After much palavering, the tall man put in a call to the "main house". "I'm sorry. There are no boys here."

"There must be some mistake. They're students at the school."

"We don't have any school here."

"Perhaps we could talk to Dr. Mehary, the school director?"

Another call. "There is no such person here."

"Or Mr. Matthews, the boys' teacher?"

Another negative. The puzzled Meyers reboarded the station wagon, U-turned and drove back to Mountainville. Deeply concerned, Marjorie persuaded her parents to contact the police.

The Chief of Police in Mountainville was an old man with a hearing aid and two canes. He made notes on a yellow pad. "These boys. Are they related to you?"

"No. We're neighbors."

"There isn't much we can do, unless we hear from the family."

At the State Police, a young detective promised to "look into it."

Ditto at the Federal Bureau of Investigation.

Unable to contact the Larrabie parents by telephone, Conrad Meyer sent off an urgent cable:

Visited your sons' school. Something is very wrong there. Jaymie and Daniel may be in danger. Urge you return as soon as possible. Call us.
                        CONRAD, HILDA, MARJORIE
                        AND JOYCE MEYER

They sent similar messages to the known Larrabie relatives: Cousins Katie and Michael, Uncle Oscar and Aunt Rosa, Uncle Leon and Aunt Laura.

"We have done our duty," declared Hilda Meyer.

"I may have made a fool of myself," said Conrad Meyer, ruefully.

[End of Book Two]

BOOK III

THE DOOM MACHINE

And the Siege of Glow Malomba

The Adventurers	Cameron, Brandon, Danny Keith, Raymond, Roger Bobby, Jaymie, Donald Jody, Steve and Troy
The Goblin	Trycon Mu Garroh
Queen of the Otherworld	Queen Hecate
Her Deputy	Ral Garyon
Her Intelligence Agent	Lyandra
Her Great Grandson	Prince Frain
Royal Lemurian Cadets	Cadets Gledd and Kollen Corporal Tramm
The Destroyer	The Mord

Goblins, Lemurians, Oreads, Animal People
High Priestess, Prophetess, Royal Counsellor
Soldiers, Jurors, Citizens of Glow Malomba
Unicorns, Rocs, Squirrels, Song Birds
Creatures Great and Small

THE GOBLIN

Day Thirty-seven

We had been eating vegetarian since we broke out of our slave collars and they fed us vegetarian here. That was a hopeful sign. If our captors were vegetarians, they wouldn't eat *us*.

We fed our leftovers to the birds and beasts in the greenhouse garden and took some of their Goblins' Bread. You get a taste for it after a while. Then Jody and Roger told us they had seen a Goblin. "A real live one," said Jody. "Honest! Cross my heart."

"He was in the garden yesterday," Roger insisted. "And now he's in the parlor."

"Okay, we'll bite. Big joke. Show us the Goblin."

We went into the parlor and darned if there wasn't a Goblin there. At least a Being that looked like a storybook Goblin. About four feet high with a very large head and very little hair. The rest of him looked human, except he had six fingers on each hand. The Goblin was seated in the throne-like chair and rose as we entered.

"I am *Trycon Mu Garroh,*" he announced.

"I'm Roger," began Roger.

"Yes. We know who you are. We have been watching you. You have broken the law by coming into our city without our consent."

Cameron said, "We're sorry. But nobody told us to keep out."

"We are at war now. We had to make sure you were not sent by our enemy. I personally believe you are harmless and arrived here quite by accident. But I have no power to release you. That must be done by a higher authority."

Trycon was an investigator. Rather like a D.A. who has to decide whether to press charges or not. He spoke fluent English, but in an odd manner. Rather like he was chanting or singing instead of talking.

"We don't mind staying here," said Keith. "We like it here."

The Goblin's face grew grave. "You will not stay here long. The war goes badly. The city is in danger."

We were prisoners of the Goblins. And the Goblin nation was at war. We hoped they weren't fighting against humans. Then they would surely fancy us to be spies.

"Who are you?" asked Jaymie. "And who is your enemy?"

Trycon looked puzzled. "You really don't know?"

"Our nation is Lemuria. The *Mu Garroh* — you call us Goblins — are only one of the peoples of Lemuria. There are the *Oreads,* the Silver People of the woods and mountains. There are the Manlings and the Animal People.

"The Manlings are the Shining Ones, the People of the Rainbow. They look like *you*——" He pointed to Donald. "Their Queen is our Empress. We are proud to be their partners."

"What do we have to do?"

"Nothing. You must wait. I am the Examiner. You will meet with the Interrogator and have a Hearing. We must be sure you are not a carrier of the *Mord.*"

"We're from Earth," said Bobby. "We're not your enemies!"

"The *Mord* can move in many ways. It can come in the bodies of the Earth people, even without their knowledge. Like a plague for which there is no cure. This is *Glow Malomba,* the City of Wonder. But when the Destroyer comes, it will be ashes."

His voice broke. I thought for a moment that he was going to weep.

"We wouldn't hurt your city," said Danny. "We'll help defend it."

He smiled condescendingly. "I am sure you would try to help, if you could. You are not of the Destroyer. There is no *Mord* in you. Nor do you come to plunder, like other Earth people."

"We have watched you playing with the animals in the garden. And playing with each other. I sense no Death in you and no corruption. You are more like innocent children. You are Earth children?"

Trycon Mu Garroh

We considered ourselves young men, not children. And we sure weren't innocent. But if being children got us a better break, so be it.

"If you are children, how did you manage to get here?"

We told him. The whole story took close to an hour. Trycon appeared to listen with growing amazement. When we finally reached the river trip and our entrance into *Glow Malomba,* Trycon suddenly was no longer there.

Keith said, "You know what I think? He never *was* here. That was just a hologram. You know — like a TV projection."

Trycon the Goblin didn't trust us. He wouldn't walk in on twelve Earthlings any more than a guy would walk into a cage with twelve wild lions. Maybe he expected us to attack him or at least seize him and hold him hostage.

He wanted to get us talking and he did. But whatever that image was, it sure looked real.

THE VOICE FROM NOWHERE

There was something wrong with Donald. His face had that same vacant, wooden look like when I first saw him in the boycatcher van. After a while, he went into the greenhouse garden and stood there rigid. When you talked to him, he wouldn't answer.

"What's wrong, Don Don?" He wouldn't tell us.

"Leave him alone," urged Keith. "He's gone autistic again. He'll snap out of it, when he gets hungry." But Donald didn't come for lunch; and when we dragged him in, he wouldn't eat. Donald followed us into the parlor, sort of like a guy walking in his sleep. Maybe that was it. Donald was sleeping with his eyes open.

If it had been any other guy, we would have doused him with cold water. But with Donald you had to be careful. He was different and might explode.

"Just let him stick around," urged Cameron. "It'll wear off."

Maybe. Or had some strange Power crept in and seized control of Donald's mind? That would not only put Donald out of action, but leave the rest of us helpless in this Unknown World.

Cameron had to take over as Gangleader again. But before he could call a gang meeting, some peculiar things happened. A door slammed. A chair toppled over. A table leaped right up into the air and flew around. A golden vase went flying past me and crashed into the wall. It was like something that a poltergeist did. If you believed in poltergeists. Was Donald doing it? There was no sign of anything in that wooden face of his.

Now a Voice came out of Nowhere, maybe out of the ceiling. "Good evening, gentlemen." It was early afternoon, so far as we could guess. But down here you couldn't tell.

"Who's there?" demanded Steve.

"I am one of you. I am from Earth."

"Where are you?" We could see nothing.

"I am right beside you," said the Voice-from-Nowhere. "I am a friend." The Voice sounded metallic, like a recording. But it couldn't be, because it was answering us.

"You are prisoners of the Lemurians. They are playing games with you. *Do not trust them. They are telling you lies.*"

"Who are you?" demanded Raymond.

"I am an American. I can help you escape."

Bobby said, "We don't feel much like escaping. We like it here."

"You're not going to like it very long. Some very unpleasant things are going to happen. You are being fattened up like a Thanksgiving turkey. The Lemurians have some rather barbaric customs and rituals."

These words were spoken in a chilling voice. We remembered that bloody altar in the Temple of the Demon-Idol. We looked at each other and shuddered.

Yet somehow it was hard to believe. The builders of this beautiful city had seemed a kindly and a civilized people. We all had tagged them for good guys. And Trycon, their spokesman, had appeared friendly and likeable. But we were foreigners, invaders, and in their eyes, barbarians. If they turned nasty, we could expect little mercy.

"I can help you escape," promised the Stranger. "But you must act quickly. You must follow orders and do what I tell you without question. . . . Behind the silver blossoms on the wall there is a lock. And hidden in the sofa is a red key. Take what weapons you can and be prepared to use them. Don't let anyone stop you, if you value your life. . . ."

The Voice faded. We searched through the apartment, including all the hidden places, but there was nothing there. No living creatures, excepting the birds and squirrels of the garden.

Cameron said, "It seems a shame to cut up this beautiful sofa." Actually, we just had to make a slit underneath. We could feel a key there.

Now we searched behind the flowers for the lock. This was the outer wall of the apartment. It might open up a secret passageway. The whole apartment abounded in secret doors and hidden places. We kept finding more and more of them. Brother Danny gave a cry of triumph. There was a light fixture here and you could pry it out. *Here was the lock.*

Keith said, "The whole thing seems pretty phony to me. This guy claims to be an Earth-American. How come he can just walk around and give us messages? The Lemurians are pretty clever. How come they don't spot him?"

"Maybe he's a Lemurian who likes little children and don't want to see us get carved up on the Altar — or whatever they do to their victims."

"Maybe he's an Enemy who wants to knock off some Lemurians and don't care if he gets us knocked off, too."

Danny took the key and shoved it into the lock. "Quiet, you guys! I can't hear."

"Hear what?"

"Hey, Jaymie. Come up here!"

I came and put my ear against the lock. I could hear music. A haunting melody, weird and unforgettable. The sweet, sad music that came to us on the rock above *The*

Dark Wonderland. The enchanting call of *The Nothing That is Everything.* The fatal strain that came before the *Leap of Death.*

Danny shuddered. My hands were shaking and I pulled myself away.

"Throw away that key!" said Danny. "And keep away from that lock. Whatever lies behind that door, it isn't freedom!"

*   *   *   *   *   *   *

All the time, Donald did nothing. He just stood around. When supper came, the guys dragged him into the dining room, but he wouldn't eat. At length, he curled up in one of the empty beds and pulled the sheets over his head.

I woke up in the middle of the night. Someone was crying like a little kid. I saw Donald now was awake, too. He was sitting on the edge of the bed, sobbing his heart out.

After a while, he walked over to the greenhouse garden. Once again, he became the autistic kid, standing there rigidly.

"Please answer, Don Don. Whatever happened, let us help! You're our leader, Don Don. The guys would do *anything* for you!"

He made no reply. Just stood there like a statue. Silent and alone.

THROUGH THE HIDDEN DOOR

Day Thirty-eight

When we woke up in the morning, Donald was gone. We searched everywhere, including all the hidden places, and couldn't find him. Did he go out by the secret door? Danny didn't think so. The wall was undisturbed and Danny still had the key.

"Donald didn't leave by himself," concluded Raymond. "Something came in and got him."

The guys were all scared at first. But after a while, they got angry. They got mad at me and Danny, too, because we talked them out of opening that hidden door. We might have escaped while we were all still together.

"Why did they pick on Don Don?"

"Because he's the Gangleader. Because without him we would have been wasted that first week. Without Don Don, we would never have made it here."

Cameron said, "Donald has always been a lone wolf. Maybe he left by himself. Maybe he had a good reason for going.

"It ain't like when they grabbed me back in *Kaah Naghallah*. That was by force. Don Don must have gone voluntarily. If he had put up a fight, we would have heard him." There was no sign of any struggle.

"Maybe they ambushed him in the garden and knocked him out."

"Maybe they doped him. He looked like he was drugged already."

"Maybe they hypnotized him." The Lemurians had mind power. Somehow, we eleven kids had done for Donald what the doctors couldn't do. Turned this autistic boy into a youth who was not only sane but splendid. Yet how easy it might be to monkey with his brain and drive him back again.

We began shouting and yelling and pounding and making a racket. Like we did back in *Kaah Naghallah* reform school. However, there was no sign that anyone cared how much noise we made or even heard us. We pleaded and we threatened, but they made no answer.

There was nothing else to do, so we held a gang meeting. Cameron was made Gangleader again, until Donald came back. We held gang meetings nearly every day. They always started with the roll call and the oath.

We were probably the World's only gang of juvenile delinquents that operated by parliamentary procedure. Cameron got a kick out of presiding. He was — or thought he was — the illegitimate son of some big shot Southern politician. Everything had to be done by the book. Like we were the City Council instead of a bunch of juvenile hoods.

Everything had to be moved and seconded. One boy, one vote. "And put your hand up, if you want to talk! Don't speak out of turn. . . . Sit down, Brother Troy! Quit jumping around.

"Come on, guys! Let's have some order here!" Cameron pounded on the table with a shoe.

There was a moment of silence. "Anyone want to make a motion?" asked Cameron, hopefully.

"Yeah!" cried Danny. "I move we knock down the chandelier!" The guys didn't wait for a vote. We tugged and pulled and pounded. The magnificent crystal chandelier crashed to the floor.

Raymond was holding an axe, Bobby a hammer. "I call the mirror," said Raymond.

"I'll choose you," said Bobby.

"Odds. One takes it."

"Hold it, guys!" yelled Cameron. "That's enough for now." And he shouted at the ceiling. "We'll wreck everything in this whole place, if you don't bring Donald back!"

"Not the garden!" cried Brandon. "That's for the animals."

"I move," said Keith, "that we don't touch the garden. We do nothing to hurt the animals."

"Second," said Steve. "We don't touch the garden, but smash up all the rest of the fucking place!"

"That's *two* motions," objected Chairman Cameron. "We'll vote on the garden first:

We do nothing to hurt the animals and leave the garden alone. Carried 11 to 0.

"Now about smashing up everything else. All in favor—"

"I take it back," said Stevie. "We might still have to live here."

"Without Don Don?"

"I ain't forgettin Don Don. Let's wait two hours. If Donald still don't show and we don't get no message, we break out."

"How?"

"Like the Voice said, *Open up the lock.* No matter what's behind it, we go right through and tear the town apart until we find Don Don."

* * * * * * *

The two hours expired. Raymond swung the axe against the mirror. Bobby swung the hammer. Strangely, this mirror didn't break, despite repeated blows. Roger struck vainly at the throne chair without making a chip in it. Jody strained hard and managed to rip a curtain. Troy pulled a tapestry down. Danny kicked vainly at the false window, hurting his foot. Brandon knocked over a table.

"Cut it!" ordered Cameron. "Everyone get yourself a weapon. I'm going to open up the lock. Do you hear anything, Jaymie?"

I put my ear against the lock. No music this time. "But I think I hear something."

"Quiet, you guys! What?"

"I hear footsteps. Real heavy! The wall is shaking a bit. I think there's something real big on the other side."

"Like what?"

"The Purple People Eater," suggested Keith. "It's about time for another Horror."

Cameron brandished the red key. "Who wants to go first?"

"I'll go first," volunteered Jaymie. If there was something deadly behind that door, it wouldn't matter if you were first or last.

"The Gangleader has to be first," Cameron decided.

"You shouldn't be. A general's never on the front line. You got to see what is happening and then give us orders."

There was a scraping sound on the other side of the wall. Something was pressing against the hidden door, trying to get in. The damn thing was beginning to move!

"Stand back! Something's coming in! Get your weapons ready!"

The Coyotes drew back in battle formation, with hammer, wrench, dagger, knife, saw and axe. The door moved just a little. . . . Then a little more. . . .

"Here it comes!"

The Thing was breaking through. The wall flew open. . . . Then, before our astonished eyes, an elderly lady entered.

"Goodness! What have you been doing? Who pulled down this chandelier?"

There was something oddly familiar about the woman. Yet I could swear I had never seen her before. Her hair was straw yellow, not white, as I had first thought. Her eyes were yellow, her shoulders broad and strong. She walked sprightly, despite her years, with an almost military bearing.

"Put those silly things down, boys! What's the matter with you?"

I recognized her now. The nurse from *Kaah Naghallah*. Or rather Karl Hasserman's nurse. I said, "Hi, Lyandra!"

"Hi, Jaymie! Hi, Cameron, Stevie, Keith, Danny, Raymond, Bobby, Troy, Brandon, Roger and Jody. And where is Donald?"

"Don't you know?" demanded Steve.

"I think perhaps I do. Do not be concerned about him. Donald will come back. Is that why you started to tear this place apart?"

We felt sheepish. Instead of bold warriors, we began to feel like kindergarten kids caught stealing toys. "You look different, Lyandra."

"This is what I really look like. On Earth, I had to wear make-up. Eye contacts. Hair dye. You see, I am Lemurian."

"You mean you had a disguise on? You were a spy?"

"Let's say I was an Intelligence agent. There are others—"

"You mean Lemuria is trying to take over the Earth?"

Lyandra laughed. "We don't need Earth. We are happy in our own land. But we have to protect ourselves. Earth numbers in the billions. We, in the thousands. All the Lemurians alive would fit into a single American city. . . ."

"Why did they take Donald? What are they going to do to him?"

"They want to ask him questions. You can be sure they won't hurt him. *You see Donald is Lemurian, too.*"

It was really not surprising. That very light hair and pale skin and gleaming yellow eyes were all signs of a race that lived in a twilight, sunless world. Yet, it was warm here. The heat must come from the Underground.

Donald was an experiment. A Lemurian zygote, transported into an Earth mother's body. A failed experiment, it was believed, and a forbidden one, proscribed by Lemurian law.

To the Earth doctors, Donald was the victim of a freakish disease. But now, after he had lived among the Coyote brothers, that moribund seed that was Donald had burst into growth.

Because of his strange and unnatural birth, it was feared that Donald might have become a carrier of the *Mord*. And we, his companions, might be contaminated, too.

The *Mord* was a fearsome thing. At its center, was a Death Machine that moved ever closer to the Lemurian heartland. Yet it also managed to infect living beings, spreading centers of decay and corruption everywhere.

No one knew just what the *Mord* was like. No one who had gone to fight the *Mord* had ever returned to tell about it.

"Why do they hate you so much, this Enemy?"

Lyandra's voice trembled. "Many years ago — many thousands of years — the Lemurians committed a terrible crime. We tried to destroy *Them*. Now they are preparing to destroy *Us*."

The *Mord*, the Mind-destroyer, was at the gates of *Glow Malomba*. "When it comes, that will be the end of Lemuria."

Lyandra didn't say *"If it comes..."* She said, *"When..."* Like Trycon, she had little hope.

Still, Lemuria did not want to die. They wanted to resist as long as possible. "You came into our city in a most surprising way. No Earthman except Karl Hasserman was able to come here and when he came, it was much easier than now.

"You made an impossible journey. The Council could not believe that twelve children — excuse me, twelve very young men — could get through, when far better prepared Earth adults had tried and failed."

"We were real lucky," said Keith.

"That's what I told them. Lucky and resourceful. But the Council wouldn't believe that. No matter how lucky, you couldn't make it. Unless — I hate to say this — Unless you were guided here by the forces of our enemy. Unless you were a carrier of the *Mord* and part of the plan to destroy us."

Bobby broke in, "But you know us, Lyandra. Can't you tell them? We would never hurt your people. Or hurt Don Don's people! You know what we are."

"I know what you were back at the school. I don't know what happened to you after you went through this Gateway. The *Mord* can creep into your bodies and possess you, regardless of your will."

"You mean we're sort of like a Trojan horse?"

"More like a Typhoid Mary, who carries the plague.

"That is why they called Donald. We Lemurians have telepathic powers. But we find it hard to read Earth minds. We could not read the minds of you boys, except on the low, outer level. We know you did not intend to harm us, except to steal the *Vrrooohn*."

Cameron gulped. "You know about that?"

"Yes. We do not blame you. You were sent to do it. Anyway, the *Vrrooohn* does not matter any more."

"Donald is Lemurian. We can read his deep, inner mind. Then we will learn how to read yours. After that, he will come back to you."

"That guy yesterday who said he was an American? Was that for real?"

"He was really a *Mu Garroh.* That was a test."

"That music we heard —" cried Danny. "The Death Music —"

"That was a test, too. Had you been infected by the Mord, it would have drawn you irresistibly. But it repelled you. That is in your favor, though not conclusive."

"What would happen," asked Keith, nervously, "if you find we are infected by the Mind Destroyer?"

Lyandra smiled, "The Lemurians are forbidden to take anyone's life or to harm their fellow creatures. But you would have to leave the city, as Karl Hasserman did. He and three companions followed the river toward the Great Sea. They took the *Vrrooohn* with them."

"Are they still alive?"

"We don't think so. They went to the *Mord.* No one who has reached the Mind Destroyer has ever returned alive."

There was a long, gloomy silence. Then Jody asked, "When will Don Don come back?"

"He is coming now," said Lyandra.

Donald came, not by the secret passageway, but by the door that turned into a wall when we came in. That door was concealed by an An-mir, an anti-mirage, like the boat on the river.

The Lemurians must have done a first aid job on Donald's mind. He was acting quite normal now, a bit embarrassed about going off and leaving us.

Being a Lemurian didn't bother Donald particularly. Nor even surprise him. The things he knew instinctively about *Bane N'Gai* — of Goblins' Bread, the healing mud, the plant and animal life and how to find water — could only come from someone who belonged here.

The thing that hit Donald was a terrible sadness. For the Lemuria that had been and would be no more. The end of the wonderful homeland he had just come to know. *Nada, Lemuria!* Donald was calm now, though still sad.

"Sorry I left you." A weak smile. "Am I still in the Coyotes?"

"Sure, Don Don. You're our leader. We all want you!"

Donald felt he was unworthy. He had been tried in the balance and found wanting.

"Well, nobody's perfect," argued Cameron. "We all loused up, including me."

Could a bunch of Earth kids have a Lemurian for their Gangleader? Well, why not? "Keep it, Don Don! We need you." He still refused.

"Tony is Gangleader again." A teasing smile. He knew Cameron didn't like to be called *Tony.*

Donald asked, "Who wrecked the room here?"

"We all did," said Cameron sheepishly. "Sorry about the chandelier."

"It wasn't your fault," declared Lyandra. "You're fond of Don Don and they shouldn't have taken him away without telling you why."

On Earth, that fancy and delicate crystal chandelier would have cost many thousands of dollars. If it could be replaced at all. But here it would be easy. The Goblins, who were master craftsmen, never stopped making things, whether they were needed or not. They must have hundreds of beautiful chandeliers piled up in storage, waiting for a place to put them.

Incidentally, they had found no trace of the *Mord* in Donald, nor in any of us. So far, at least. But the decisive test was yet to come.

AMERICAN STYLE JUSTICE

The Thirty-Ninth Day

We had a great meal that night. Lemurian food, served with rare spices, herbs and sauces. This would be our last night here, if we were found guilty and kicked out.

Lyandra joined us. We asked her how the food came. Secret passages, of course. There were lots of them we hadn't discovered yet. The Lemurians loved these things.

There were openings in the walls, concealed by an anti-mirage. There were locks "put in the *Quayne,*" which is a kind of time warp, hidden to the eyes and touch of ordinary men. How do you make an *An-mir* or a *Quayne*? You do it with your mind. Could an Earthman do it? With the *Vrrooohn,* he might. It takes an awful lot of Mindpower.

Lyandra was real sweet and friendly, but she actually told us very little. We kept forgetting we were suspected of being Enemy spies and Terrorists.

If we *did* get kicked out, where would we go? We could try to find our way back to the Gateway, which almost certainly would be sealed against us, even if we could make it through the Labyrinth. Maybe we could find the *Garden of Eden* again; this time, hopefully, without any Horrors.

What should the well dressed youth wear to his trial for treason and terrorism? A Lemurian would spend a good deal of time choosing the correct costume, which would be furnished at state expense. You could keep it, even if you were sentenced to be thrown out.

Trycon, the Goblin, told us not to worry. We would receive "American-style justice" and get as fair a trial as we would on Earth. That sounded pretty ominous to us.

For our "American-style justice", they got us blue jeans, blue T-shirts and sneakers. Lyandra must have picked them out. The Lemurians wore all kinds of peculiar clothes, often looking like they were going to a fancy dress ball.

"Will there be a jury? Will we get a lawyer?"

"You already have a lawyer. Lyandra. She has already

talked to the jury."

"Without us being there?"

"They have seen you. The jury has been watching you."

They probably watched us trying to wreck the parlor. That, however, turned out to be a point in our favor. They expected Earth people to have bad manners and a bad temper. Had we been infected by the *Mord*, we would instead have acted smooth and sneaky.

A delegation came to lead us to the Judgement Chamber. Besides Lyandra and Trycon, there were two young men in fancy military uniforms, with lots of gold braid, lace and medals.

The fifth individual, I swear, looked just like a kangaroo and hopped like a kangaroo. The citizens of Lemuria included a number of intelligent animal races. The lady kangaroo, though, had hands with fingers. She was the only one who carried what looked like a weapon. A black box with a long handle. She talked into it, making funny noises.

They must have done something to our hair and ears, though we didn't feel it. We each had a red and yellow glow around us. That was to warn people we were going on trial as suspected criminals. Don't abuse us. But don't trust us or get too friendly.

"You lead, Don Don." Donald didn't want to.

"Okay," called Cameron. "Form column of twos and follow our escort."

And the procession of twelve Earth youths, three Lemurians, one Goblin and one Kangaroo Lady moved out onto the boulevard.

When we first came to *Glow Malomba*, the city appeared empty and deserted. Now it was teeming with life. Somehow, our first arrival had triggered an alarm. People got out of the way, went into hiding or concealed themselves behind an anti-mirage. They thought, or feared, we were part of the *Mord*.

Now there were many Lemurians on the streets, all with tall bodies, straw-colored hair and yellow eyes. There were also a number of Goblins and elf-like Oreads, clad in

bright garments, with feathered hats. People were looking at us curiously. Lemurians are too polite to stare. But
you could see them give us a quick glance and then turn
away. You could almost hear them talk:

"Those are the prisoners?"

"The Invaders."

"We captured them before they could start anything."

"So *that's* what Earth people look like."

"They're going on trial."

"They don't look very dangerous."

"You never can judge by appearances."

"They don't look too different from us."

"Their minds are different. The Earth people are still
savages."

We arrived at the Courthouse. Two young men in fancy
blue uniforms came forward to receive us. They had even
more gold braid decorations than the first two. The four
musical comedy soldiers exchanged greetings. It wasn't
exactly a salute. More like thumbing their noses at each
other. In Lemuria, apparently, that was a gesture of respect. Cameron punched Roger to keep him from giggling.

A group of people with cow-like heads and horns came
prancing by. They m-o-o-o-o-ed at us and we m-o-o-o-o-ed
back politely. We had to be careful not to insult anybody.
They might be on the jury.

A brown setter dog, or what looked like one, guided us
inside. Like all the intelligent animal races, she had
human-like hands. She talked, too, in musical Lemurian,
with just an occasional bark. Then the soldiers and the
Kangaroo lady barked back and everybody laughed. We
didn't get the joke.

We got on a ramp on a spiral escalator. All at once, we
found ourselves in a large room, without ever going
through a door. A lady *Oread*, with antennae on her head,
checked off our names. "The accused will face the jury."
But we couldn't see any jury. Just a blank wall.

To the left was a tremendous mirror. I think there were
people behind it, watching the trial. That way, they could
view us without appearing to stare. Jody stuck his tongue

out at the mirror. Troy made the *Fuck You* sign. There
was no response.

On the right side, there was a complicated machine,
with all kinds of dials and discs and keys and pushbut-
tons; flashing lights, printers, recorders and moving
parts. We guessed it must be some kind of a computer.

"Are we being tried by computer!" protested Keith. "I
thought we would get a jury trial!"

"You will have one," assured Trycon. "That — computer, as you call it, is merely to assist the jury —"

"Be seated, please!" The Setter Dog Lady spoke in
English. There were twelve chairs. We took our seats in
no particular order.

Now the Court Attendants, two more *Oread* Elves,
placed something over our heads. It looked like an electric
hair dryer, but with no wires attached. I feared this might
be an instrument of torture and we would be coerced into
confessing. But the contraption caused no feeling and
was almost noiseless. There was a faint roaring sound,
like a sea shell held against your ear.

Somewhere in the distance, a bell sounded and the trial
began. It was a strange trial. No word was spoken and no
evidence presented. We sat there in silence. Roger started
to giggle again, but the rest of the guys were grave and
nervous. Troy kept wriggling and jumping out of his
chair. Cameron socked Roger and Troy and they became
quiet.

Jody was sucking his thumb. Bobby was biting his
nails. Donald's pale face was paler still. Brother Danny
was sweating. Stevie wiped his nose with his sleeve. Keith
stared anxiously at the computer. Raymond kept tighten-
ing his shoe laces. Brandon shivered, though the room
was warm.

Cameron's heart was beating so loudly you could hear
it. You could hear Jaymie's heart beating, too. . . . . .

That head piece they had on us must be a brain scanner,
a deep-mind reader. By now, they must know *everything*
about us.

THE VERDICT

The computer was talking. Or something was talking. In English. I couldn't tell if it was speech or telepathy into our minds. The sentences were a translation from the Lemurian and came out awkward and funny. *The examination has been completed. The jury has finalized its deliberations.*

We could see the jury before us, though we knew they weren't really there. Like Trycon in the beginning, this was a hologram. One Lady Goblin, One Elf with pointed ears, Three Lemurians; one man, two ladies. And the sixth juror looked like an enormous black cat, wearing a diamond necklace.

"Will the defendants please rise and face the jury." Though spoken politely, that was a command, not a request. We all stood up.

"Pronounce the verdict, please." The whole thing was crazy. Scarey and at the same time comical. The Coyote boys, though, were all nervous and shaky.

Now another voice, louder and deeper, spoke out of Nowhere. I heard it in my ears, yet felt it must be in the mind.

"The Neophyte Earthling, Cameron of Westcott-Naghallah (*a pause*) *Innocent and Acquitted.*" Cameron gave a deep sigh of relief.

"The Neophyte Earthling, Steven of Scanlon-Naghallah — *Innocent and Acquitted.*" Stevie rubbed the sweat off his face.

"The Neophyte Earthling, Keith of Caldwell-Naghallah — *Innocent and Acquitted.*" Keith looked like he had gotten a reprieve from hanging.

"The Neophyte Earthling, Robert of Alliconda-Naghallah — *Innocent and Acquitted.*" Bobby looked bewildered.

"The Neophyte Earthling, Raymond of Ridgeway-Naghallah — *Innocent and Acquitted.*" Raymond broke into a weak smile.

"The Neophyte Earthling, Daniel of Larrabie-Greenwood — *Innocent and Acquitted.*" Danny pulled up his pants and grinned.

"The Neophyte Earthlings, Brandon, Troy, Jody, Roger and Jaymie. All *Innocent and Acquitted!*"

Silly Roger giggled again. This time, nobody socked him.

What about Donald? There was a momentary pause. Then a separate announcement. "The Neophyte Transling, Donald of Turrentine Glow-Malomba Crossways — *Innocent and Acquitted.*"

The guys all broke into cheers.

Such an outbreak of rowdy behavior shocked the Lemurians, who took these occasions very seriously. Noisy yelling in the Courtroom was the very height of bad taste. Earth people, of course, were known to be crude and vulgar. But even so! Even the Pussycat looked shocked.

Fortunately, we were not on trial for bad manners. Then we would have been found guilty for sure.

THE ASSISTANT DEPUTY CHANCELLOR

The Setter Dog Lady came in and woofed for attention. There was going to be another trial. Lyandra said we could stay and watch it, if we wanted to. Nobody particularly wanted to. Lemurian trials might be fair, but they were boring.

"This trial is about chandeliers." Someone was suing the Queen.

"Suing the Queen!"

"It's ridiculous," said Trycon. "They have to give him a trial, if he asks for it. But they'll throw the whole thing right out."

It was a nuisance suit brought by one of his fellow Goblins. He had made chandeliers for the palace and didn't get paid; or rather overcharged outrageously and didn't get paid enough.

Would the Queen herself appear? Not in so trivial a matter. The Queen would be represented by the Second Deputy Assistant Royal Chancellor, whose name was Ral Garyon. A friend of Lyandra's. Ral looked like a high school student. But Lemurians are always older than they look.

We decided to stay. It might be good for a laugh. And it was. Ral and the Goblin kept yelling at each other in Lemurian. And the Setter Dog Lady kept butting in and woofing.

The Goblin kept jumping up and down. His manners were as bad as the Earthlings. A most undignified trial!

They had the same jury as we did, including the Pussycat. The jury did give the Goblin something, but not much.

Days Thirty-nine to Forty- one

Now that we were acquitted, everyone was real nice to us and sort of apologetic for putting us on trial as Enemy agents. Ral Garyon guided us and showed us the City. He told us we could stay here now, if we wanted to. We could learn basic Lemurian and become students. There were a lot of people who would like to study *Us*, if we didn't mind.

"You mean go to school?" asked Stevie, who didn't particularly relish the idea.

"If you wanted to. Students get paid."

"What would happen," asked Keith, "if you took the pay and didn't study? Suppose you flunked everything. Would they kick you out?"

"They wouldn't kick you out," said Ral. "But people would laugh at you." The Lemurians didn't like to be laughed at.

Ral feared, however, that our school wouldn't last very long. The *Mord* — the Mind-Destroyer — was only fourteen miles from Glow Malomba.

We had dinner one night with Lyandra, one night with Ral and his family, and on the third night with Trycon, the Goblin. Those man-made mountains stretching across

A most undignified trial.

the City were the abode of the Goblins, who liked to live underground. They never felt altogether comfortable on the surface world.

We told our new friends all our adventures, most of which they knew already. And they, in turn, told us the story of Lemuria.

THE ENDLESS WAR

Long, long ago, when the Earth people were still living in caves and trees, there was in the center of the Galaxy a great civilization: *Lemuria.*

The Old Lemurians were a dark-skinned people who lived on a hot planet with two suns. They built great cities, developed space travel and worshipped *The Great Mother.*

The Ruler of Lemuria, elected by the citizens, was known as *The Guardian.* In time, he became *The King.* Then, as Lemuria expanded, *The Emperor.* Now, no longer chosen by the people but by a hierarchy of nobles.

In the beginning, the Empire spread by trade and persuasion. New peoples and planets were taken into a union of equals and given full citizenship in the Lemurian Empire. "But in time, we became arrogant. Those who resisted were annexed with brutal force."

A change came over the Lemurians. They became a warrior nation, cruel and ruthless, yet glorious and irresistible. The Supreme Ruler became *The Holy Emperor, God-King of the Universe, Lord of the Space-Ways, Monarch of the Cosmos.* That was his modest title. He abandoned the cathedrals to *The Great Mother.* Instead, he built temples to the Demons of Power and Might, and conceived himself to be one of them.

"Everything fell before us until we reached the Silicon Planet. The Machine People of the Silicon Planet would not yield to us. So we destroyed them, utterly and completely. Exterminated every one of them and turned their home planet into a fiery wasteland. *Thus shall perish all those who defy the Lemurians!*

"That was a hideous deed, a horrifying crime. An evil for which we met a horrifying retribution.

"They were wiped out, our enemies. So we thought. But a few escaped and lived on on the very edge of the Galaxy. There, they swore eternal vengeance. To destroy the Lemurians utterly and completely, as we had done to them — or tried to do.

"For centuries, they lived in hiding. Then they gathered their strength and with strange new weapons, struck back at us. The Lemurian Empire frayed and crumbled. Our outposts were overrun; our forward defenses were shattered. Year after year, we fell back. Withdrawing, they kept saying, to a more defensible position. Then, in what must have been the greatest battle in all Creation, our Space Fleet was wiped out, leaving us helpless.

"The Emperor prepared to flee. His Demon-gods did nothing to save us. Their temples had become increasingly corrupt and evil. Shameful to say, there were human sacrifices there.

"The people now rose in revolt. Mobs attacked the palace. The Holy Emperor, God-king of the Universe, was dragged through the streets and hanged.

"The oppressed serfs and slaves put their Masters to the sword. The priests of the Demon-gods were slaughtered on their own altars and their temples burned to the ground."

After years of anarchy, a revolutionary government was formed that sued for peace. "But our enemies were determined to destroy us utterly. To exterminate every last Lemurian and all our allies. The Enemy could have taken over all the wealth and wisdom of the Old Lemuria. Instead, they wiped it out.

"But Lemurians are resourceful. They escaped in whatever space ships they could muster. They scattered in all directions and broke off communications, making it hard to track them. Enemy warships hunted them down relentlessly. Many were destroyed, but some escaped.

"For many centuries, the only way to survive was to keep moving. Wherever there was a permanent settlement, the Machine People would discover it and wipe it out."

We realized now that Ral was no longer speaking, but was projecting an image. We could see it all with our mind's eye. The decay of a once glorious civilization. The colossal space battle in which billions may have perished. The crazed tyrants and cruel priests of the Temple of Terror and Death. The frenzied mob of oppressed peoples rising to slaughter their oppressors. The fanatical and merciless invaders with their Hellish weapons. The doom and ruin of the Great Galactic Empire. And the desperate flight of a few survivors. It had all happened here on Earth, too. Not quite the same way.

Ral was speaking now: "About thirty thousand Earthyears ago, three small Lemurian space ships landed on the continent of North America. With them, were a group of *Oreads* and *Mu Garroh* and some of the Animal People, ancient allies who chose to stand with the Lemurians in adversity.

"Here, for a thousand years, hidden in the forests and mountains, the fugitives lived in peace and safety. Until the deadly eyes of the Enemy scout machines came over the land and marked them for extinction. These were robot ships, without pilots, spying the entire Universe.

"In the vastness of Space, we had about a hundred years before the signal was transmitted and the Enemy destroyers came over the land. We were the last Lemurians, as far as we knew. All the others were gone. In a hundred years, we would be gone, too.

"Desperate and without hope, the Lemurians came upon the Gateway, the *Kaah Naghallah* passage to *Bane N'Gai*. An Alternate World in a new Dimension, parallel and perpendicular to the Universe we had known. Into this new dimension, the spy ships of the Machine People would be unable to follow us. They would send back a message that Lemuria was no more.

"Then we destroyed all traces of Lemurian settlements;

turned our villages back into field and forest."

The Lemurians abandoned the continent about a thousand years before the Indians crossed the Bering Straits from Asia. They had done their task of concealment well, leaving behind no ruins nor artifacts. "We destroyed every building, every landmark, even our burial grounds, that the Machine People could not trace us. . . . ."

THE COMING OF THE MORD

"The World is of the nature of Mind. And by our minds, we created a new Lemuria. A Place joined to Earth, yet not of Earth."

In this Alternate World, by the power of the mind, the Lemurians could anticipate any attack by material weapons, and counteract it.

Living close together, in their centuries as fugitives, the Lemurians developed a collective consciousness. Even in the vastness of *Bane N'Gai*, they continued to live close together, as in their space ship days. In this weird but lovely world without a sun, their hair and skin became very light, their eyes yellow and glowing.

"We are an ancient people. We have mastered both the lore of the ancient sorcerers and the principles of the higher sciences. Yet for the evil we had done, we would atone. So we swore never to use our knowledge to oppress our fellow creatures, nor to destroy any living thing possessing mind or spirit. We hoped now to turn our hands to creating beauty and our minds to Transcendental Thought. But our ancient enemies would not let us be. . . . ."

Ral's yellow eyes now stared trance-like into the sky. "I sometimes think there is a Devil. Or that those Demon-gods we once worshipped are real and seek revenge on us for destroying their priests and their temples. Only a diabolical Power could have created the *Mord.*"

The *Mord* ravages the mind instead of the body. The highest and most intelligent minds were the most vulnerable.

No one who had witnessed the *Mord* had come back to describe it. The *Mord* was known only by what it did. First, there was a terrible fear. Then Madness. Then a mindless state, leaving the body an empty shell. At last, the mindless body decayed and perished. Those who were infected by the Mind-Destroyer seemed to have the Power to infect others.

The *Mord*, said Ral, had been tuned to the Lemurian mind. "Conceived to track us down anywhere throughout the whole of Creation."

About a thousand years ago, it crossed the Veil; moving slowly but inexorably toward the Lemurian heartland. In the *Endless War*, a few centuries did not matter. All that mattered was the final ruin and obliteration of Lemuria.

Sometimes, the Mord moved in inches; sometimes, in miles. That was part of the terror. You never knew when it would come or how. You knew only the certainty of impending doom. *And now the Mord was at the very gates of Glow Malomba!*

When we twelve strangers came down the river and entered the city, many feared we might be the bearers of the Mind-Destroyer. That was why people hid themselves and watched us fearfully. Fortunately for us, they didn't kill us. The Lemurians are forbidden to take the lives of their fellow creatures. Anyway, killing us would have been futile. If once the *Mord* reached *Glow Malomba*, the heart of Lemuria would perish.

"But come," said Ral, "I talk too much. The *Mord* has not yet come. *Glow Malomba* is still here. Perhaps *The Great Mother* will give us another miracle, as when She revealed the world of *Bane N'Gai* to us.

"Come, let us see the City!"

THE CITY OF WONDER

Glow Malomba was like a wild, fantastic dream. No human Earthman had ever looked upon such a place; nor even imagined it. Except, perhaps *The Heavenly City* in the Book of Revelations.

Glow Malomba was more than four times as large as the Biblical *City of Heaven* in which the elect would dwell. Within its enclave, lived about half a million Lemurians, a hundred thousand of the *Mu Garroh* Goblins, about an equal number of the elf-like *Oreads* and some sixty thousand of the Animal People. More than half the inhabitants of the Lemurian nation. There were no accidental births. All births were planned. The Lemurians had extended families and shared children. Thus the population grew slowly, if at all.

Stretched out before us were buildings of every conceivable style and structure. Yet they blended together in a mosaic of radiant beauty. Many appeared to be growing right out of the ground, surrounded by living things. Trees came up through the roofs. Flowers and vines and vegetation covered the walls and ledges. Plants grew right out of stone. And every few blocks there were woods, parks and lakes.

Steeples and towers rose magnificently upward. Here, birds gathered fearlessly and nested. And beyond it all, great rainbow arches climbed upward, as far as the eye could see.

Transportation was in tunnels below the streets. Here, wheel-less carts moved, powered by some hidden energy and bearing goods and people. There were also occasional carts that moved right through the air in apparent defiance of the law of gravity. They travelled slowly and without noise. Each graceful, like a living creature; apparently designed for beauty rather than speed. The Lemurians never seemed to be in a hurry. Their garbage and waste was transformed into energy and building materials. Ral explained how this was done, but we couldn't understand him.

The Queen's palace, made from that delicate gossamer material, resembled a magnificent sunset. That is the only way I can describe it. Like the chiming of a silver bell. A summer dream.

The palace of the Oreads dazzled the eyes, Can you imagine a diamond of a million---no, a billion---carats? Hollowed out? With doors and windows and taking up a couple of city blocks? Surrounded by rubies, emeralds and sapphires, each as big as a truck? That's what it looked like. And the whole thing wasn't standing on the ground. *It was floating.* The colossal gem flared up like a million lights. They called it *The White Sun of Lemuria.*

Ral Garyon thought the Oread palace was vulgar and ostentatious. *Showing off!* "The Oread Queen tried to go our Queen one better."

Did the Goblins have a palace, too? Oh, yes. Under that biggest mountain with a crystal peak. It was a man-made — or rather Goblin-made — cave. The *Mu Garroh* loved to create caves. Probably, a lot of the caves we discovered in our journey were built by the Goblins.

There was a library here that contained several billion books. No micro-films. All hard cover, made of some fine-spun metal and colored glass. When no one was reading them, the library books were *"put in the quayne"*. That meant they were put in a "time warp" and took up no space at all. To read them, you take them *"out of the quayne"*, that is materialize them. It's not done with any gadget. You do it with your mind.

A scholarly Elf-lady showed us around. One section of the library was devoted to books from Earth. Just for a laugh, we asked for Dr. Mehary's *Behavior Modification of Defective and Delinquent Juveniles.* They had it. They had Karl Hasserman's book, too.

Outside the city, there was a sanctuary that contained perhaps the strangest life form anywhere. Flying trees, all verdant green, including trunk and branches. In their young state, the creatures were avian and flew like eagles. Then they developed roots and anchored themselves into the earth.

The bird-trees grew very old and maybe once every hundred years, they grew egg-fruit that developed into a new bird tree. But there were very few of them left. The original colony in the Second Continent was destroyed by the *Mord*. Only the still avian bird-trees escaped.

The oldest bird-trees had lived for many thousands of years and were said to be the wisest creatures in Creation. Though they gave their knowledge very rarely and only to a very few. Now, alas, all their great wisdom had been lost.

Those rainbow arches, we learned, were more than just a decoration. They were part of a dome, made of secret material, to protect the City against the *Mord*.

No one really believed that dome would stop the Mind-destroyer. No wall, no barrier had stopped it yet. But it gave the people hope — although a faint one. And it was better to do something — *anything* — than just wait.

"The High Council," said Ral, "is planning a general mobilization. All able-bodied young men and women will be called up — including me. If the Dome does not stop the *Mord*, perhaps a mass attack can overwhelm it. There will be terrible losses. . . ."

This would be the first battle the Lemurians had fought since landing on Earth. And perhaps the last battle they would ever fight.

It would be Life against Death. *The Heavenly City* against the Powers of Hell. And in this corner of Creation, it looked like Hell was going to break through.

THE VRROOOHN OF MARL'HAI

Ral took us to his home and we had dinner with his parents and his sisters. They tried to entertain us with a Lemurian game. Each team got fifty pieces with different shapes and colors, moving in three dimensions. We couldn't understand it. It was like playing chess with a two year old.

When they saw how dumb we were, they tried something else. They showed us scenes of the wonders of *Bane N'Gai*. The scenes were all around you, just like you were right in the picture, with all the sounds and tastes and smells and feelings like you were there. And the strangest thing was we all experienced something different. You felt like you were flying and had wings. You were walking on the sky; or on the bottom of the Great Ocean and could build things just with your mind.

Still, for all the wonders of *Bane N'Gai*, Ral seemed to think Earth was more interesting.

Cameron said, "You should have come to Earth, Ral."

"You couldn't go without the Queen's permission."

"What would happen if you did? Just got up and went to Earth?"

"They wouldn't let you come back to Lemuria. You'd have to stay on Earth for the rest of your life."

To the Lemurians, Earth was like the Canals of Mars to us. A great place to explore, but pretty awful to be stuck in.

Lyandra also invited us to her place. It was like living in a garden. The walls were covered with wildflowers and growing plants. And red and yellow birds were flying around.

Lyandra sang to us and played a musical instrument. It sounded sometimes like a violin, sometimes like a trumpet and sometimes like a full organ. A rhapsody of magic and enchantment. Then she played some lively tunes and had all twelve Coyote boys dancing and hopping around. Lyandra made us sing, too. We sounded like — well, a pack of Coyotes.

Lyandra said we could stay in our apartment — at least as long as the city was still there. Our place was designed for Earth people. Karl Hasserman had lived here. He complained about the place.

"Gosh!" said Troy, "you mean it wasn't fancy enough for him? How much fancier could it get?"

"It wasn't protected enough. Karl Hasserman was constantly looking for enemies and was afraid of being assassinated."

"Whatever happened to Hasserman? And what happened to the *Vrrooohn?*" asked Stevie.

"Do you intend to steal it?"

"The Masters wanted us to steal it. They'll be awful mad, if we come back without it. But even if we bring them the *Vrrooohn,* they may knock us off, because we know too much."

Bobby said, "I'd just like to get back to Earth and be an ordinary kid again. I wouldn't mind going back to *Kaah Naghallah*, if it was like when we first came. We got muckled and pushed around. But we had a lot of fun, too.

"Anyway, we wouldn't know how to steal the *Vrrooohn.* Nobody ever told us what it looked like."

"What did the Masters tell you?"

"Nothing," said Cameron. "We were just told to follow orders. They said to come back with Karl Hasserman's treasure or don't come back at all!"

"I will tell you," said Lyandra. "But it will not help you. Karl Hasserman's treasure has been lost."

THE LOST TREASURE

"The *Vrrooohn* is a rainbow crystal with the horns of the Laranak, the sky beast. A mythical creature. At least that is the shape in which most people see it. It has the capacity to greatly enhance the powers of the mind. But there are dangers to using it, for the *Vrrooohn* enhances not only the powers of reason, but all of the mind's darker and irrational cravings. Megalomania, paranoia and uncontrolled lust. It was by the *Vrrooohn*, many believe, that we were led into *The Endless War*.

"There were once many *Vrrooohns* used to train adepts in the service of *The Great Mother*. They were seized and corrupted by the High Priests of the Devil-gods. In the diaspora following our defeat, all the *Vrrooohns* were lost or destroyed, except the one carried by our ancestors to North America.

"In *Bane N'Gai*, we found we did not need the *Vrrooohn*. By the Discipline, we were able to develop our minds to a higher state, without external props or the danger of corruption. The *Vrrooohn* was held in the *Temple of Marl'Hai* as an ancient relic."

On occasion, there had been Earthmen who stumbled on one of the Gateways to *Bane N'Gai*. If they managed to return, they were able to remember very little.

"You mixed their minds up?" asked Brandon.

Lyandra just smiled. "But there was one of them, a Sorcerer named Kalda. He thought the Lemurians were Powers of the Underworld. He wagered his soul against the *Vrrooohn* and lost. So it is told. Then, not keeping to his bargain, he stole the *Vrrooohn* and returned to Earth. Here, he amassed great wealth and became a Grand-duke. The brutal ruler of an unhappy land.

"Kalda was a cruel and wicked man and the *Vrrooohn* made him more so. He oppressed and tormented his people and conducted vile and depraved orgies."

"What kind of orgies?" asked the Naghallah boys, eagerly.

Lyandra refused to describe them.

Lyandra

"One night, the Grand-duke held a great feast, when seven fiery Devils, with flaming torches, burst into the banquet hall."

"Not real Devils," said Roger. "They were Lemurians dressed up. Right?"

"Yes, Roger. But the terrified guests fled screaming and the Sorcerer, it is said, died of fright. The Earth people, however, believed the Devils had carried Kalda off to Hell. The *Vrrooohn* was recovered and thereafter closely guarded.

"Some fifty years ago, a young man named Karl Hasserman penetrated the Veil and entered *Bane N'Gai*. That was when the Mind-Destroyer was already moving on *Glow Malomba;* though still far away. Karl Hasserman persuaded the Queen and the Grand Council to let him take the *Vrrooohn* from the *Temple of Marl'Hai.* He had a plan to stop the Mind-Destroyer and turn it back forever.

"They should have known he was lying. Or perhaps he really meant to do it, but greed and fear overcame him. Having secured the *Vrrooohn,* he returned to Earth with it and abandoned the Lemurians.

"By the *Vrrooohn,* Karl Hasserman amassed a tremendous fortune. But he found no joy. He lived without love or friends; in constant fear, thinking all men were plotting against him.

"Hasserman trusted no one. He began to believe that his closest associates were scheming to destroy him. Perhaps the poison of his thoughts made his fears come true.

"In the end, Hasserman fled for his life. Sick and slowly dying, he returned to Lemuria, bearing the *Vrrooohn.* For many months, he lived in lonely solitude. Then the idea came: To make atonement for his past betrayal.

"That lying promise Hasserman would now fulfill. Though now weakened in body, lame and half blind, he tried to use the power of the *Vrrooohn* to strike against the Mind Destroyer.

"It proved to be the wrong thing to do. The *Vrrooohn* could raise the mind of an Earthman to a near-Lemurian level. But the higher minds are all the more vulnerable to the *Mord*, more easily destroyed."

Lyandra's voice broke. She must have cared for the old pirate. She and Karl Hasserman must have confided in each other. Perhaps, even after he returned to Lemuria, she had a way of sending him reports about what was happening on Earth. About the phony Karl Hasserman and the scheming Masters of Naghallah. Maybe about Dr. Mehary and the juvenile punks in his nutty school. Maybe we gave him a laugh. Too bad we never got a chance to meet him.

"Several months ago, Karl Hasserman went against the *Mord*. With him were three other Earthmen, Dean Harlow and his wife, Alice, and Jerry Golding."

"They were witnesses to Karl Hasserman's will. But we saw their graves."

"Their companions abandoned them for dead. But the *Oreads* found them and restored them to life. The *Oreads* have the power sometimes to restore the dead. But it must be done quickly, before the soul departs from the body."

"What happened then to Karl Hasserman?"

"He was stricken down by the *Mord* in the Hollow of the Giants. The Harlows and Golding must have perished with him."

Thus ended Karl Hasserman, a Lemurian hero. At least they let him be remembered as a hero. But perhaps they discovered the *Mord* in him and drove him out.

THE CAVERN OF THE GOBLINS

Trycon *Mu Garroh* also gave us an invitation. Ral and Lyandra came along. Also present was the Setter Dog Lady, a green-haired Oread and a tall, distinguished lady who was Counsellor to the Queen.

Trycon lived in a Goblin-made cave under the city, along with five lady and four men Goblins. The Goblins, it seemed, married several people and each spouse married several people. Among humans, that might cause trouble. But among Goblins, the whole household lived happily together.

There were six little Goblins, too, who were everybody's children. In Lemuria, kids were part of everybody's family, not just their parents. There were no homeless waifs like us. The young Goblins climbed up on the walls and could even crawl on the ceiling. When the Naghallah boys tried wall climbing, we took a flop.

Trycon asked us what we would like to eat. When we told him *Goblins' Bread*, he looked surprised. That was for the animals. The Goblins put it in every cave they made. As soon as it was eaten, it grew right back again. That way, no living creature in *Bane N'Gai* would have to starve. The Goblins themselves ate cakes and ale, nectar and ambrosia. Stuff like that.

What a wonderful cave this was! With many halls and chambers opening in every direction. Each of them full of shining and gleaming stalagmites, like delicate statues. There were all kinds of jewels here, even more magnificent than in Karl Hasserman's treasure chest. In fact, in Lemuria such jewels are not rare at all. The Goblins make them from raw materials they dig in the Underground. The *Mu Garroh* are always making beautiful things and then had to build more caves to put them in.

Wild music came out of Nowhere, and the entire company joined in a merry dance. In a Goblin dance, everyone does their own thing and dance pretty much by themselves. The Goblins leaped over each other and did somersaults and cartwheels.

But after a while the Group became somber and, as everywhere in Lemuria, talk turned to the Mind-Destroyer. The Shadow of Doom that hung over every thought and action. Not only for the Lemurians, but for their friends and allies. The *Mord* had advanced again and was now only thirteen Earth miles away.

"Could the *Mord* strike you down here in the Underground?"

"Yes," said Trycon, sadly. "It can follow you anywhere."

"In a few days, the Dome will be closed down." Then nobody would be able to leave or enter *Glow Malomba* except by the Goblins' tunnels. And these would be closed, too, if the City is under siege. "In a quarter-year, or maybe less," predicted the Counsellor, "it will all be over — one way or the other."

On Earth, people would be fleeing wildly and in panic. Frantic fugitives would be clogging all roads in mindless flight. Here, there was no panic. Only a calm and melancholy resignation. For some time, refugees from the North and West had been pouring into *Glow Malomba*. But from the beleaguered City no one even tried to escape. Perhaps the *Mord* destroyed the Will before it destroyed the Mind.

Bound together by a collective consciousness, the Lemurians shared each others' feelings and perceptions. No matter how distant, none could escape the fall of the Lemurian heartland. They and their sister peoples were destined to be saved or doomed together.

"Why couldn't you come to Earth?" asked Keith.

I pictured a vast migration out of *Bane N'Gai*, back through the Gateway; to the utter astonishment of the Earth dwellers. The entire Lemurian nation, including *Oreads, Mu Garroh* and Animal People numbered not much more than one million and could easily be absorbed in America alone. What wisdom and wonders they could bring with them! With their great mental powers, they might soon become our leaders and governors, converting the World to Vegetarianism and Peace.

"If we came to Earth," said the Counsellor, "the *Mord* would only follow us and destroy Earth, too. We cannot impose our fate on others."

What about escape into the vast unexplored lands of *Bane N'Gai?*

"It wouldn't help! Not if our city is gone!" The Setter Dog Lady gave a mournful howl.

Glow Malomba, the City of Wonder, was the soul of Lemuria. The life of the nation would perish with the City.

Would the Machine People delight in their triumph? The Counsellor didn't think so. "We believe they no longer care, or perhaps are even regretful. But the Death Machine now has a life of its own and cannot be called back."

The fanatics who developed the Mind-Destroyer, said the Counsellor, were among the victims of the Mind-Destroyer. The Doom-Machine spares none within its deadly power. Destiny moves with a strange irony. How often in history do inventors become the victims of their own inventions!

"The rest of the Machine People now have dwindled and scattered. To them, the Lemurians now are but an ancient legend. But their Death-Machine moves on, immortal and invulnerable, on its Hellish mission."

"How stupid do you have to be," asked Steve, "to be immune from the *Mord?*"

The Queen's Counsellor didn't know. It would depend on how strongly you were exposed to it. She thought no life form would be completely immune, though some would be stricken very slowly. But no Lemurian could go near to it. Even the youngest children would be ravaged after a few seconds.

"What about Earth kids?" asked Stevie.

The Queen's Counsellor looked puzzled. "What Earth kids?"

"I mean *us.*"

She gave us a look of amused tolerance, as a grown-up might view a four-year-old with a toy sword who proposes to slay a mass murderer. "It would tear your mind to pieces.

Many of our best and finest have tried to stop the *Mord*. But no Lemurian may look upon the Mind-Destroyer and live."

"We ain't Lemurians. We're just dumb Earth kids. Where is the *Mord*?"

"North of the City, there are a series of Hollows, surrounded by mountains. The *Mord* has now reached the nearest Hollow. One more mountain range and then there are but twelve short miles to *Glow Malomba*. That much we know. But we know nothing about the nature of the *Mord*. Only that it paralyzes, then poisons, all intelligent life within its wake."

We looked at each other and started to laugh. Our hosts looked shocked. "Sorry," said Bobby, "We were just thinking. If you got no intelligence, the *Mord* can't kill you. What would we get, if we could save Lemuria?"

"It is too late for that. No one can do it any more."

They had lost all hope and were desperate. They didn't want our destruction on their heads. But they didn't forbid us to try. Their faces lit up just a little. *If we could save them, we would receive the highest honor they could bestow. They would make us free and equal citizens of Lemuria.*

"Suppose we wanted to return to Earth?" asked Raymond.

"That would be foolish." But they would not try to stop us. *We could return to Earth and take with us whatever we could carry. That was a sacred promise in the name of the Queen.*

THE COYOTES GO TO WAR

The Forty-Second Day

"We'll have to case the *Mord*," said Danny.

Few Lemurians would go anywhere near it. And those who did made a one-way trip.

We took along an assortment of tools and supplies and miscellaneous weapons. There was no way of knowing what we were up against. Something that moved slowly and could strike over a wide area. Maybe it was something like a Trojan horse, with people inside. Killer people or killer animals. *Unlikely.* The Mind-Destroyer had been around for hundreds of years. People, or anything living, would have to eat and get supplies. Someone would have spotted them. The *Mord* just moved by itself, with perpetual and unlimited power.

The enemies of Lemuria were the Machine People. They would probably devise some kind of a machine. Something that threw out waves or rays, like Death Rays. Only, these rays killed the mind instead of the body.

Cameron said, "You lead, Don Don. We're going back into your territory again." However, Donald didn't want to. We wondered if Donald should come at all. He was a Lemurian and sensitive to the Mind-Destroyer. But Donald wanted to come.

Raymond said, "Let Don Don come. He's got a dumb Earth mind, like us."

"Okay," ordered Cameron. "Form column of twos and follow me. We're off to battle!"

The city was still amazingly calm. A few now were departing in threes and fours on those floating airships piled with household goods. But most people just waited. Was it because they hoped some miracle would save the City? Or was it that their doom now seemed inevitable? When the Mind-Destroyer had overrun *Glow Malomba*, it would explode in all directions. All *Bane N'Gai* would fall. There would be no place to run, no place to hide. Neither the *Mu Garroh* in their caves, nor the *Oreads* in their forests, nor the Animal People in their hide-outs would escape. For they were allies of the Lemurians and likewise doomed.

Yet there was no fear among the people. Just a quiet sadness. Perhaps because they knew in their inner selves that Nothing can die forever. Somewhere within the *Great Mother*, the Eternal Mind, they would be born again.

Ral drew a map for us and brought us a boat. "About seven American miles downstream. Then go left toward the highlands. There's a whole grid of Hollows, running on for many miles. We don't know just where the *Mord* is now. It keeps moving, not always in a straight line."

"But never backwards?"

"No," said Ral, grimly. "Never backwards."

Like many young Lemurians, Ral had once scouted the *Mord*. "I didn't get close enough to see it. I'm afraid I wasn't much of a hero. My body was starting to get paralyzed. Two *Oreads* who were with me pulled me away."

"How do you look for the *Mord*?"

"It's easier to find it than to avoid it. You will hear a humming sound, then feel a chill. Then, like a whirlpool, something will suck you in. As you get close, you'll find it hard to stop and get away."

"If you start feeling cold and shaky, turn around and break away, while you still can. Good luck, guys!"

"Good luck to you, Ral."

"We'll both need it. I'm being mobilized tomorrow. We're going into training and don't know what to train for. Fighting the *Mord* is like fighting the Invisible Demons of the seven Hells."

Ral had the rank of Assistant Groupleader. "I guess that would be a lieutenant in an Earth army. All I know is what I read in books on Military History — mostly about Earth wars. I feel sorry for the guys I'm commanding."

Along the riverfront, there was a group of young men and some young women, too, in green uniforms, marching in array. The first outward sign of war. We saluted and cheered each other.

The Coyotes go to War.

Thus did the Coyotes depart into battle. As our boat pulled down the river, people waved and shouted. Troy pulled off his blue shirt and waved it as a banner.

We were off to the war.

THE DIRGE OF DOOM

We floated down the river. Ral turned and joined the soldiers. They were joking and laughing together. Ral was a lieutenant and the others were privates. But there were no social distinctions in the Lemurian army.

Ral looked younger than most of the soldiers. About eighteen, though he must be a lot older. *Bane N'Gai* didn't have years like Earth. No seasons. In *Bane N'Gai*, it was always Spring and always Autumn; for the flowers ever bloomed and the fruits ever ripened.

Earth was a round ball. *Bane N'Gai* was more or less flat. With deep ravines, seas and towering mountains. But the land didn't go on forever. If you travelled long enough, you curved around and came back to where you started. Straight lines curved in *Bane N'Gai*.

How could that be? If you asked a Lemurian, they would draw you a page of mathematical equations that you couldn't understand. If you asked some more, they would shrug and say, "That's the way the *Great Mother* made our World."

The land beyond the City was perhaps even more beautiful than *Glow Malomba*. The hills and meadows were ablaze with flowers. The magnolia, the lilacs, the hibiscus, the dogwood and the roses were in blossom; along with a vast variety of multi-colored vegetation, unknown on Earth. At intervals, there were more magnificent houses. But most of them were now abandoned.

Song birds gathered on the trees and roofs, but their melodies were mournful. This enchanted land of eternal Spring was destined to become a memory. A forgotten memory with no one to remember.

About seven miles downstream, we left the boat on a

sand bank and waded ashore. Danny suddenly gripped my arm. "Do you hear that, Jaymie? The Death Music!" *The Dirge of Doom.* And I heard it for the third time.

There was no music really. No one else heard it. The *Mord* was beginning to work on us, pulling our minds apart. The other guys began to hear things, too; but different things. Brandon could hear a scream. Bobby could hear his grandmother weeping. Raymond felt things exploding inside his head.

"I hear stuff, too," said Cameron. "We got to snap out of it. We're still miles away from the *Mord.* By the time we reach it, we'll all be nuts.

"Remember, the *Mord* can only hurt people. It can't hurt us."

"Why not?"

"Because we're animals. We're a pack of Coyotes. What do coyotes do?"

"They howl," said Jody.

"What else?"

"They growl," said Keith.

"They yowl," said Roger.

"They prowl," said Stevie.

"Okay. We'll howl and growl and yowl and prowl. Leave your stuff here and follow me. Come on, Coyote pack! Run!"

We stacked our stuff in a small cave and followed Cameron. We howled and growled and yowled. Then we prowled, jogging at a fast pace. Pretty soon everyone was panting and breathless. Our minds cleared and we didn't think of anything except keeping up with the others and not falling behind.

We jogged across the meadows and over a series of rocky hills. Toward the Hollows and the white crags that surrounded them. Now we could feel it. A force — a power. Something that was drawing us forward.

"The *Mord!*" cried Troy in alarm. "It's pulling us in!"

"It ain't pulling us in," retorted Cameron. "We're tracking it. Come on, Coyote Pack! Follow the scent of the *Mord!*"

THE MIND DESTROYER

We were climbing now. Over a range of barren hills. The pull on our bodies became stronger. Like a whirlpool that sucks you in. Some unearthly power was dragging us forward. We locked arms and dug our heels in to resist it.

The *Mord* must be very near now. There was no bird or animal life to be seen here and only sparse vegetation. Most of the trees were bare and dying. The *Mord* might work but slowly on the lower forms of life. But in time these, too, would wither and perish. Everywhere, there was the stench of decay and death.

We should have brought the rope. Instead, we locked our belts around the next guy's belt. That held us together so that no one guy could be sucked in. Cameron moved sideways until we reached a line of boulders. We climbed again and braced ourselves behind them.

We were now on top of the mountain, looking down on a wide Hollow. Below, there was something that looked like a series of blurs. I felt a buzzing in my ears and a sudden nameless fear.

Finally, the blur came into focus. In the vale beyond, were a series of greyish discs — eight in all. They were ranged in a circle, like the eight points of the compass and connected by some thing that looked like wire or rope. Two wires between each disc.

"This is *it!*" cried Raymond. The *Mord*, the Mind-Destroyer.

The front of the disc had an eerie sheen that seemed menacing and evil. All at once, the air grew cold and a freezing wind went through our bodies. There was a strong impulse to turn and run, but we forced ourselves to look.

The *Mord* looked like some kind of a weird machine. It floated in the air with nothing to hold it up. The fantastic structure rose up to the height of a building, and then sank again, never quite touching the ground. The *Thing* might destroy rational thought, but it moved in a planned pattern, in three movements. Up and down, revolving slowly, and forward — ever forward. Ever nearer to the City. Ever closer to the destruction of Lemuria.

Each disc in size was about the spread of two human arms, and the circle formed by the connecting wires about sixteen paces across. Those weird grey discs were sending forth emanations, deadly rays in all directions. Now, the discs were tilting to the ground. Now they swerved upward into the sky. The *Mord* swept the land in all directions. Ground, sky, surface. Nothing could escape.

It was said that there was no way to attack the *Mord*. Weapons are useless against it. Whatever the Thing was made of, it appeared invulnerable. Desperate Lemurians had attacked it with guns, rockets, bombs, explosives. Even with knives, hammers and axes. But that was the last thing they did before the *Mord* got them.

The *Oreads* had invoked psychic weapons. Their witches had pronounced dire curses and enchantments against the *Mord*. But their spells and curses always failed and indeed rebounded against their makers. Those who laid a curse against the *Mord* would perish by the curse. So it was told.

The *Mord* was moving slowly now, apparently in no hurry to reach *Glow Malomba*. The Intelligence behind this weird machine seemed to savor this moment of triumph over their ancient enemies and to draw it out as long as possible. The *Thing* could leap forward suddenly or crawl along interminably. The citizens of Lemuria would never know whether any night would be their last.

By tomorrow, the protecting dome would be lowered over the city. But nobody really believed that would stop the *Mord*. "The Thing will go right through it, and poison the City. The people will perish. Their minds will be destroyed and their mindless bodies will rot and fall apart." So Trycon had predicted in a pessimistic moment.

The *Mord* worked slower on us inferior creatures than it did on the Lemurians. But it was working now. The air grew unbearably cold, the noise in our ears grew painfully louder and that terrible fear grew worse.

Danny was trembling and his lips were blue. Troy and

Stevie were shivering and shaking. Brandon's pale face had turned a ghastly white. Roger was gasping for breath. Keith's heart was beating furiously. Bobby clutched his head, trying to ward off dizziness.

But on Donald the effect was the greatest. He struck wildly into the air as if something were attacking him. Then he put his hands to his ears and started screaming. Then his knees sagged and he collapsed. Raymond and Jaymie held him up.

Cameron gave the signal for retreat. "About face! Let's get out of here. Back where we came from. Run!"

We couldn't run. After a few steps, Donald collapsed completely and we had to carry him. He said later he couldn't endure the noise of the *Mords*. They were screeching into his brain, drawing out his life power.

None of the rest of us got it as bad as Don Don. But we developed headaches and painful cramps. Like a deep sea diver who gets the bends from being down too long.

We got out of there in a hurry, limping and staggering rather than running. We moved as fast as we could, carrying Don Don. We were glad to get away alive. Then slowly we became warm again and our terrible fear was gone.

"He who fights and runs away
  Will live to fight another day," quoted Keith.

"'We didn't even fight. We just ran."

"Better to be a live coward than a dead hero."

"'That," said Cameron, "was a reconnaissance, not a battle. Sure you get away as fast as you can, after you have fulfilled your mission."

"What did we do? Besides run?"

"We found out what the *Mord* looked like. That's more than anyone else did who got away alive."

Back at the cave, we slept in a circle that night. Like we usually did when there was danger. There was just a chance that the *Mord* might come after us.

But it didn't.

A COUNCIL OF WAR

The Forty-Third Day

Back by the river, we held a council of war.

"What did we learn from our reconnaissance?" Cameron asked everybody.

"We learned shit," said Stevie. "Just how to go nuts without even trying."

"What do we know now about the *Mord* that we didn't know before? Everybody try to remember."

We had learned that the Mord consisted of eight plates or discs, ranged roughly in a circle and shooting out rays or emanations. Each disc was connected to the next one by some kind of wires or cords.

"Yeah," said Bobby. "And the fucking thing keeps moving."

"How does it move?"

"Up and down. Tilting. Changing angles. Throwing the lethal rays in all directions. . . . And forward. Zigzagging sometimes, but always forward. . . . Toward the heart of Lemuria. . . . . ."

"And one more way. Rotating around in a circle."

"Why should the thing rotate?" asked Cameron. "Why not just forward and up and down?"

"Why must there be a reason? Whoever built this contraption must be a bunch of mad men."

"Then they have a mad reason. Come on, Gifted Child. Can't you think of something?"

"Why the *Mord* turns?" I tried to think. We all did. The Doom Machine had been going for over a thousand years, hunting Lemurians and casting rays that shrivelled up the mind. It must get its power from somewhere. Not energy like we had on Earth. But some kind of force.

It was Danny who had an idea. I always said on practical things he had a better mind than me. Power! That was why there were eight *Mords* that turned around. Each of the Mind-Destroyer discs, Danny figured, threw out power to the front and sides and recharged as it reached the rear. The land behind had already been wasted. You didn't have to waste it over again. An advancing army doesn't shoot behind them.

"If that's true," said Keith, "we could circle around and attack the Mind Destroyer from the back. We might still get some of the *Mord* rays, but not nearly so much."

"How come dumb Earth kids like us think of that and the Lemurians didn't?"

"They never got close enough to the Mind Destroyer to see it turn. And those who did got their brains knocked out and were wasted."

"We got a battle plan now," said Cameron. "Come on, guys. Get the tools and weapons. We'll hit the *Mord* from the rear!"

Should Donald come? It might be the end of him. But we hated to leave him behind. Somehow, as long as the twelve of us were together, no matter how rough it got, things turned out all right. Maybe, like Ral Garryon said, we were blessed by *The Great Mother.* Maybe it was just dumb luck.

"Donald come," he announced. "Donald go with brothers." He was staring into space now with that dreamy look, as when he had foretold our nightmare journey into the Underworld.

"Can you see the future? Do you know what will happen, Don Don?"

"Yes, I know. --- It will be the end. . . ."

"The end of the War?" we asked anxiously. "The end of Lemuria? The end of the Coyotes?"

"No," said Donald. *"The end of the Mord!"*

We cheered.

TWELVE AGAINST THE MORD

We returned to the *Mord* by a circular route to hit it from the rear. We crossed the *Hollow of the Bats,* the *Hollow of the Lizards,* and the *Hollow of the Mountain Goats.* But there were no bats, nor lizards, nor mountain goats anywhere around. The denizens of these Hollows, human or animals, had long since fled or perished by the *Mord.* Nor was there any healthy plant life remaining. Everything looked withered and dying.

At length, we came to the *Hollow of the Great Pines.* These magnificent trees, with silver needles instead of green, rose hundreds of feet into the air. But now, the branches had blackened, the needles were falling off, the bark peeling. All the once majestic growth looked bare and burned, as if a forest fire had passed over it. Even the rocks that lined the Hollow were scorched and crumbling.

The *Mord* had passed here about a week ago and had now reached the *Hollow of the Lost River.* This was the last of the Hollows. From here on, there were nothing but open fields into *Glow Malomba.* Up to now, the cliffs and mountains of the Hollow country perhaps had served to slow the advance of the Doom Machine. There would be nothing that could stop or slow it now.

There was no water in the Lost River. Instead, there was a river bed about nine or ten feet deep, where a stream had once flowed. Cameron said we would enter and advance along the river bed. That way, the earth would shield us from the Doom rays, at least until we got close.

"And quiet, everyone! Move in silence!"

The *Mord* was cunningly constructed and appeared to move by some intelligence; following the contour of the ground and sweeping relentlessly toward the Lemurian heartland. The *Thing* might have built in sensors to give warning, if someone approached.

"You mean like radar?"

"Maybe, but something more. Radar couldn't tell a man from a mountain goat. The lower animals don't set off an alarm. If people trigger an alarm, there has to be some special gimmick. How could a machine tell a man from an animal?"

"Smell, maybe," suggested Bobby. "Or maybe human speech. People talking."

"Good thinking, Brother Alliconda." We rubbed ourselves with foul smelling muck so as to cover up any human scent. We rubbed the muck over our faces, too, and our hands and arms and neck and hair and over our clothes, making us look like swamp creatures out of the fen. That muck might protect us just a little from the Doom rays.

"And no talking," ordered Cameron. "No human speech. At least until we get inside the circle. *If* we can get that far."

We would communicate by Coyote howls. One howl, *Attention.* Two howls, *Do as I do.* Three howls, *Get the Hell out of here fast!* "And if you absolutely have to talk, just whisper and then make animal noises. That ought to mix the Doom Machine up."

We moved across the river bed, trying to keep low. About half way across the Hollow, Cameron put his head up We were less than fifty yards from the *Mord's* deadly circle. Cameron watched as the *Mord's* eight discs came downward, then rose again. Now two Coyote howls. *Do as I do.* That last fifty yards we'd have to cover in a fast run.

Once inside the circle, Cameron reasoned, we would be shielded from the Mind Destroyer. The emanations were all pointed outside the circle. If the *Mord* acted like ordinary energy rays, we would be out of range, or at worst receive only a weak reflection of the Doom vibrations.

Down in the river bed, we had been relatively free from the *Mord.* Now out in the open, it came on us again with all its full horror and power. The screaming in your ears, the deadly chill, the terrible fear and weakness. As we ran, Donald staggered and I thought he might fall. But he braced himself and recovered.

A few seconds and the twelve of us were inside the circle. Cameron had calculated well. Inside now, the dizziness and the screaming stopped. The chilling cold was gone. Only the fear remained. Then even the fear vanished as we gave a triumphant Coyote howl.

We were in the Eye of the storm that was raging all around us. The Eye was tranquil, while the *Mord* rays swirled outwards in all directions, carrying Doom and Death.

Seeing the *Mord* from the inside was a surprising revelation. We had expected a very complicated machine, with many parts. However, this contraption looked absurdly simple. Eight huge plates, each spreading like a roc's wings and connected by two sets of wires to the plates on either side. Sixteen wires or cords in all. Probably, the Thing was far from simple. Some hidden mechanism must be built into each plate and covered up.

Something like a complicated screw seemed to hold the wires in place. What would happen if we were to break the connections?

That might wreck it and it might not. The plates might go flying off in all directions, objected Keith. Then we would have eight *Mords* instead of one, spreading the Doom rays.

We found ourselves talking now. First in whispers then in a normal voice. We hadn't triggered any alarm. However, we were beginning to feel a little woozy. Even inside the circle, the *Mord* would get us, if we stayed long enough.

We examined the connections. The upper ones were marked by what looked like an eye. The lower ones, by two rows of jagged teeth facing each other.

The *EYE* and the *JAWS*. Each *EYE* was connected to another *EYE*. Each *JAW* to another *JAW*. Why should that be?

"Maybe it's like positive and negative on a battery," suggested Raymond.

Stevie said, "When you charge a car battery, you got to put the positive on the positive pole and the negative on the negative. Otherwise you fuck up the battery."

"Yeah," said Troy, "I know a guy who put the positive cable on the negative pole and blew the whole thing up."

"What would happen," asked Cameron, "if we put the *EYE* on the *JAWS* and the *JAWS* on the *EYE*?

"We might fuck the Mord up, or blow it up and blow ourselves up, too."

"We don't know what else to do. Let's try it and get the Hell out of here. We can't take these rays much longer."

We acted fast, fighting off nausea, dizziness and pain. One end of each wire was disconnected and reconnected to the opposite marker. *EYE* on *JAWS; JAWS* on *EYE*. Danny, Steve, Keith, Raymond, Cameron and Bobby worked with the Goblins' tools. Screwdrivers, pliers, joiners, wrenches, couplers, splicers, connectors and disconnectors of varying shapes and dimensions. The rest of us struggled to hold the *Mord* in place. The Thing was getting hot. We had to use grippers to hold it. We shouted at the top of our lungs to drown out the screaming of the *Mord*.

The whole operation took about four minutes. Fourteen wires had been switched around. Two wires still hung loose. Now sparks were coming out of several discs. The contraption was beginning to smoke.

"Quick!" yelled Cameron. "Run!"

We sprinted back to the river bed. Donald was limping and staggering. But he made it.

All twelve of us were a wreck. We looked like we had been hit by a truck — or maybe a bomb. The blood was coming out of our ears and noses. Our eyes were bleary and our bodies felt like we were burning up.

I was choking and coughing and felt a sharp pain in my

chest and heart. Still we kept running. Back down the river bed and out of the Hollow. And the terror and pain and bleeding gradually stopped.

THE LAST BATTLE

We kept going into the next Hollow. The ground was shaking under us. We crouched behind a row of rocks. Huge billows of smoke were rising into the air.

Now there was a rumble and a roar. Flashes of lightning exploded on every side. The earth trembled violently. The sides of the Hollow split apart and collapsed. We were in the middle of a whirlwind with dust and stones and debris swirling in all directions. Rocks were flying into the air like pop corn. I feared for the moment we would be buried in a landslide. But the *Great Mother in Heaven* or just dumb luck saved us again.

A giant tree, torn up by the roots, crashed down on top of us, fortunately not all the way. A rock broke its fall and kept the tree from crushing us. The branches covered us and warded off the falling stones.

Two huge boulders landed on either side of us. The ground split open where they landed. But Destiny or dumb luck protected us again. Finally, there was silence. . . .

Donald was the first to climb out and look down into the *Hollow of the Lost River.* There was no longer any sign of the river bed. Just a huge pit fifty feet deep.

Donald gave a cry of victory. "Lanna' Hai!" he yelled, triumphantly. "Nada *Mord!*"

The *Mord* was gone. There was no sign of it. No trace remained of the death plates, nor the connecting wires, nor the mind-destroying radiation. The Doom Machine had vaporized and simply vanished. The fear, the chill, the cramps and nausea, the deadly screaming in our ears, was gone.

Everything was still. There was no sound except for the triumphant cries of the Coyotes. Thus ended the last battle of the Sixty-thousand year war.

Cameron checked his men one by one. "Anybody hurt?"

"I'm crazy," announced Troy.

"That wasn't the *Mord,* Brother Troy. You were that way all the time."

"I'm stupid," lamented Bobby. "That thing blew all my brains out."

Somebody asked, "What brains?"

Cameron said, "We all lost most of our brains here. But we didn't have much to lose. Maybe now, if we can find Karl Hasserman's *Vrrooohn,* we can get smartened up again."

THE HIDDEN CAVE

The Forty-Fourth Day

We made camp in the *Hollow of the Great Pines,* which the *Mord* had ravaged the week before. These once magnificent trees were now all bare and withered. Yet now, for the first time, we could see new shoots coming out of the roots. By morning, the new silver shoots were over a foot high. In this incredibly fertile land, within a few years, the Great Pines would arise again.

We slept restlessly. As the exhilaration of our triumph wore off, we began to feel the first effects of the *Mord.* Weariness, cramps and chill. We shivered, although the air was warm. We couldn't make our hands and feet move the way we wanted to.

Cameron was a gallant leader, if there ever was one. He was the first to enter the deadly circle and the last to leave it, making sure everyone else was safe. The first to put his hands upon the Mind-Destroyer to disconnect the wires. Whenever there was a risk, Cameron took it first himself. Cameron seemed invulnerable. We never expected anything could happen to him.

Now that we started our search for the *Vrrooohn,* Cameron had trouble walking. Cameron's legs wouldn't move. He had to pull himself along with his arms.

Cameron had trouble seeing, too. He put his hands in front of his face, as if to ward off a blow. His skin was turning a dull grey. The blood began to flow from his nose and ears.

Cameron gritted his teeth. He pulled himself up, then took a step, or tried to; then he lurched forward and collapsed. He lay on the ground, unable to rise.

"Don Don!" he called. "You lead now! Take over!" Then Cameron blacked out.

We looked at each other, wondering who would be next. But no one was next. The rest of us were still on our feet.

"What will we do, Don Don? Shall we carry him?"

The "retarded boy" became a leader again. "Form column of twos and follow me. Fast!"

Cameron must weigh at least as much as Donald. But the Lemurian youth lifted Cameron's unconscious body squarely across his shoulders and carried him unaided.

Donald didn't say where he was taking Cameron. He had a destination. Easing his way rapidly through the fallen trees and rocks, Donald crossed the Hollow. Finally, he reached what looked like a blank wall. "Dig!" he ordered.

We had abandoned our tools in our last mad dash for safety. We used our hands and branches to clear away the rubble, pulling the rocks and scooping the dirt away. There was a cave here. Donald must have a clairvoyant power. Surely he had never been here before.

In the cave was a spring of clean water to wash off at least some of the muck. And that healing, miraculous wonder that we called *"pink mud".* We stripped off Cameron's clothes and rolled him in it. Cameron's eyes opened and he came back to life. The rest of us rubbed the wondermud over our bodies, too.

Cameron stretched his hand out. "Thanks, Don Don."

"How did you know the cave was here?"

388   *No Traveller Returns*

"Donald can see things."

"Maybe you can find the *Vrrooohn,* too? Can you?"

"Yes, I can. I see it."

Keith handed him Ral's map. "Don't need map. *Hollow of the Giants.*" Donald pointed. That was where Karl Hasserman and his companions died.

There was a moment of astonished silence. Then Cameron said, "I guess you got yourself a job as Gangleader, Don Don."

"No! *Tony* Gangleader!" Said with a teasing grin.

"Okay, I'll be Tony, if you want me to. We'll be co-leaders, Don Don. All right? But you got to do the leading around here."

We had to hold a Gang meeting, according to the Boy-law and elect them co-Gangleaders. The vote was 10 to 0. Our co-leaders modestly refused to vote for themselves. They were as great a pair of leaders as any youth gang ever had.

Cameron still couldn't walk too well. He hobbled along, using two sticks as canes. "We better get the *Vrrooohn* while we can, before someone else grabs it." Cameron wouldn't rest. He had to go along. "The Coyote pack has to stay together. As long as we're together, we're invincible."

We had lost our food supplies, too. But there was Goblins' Bread in the cave. That was three things the *Mord* couldn't kill. The Great Pines, Goblins' Bread and the Naghallah boys.

THE HOLLOW OF THE GIANTS

We entered the ravine to the *Hollow of the Giants*. Who or what were these Giants of the *Mord*-ravaged Hollow? Were they living creatures? Were they friendly, indifferent or a new kind of man-destroying horror? Donald knew, but he wouldn't tell us. "You will see Giants."

The Giants proved to be stone statues about seven times the size of an ordinary man. There were seven of them, ranged in a quarter-circle. Six were bestial, weird and misshapen, with tentacles and extra heads and feet and eyes. The middle one was an enormous android, with tremendous jaws and spikes on its back and chest.

They were indeed the same seven as we had encountered by the altar of the desert Temple. That spiked middle Thing was the one that came to life and hunted us. But there was no sign of life or movement in it now.

These, I thought, must be the Devil-gods, the cruel Powers of Fear and Violence that had lured the Lemurian Empire into the *Endless War*. But they were just stone idols built by man. There were men, Lyandra told us, who were possessed by the *Mord* and became maddened and dangerous. Like the Werwolves of Earth, they had lost all control over their actions. The Lemurians did not kill them, but drove them into exile. In the wilderness, perhaps, they revived the cult of the seven Demon-gods of Death and Destruction. Then, in some crazed ritual, they sacrificed each other and themselves.

Yet, as we looked at the statues now, they no longer seemed evil. More like the grotesque gargoyles that joke-playing medieval sculptors put on cathedrals in place of angels. Costume demons at a carnival, rather than the real thing.

Troy thought the seven of them appeared to be laughing. Stevie thought they looked stoned. Jody thought they looked drunk. "That Insect-man looks like my stepfather." He was awful mean to Jody when he was sober. But when he was drunk, he used to give Jody treats and money. Then take it back, or try to, when he became sober again.

The stone Giants looked pitted and weatherworn. Some had cracks in them. Maybe that was from the *Mord*, when it passed by. Roger threw a rock at the three-headed snake and knocked the middle head off.

The other guys all started chucking rocks, too. "Hold it," called Cameron. "Let's find the *Vrrooohn* first!"

At the far end of the *Hollow of the Giants,* we discovered a grotto. This must be where Karl Hasserman took refuge after his failed attack on the Mind Destroyer.

He was lying there on the floor of the grotto with his white hair and pointed goatee and a dueling scar on his right cheek and a monocle still in his eye. Like his picture on the wall at *Kaah Naghallah.* Though he had been dead for many days, the body was remarkably preserved. Almost like he was a statue himself.

For a moment, we thought he might still be alive. But the signs of bodily decay, although delayed, were unmistakable. There was nothing we could do for him any more. In the presence of death, Bobby crossed himself. Donald made a circle around his heart, an ancient Lemurian gesture.

Behind a pile of rocks, we found another body. — A young man not much older than us. There was still a defiant smile on his face. Jerry Golding, perhaps. The third witness to Karl Hasserman's Will. Too bad we never got to know him.

In the back of the grotto was the body of an older woman. That must be Alice Harlow. There was no sign of Dean Harlow, her husband.

"He probably didn't make it to the grotto. He's buried in the Hollow somewhere." The ground had split open and a rock slide covered part of the land.

At Hasserman's feet was a black leather bag. A pale silver glow came up from the inside. "Is that --- *It?*"

The Masters called it, *The Thing Without A Name.* "A Thing of great Power, but only to those who know how to use it. In the wrong hands it could be very dangerous. . . ."

We eyed the black bag warily, like it contained an unexploded bomb.

"*Vrrooohn,*" said Donald.

We had not hesitated to lay hands on the death plates of the Mind Destroyer. But no one dared to be the first to touch the *Vrrooohn.*

"You found it, Don Don. You're the Gangleader. You open the bag."

"No!" said Donald, emphatically. No one else wanted the honor either.

"Maybe there's a curse on the *Vrrooohn,*" suggested Troy. "First guy to touch it gets the curse."

"If there's a curse on it, it's on all of us. We swore to share everything."

"Come on, Cam. You do it!"

Even Cameron balked. Instead, he drew a line in the dirt. "We'll throw pebbles. Whoever gets closest to the line will be the first to hold the *Vrrooohn.*"

"Go ahead, Gifted Child. You get first throw."

It was a shitty throw, nowhere near the line. But the other guys all deliberately threw even worse than me. Raymond was the only guy who even looked like he was trying. Ray Ray is the champ at pebble pitching. He managed to throw just about three inches further away than me.

"Jaymie gets it!"

"Jaymie will be the first to hold the *Vrrooohn.*"

"Jaymie gets the honor."

"And the curse."

I opened up the bag. Inside, was a pale blue crystal, about the size of a soccer ball. Streaks of light kept moving on the surface, in ever changing colors and patterns.

From the top of the Crystal there arose a pair of antlers made from the same sky-blue material. The horns and ball appeared as one. It was as if the antlers had grown right out of the Crystal.

I held the Crystal by the horns above my head. And when I did, a golden light flooded the cave. *The Vrrooohn of Marl-Hai!*

The Vrrooohn of Marl'Hai now had fallen into the hands of the Slave-boys.

Men had died for it and killed for it. The schoolboys of *Kaah Naghallah* had been kidnapped for it, suffered torture by the slave collars and faced the horrors of the Labyrinth.

The Masters of *Naghallah* had plotted for it to bring them unlimited wealth and power; believing *He who holds the Vrrooohn can rule the World.*

Now by a curious quirk of Fate, the Horned Crystal had fallen into the hands of twelve juvenile delinquents. Twelve runaway urchins who really didn't want it, but were afraid to let it go. It would be less dangerous in our hands than in anyone else's.

A golden light fell over each of us and the whole grotto gleamed with rainbow colors. Our fear changed to triumph. *The Triumph of the slave boys!*

"The Slave boys got the *Vrrooohn.* The Masters got screwed!"

We were cheering and shouting and leaping around. Then we remembered the dead and became silent.

"Should we say a prayer for them?"

"It can't hurt," said Cameron.

We recited the Lord's Prayer. Donald chanted something Lemurian. Then we filed out silently, leaving the grotto to the dead.

The dark cloud that had covered the sky now had vanished. The three moons gleamed brighter than we had ever seen them before. A silver radiance fell over the statues of the seven Devil-gods, as if they, too, had been freed from an evil spell.

We no longer felt like smashing the Giants or even throwing rocks at them. In fact, Brandon climbed up on the Snake-man and stuck the missing head back on with mud and clay. Brandon came down fast. He swore the snake heads hissed at him.

We held the *Vrrooohn* up and paraded before the ancient idols. "We got the Power now! Bow to the conquerors!" And Troy swore the Crocodile-man did bow, or at least nod.

We all took turns holding the *Vrrooohn* and all made a

wish by it. Most of the wishes were silly and didn't happen. Roger wished for an ice cream cone, Danny for a stein of beer, and Raymond for a flying machine to ride in. Just wishing didn't make the *Vrrooohn* work.

I made a wish, too. *May the Horned Crystal hold the twelve of us together and not drive us apart.* And from the Giants that towered above us there came a silent voice, as if in answer.

"From this day hence, ye twelve are bound together. There is nothing you can ever do to break away. By the *Vrroohn,* the twelve of you shall be joined and inseparable forever. That is the curse we put on you. *The Curse of the Giants.*"

I thought, if that's supposed to be a curse, it's pretty creampuff. I didn't mind it at all.

REJOICE ALL CREATURES GREAT AND SMALL

The Forty-Fifth Day

We went inland, instead of to the river. We came upon a broad highway that led to a chain of Lemurian villages, abandoned and later devastated by the *Mord.* Lemurian vehicles did not move on wheels. Rather, they floated in the air, propelled by some unexplained power. The highway was not a paved road, but a broad strip of silver grass, lined by forests, lakes and meadows.

The smell of death was still there. Withered trees and scorched land; wrecked vehicles and unburied bodies. Not only Lemurians, but *Oreads, Mu Garroh* and Animal People. Some had household pets with them who perished with their families. We came upon at least two dozen wrecks and stopped counting. The Doom Rays struck far and wide and high into the air. Those who took to the sky found no safety.

We stopped by each body, but all seemed to be beyond help. Long dead. At least no more would die like this. There was no sign of any living thing here. Even the silver grass was shrivelled and dying.

We walked for miles down the empty road toward *Glow Malomba.* At long last, the highway became silver again, lined with wild flowers. The Doom Rays had not reached this point and now they never would.

We reached a grove of trees beside a lake. Fruit trees that grew red peaches the size of pumpkins and a banana-like fruit in heavy clusters. The fruits were all on the upper branches, out of the reach of most animals, but an easy climb for the Coyote kids. We found some *gai'nabs,* too, and feasted.

No birds or mammals could be seen yet. But there were ladybugs and fireflies and great moths with wings of blue and gold.

"Camp here," decided Donald. We were glad to rest. Everyone was pretty well exhausted.

We were still covered with muck and grime and looked more like Abominable Swamp Creatures than human boys. We washed the dirt off our skin and clothes as best we could. Then went swimming in the lake. And it felt good.

Day Forty-Six

In the morning, we got woken up early by chirping crickets and croaking frogs. There were song birds on the trees and no fruit left. The countryside had come to life again.

No *gai'nabs* left, either. But Donald found us some wild carrots. When we got back to Glow Malomba, they ought to feed us well.

We started down the highway. The road seemed longer than we expected. But you can never figure distances in *Bane N'Gai.* We saw now there were birds overhead. A whole flock of blue and red birds. And those silver birds from the mountains. And speckled birds with yellow wings. And quails and gulls and swallows. They were flying all around us. More and more of them, making loud noises. They kept following us. I was afraid they might swoop down and attack us.

Donald started making bird noises, too. "Birds are friends," he told us. "They are happy that the *Mord* is gone. They fly over us to protect us."

"Protect us? From what?"

"From *Anything.*"

Small animals now were following us. Rabbits and squirrels and raccoon-like creatures. And beyond them came flocks of deer and three-horned goats and leaping llamas. And prancing unicorns and jumping kangaroos. The plains on either side of us were alive with animals of every kind. A veritable zoo. But these were no zoo creatures. They were wild beasts of nature, running free, like the Coyote kids.

They moved along beside us on the highway. All craning their necks, trying to look at something. Though there was nothing worth looking at, so far as we could tell. It took us a long time to realize they were looking at *us*.

Still more animals kept coming. Cats and cows and camels. Buffaloes, bears and beavers. Dogs, ducks and donkeys. Trumpeting elephants. Possums, pigs and peacocks. Orioles and ostriches. Porcupines, pandas and monkeys in the trees. Turkeys, toads and turtles. Giant snails and silver wolves and things with fur and feathers that moved on many legs. Walking mushrooms, with eyes and arms. Screeching pterodactyls, a pair of giant octocorns and a great roc hovering high above.

All the creatures of Lemuria appeared to be assembling around us, making mighty noises. Donald said they were celebrating the end of the Sixty Thousand years War. Every creature made its own kind of noise. It sounded like they were giving us the razzberry. But Donald said it was their way of cheering us. We waved and the noise grew louder.

For several miles along the highway, the commotion continued. The animals crowded around us so it was hard to walk without stepping on them. Gradually, the animals moved further away and turned back into the fields and forests.

Rejoice, ye Creatures Great and Small!

Your Land is Saved.

We rounded a hill and there were people waiting and shouting. Many were soldiers in uniform. We were a ragged-looking crew. "Form column of twos," ordered Cameron, "and try to march in step."

We made a botch of it and began tripping over each others' feet.

The people began yelling *"Lanna' Hai!"*, the Lemurian cry of victory. *"Lanna' Hai!"* we yelled back. Then Ral and Lyandra and Trycon came up to greet us and the people all crowded around.

They had felt the explosion and didn't know what happened. They figured us for goners and thought the *Mord* had broken through. Their clairvoyant powers finally told them that the *Mord* was gone and that we were alive and coming back down the highway. But they didn't dare believe it.

The explosion was felt all the way into *Glow Malomba*. It hit the city like an earthquake. The rainbow arches had collapsed and the palace roof had fallen in. They were still counting the damage and the casualties. But nothing could dampen the wild joy of the people at the end of the Sixty Thousand Year War.

More people gathered, waving and shouting. It looked like half the citizens of Glow Malomba were coming out to see us. I was afraid we would be mobbed and maybe somebody might grab the *Vrrooohn* in the confusion. But Lemurians are always polite. They stepped aside for us.

Some doctors and nurses came with what I guess was an ambulance, Lemurian style. We told Ral we were okay. Tell the doctors we didn't want to go to no hospital. Please take us home. They put us on one of those Lemurian magic carpet vehicles and took us back to the apartment.

The birds still followed us and flew over the city. With them was the Great Roc — now a pair of Great Rocs — and their five chicks. The smallest chick with the blue stripe was the one Donald had rescued.

Day Forty-seven

We went to bed and stayed there nearly all day. Doing noble deeds sure makes you sleepy. Lyandra came around and looked in on us, but we were too lazy to get up.

Outside, silver bells tolled in the Cathedral in Thanksgiving to *The Great Mother* "for having sent us these twelve heroic young men who saved us." In a few weeks, we had been transformed from gutterpunk juvenile delinquents into *Blessed Deliverers*. The change was just too screwey to be real.

We had a visit from Ral and three soldiers. Two privates, Gledd and Kollen, and Corporal Tramm. They were supposed to be on guard duty, but nobody told them what to guard, so they decided to come and guard *us*. They all spoke English. When people have mind power, they can learn a language easy. We gabbed for a couple of hours.

When the *Mord* exploded, the Dome was down over the City. The *Mord* blew a hole right through it. The Rainbow Arches collapsed.

People thought the *Mord* had broken through. For twenty-four hours, the soldiers went charging all over the place, repulsing imaginary invaders. Sometimes, they attacked each other by mistake. The Military, said Lyandra, was the only thing in the country that was run by men instead of women. No wonder the Army got all fouled up.

Many buildings in the City had been damaged. The great Royal Library, with its ten billion books, was split apart. Fortunately, the ten billion books were *"in the quayne"* and uninjured. But they got all mixed up and it would take years to sort them out again.

The tower fell off the town hall. The diamond palace of the *Oread* Queen had toppled over on its side. Instead of calling in Lemurian repair men, the *Oreads* tried to put it back by spells and enchantments. And their spells all didn't work! Ral and the soldiers thought this was highly amusing.

Fortunately, no one in the City had been killed in the explosion and only a few had been seriously injured. Among the injured was the corporal, who had a tremendous bandage around his head. He had been ray-gunned accidentally by his own men.

For his gallant services, the corporal had received a huge gold medal, studded with diamonds and rubies. The *Third Class Military Medal* with three moons and stars:

Glorious Defender of Lemuria

Ral and the privates just got the *Fourth Class Military Medal.* Gold with just diamonds. No rubies and only two moons and stars:

Stalwart Defender of Lemuria

"Gosh!" said Bobby. "If that's Third Class, what can they give you for Second and First Class?"

"Second Class," said Gledd, "is the one the generals give to each other. The Rainbow medal with the Tree of Life."

Hero of Lemuria

"The generals," said Kollen, "didn't deserve that medal. What did they do anyway?"

"They didn't do anything," said the Corporal. "They just kept yelling out orders. 'Go here! Go there! What did you find?'

"'We haven't gotten there yet, sir.'

"'Well, hurry, Soldier! Get moving! This is a war, not a picnic!'"

"How about a first class medal?" asked Troy.

"*Glorious Hero of Lemuria,*" explained Gledd. "They give that to a guy after he is dead."

"You'll see it for yourselves," predicted Tramm. "That's the one they're giving *you.*"

"But we ain't dead," objected Bobby.

"Are you sure?"

With their blue and gold uniforms and their many medals, the Royal Lemurian Defense Corps seemed like a comic opera army. I guess that's what they were right now. But in a really rough and long drawn out conflict, I would sooner fight the devils in Hell than the Lemurians.

GLORIOUS HEROES OF LEMURIA

The Forty-Eighth Day

We were summoned to appear before the Queen of Lemuria, *by the Grace of the Great Mother, Queen Hecate X, of Marl'Hai-Glow Malomba and the lands beyond.* She sent her great-grandson, Prince Frain, to escort us.

Prince Frain had a reputation for being a joke player. He had been in the dog house for playing silly tricks on some V.I.P. from Earth. The Big Shot got real insulted. What Earth Big Shot? It could only have been Karl Hasserman. He was the only one from Earth who got here without being carried. Except the Naghallah boys.

The Queen was a stately, elderly lady, nearly seven feet tall, dressed in a flowing robe of blue and gold. Instead of a crown, she had a large black bird sitting on her left shoulder. The bird, we were told, was a royal crow and would only sit on a queen.

Her Majesty beckoned us forward. We kneeled down, but the Queen gestured to us to rise. Then she kissed us each on the top of our heads and rubbed something that looked like lipstick on our foreheads.

Now the Queen made a speech in *Marl-Haic,* the official Lemurian tongue. It has more words than any other language. Whenever they find a word they like anywhere else, the *Lemurian Linguistic Council* puts it in the Imperial Dictionary and makes it a Lemurian word, too. They took a lot of English words, like *glorious, valiant,*

Queen Hecate of Lemuria

stupid and *ridiculous*. They also took words from the Goblins, Oreads and the Animal People.

Sometimes, the Queen woofed like a dog, brayed like a donkey, roared like a lion and chirped like a bird. Sometimes, she sounded like a bugle or a violin. Then suddenly, for no apparent reason, the crowd would cheer and applaud and the crow would caw and flap its wings.

Now, a trumpet sounded and the drums began to roll. The people yelled and shouted. One by one, we stuck our necks out, feeling a bit like the people going to the guillotine. The Queen declared, "I hereby dub you *Glorious Heroes of Lemuria,*" and hung the medal of Highest Honor around our necks.

It was the most golden thing I have ever seen, like a piece of the sun, throwing an aura of radiance around it. On the one side was the Spiral Nebula, the Grand Seal of Marl'Hai. On the other, the inscription, mostly in English.

> *Glorious Hero of Lemuria*
> *Daniel of Larrabie, Earth-America*
> *Lanna'Hai!*

Danny got the one that was meant for me.

The whole thing was embedded in a translucent blue stone, the *Star of Lemuria,* a jewel unknown on Earth. The chain was made of the same thing. Brother Danny was already thinking what he could get some day, if he hocked it. Since we gained the *Vrrooohn,* I was beginning to read minds a little.

Now the Queen took a golden vessel and poured oil on our hair. That made the crowd cheer even more. At that last cheer, the crow flew off the Queen's shoulder and landed on Donald's head. The crowd roared and shouted. Then the crow flew back and settled on the Queen again. The crowd applauded. No matter what happened, it brought a cheer.

Now, they mounted us on unicorns and rode us around. Prince Frain led the procession. He was mounted on what looked like an enormous white frog. The creature jumped like a frog. Prince Frain rode it perfectly, holding on with just his legs. He was dressed in an all white uniform, white shoes and helmet. When they jumped, Frain and the frog seemed almost like one animal. It was a magnificent creature, as big as a horse. The ancient Lemurians used to ride such frogs into battle.

A procession of those magic carpet vehicles floated noiselessly overhead. And around them floated thousands of golden bubbles and gossamer clouds of rainbow colors.

We rode down the *Boulevard of the Beautiful Maidens*. The unicorns had no saddle and no stirrup or bridle. Me and Roger almost fell off. Which would have looked pretty stupid for a hero. Streamers and confetti rained down upon us. And showers of colored lights and sparkling bubbles. Groups of Lemurian kids were throwing flower petals at us. They cheered and we waved and they cheered some more.

Now they were throwing not just petals but whole flowers and bundles of flowers. A bouquet of lillies hit Keith in the face and he nearly fell off his unicorn. We started catching the flowers and throwing them back. Great fun! That made the crowd go wild.

We went down the *Lane of the Noble Elves* and the *Highway of the Marvelous Mothers* to the *Street of the Gallant Youths* and the *Road of the Wise Philosophers,* across the *Terrace of the Eloquent Poets* to the *Avenue of the Oreads.* The Queen of the Oreads wanted to honor us, too.

The Queen looked just like a story book fairy queen. All silver, with a wand and shining crown. She hit us each with the wand on both shoulders and the Elf People cheered. She hung a wreath of flowers around our necks. Red roses. That made us feel like a winning race horse and looked real pretty. But somebody forgot to take off the thorns.

Prince Frain said to get down on our knees and salaam the Queen. I guess that was his idea of a joke, because when we did, all the spectators began to laugh.

Prince Frain, mounted on his Battle Frog.

Now the Queen made a speech in Elf or Faerie that sounded rather like a piano a little out of tune. The crowd cheered and applauded. A band played and people sang the Oread anthem. The Elf drums rolled and the crowd danced around us. Then they anointed us and dumped incense and oil on us, and made us smell like a perfume factory. Then they put us back on the unicorns to parade some more.

We went up the *Boulevard of the Friendly Animals* into the *Place of the Laughing Dryads*. We kept on waving. The flowers and confetti and gleaming bubbles kept coming. And the bells tolled everywhere we went. We rode on through a blizzard of streamers. And here were the Cow-like People mooing and the Donkey People braying and the Penguin People squawking and flapping their wings.

The people stared at us with their mouths open, like they couldn't quite believe it. *These are heroes?* For hundreds of years, they had been living in terror. And a bunch of stupid kids come blundering in from Earth and end the terror. All in a couple of minutes. Because our minds were too weak to be destroyed by the Mind-Destroyer. The *Mord* was geared to kill off the higher minds. We were like those bacteria that can live without air or water. We were so low on the evolutionary scale that we survived.

We reached the *Avenue of the Faithful Friends*. The street was lined on both sides by Lemurian cadets in their blue and gold uniforms. They had been mobilized to defend the City and now they didn't want to go home.

The cadets were waving banners and were jumping up and down. Our unicorns began jumping, too. For some reason, my steed stood up on his hind legs and dumped me off. The crowd cheered and applauded. I grabbed the unicorn's horn and climbed back up. The crowd cheered again. They cheered anything. And the unicorn went prancing around, shaking his head like he was taking a bow.

And there were a group of girl cadets, shouting and laughing. And in the middle of them were our soldier friends, Gledd, Tramm and Kollen. The girls had on those same blue and gold uniforms with ray guns, ribbons and medals. The only way you could tell the girls from the guys was their hair was longer.

We entered the *Square of the Mu Garroh*, the Goblins, that is, where Trycon greeted us. The Goblin Queen wanted to present a gift to us and to honor us in the traditional way the Goblins always honored their heroes. The gift turned out to be something real nice and very useful. A silver knapack for each of us, real light and strong and roomy. Good to put our jewels in and hide the *Vrrooohn.*

It's hard to tell with Goblins, but I thought the "Queen" might be a man. He or she was wearing trousers and spoke with a deep voice. However, Goblin ladies sometimes do that, too.

The Ruler made a speech in English, praising our valor; then conferred a blessing on us in Goblinese. Then, he (or she) said, "On this great day, let us honor our heroes for their noble deeds."

We were standing at the edge of a pool with reddish water. And darned if they didn't throw us in. All twelve of us. While the assembled Goblins cheered wildly.

Trycon said this was the very highest honor the *Mu Garroh* could bestow. Only the most worthy received that honor. No one else had been dunked in that pool for seven years.

The Goblins were dead serious, but Prince Frain was laughing. Cameron said they ought to honor Prince Frain, too. Surely the Queen's great-grandson deserved as much honor as a bunch of foreigners!

The Goblins appeared embarrassed. They apologized to Prince Frain then grabbed him and tossed the Prince into the sacred pool, too. Nobody intended to honor the big white frog. But when Frain got doused, the creature jumped in after him.

We were all dripping wet and covered with some greenish water plants. The Prince had lost his helmet in the pool and nobody offered to get it. The frog creature, however, jumped in again and, in the manner of a retriever

The Goblins bowed to Prince Frain,
then doused him in the slimy pond.

dog, brought the helmet back to the Prince, wagging its short, stubby tail.

Acting with aristocratic grace, Prince Frain bowed in a courtly manner and thanked the Goblins for the great honor they had bestowed upon him. And the copy-cat Coyote kids did the same.

The unicorns went back to the royal stable. "Just let them go. They know the way." We thought they might run off and join the herds of wild unicorns out on the prairies. "Why should they? They like it here."

THE PALACE BANQUET

The Forty-Ninth Day

Next morning, Prince Frain appeared again, this time in a sky blue uniform replete with ribbons, braid and sashes. Nearly everybody, it seemed, had one medal. The Prince had three. The Second, Third and Fourth Class Military Medallions. Also, a scarlet heart for being injured in battle.

"What happened?" asked Bobby. "Did someone shoot you?"

"He got kicked by a unicorn."

"He got jumped by a frog."

"No. Guess again."

A piece of the Rainbow Arch had fallen on Prince Frain's head. Fortunately, the Prince was wearing his helmet.

We, Glorious Heroes of Lemuria, were to be the guests of honor at a royal banquet in the palace gardens. A feast of celebration and rejoicing. "Come just as you are." We barbarians were expected to wear our native clothes, which were blue jeans, T-shirts and sneakers.

One of those flying vehicles took us to the palace grounds. The whole area was a great garden, with crystal fountains and groves of flowering trees. Unicorns and other animals wandered freely through the gardens. Red, blue and yellow birds were all over the place and those big riding frogs were jumping around.

The Queen's table, all blue and gold, was on an elevated platform. Lyandra, Ral and Trycon were there. And the Pussycat lady juror. Also, the High Priestess, members of the Grand Council and the royal family. And the *Prophetess of the Oracle of Wisdom,* or something like that. When everyone else was in despair, she had predicted that strangers would come by the river and save the City. And who should come along but the Naghallah boys. Now the Prophetess was in high standing. Everyone forgot about all the things she predicted that didn't happen.

Her newest and startling prediction was that the next Queen of Lemuria would be a man. Lemuria, in a nice way, was a sort of Matriarchy. Everyone was theoretically equal, but the girls were a bit more equal than the guys. Men could be charming, creative, brave, adventurous; do deeds of daring; explore unknown lands; build and fight. But when it came to something really serious, there was always a lady in charge.

Men voted for women. They didn't trust each other. It had been that way ever since the Lemurians crossed the Galaxy. After the patriarchal Lemurian Empire started the Sixty Thousand Year War and couldn't stop it.

Of the nineteen members of the Grand Council, only one was a human male. That was the King Consort, the Queen's husband. He had perished fighting the *Mord.* We stood for a moment of silence in his memory. The other males were an Elf, a Goblin and a Bear-man. There were also fifteen lady members, including the Queen's sister.

There were thousands of guests at the banquet. About a third of them were from non-human races. Goblins and Oreads and Animal People. Donald's *Lady of the Forest* was present with a small Octocorn, maybe a calf of the big one.

There were Cat and Dog People, wearing lockets and necklaces. Giant Robins, Bluebirds, Penguins, Owls, Parrots and Blackbirds. All feathered, yet somehow manlike with human hands. There were Goat and Deer People with horns and antlers, but with fingers and booted feet. And here was a white rabbit, a perfect model for the Easter bunny. Some even had shells like a snail and many eyes. They all mingled easily with everyone else. We were the ones people stared at. Politely, of course.

Whatever their violent past, the Lemurians had now achieved a wonderful harmony. All at once, we felt very glad and very proud that this happy corner of Creation had been saved.

The Queen was wearing an enormous hat, covered with flowers and ribbons and the royal crow was sitting on top of it. She greeted us each by name and introduced us to the guests. The crowd cheered and applauded. Also woofed and chirped, squawked and bleated, bellowed and made musical noises. The High Priestess chanted out the Benediction. The *Oreads* did a ritual dance and the Feast began.

The royal table was like a triple horse shoe. We, guests of honor, were seated in the middle, next to the Queen. She asked us about Earth and about our travels. We told her everything, from the boy-catcher van to *Naghallah* to the Gateway to the destruction of the *Mord.*

"I suppose now you will go back?"

"Yes, Your Majesty."

"You don't have to. You could stay if you wanted."

The Prophetess said, "They *will* go back. It is their Destiny."

The Priestess said, "Men make their own Destiny."

There were endless tables of goodies here. What they call a *buffet.* Everyone served themselves, including the Queen. Pies and puddings and tarts. About twenty different kinds of cheeses. Even something that tasted like ice cream.

Everything was vegetarian and delicious. There must have been at least fifty different vegetables. Corn and potatoes, artichokes and asparagus, beans and peas and platters of things that were never seen or tasted on Earth.

Tables were piled high with fruits and jellies and salads and spices. We tried everything, including the sauces. There must have been fifty different kinds of those, too.

Prince Frain passed us a gooey sauce. Pretending to be clumsy, he managed to dump most of it into Cameron's lap. Some of it spilled over onto Brandon, Stevie, Bobby and me.

"I'm frightfully sorry!" That's what Prince Frain said. But I think what he really meant was "That makes us even." For getting Frain dunked in the Goblins' murky pool.

The polite Lemurians pretended not to notice it. But the crow cawed loudly and flapped his wings. Then he flew off the Queen's hat, landed on Donald's head, cawed some more and then flew back again to the Queen. You couldn't help noticing *that*. Ral Garyon was trying not to laugh. The Queen gave Frain a dirty look.

We were told to walk around and show ourselves. "You don't have to talk. Just wave and be friendly." Like we were campaigning for public office. People stared and smiled at us.

"So that's what Earth people look like."
"They look almost human, don't they?"
"I thought Earth people were primitive savages."
"They are not as backward as we thought."
"A bit smaller than us."
"These are neophytes. Not full grown yet."
"Are they all male?"
"It's hard to tell with their clothes on."

A group of Animal People crowded eagerly around us. The Setter Dog Lady embraced us and licked our faces. The Kangaroo men mounted us on their shoulders and went leaping around all over the gardens, jumping over chairs and tables. A group of nine foot Bearmen cheered us then threw us up into the air, shouting "Yahhoo Hweee! Yahhoo Hweee!" That's what the Bearmen did to the cubs to show affection. I was afraid they might muff the catch and drop us, but they caught us every time.

Then they lifted us onto their heads and carried us back to the royal table, saluted us and bowed to the Queen. In *Glow Malomba*, there is only a narrow line between being honored and being assaulted. I noticed Prince Frain

ducked out of the way. He didn't want to be honored, too.

Lemonade and punch were in abundance. There were innumerable pitchers of fruit juices and delectable beverages, along with cakes and confections. Goblins' Ale and Dryads' Mead flowed freely and there was a marvelous drink that looked like milk and tasted like Firewater.

The Elfin orchestra made merry music. There were no visible loud speakers, but the sound carried all over the palace grounds. The merry-makers grouped into pairs and trios; then lined up in a long chain of dancers, like a snake dance or a congo line. About a thousand people long. They called it a *Revel.*

Lemurians and Oreads, Goblins and Earth kids and Animal People. Everybody got into it. Around and around we went, leaping and whirling. Some almost flying. The older people watched, beating time with their hands and feet. Some dancers dropped out, gasping for breath. The Earth kids were still going when the music stopped.

Now her Majesty was getting sleepy. She yawned several times, then looked anxiously at the assembled celebrities. Reassured, she graciously waved *Good Night.* Then, with two royal Counsellors, she departed on one of those sky boats to a private palace outside the city. The royal crow was still sitting on her hat.

"Long live the Queen!" everyone shouted. "Long live Lemuria. *Lanna'Hai!*"

Goblins' Ale is strong stuff and Dryads' Mead is even stronger. Lyandra warned us not to take too much of it. We should have heeded her advice.

There was more chain dancing. One *Revel* after another. The Earth kids were always in on it, grabbing anybody for a partner. We danced in a *Revel* and we danced by ourselves, even after the music stopped. People cheered us, but they were really laughing.

Stupid Donald got into a dancing contest with some Elves and stupid Cameron got into a drinking contest with Prince Frain. They both came out second best.

At the end of the Festival, at least four of us *Glorious Heroes of Lemuria* had passed out and had to be carried home. As heroes, we make good comedians.

FAREWELL

The Fiftieth Day

We prepared to return to Earth, bearing the jewels and the *Vrrooohn.* The Lemurians never stole things. Maybe because they had enough of everything. Or maybe because they could read each others' minds and any theft could be readily detected. But from here on, we would have to guard our treasure well.

We all felt sorry to go. We had grown to love this beautiful land and its friendly citizens. But some powerful force was pulling us back to Earth.

We thought of all the marvels we had seen here, unknown on Earth. We took with us just two: some Goblins' Bread and some of that healing pink *Wondermud.*

Before we departed, we went to the Cathedral of *Marl 'Hai,* where we were greeted by the High Priestess. She wore a silver robe and a black veil that covered her long, white hair. Nobody told us to kneel, but we did. It seemed the right thing to do.

The High Priestess spoke to us silently. She seemed to be telepathing her thoughts:

"The World is of the nature of *Mind.* Each World is an *Eternal Mind.* All Worlds and all Realities are united in *The Great Mother,* the Creator of all Being.

"There is no death within *The Great Mother.* All things that have been are remembered and will be again. The *Tree of Being* shall branch and re-branch, becoming ever greater. All Realities shall multiply and grow forever.

"But the Present can be hard and filled with fear and torment. We cling to the life we know, even if we are destined to live again. . . . . "

The High Priestess of the Temple of Marl'Hai

She smiled and stretched her hand out and touched each of us. With her touch, a warm radiance flowed through our body.

"Go forth now freely. You have given us back our life. We can never repay you. But select from among our greatest treasures and take whatever you can carry, with our blessing.

"You may take the *Horned Crystal* with you, but beware of it. On Earth, the *Vrrooohn* will give you great power. But Power can fester and become deadly. As you act, so shall you become. . . . .

"Stand together always, as you have here. Together, you are a hundred times stronger than alone. . . . .

"You face grave perils and a terrible ordeal, but with the help of the *Almighty Mother,* the Infinite and Eternal Mind, you shall prevail. Remember, all things are in the *Eternal Mind* and the *Eternal Mind* is in you.

"May Hope and Love and Faith be with you forever. *Farewell.* . . . ."

BAD NEWS

Mitch and Pamela Larrabie did not expect to meet Mr. Bartlow at the airport. But he was there, accompanied by a man he introduced as "Major Powell." The Larrabie parents had not informed Bartlow of their return from Europe. However, a man with Mr. Bartlow's connections had ways of finding things out.

Powell was stony-faced. Bartlow looked very grave. "I'm afraid we have some rather bad news for you."

"About the boys?"

"Yes. They have run away from the school."

"Run away?" cried Mother. "I thought the boys were not unhappy there. In fact, Jaymie wanted to stay---"

"I would have taken Jaymie out," said Mitch. "If he wanted to leave."

"It wasn't just Jaymie and Daniel," declared Bartlow. "There were ten other boys involved in the runaway. They were very wild, rebellious youngsters who couldn't take even the mildest discipline.

"In fact, these boys were emotionally disturbed and borderline psychotic. Not Jaymie. But Jaymie is a follower, not a leader. He goes along with whatever Daniel, or Westcott, or Scanlon tell him. Some of these boys are bad actors. They decided to leave and they dragged along the younger boys and that retard, Donald---"

"It shouldn't be hard to trace twelve boys," said Mitch. "After all, where can they go?"

"We think they went into the mountains."

"They probably will come back by themselves, as soon as their food gives out. A few cold nights and a few days of hunger and they'll return with their tails between their legs."

"I'm afraid you don't understand. Tell them, Major."

"The boys have been missing for a month. We have searched the entire region, both by plane and on foot. We have not been able to find any trace of any of the boys."

Mother now grew excited and angry. "And why didn't you let us know when they were missing?"

"We didn't want to alarm you unduly. We had every hope of finding the boys promptly. We are doing everything we can---"

"I don't believe it!" interrupted Mother. "I think you can do a great deal more!"

"We will do our very best," pledged Major Powell. "I give you my word---"

"I don't want your word!" shouted Mother. "I don't think this concerns you at all. I want to talk to the man who is Head of this school and find out why these boys ran away. What is going on here anyway?"

"You mean Dr. Mehary?" asked Mitch, meekly.

"Yes, Dr. Mehary. That silly psychiatrist. The one who takes kids apart and puts them together again correctly. He's the one responsible for this peculiar school. Why isn't he here?"

Powell and Bartlow looked at each other. Then Bartlow said, "I'm sorry. Dr. Mehary has disappeared, too."

Mitch looked astounded, Pamela incredulous. He caught her arm to keep her from falling. But she broke loose.

"We must call the police!" shouted Mother. "Right away!"

"We have already called them," Bartlow assured her. "The State police, the County Police and the Bureau of Missing Persons are all working on the case."

Mitch said, "We must offer a reward, Bartlow."

"Yes, we will. In fact, Karl Hasserman has already offered a reward. One hundred thousand dollars for the safe return of the boys."

"That's not very much for *him*," protested Mother. "After all, he was the sponsor of this weird school. He is responsible. We must see him!"

"I'm afraid that would be impossible," said Mr. Bartlow. "Karl Hasserman is gravely ill and is not permitted visitors."

"We must go to the school as soon as possible."

"That would not be helpful," said Mr. Bartlow. "Go home now. You may receive some important messages."

"What kind of messages? Do you suspect kidnapping?"
"One never knows. Go home and wait."
Mitch said, "I think we better do it, Pamela."
When the parents had departed, Powell said, "I think that Larrabie woman may be hard to handle."

* * * * * * *

"I don't believe there was a runaway," said Pamela.
"I'm not sure I do either," answered Mitch. "Bartlow can be very ruthless and very nasty."
"Do you think he knows where the boys are?"
"I'm inclined to think he does. Believe me, Pamela, our chances of getting the boys back alive are a good deal better if we don't try to cross him. There is no point in rushing up to the school. We would learn nothing. And besides, *it could be dangerous.*"
"Is it really that bad?"
He nodded.
"Why, oh why, did you ever get involved with a man like that?"
Mitch didn't answer. His face had a drawn, haggard look.
"I will wait one more day," agreed Mother.
"At least call the family," urged Mitch. "Oscar and Rosa, Leon and Laura, Katie and Michael; also, Dr. Weinberger and the Meyers. Don't do anything alone!"

RETURN TO EARTH

We loaded our stuff onto one of those magic carpet vehicles. A few hours flying would save us weeks of walking. Would we have to go back the way we came? No, there was another Gateway. Lyandra knew it well. She piloted the sky boat. Ral sat beside her. Prince Frain and his friends followed in a second sky boat. Trycon and his Goblins came in a third one.

The three airships took off straight up into the air over *Glow Malomba*. We were now in one of those shining chariots we had seen from the land. We thought then they were driven by gods or demons. Or else, had a life of their own. Flaming monsters of the sky, seeking their prey. Now, we knew it was just another man-built machine.

The airships moved silently, propelled by forces Ral tried to explain, but which we couldn't understand. Actually, the sky boats were even easier to drive than the amphibians by which we had traversed the tunnels. Ral said they couldn't crash. There was a built-in anti-collision. We all took turns driving the vehicle.

We were now far higher than the highest mountains. But the three moons and the stars appeared ever further away. No matter how high you rose or how far you went, those celestial bodies never seemed to get any nearer. That was one of the mysteries of *Bane N'Gai*. In this Alternate World, distances didn't follow Earth geometry. Straight lines finally curved and curved lines spiralled. What spirals did was something only a Lemurian mathematician could figure out. But the end result was those sky bodies were unreachable. "You just can't get to there from here." If you kept going higher long enough, after a while you started coming back down.

Ral thought, "The *Infinite Mother* who created this world is a bit of a jokester. She doesn't like to be explained. Whenever anyone tries it, She makes them look wrong and foolish. But She has given us a good world." Those distant celestial bodies gave forth rays that let the plants grow and made the land rich and abundant.

As we watched the land below, the scene was like a movie reel run backwards. Here was the city and the river and the high mountains we had crossed before. . . . Huge cliffs and crags and jagged peaks. . . . Over the nesting grounds of the pterodactyls. For a while, two great rocs and five smaller ones flew beside us, watched the ships curiously and then veered away. . . .

We flew on. Over the desert and the silver forest and the endless fen. . . . Over deep hollows, ravines and chasms. . . . Over plains and meadows with grazing animals. . . . Over the *Garden of Eden*. . . . And the Swamp of the Brontosaurus. . . . And the Woods of the Great Coyote. . . . And the high rocks with the Cave of the Giant Rats. . . . Toward the Abyss.

But now we turned sharply leftward and came to a region we had never seen before. . . . A towering mountain range with bare peaks of gleaming red stones.

We landed on a high plateau. Before us was a tremendous towering peak. The summit was lost in a grey cloud that hung above us. *"This is It. The Second Gateway. Goodbye friends. Come back some day."*

"We hope we can. If you ever come to Earth, be sure to look us up. Thanks for everything!"

We all felt sad. But Donald looked the saddest. There were tears in his eyes. We didn't then know why.

There was a door here. At first glance, it looked like just part of the mountain. Lyandra did something and it opened up. Beyond the stone door was a spiral ramp that climbed up endlessly, dimly illuminated by a silver light. We walked in silence. Donald hung back and dragged his feet. His head drooped and his yellow eyes weren't glowing any more.

After about an hour, we reached a level passageway. Then a stone stairway and later another spiral ramp. We halted now to eat and drink.

Another stairway. Then still another ramp that led into a wide, circular chamber, covered with curious markings. From here, a curving tunnel ran downward. The tunnel ended abruptly in what seemed to be a solid rock wall.

"Dead end," said Keith. "We must have taken a wrong turn."

"No," said Donald. "This is the Gateway." He put his arm out. The rock parted and seemed to flow around him, like heavy mist. "Go!"

"You lead us, Don Don."

"I can't. I have to go back." Donald's voice broke. He gave a choking sob.

It was hard to understand what Donald was saying and why he had to go back. He started talking what appeared to be Lemurian. It seemed, however, that the Prophetess had made trouble for us. She had predicted that a man would be the next Queen. That man would come by the river and save the city and the people.

Now we had come by the river and saved the City. Not because we were so wise, but because we were too stupid to be wasted by the Mind Destroyer. The Queen, of course, would have to be Lemurian. That let the rest of us out. Donald was only sort of half Lemurian. But he fitted closest to the prophecy. Besides, that royal crow had sat on Donald's head, not once but *twice.* Royal crows, according to tradition, will only sit on a Queen.

The old Queen had a lot of life left in her. But she was getting weary and talked about retiring to her mountain lodge to grow Bird-trees. The Queen-makers had their eye on Donald for the future. They wanted to groom him as a Lemurian Princess. That would take a lot of training and education.

"Do you *want* to be a Lemurian Princess?"

No, Donald didn't. "But I promised---"

They had left one airship for him on the plateau.

"They can come back and get it. And if they want a guy for Queen, what's wrong with Prince Frain?"

"I gave my word," said Donald. "I can't break it."

"Then we'll have to kidnap you. Anyway, they promised us if we got rid of the *Mord,* we could go back to Earth with anything we could carry. We'll have to carry Don Don."

"They will be waiting for me."

"They can read your mind. Send them a message that you can't come. You're being kidnapped."

Donald turned slowly, as if to go back. "Come on, guys, grab him!"

Donald resisted with all the power of a two year old who doesn't want to go to bed. Cameron, Stevie, Keith and Danny each grabbed an arm or a leg and lifted Donald up.

"Wait! I'll walk."

We half dragged half shoved Don Don, and the Gateway opened up around us. Donald moved along without resistance. After about ten minutes, he halted again. "Hold it!"

Donald had received a message. Telepathic, of course. Donald's mood changed and he began to laugh. "It's from Ral Garyon. He says I'd make a *lousy* Princess. They won't tell the Grand Council I ran away. Ral will say they kicked me out."

We began moving again through a long dark tunnel. The mist around us grew denser and thicker. We had to struggle to break through. All at once, we were out of it. The mist ended. The sides of the tunnel fell away. Now we were no longer in the mountain, but in an open hollow underneath the sky.

A dazzling light exploded around us. The sky was on fire. A searing yellow ball hung over our heads — enormous and unbelievable. That fireball blinded our eyes. We put our hands over our faces and turned away.

It was several minutes until we opened our eyes and could see again. "Where the Hell are we?"

"We're back on Earth," said Keith, "And that fireball is the sun."

[End of Book Three]

BOOK IV

THE INCREDIBLE TREASURE

And the Triumph of the Coyotes

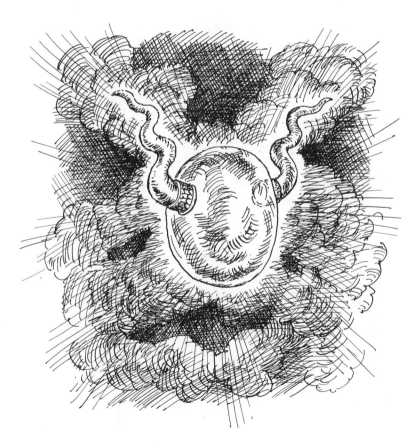

The Coyotes . . . . Danny, Raymond, Keith, Stevie
Bobby, Jaymie, Brandon, Donald
Cameron, Roger, Jody and Troy
The Larrabie Parents . . . . Mitchell and Pamela Larrabie

Relatives . . . . Uncle Oscar and Aunt Rosa
Uncle Leon and Aunt Laura
Cousin Katie and Cousin Michael
Neighbors . . . . The Meyers, The Weismanns,
Dr. Weinberger and Family, The Grouchy Man

The Masters of Naghallah . . . . "Commander" Bartlow,
"Major" Powell, "Colonel" Lammington, "Captain" Craig
"Captains" Striker and Klayborne

The Gay Poet . . . . Rodney Desmond
The Inspector of Police . . . . Inspector Smith
Lady Detective . . . . Officer Caroline
The Baby Nurse . . . . Miss Ferris
Hunted Fugitive . . . . Franz Hasserman
Night Watchman . . . . Larry
Professional Murderer . . . . The Boss
Hired Killers . . . . The Creeper, Buggsey, Wires, Harry,
The Fish, The Hop Toad and Others

Lady Ranger, Caretaker, Dog Handler, Conspirators,
Kidnappers, Youths, Girls, Friends, Merrymakers,
Citizens, Police, Visitors

THE FOREST PRIMEVAL

How much Earth time had passed since we went away? By our body time, it was nearly night. But by the sun it must be around high noon. Just gaining or losing seven hours going in and out of an Alternate Universe wasn't very much. But what about the date?

We had come out toward the bottom of a rock-covered mountain. Around us was a vast forest, extending as far as the eye could see. The autumn foliage was now in full glory; a magnificent panorama of orange, red and yellow. A vista truly as splendid as the forests of *Bane N'Gai,* only it wouldn't last more than a few days. There was a heavy carpet of fallen leaves already.

It was now the high tide of the Indian Summer. Late October. That checked. They put us in the dungeon around the 10th of August. We spent maybe nineteen days in the dungeon and fifty-one days in *Bane N'Gai.*

"But how do we know what year it is?" wondered Brandon. "Maybe we're like Rip Van Wrinkle and it's twenty years since we left."

The whole area looked wild and primitive, with no sign of human civilization. "Maybe," reflected Troy, "we're in a Time Warp and back in the days before Columbus."

Raymond was carrying the *Vrrooohn* and talked to it. "*Oh, Horned Crystal, guide us.* It says to go South."

"I didn't hear it say anything," objected Steve.

"It talks to your mind," insisted Raymond.

The *Vrrooohn* was supposed to give us awesome power. We soon found several things it couldn't do. It couldn't make you levitate or walk on water. Stevie tried to fly and fell on his ass. Bobby tried to walk across a swampy pond and got a dowsing.

If this really was the Forest Primeval, we were in trouble. There were no gai'nabs or Goblins' Bread in this Earth world; no sheltering caves. And it was getting cold. It was too late to go back to *Bane N'Gai.* The Gateway closed solid after we left it. The Lemurians didn't want people going in and out. Not even their friends.

We stumbled through the heavy brush, half expecting to run into a saber-toothed tiger or at least a grizzly bear. But we didn't spot even a moose or a racoon. Just a small white lizard on a rock and a rabbit in a clump of ferns.

We kept going south by the sun. Raymond was in the lead. For several hours, we broke our way through briar and marsh, looking vainly for some sign of human habitation. Finally, we hit an overgrown trail and a few trees that had blue markers.

About a mile down the trail, we reached a brook. Here was a burned out campfire with some broken bottles, empty beer cans, discarded cigarette butts and a heap of rubbish. The guys cheered. We weren't in the Forest Primeval nor in some far-out world of the future. We were back in civilized America!

We made camp. It was chilly here. A lot colder than in *Bane N'Gai.* We tried to start a fire with no matches, using mind power and rubbing two sticks together. It didn't work.

Brother Danny cursed. "This fucking *Vrrooohn* made Karl Hasserman a billionaire. But it can't keep us from freezing."

It was getting colder. We huddled together in a heap, like the deer do in the winter. That helped a little, but not much. We were all shivering in our light Lemurian clothes.

"You got to talk to the *Vrrooohn,*" Raymond insisted.

"We did talk."

"It didn't hear you." Raymond put the *Vrrooohn* down in the middle of us and said, "Oh, *Horned Crystal,* give us heat!"

Absolutely nothing happened.

Raymond tried again. "You got to talk to It real respectful-like. *Oh, Great Crystal, with the horns of the Laranak, the Sky Beast, give us your Power! Save us, your devoted servitors, from freezing!*"

All at once, the Vrrooohn began to glow. It warmed us up until we were almost sweating. There was frost on the ground around us and ice on the pond by morning. But the twelve Naghallah boys slept warm and comfortable throughout the night.

In the morning, we were awful hungry. We ate up almost all the food we brought with us. We even started nibbling on the Goblins' Bread that we were going to donate to Science. We were wet, too. It must have been raining.

We found a couple of small caves. We seeded them with Goblins' Bread. Maybe it will grow and spread, but I doubt it. The climate is too cold.

We followed the trail with the blue markers. About an hour later, we reached the Ranger's cabin.

THE CABIN OF DEATH

We had been striving to get back to Earth and had given little thought to what would happen when we got there. We would have to give them some kind of story. *We were hiking in the woods. We got lost.* We must at all accounts keep the *Vrrooohn* and the jewels hidden.

Don Don carried the *Vrrooohn*. The jewels we split up among the rest of us. We carried our treasure in the Goblins' silver knapsacks, wrapped up in our extra clothes. To Jaymie was entrusted the Testament of Karl Hasserman, a brown envelope sewed into my jacket.

The Ranger in a brown uniform was a lady. She was a handsome woman, though hefty, and all muscle. The kind who had to show she was as good or better than a man.

"Are you the Naghallah boys?" We had been reported missing. We had gone into the mountains and didn't return.

"Tell me what happened. Did you guys run away from the school?"

We let Cameron do the talking. He didn't trust the Ranger. None of us did. She was a grown-up. The Masters were grown-ups. They would be believed ahead of us.

"I guess you might call it a runaway," said Cameron. "We just took off and went into the woods."

"Why did you leave the school?"

"The school was pretty shitty — I mean lousy."

"Did they abuse you?"

"They kept us locked up all the time. They wouldn't let us do nuthin'. We got sick of it."

"Are you ready to go back to the school?"

"We ain't goin' back!" said Stevie emphatically. "We all live down near Greenwood. We're going home."

The Lady Ranger sighed, "I understand you boys were placed in the school by the Juvenile Court. You can't just walk away. The police have been searching for you. I will have to inform them."

Cameron said, "We're awful tired and hungry, ma'am."

"Why, of course. And you're wet, too. Make a fire and dry out. And help yourselves to food. You boys have been in the woods for over a month. And you look pretty healthy. Where did you get your supplies?"

"We take the Fifth Amendment on that, ma'am."

"You stole them from the school, no doubt. Or from somebody else. Well, that's not my concern. You must be twelve real good woodsmen. Where did you hide out? Or don't you want to tell me?"

Cameron just smiled.

"A secret hide-out? I'm sorry if I talk so much. You must be hungry. Go ahead and eat."

We built a fire and scavenged in the kitchen. There were lots of canned goods and edibles here. Enough to feed a small army. We started cooking. Each of us made our own thing and got in each other's way. Brandon was making pancakes; Troy, hot cocoa; Keith, mushroom soup. Bobby was cooking up fried potatoes. Roger struggled to open up cans of pears and peaches with a can-opener that didn't work.

Me and Cameron studied the Ranger's maps. We were about fifty miles north of Mountainville and thirty miles north of *Kaah Naghallah*, where we started from.

We ate, then lay around in front of the fire and dozed a

while. We were short on sleep. Then we went back and ate some more. We decided to stick around until tonight. We'd take off and disappear after the Lady Ranger was asleep. We didn't know she had a short wave radio transmitter. We didn't know she had sent a call out. We were too busy eating and loafing.

There was a narrow road on the far side of the cabin. A yellow vehicle splashed through the mud. The car halted and four men approached the cabin. They wore trench coats and brown uniforms, but they weren't rangers. We knew them and knew there was going to be trouble. It was "Commander" Lammington. With him were "Captains" Klayborne, Craig and Striker.

Twelve kids against four men. And we weren't ordinary kids. We had been in *Bane N'Gai* and we held the *Vrrooohn*. In a showdown, we could hold our own.

Lammington was carrying something, but it wasn't a gun. They might have guns concealed on their person. Or the Lady Ranger might have firearms. It was hard to tell if she was one of *them*, or just a buttinsky.

But now there was a second car coming up the road. There were five men in it. These men didn't come to the cabin. They were waiting outside and *they* had guns.

What fools we were, getting caught like this. We who had vanquished the Fen-Horror and the Terror-Idol and the Spider-Monster and the Mind-Destroyer had fallen into a stupid trap on Earth.

Commander Lammington led the procession of four into the cabin. The five gunmen spread out, waiting for a signal. The twelve Naghallah kids were sitting at the table. Brandon had made us a jello desert.

"Don't get up, boys." We expected Lammington would threaten and abuse us. But his manner was surprisingly genial.

"Well, boys, I can't believe it! All twelve of you back from the lower regions. Did they tell you where they were, Ranger?"

"No, they didn't."

"Down in the caves. There's a network of caves and an

old iron mine near Thunder Mountain."

"I know the mine," said the Lady Ranger. "I searched it. There were no boys down there." There was an edge of disbelief and suspicion in her voice. I figured she wasn't one of Lammington's agents. At least, she wasn't in the know.

Craig seemed genuinely friendly. Striker nodded at us. Klayborne gave us a cold look, like an undertaker sizing up a corpse.

There were a series of rifle shots. "Somebody's hunting out of season," said Craig.

"Sounds pretty close, too."

"You folks better go out and see what's going on," said Lammington. "I want a chance to talk to my boys in private."

He spoke like a doting father, planning a man-to-man talk with his prodigal sons. The Lady Ranger departed with Striker and Craig. Lammington nodded at Klayborne and he remained. He stood back against the wall. His hands were in his coat pockets. Above him, a magnificent moosehead was mounted on a heavy wooden slab. A hunter's prize trophy. What a shame! To kill the noble creature for an ornament! Klayborne might be holding a gun. Lammington didn't trust us and had Klayborne there for protection.

"Now," Lammington asked eagerly, "Did you find it?"

"Find *what?*" asked Cameron.

"You know what I mean. Karl Hasserman's treasure."

"No, sir," said Cameron. "We went all over the place and finally got out near Thunder Mountain."

"I don't believe you. You couldn't have gotten out without the ——"

"The *Vrrooohn?*"

"How do you know the name?"

"Mr. Smeer told us. He is dead."

"Dead?" The mention of Smeer's name left Lammington a little shaken. "Did you kill him?"

"No, sir. We tried to save him. He was bitten by a poisonous worm."

"Where is the *Vrrooohn* now?"

Cameron didn't answer. We were all silent.

"Remember the reward we promised you. One million dollars."

"For *each* of us?"

"Yes, for each of you. Did you see Karl Hasserman?"

"He is dead, too."

Lammington looked relieved. "That," he started to say, "simplified matters." But he cut himself short.

"Is it a bargain? Twelve million for the *Vrrooohn*?"

"When will we get the money?"

"I will arrange it with Bartlow. The twelve million will be deposited for you in the Hasserman bank. Since you are minors, the income will be paid to your guardians until you are eighteen. Then you will receive the principal."

I knew what Cameron was doing. Trying to bluff Lammington and make him think we had hidden the *Vrrooohn* somewhere. Then he had to give us a chance to go and get it. And all the while Donald was holding it under the table.

At some point, Lammington sensed we had the *Vrrooohn* with us now. But we were stupid, ignorant kids who didn't know what to do with it.

He gave us a friendly smile. "I can't pay over the twelve million dollars now. But I'll give you boys each something on account."

From his wallet, he pulled out a roll of fifty dollar bills and peeled off two for each of us. "That'll buy you kids a lot of bubble gum.

"Oh, I forgot. You're men now. You have been through *Bane N'Gai*. No more bubble gum. Let me get you something for a man."

Lammington went into the kitchen and came back with twelve gold-leaf glasses. Then he returned and brought in a fancy bottle of brandy and another glass already filled. "Join us, Klayborne?"

"No, thank you." Klayborne just stood there under the moosehead. His face looked unnaturally white.

Lammington poured out the brandy into the gold leaf

glasses. They were real fancy and expensive. The kind of stuff you'd expect to see in Karl Hasserman's mansion.

Lammington lifted up his glass. "Too bad you won't join us, Klayborne. This is Karl Hasserman's finest brandy." He raised up his glass. "I drink to twelve brave young men. I never thought you had it in you. You are men now and I am giving you a man's drink."

He touched his glass against his lips. " Come, my young friends. Let us drink together."

Both Danny and Stevie were reaching for their glass. Bobby and Raymond, too. Then Donald shouted out the deadly warning. "*Xi! Nada Coy!*"

The hands were drawn back. The twelve glasses stood untouched on the table. Lammington gazed at Donald with contempt. "The dummy still can't talk right. He still speaks gibberish, doesn't he? I guess he'll never learn."

There was a moment of silence. Then the door opened. Striker came back in, followed by Craig and the Lady Ranger. Striker appeared chilled. He rubbed his hands and walked over to the table.

"*Paragon's Emperor brandy!* Don't waste that stuff on kids!" He picked up Jody's glass and drained it down.

Lammington said nothing. He stood there impassively. I thought later that we murdered Striker. We knew the stuff was poisoned and did nothing to stop him.

"Why don't you give the boys a little beer?" suggested Craig. He picked up the brandy bottle. There were still a few glasses left in it.

We didn't murder Craig. We remembered his kindness when we were locked up in the dungeon. How he brought us food and tried to cheer us up. And how he wrote our song. I got up to knock the bottle out of his hand. But Bobby knocked it out first. The bottle cracked and shattered on the stone floor.

Craig cried out, "What did you do that for, lad? What's the matter with you!"

However, at this instant, Striker broke into a raging bellow. "You swine, Lammington. You rotten, filthy swine! You poisoned me. You tried to poison the kids and it was me——"

He reached forward, clawing the air; then groaned and collapsed to his knees. "What did you give me? Water! Get me water! My insides are burning up!"

Striker was fumbling in his clothing. Now he drew forth a gun. "Help me! What did you give———"

"You're sick," said Lammington. "I'll call a doctor." He started to leave the room.

Striker's gun spurted flame. The shots struck Lammington in the back. It was Striker's last act. His body was in convulsions. His gun hand fell forward motionless. Lammington was badly hurt. He staggered and then went down.

The Lady Ranger reached for Striker's gun. But Raymond was too fast for her and got it first.

"Give me that gun, boy!"

Raymond grinned. "Sorry, ma'am. We need it!"

"*Hold it!*"

Klayborne had a gun, too. And he pointed it. This one was an automatic. There were enough shells here to mow down all twelve Coyotes. And the Lady Ranger and Craig, too.

I think he might have done it, wasted all of us. I think he was going to. Klayborne's face was cold and merciless. But his expression suddenly changed to amazement.

Donald had taken out the *Vrrooohn* and was holding it. The Horned Crystal had a red and angry glow. Klayborne's fingers tightened on the trigger. Donald did something or thought something. There was a flash of purple light and the great moosehead came crashing down on Klayborne's head. Two shots went wild as he fell. One hit the ceiling, the other went out the window. Then he keeled forward and lay senseless on the floor.

You have to hand it to the Lady Ranger. She went into action fast. She grabbed Klayborne's automatic and sent out a call for help. *Red alert! Red alert! Grave danger! We're being attacked by criminals. Come quickly!*

"I'm sorry, boys. I didn't know. But you will be safe now. I have sent for help. The State Police are coming."

Striker was dead. He had expected the guns, but not the poison. Lammington lay there dying. Nobody went to his aid. Craig was stupidly gathering up the poison brandy glasses and dumping them into the kitchen sink. He washed out each glass, then smashed it and threw the shards into the garbage.

Those five gunmen outside must have been waiting for some kind of signal and didn't get it. Or maybe those two shots that Klayborne fired was the signal. They were coming into the open now; but very cautiously, taking shelter behind an abandoned chicken coop, a toolshed, a large maple tree and several stacks of firewood. They seemed content to wait until they found out what was going on.

One of them, the guy behind the coop, got impatient. He was a trigger-happy oaf with bushy hair. He was firing into the kitchen window. One shot split open the clock on the kitchen wall. Another smashed into a pile of dishes. Somebody yelled at him to "Cut it!"

Captain Craig had changed sides. He was our protector now. He had the Ranger's hunting rifle, though he didn't seem to know how to use it. He left the safety catch on. "Keep down, lads! Help is coming soon."

That trigger-happy oaf was shooting again. This time, he hit the solar collector on the roof. Raymond shot back and hit a window in the chicken house. The bushy-haired oaf ducked down fast. Captain Craig yelled out some British insults at the "bloody thugs and ruffians." There was a volley of shots from behind the woodpiles, causing the plump captain to do a nose dive.

The Lady Ranger grabbed a bullhorn. "You out there, whoever you are. The State Police are on the way. They are coming by plane and will be here any minute. Your leaders are dead or captured. Hold your fire and get away while there is still time."

As if in answer, you could hear the roar of a helicopter overhead. It didn't try to land. It hovered above the cabin, waiting for reinforcements. The gunmen saw it, too. The bearded man behind the maple tree was retreating to the cars.

Donald and Cameron exchanged signals. Or maybe they exchanged thoughts. With the *Vrrooohn*, it's sometimes hard to tell a thought from a deed. "Coyotes, grab your stuff," called Cameron. "We're getting out of here!"

"But you can't!" protested the Lady Ranger. "Those men outside will shoot you down."

We grabbed our knapsacks and some provisions from the Ranger's kitchen and prepared for a breakout. Donald had the *Vrrooohn* now under his jacket. Craig saw we had it and his eyes popped. "Good luck, lads!"

There was a roar of a second plane. The State Police were surely coming. They wouldn't shoot us down, but they could take our stuff away and take us into custody.

The Lady Ranger thought we didn't trust her. That was why we were leaving. She tried to reassure us. "The Police will protect you boys. You won't have to go back to *Kaah Naghallah*. I don't think there will be a school there any more."

Two Masters lay dead. Striker lay stiff and rigid. Lammington was sprawled out in a pool of blood. Klayborne seemed to have recovered consciousness. He was playing possum, but inching his way toward the door.

A police helicopter had tried to land. A gunman behind the toolshed fired and drove the plane back into the air.

The gunmen were firing now to cover their retreat. They were shooting at us from the front of the cabin. Cameron determined to break out the back.

"*Anmir!* See if we can make an anti-mirage. Don take the lead. We're going to be an anti-mirage. Close formation! Move fast! Break when I say."

I realized suddenly that Cameron hadn't spoken at all. He had thought the words and we had received his thought. With the *Vrrooohn*, we could talk to each other without speaking.

We were grouped at the back door. Cameron gazed into the hall mirror. He watched while the reflection of
twelve youths faded and disappeared. Donald stood
there with the *Vrrooohn*, poised like a hunting dog,
waiting for the command of his master.

"Break!" yelled Cameron.

With the power of the *Vrrooohn*, the twelve Coyotes
broke out of the cabin. An anti-mirage works only on the
mind. It doesn't change anything physical. They could
still have traced us with radar or with an electronic
camera. And it only works from the distance.

Our anti-mirage wasn't perfect and the break-out
wasn't timed quite right. Somebody must have seen us
when the door opened. They yelled something and then
we vanished. It was a hundred yards into the forest and
we covered that distance in record time. A strong wind
was blowing, so they couldn't tell anything by the trees
and grass moving. That trigger-happy oaf with the
bushy hair had an angle shot at us. But by the time he
got around to shooting, we were gone.

There were three helicopters overhead now and one of
them was landing. The gunmen had no stomach for a real
battle and fled to the cars.

From the helicopter, they must have seen us disappear, too. I will never forget that pilot's puzzled expression. It must have been telepathic because I couldn't see
him physically through the plane. You have to learn how
to handle the *Vrrooohn*. It mixes up the people who use
it almost as much as it mixes up our enemies.

Craig and the Lady Ranger watched us disappear and
stared at the haze where the twelve Coyotes had been
before. Klayborne, taking advantage of their bewilderment, dashed out of the door to join the fleeing gunmen.
And the State Police landed by the Ranger's cabin.

The Coyote kids broke their way through the thick
forest. We tried to stay an *Anmir*, but since we could see
each other, there was no way to tell if we were suc-
ceeding.

Donald held the *Vrrooohn* and Raymond held Striker's

gun. If we got caught with it, we would have a lot of explaining to do. But we didn't intend to get caught.

As Stevie said, you couldn't count on the *Vrrooohn* alone. "That fucking thing may not work when you need it most."

THE NATURE GIRLS

We crossed through the woods for several miles. Then we climbed a small mountain that had a log cabin shelter on the summit. Newly erected by the State Department of Parks. There was a running spring here and a concrete fireplace. Just right for the Coyote boys to spend the night.

The only trouble was the shelter was already occupied. By a group of Nature Girls in their green uniforms and three lady counsellors. They had a fire going and some stuff cooking. Not all the Nature Girls had their uniforms on. Some had taken their clothes off and were bathing in several buckets of warm water.

We had forgotten we were an anti-mirage. We must have popped into view all of a sudden. When you're an *An-mir* and other people cannot see you, you can't see very well yourself. You don't hear too well either. We didn't hear the girls laughing and giggling and the chief Counsellor yelling. We just heard the wind in the trees.

We were heading for the fireplace, because it was real chilly. That's right where the girls were taking a bucket bath. They were real shapely, too, those girls. But we didn't get much of a chance to look at them.

A red-headed lady, the Nature Girl Leader, thought we had been sneaking up on the girls. We were Peeping Toms, slinking around so we could gawk at girls with no clothes on.

We must have looked pretty shitty; twelve ragamuffin boys, all messy and dirty. A bunch of juvenile hoods. You would think the ladies would have been a bit scared of us. But not *these* ladies . They were yelling and shouting and calling us names. "Aren't you ashamed of yourselves, you punks! Go find your own shelter and leave us alone!"

Cameron tried to sweet-talk the Girl Leader. "Please, ma'am. We got lost in the woods. We're awful cold and tired."

But the Nature Lady said, "You can't stay here. There's no room. There's another shelter on Eagle Mountain over there!" She pointed. This shelter was reserved for the Nature Girls only.

Cameron asked how about *us* joining the Nature Girls? Why don't you let boys in? It was old-fashioned to segregate the sexes like that. "Everything is co-ed now."

The Nature Lady said we could come back tomorrow and talk about it. But now we'd have to go. "Be good boys now and don't make any trouble. Follow the red-dot trail to Eagle Mountain." She sure was bossy, that Nature Lady. But she gave us a guide-map so we wouldn't get lost again.

I think the girls were sorry to see us go. They were all smiling and waving at us. We would have come back tomorrow. But things happened that prevented it.

THE BATTLE OF EAGLE MOUNTAIN

It was a moonless night and real dark now. We had no lanterns or flashlights. The *Vrrooohn* could light the way for us, but we didn't dare use it. We were afraid of being spotted. Fortunately, our eyes had been trained in *Bane N'Gai* to see in very little light. Once again, we formed an anti-mirage.

We passed a high cliff. Some guys had written their names on it. . . *The Raiders* . . . *The Falcons* . . . *The Mountain Men.* . . . I had a momentary impulse. We all did. Of writing our name high on the cliff above all the other names. With the mark of the Shell and the Arrow.

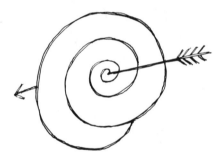

THE COYOTES WERE HERE

It was a strong thought. But of course we didn't do it. We were fugitives and hiding out.

Finally, we came to Eagle Mountain. We were lucky this time. The shelter was empty. We flopped down and fell asleep.

We wondered later how Klayborne and his gunmen found us. Was it sheer luck, bad luck for us? Or did the Masters of Naghallah have an organization that could track us down, no matter where we hid or ran? At that time, we gave them credit for being supermen. The Police, the Rangers, everybody was working for them. Perhaps even the Nature Counsellor was their spy. It was the Coyote Kids against the world!

Actually, it was our own dumbness that gave us away. We were in an anti-mirage and the *Vrrooohn* was active. We thought and talked about putting our name and mark on the cliff. And our thoughts were projected into reality. In the morning, our Coyote mark was on the cliff, higher and larger than any of the others.

Klayborne and his gunmen spotted it. They must have thought we were awful dopey kids who couldn't resist making graffiti. It shouldn't be too hard to terminate us and get the *Vrrooohn*.

We were like the Sorcerer's Apprentice and couldn't always control what we were doing. Later, we learned to be more careful.

We slept real late and ate well. We let our guard down and received an unpleasant surprise.

There was an old logging road below and a car drove up on it. No cars were allowed on the road, except the Rangers'. But when you're planning some murders, you don't worry about violating the traffic rules. We shouldn't have been trapped like that. The car was the same one as came to the Ranger's cabin. We were too busy eating and gabbing to spot it. If we had time, we could have retreated into the deep woods. But the shelter was on a bare hill, with no cover to hide or flee.

Brandon yelled and we ran into the shelter. They figured they had us trapped and at their mercy. The whole mountain was in their gun sights. Any guy who tried to run would be blasted.

Klayborne was leading the gunmen. He had a bandage on his head, but still could walk around. Klayborne shouted into the megaphone, "Boys! We don't want to hurt you. Give up what you took from Karl Hasserman and we'll let you go safely." I didn't think they would. They couldn't let us go. We knew too much and were too dangerous.

They didn't charge right in and shoot us up. They didn't know what weapons we had. Raymond brandished the gun we took from Striker. Then he started cursing. The damned thing was jammed and wouldn't shoot.

Our enemies didn't fire either. Not right away. Gunfire might attract attention. It would be better if they could get us to surrender.

"We'll give you one more chance, boys. Come out with your hands up and we'll give you safe conduct to the nearest town.

"This is your last chance," continued Klayborne. "This is your last warning! I'm counting to ten——" Then they began to fire. They were shooting to frighten us rather than kill us. *That* could be done later. Now they were careful in their shots. They didn't want to damage Karl Hasserman's treasure.

There were three gunmen and Klayborne on the door side of the shelter and two more gunmen on the rear side, in case we tried to break out the back. Cameron waved a dirty white towel. "Wait! Don't shoot! We'll talk." I thought first Cameron had gone chicken. But he was stalling for a reason. Donald held the *Vrrooohn*. It had worked for him before. We only hoped it would work now.

Klayborne called back, "You've had time enough. Come on out and stack your things, if you want to stay alive. This is your last chance! Or we'll get very nasty!"

Cameron stood next to Donald and put his hand on the *Vrrooohn*, aiming his mind at the gunmen. And he shouted, "You're a liar, Klayborne and a double-crosser! You destroyed all the others, Vedemore and Smeer and Eberle and Striker and Lammington! They're all dead now."

"Shut up!" cried Klayborne.

"You murdered Dr. Mehary and betrayed Karl Hasserman——"

"You loud-mouthed punk, I'll burn you!"

But Cameron continued. "You guys out there! Whatever he promised you, don't believe him! He'll betray you, too, and turn you over to the cops. While he runs off with Karl Hasserman's loot."

The gunmen wavered a bit. Cameron was furiously throwing out his thoughts, hoping to reach the minds of the gunmen. We all joined in, trying to turn the men against their leader. *If ever the Vrrooohn could sway the minds of men, do it now!*

It didn't work. Klayborne gave them orders to blast their way in. This time, they would shoot to kill.

"Get that little rat! Get all of them! Splatter their guts!"

Their guns were pointed. Whoever heard their shots would think they were just hunters, jumping the November season. It would all be over long before anyone could come to our aid. We could make a desperate try for a break-out. Of the twelve of us, one or two might make it.

They were shooting for deadly real now. A stream of bullets tore into the shelter. Roger cried out. His face was covered with blood and he went down.

Donald lifted up the *Vrrooohn*. He shouted out something that sounded like a curse in a foreign tongue. There was a scream and a roar and a blast that shook the cabin. The faces of the three gunmen were jerked upward and turned deadly white. Whatever they saw filled them with terror. The shadow of some enormous creature fell over the gunmen. The men shot wildly into the air now, instead of at us. They turned and fled down the mountain in a panic. I watched them run and got a bullet in my neck.

On the other side, that bushy-haired guy and a man with side-burns were firing through the shattered window. Donald turned and yelled that curse again. For a moment, he looked more like a demon than a human boy. Those yellow eyes glowed and blazed like fire. If Roger or Jaymie died, he was going to avenge us.

Donald ran to the window. There was a tremendous flash, but it wasn't lightning and a terrible crash, but it wasn't thunder. Then a scream. And the two gunmen went down. Bushy Hair put his hands to his head and collapsed. Sideburns staggered, took a few steps and dropped.

That was the last I saw. I felt a bad pain and was leaving a trail of blood. Then I fainted and passed out.

The guys carried Jaymie and Roger away. Next thing I knew, me and Roger were in the pine woods. Donald was working over us with the *Vrrooohn*. The *Vrrooohn* can heal as well as kill. Otherwise we both might be dead.

The guys also used up all that healing pink **Wondermud** on us. That queered our chances to make medical history. Now Pasteur, Harvey, Freud and Fleming would never have to move over for any of the Coyote kids. But maybe it saved Roger's life — and mine.

As it turned out, those two gunmen, Bushy Hair and Sideburns, weren't dead. They were just knocked out. We took their guns and left them there. Later, a police helicopter spotted them. I was glad they weren't dead. They were hired killers. But they crummed it up and didn't manage to kill anybody, except themselves — almost. Now nobody would give them another job. Maybe that would teach them not to mess with the Naghallah Boys.

By the Nature Girls' map, we were about eleven miles west of Lake Wahehla. Wahehla was a village at the edge of the State Park, near a highway that could lead us to Greenwood. Klayborne would be expecting us to go the way we knew, through Mountainville, and would be watching for us there.

The Coyote kids would have to hike to Lake Wahehla. The *Vrrooohn* could do many things, but it couldn't move heavy objects. At least, it couldn't move *us*. No teleportation.

Roger was grinning gamely. Cameron lifted the kid onto his back. "We'll have to make a litter to carry Jaymie."

"I'll walk," said me.

"No, you won't," said Brother Danny. "Shut up and get on the litter."

They made a litter out of branches. Stevie and Danny carried it. After a while, I said, "It hurts to lie still. I feel better when I walk."

"Suit yourself," said Danny and I walked. Then Roger insisted on walking, too.

THE ESCAPE OF THE COYOTES

We fancied then that Klayborne and his organization had spies everywhere. All the Northland was hostile territory where paid assassins lurked to waste us. The Masters of Naghallah ruled here and everyone was either on their payroll or too terrified to oppose them. "If we could only get back to Greenwood——"

I wondered if our parents were back from their trip. Maybe our house was empty. None of the other kids had any home to go to. We had a big, rambling old house. There was room for all of us.

We hit a trail now. It was taking a chance travelling on a trail, though easier going. We didn't dare stop to rest for very long. A sign said:

LAKE WAHEHLA — 10 MILES

There was a helicopter in the sky now, searching for something. Cameron decided we better form an anti-mirage again. We didn't want to over-work the *Vrrooohn*. But we were hunted prey and couldn't take a chance on being spotted.

"*An-mir!*" said Cameron. "Go slow and keep together. We'll hit Lake Wahehla by tonight."

"And then what?"

"We'll have to find some way to get to Greenwood. Some quiet way. Not bus or railroad. Our enemies might be watching those."

"We could steal a car," suggested Bobby, grinning.

"That's what they expect us to do. They'll be watching for a stolen car," declared Keith. "They might even leave a couple of cars around for us to steal."

"If there were only some guy we could trust. A guy with a van or a truck."

Brandon had an idea. "Rodney Desmond." The Gay Poet. "He once said he'd do anything for me. . . ." Rodney had a station wagon that could hold the twelve of us. But how could we call him?

"The *Vrrooohn* might do it," urged Brandon. "A telepathic wave."

Brandon took the *Vrrooohn*. "I'll know if I get through. Yeah, he's sleeping. Rodney is up all night and sleeps most of the day."

Brandon was speaking. He didn't make any physical noise, but we could hear him. . . . "*Rodney . . . Rodney Desmond! This is Brandon. Brandon Zuchtig. . . . The kid who haunts your dreams . . . I'm haunting them now. . . .*

"*You got to help me. I'm in bad trouble and great danger. We're all in danger. Me and my eleven brudders. . . .*

(He hears me. I'm getting through.)

"*I'm talking to you by telepathic wave. This is for real, Rodney. We need your help, Rodney, and we need it bad.*

"*Do you still have that blue station wagon?* (He does) *Get a road map. There's a village called Lake Wahehla on the northern edge of Grey Mountain State Park. There's a motel there . . . Go there, Rodney. Start now. You should make it by tonight. Check in at the Wahehla Motel. . . .*

"*Do you still have those red towels?* (He does) *Hang a couple outside your window. . . . We're in danger, Rodney.*

*People are trying to kill us. . . . You'll be in danger, too. . . .
Goodbye, Rodney. I can't hold it any longer. . . . . "*
"*I'll do it for you, Brandon. For you and your brothers. I
won't let you down.*" You could almost hear the sleeping
poet saying that. His face changed from the dreamy
esthete to the resolute man of action. Then everything
faded.

THE PHANTOM HITCH-HIKERS

Rodney Desmond believed in visions and intuitions.
Otherwise he wouldn't have come. Probably on a fools' errand. It was well after dark when he checked into the
Wahehla Motel and hung out two red towels. There was
no sign of Brandon and his brothers and no message for
him.

He purchased and scanned the *Grey Mountain Evening
News.* A late item reported:

TWO HUNTERS STRUCK BY LIGHTNING

They were picked up by helicopter on Eagle Mountain
and were still unconscious, "in critical but stable condition" . . .

A curious headline:

MYSTERY MAN REPORTED MISSING
Where is the Billionaire Recluse, Karl Hasserman?

The Gay Poet ordered and consumed a cheese sandwich
and several bottles of beer. Then, without taking his
shoes off, he lay down on his bed and fell asleep.

Moments later, he was conscious of people in the room.
There were twelve shapes vaguely resembling human
youths.

"Rodney, wake up!" The leader of the youths resembled Brandon. A pale, wraith-like shape. A spirit manifestation.

Rodney had always believed in psychic phenomena and believed himself to be a sensitive. But he had never experienced an honest-to-goodness spirit. Only a vague presence. He had held seances at times and worked the ouija board. But to be truthful, he cheated.

Now suddenly, he felt himself in the presence of genuine phantoms. Spectral figures from another plane of Being. Twelve dead youths who had chosen to appear to him, perhaps at the very moment of passing from their physical bodies into *The Great Beyond.* He watched them for a moment with both fear and fascination.

"Get up, Rodney! We ain't dead, if that's what you're thinking. But we may be, if you don't get moving!

"These are my brudders——" The Poet had to touch all twelve of us to make sure we were alive.

"I heard things about *Kaah Naghallah.* Was somebody killed?"

"A couple of people. But not *us.* We'll tell you what happened, but not now. You wouldn't believe it anyway."

Rodney said he was awful tired. He had been driving all day on this crazy hunch. "You can sleep in the car," said Bobby. There were four or five experienced car thieves here. "We can drive. You just have to take the wheel when we go through the tolls."

Keith drove until we hit the Thruway. The toll taker noticed a long-haired man with a red scarf around his neck, driving a station wagon crowded with messy-looking youths. "Camping with the boys?" he asked.

"Up in the mountains," said Rodney.

"Grey Mountain Park? Heard there were a couple of murders up there. A big shoot-out."

"Really?" asked Rodney. "Things were real quiet where we went. How much is the toll to Riverport?"

"Riverport? End of the line. Nine bucks."

The garrulous toll taker might remember us, but he wouldn't know where we were going.

First chance he got, Rodney pulled over and let Bobby Alliconda do the driving. Bobby took us right down to the West Greenwood Exit. Real slow and careful. There were traffic cops around, even after midnight.

"What have you guys got in those bags?" asked Rodney.

"Jewels," said me. Sometimes the best way to keep a secret is to tell it. Then people will think you are kidding.

It was dawn when we hit Greenwood. Our parents must be home. The night lights were on.

Rodney dropped us off. We each gave him one of our fifty dollar bills. He didn't want to take it. But Cameron said, "We might need you again, Rodney. Real soon."

"Sure, fellers. Brandon knows the place. Come and visit me."

"We weren't thinking of visiting. We might need a place to hang out. You got room for twelve guys, Rodney? We can sleep on the floor."

"Sure, sure," said the Poet, without enthusiasm. Even for the boy-loving poet, the twelve of us seemed a bit excessive.

"Thanks for saving our lives."

"My pleasure," said Rodney. "Thanks for the adventure."

"Write a poem about it," Brandon urged.

"Maybe I will." And he did. Only in the poem, he made us ghost boys who vanished at the end of the ride.

"The Phantom Hitch-hikers."

THE HOME COMING

Pamela Larrabie was sitting in her bedroom, looking into the mirror. Sometimes, she could see things in the mirror that nobody else could see; things that "weren't really there." Now she could see Jaymie standing in the doorway.

These visions in the mirror had come to her ever since girlhood. She no longer told anyone else about them. People considered it odd. Mitch had grown excited and wanted her to go to the hospital.

Several times since they went away, Pamela had seen one of the boys in the mirror. The last few times, there was a heavy shadow over them. There was no shadow now over Jaymie. There was a bright light instead.

Now there was a yellow-haired youth standing next to Jaymie. That must be Danny! This vision was different. It didn't fade in and out like things usually did.

A voice this time said, "Mom!" She turned slowly and embraced the boys. Pamela had never had a vision that she could touch before. It was a full minute before she knew that we were real.

"Jaymie! And Danny! I love you! Promise you won't go away again. Ever!"

"We won't, Mom. We have some friends. Can they stay here, too?"

"Of course. They were with you at the school? You all ran away? It must have been pretty awful."

"It got kind of rough at the end," said Danny. "But we didn't run away. They turned us into slave boys."

"How did you get away from them? No, don't tell me yet. Bring your friends in. They must be hungry and tired. Have you been up all night?"

Danny went to get the guys. And Mitch came in through the opposite door.

The Homecoming

Dad said, "I'm sorry, Jaymie. I didn't know. Please forgive me. I'll do anything I can to make up for it. Tell me what I can do."

I said, "Dad, there are ten kids here. None of them have any home or any family. Let them come and stay with us."

Dad looked at the crew. "Ten, Jaymie? And you and Danny make twelve. Twelve boys would be a little much."

"I guess twelve guys would cost quite a bit of money, Dad. Just feeding us and buying the clothes. But we didn't come here empty-handed."

I opened up my knapsack and revealed the jewels. The other guys opened up their knapsacks. The whole room was filled with a dazzling fire. Red, green, blue, silver, gold, orange and white.

Our parents stood there in stunned amazement. Mother trembled. Father gasped. At last, Dad said, "These look real, son. Where did you get them?"

"From Karl Hasserman. As a reward for bringing back some papers for him. His *Last Will and Testament*. Karl Hasserman is dead ——"

Jaymie had the papers. Donald still held the *Vrrooohn of Marl'Hai.* "Karl Hasserman's treasure." But the *Vrrooohn* was one thing we kept hidden.

Dad knows about jewels. "Incredible! Fantastic! These must be worth many millions." We would have to sell them off real slowly so as not to break the market.

"We ought to put them in a bank vault. I'm surprised you didn't get attacked and robbed."

"They did attack us," blurted out Jody. "They shot Jaymie and Roger!"

I didn't want to go to the hospital. "It's okay. They just nicked me."

"They just nicked me, too," declared Roger.

Mother insisted a doctor look at us. "And don't worry about your friends, Jaymie. We have a big house and lots of empty rooms. You boys don't mind sleeping three to a room?"

"We slept twelve to a room back at the School."

Mother said, "If these jewels are really so valuable, we can add more rooms. Can't we, Mitchell?"

Dad said nothing. He just sort of nodded. Up to now, Father had been the boss in the family. But now, Mother was taking over. She laid the law down. "I want the boys to stay in this house, Mitch. All twelve of them. We almost lost Danny and Jaymie. But the Good Lord has brought them back to us. Their friends are welcome here for just as long as they want to stay." Mother smiled. "I wish we could adopt *all* of you."

Cameron said, "Why don't you?"

"Hey!" said Stevie. "That would be great!"

And, surprisingly, Dad agreed to it. Donald can use the *Vrrooohn* better than anyone else. Maybe he worked on Dad's mind, though Donald said he didn't. Dad was really sorry about what happened and wanted to make up for it. He wanted us to like him again.

Also, Dad likes money and those jewels gave him a hungry look. The more he looked at them, the more amazing and valuable the jewels appeared. And we held back about half of them.

Dad probably figured twelve boys wouldn't be any worse than just me and Danny. He was stuck with us anyway.

The rest of the family approved. *"How lovely!"* wrote Aunt Laura, whose handwriting is rather hard to read. Our parents first thought she wrote, *"How lousy!"*

"That's great news!" said Uncle Oscar. "A dozen sons! You'll be a patriarch, Mitch, my boy!"

"Twelve sons!" exclaimed Cousin Katie. "I think that's wonderful! Don't worry if they're not Children of the Blood. They will carry the Larrabie name to future generations. You'll be a famous ancestor, Mitchell."

And Uncle Oscar promised to leave his twelve grand-nephews "all my money." Which was a joke of sorts, because Oscar was always broke.

*   *   *   *   *   *   *

We moved our gear into the rec room, which is really two rooms put together and put all our beds there. Mother couldn't understand why we jammed into one room, when there were half a dozen empty rooms around. We felt safer that way. We ranged our beds in a circle, like the covered wagons of the besieged pioneers. We kept on expecting to be attacked.

We put the *Vrrooohn* into an anti-mirage and *quayned* it. *Quayne* is a Lemurian word meaning putting a thing into a time warp. It vanishes, but it's still there. Nobody can see or hear or feel it, until you take it out. We do that with our minds. All twelve of us have to work together to open the *Quayne*.

Quayning was a trick Donald showed us. Don Don had as many tricks on Earth as he did in *Bane N'Gai*. We sure were glad to have him on our team.

We quayned about half of the jewels, too, and gave the rest to Father. We still didn't trust Father completely. Like Bobby says, "Never trust anyone over twenty."

If you look where the *Quayne* is, all you can see or feel is a solid wall.

THE PATRIARCH

All kinds of rumors were circulating about *Kaah Naghallah*. The School Director and several of the Masters were "missing." The twelve boy students were "missing." Mr. Matthews, their teacher, had a nervous breakdown and was in a mental hospital. The cooks, Johanna and her sister, Minnie, were in hiding, too terrified to talk. Old George did talk, but nobody believed him. About an underground Terror that swallowed people up. And a hidden tunnel into another world, where Demons lived. People thought he had blown his top and belonged in a funny farm.

Still, people felt that there was something very wrong about *Kaah Naghallah.* Judge Tuffney was severely criticized for sending the welfare kids to "that House of Horror." He was mightily relieved when the twelve boy students turned up unharmed, and made it easy for Dad and Mom to take the kids.

Mitchell and Pamela Larrabie were named *Guardians of the Person* of:

> *Roberto Miguel Alliconda*
> *Keith Gerald Caldwell*
> *Troy Jeffrey Feroldi*
> *Jody Guy Kallinger*
> *Roger Darrin Newland*
> *Raymond Joshua Ridgeway*
> *Steven Dale Scanlon*
> *Donald Lance Turrentine*
> *Cameron Anthony Westcott*   and
> *Brandon Wolfgang Zuchtig*

"You want to adopt these punks? Really? *All of them?*" Judge Tuffney was a bit incredulous. "We'll hold a Hearing a week from Monday. And if no one objects, the punks are yours.

"Why should anyone object? Who else would want them?"

"You never legally adopted Daniel? Well, we'll put him down on the list, too."

Father recruited our good neighbor, Mr. Meyer, to handle the legal details. He was an attorney and a partner in the firm of Meyer, Greenbaum, Perkins, O'Leary and Untermeyer. To them, we entrusted the Last Will and Testament of Karl Hasserman. That Will was going to mean a bundle of trouble and probably years of litigation, but also a fabulous fee from the Hasserman Estate.

"We will have to prove it by the writing and the signature of the witnesses. Could I ask how you boys got a hold of this document?"

"We found it," said me, truthfully. "Hidden in a closet."

"At least, it's handwritten. That should make it easier to establish."

Having my Coyote brothers as my true and legal brothers was more than I had dared to hope for. The guys were all happy about it.

Keith said, "It's good to be in a family and have parents as a cover. It's a grown-ups' world. Kids on their own get muckled." But it wasn't just as a cover that Keith wanted parents. He wanted a home and a family — a place to belong. All he had had in his life so far was a series of dreary and uncaring foster homes and institutions. Keith's only kin had been his foster brother, Stevie.

Mother bought us each a new blue suit for the Adoption Hearing. The guys had all been in Judge Tuffney's court before. This Hearing was in chambers and no one was on the griddle. Still, we all felt nervous.

I kept fearing that something was going to happen to queer the adoption. It was too good to be true. Would "Commander" Bartlow and the Masters of *Naghallah* come after us? Or would one of the relatives who had dumped the Naghallah boys, having heard rumors of our new-found wealth and treasure, come around and claim the kid now? Or would one of the guys be busted again for some new offense?

We took the *Vrrooohn* along, concealed inside a knapsack — just in case.

Judge Tuffney was genial, though a bit patronizing. He kept telling the boys how lucky they were. Then he wiped his glasses and read the list of names.

"Tony Westcott. That is Anthony Cameron Westcott. Do you wish to become the lawful son of Mitchell and Pamela Larrabie?"

"Yes, Your Honor."

"And your name will be legally changed to Tony Cameron Larrabie?"

"Make Cameron my first name please, Your Honor."

"Very well. . . . Brandon Wolfgang Zuchtig . . . Roberto Miguel Alliconda. . . . One by one, each guy became a Larrabie.

When he reached Donald, whom the Judge knew only as "the retarded boy," Tuffney squinted over his glasses. "Do you understand what is happening here, son?"

The *Glorious Hero of Lemuria* just smiled.

The Judge said, "He doesn't talk yet, does he? Can he comprehend what we are saying?"

Counsellor Meyer broke in. "I have found Donald a very intelligent young man, Your Honor. He read and signed the petition you have before you."

"Did he really? I thought someone signed it for him." He thrust a piece of paper at Don Don. "Can you write your name, son?"

Don Don wrote in a clear hand:

> *Donald Larrabie*
> *And how are you, Judge Tuffney?*

"Very good, son! He learned to write at Dr. Mehary's school? At least that's one good thing that came out of Dr. Mehary's school. What has happened to Dr. Mehary anyway?"

Nobody told him.

Judge Tuffney signed the rest of the papers and handed them to Mr. Meyer for filing. We thanked him and started to leave. But he couldn't resist giving us a lecture on Brotherhood, Decency and Filial Devotion. Father yawned and looked at his watch. My new brothers all looked hungry.

All at once, one of the drawers of the Judge's desk flew open and the contents spilled out all over the floor. Among the stuff, was *Whoops!*, a sex magazine, with a naked girl on the cover. Judge Tuffney quickly grabbed the sex magazine and stuck it back in his desk. *End of Lecture.*

Donald swore he didn't make that drawer open. He didn't do *anything*. When you have a power, like Don Don, you get the credit — or blame — for things of which you are quite innocent.

We had a fine lunch at the Greenwood Inn to celebrate. Cousin Katie's husband is the Manager at the Inn, but that don't mean we get a free meal. Counsellor Meyer insisted on grabbing the check. His daughters, Joyce and Marjorie Meyer, are having another party and all twelve Larrabie boys are invited.

People used to think Mitchell Larrabie was some kind of nut for sending his sons to "that miserable, phony boarding school." Now they thought Mitch was a nut for adopting all these homeless kids. "Twelve juvenile delinquents right out of reform school. Well, ten really. He had Danny and Jaymie already."

But before, people thought Mitch was a mean nut. Now they thought he was a nice nut. Said our good pastor, the Reverend Jenkins, "I wish more people were crazy like Mitchell Larrabie."

RUMORS AND QUESTIONS

All the neighborhood guys were mighty curious about what happened up at *Kaah Naghallah.*

Rudy Leone asked, "What was that nutty school really like? Was *Kaah Naghallah* as shitty as they said it was? How come you guys got released? Do you get muckled or do they straighten you out? I heard they turn you inside out, but you guys don't seem any different."

"They didn't have a chance to correct us," said Jaymie. "Me and Danny and our friends wrecked that school before it could straighten us out."

The police, of course, asked a lot of questions. We told them we couldn't remember very much. We had been imprisoned down in a dungeon. Why? We found out Karl Hasserman was missing and Dr. Mehary had been killed.

They sent us into the tunnels to find something. They didn't tell us what. They put slave collars on us and we managed to break them off.

From here on, everything was vague and cloudy. We came into an underworld land and crossed a ghost river.

We told them of our battle with the Fen Monster and the Giant Spider and the Terror Idol. We told them of the silver plains with the wild unicorns. And the mountain crags with the great Roc and the Pterodactyls. Of the Brontosaurus, the Octocorn, the crawling stones and the Bird-trees. And the shining caves where we met the Goblin People who sheltered us and guided us back to Earth.

The Police listened patiently, but they didn't believe a word of it. They searched the underground at Kaah Naghallah and found our dungeon. But they didn't find any tunnels. The dark Gateway into *Bane N'Gai* had been sealed up. There was only a solid wall of rock.

The Police concluded the boys had been in the dungeon the whole time, until they somehow managed their escape. We were the victims of a mass hallucination. They must have fed us LSD, or something like that.

Still, some reporters got the story:

KARL HASSERMAN DISAPPEARS
Death of Eccentric Billionaire Reported and Denied

and:

YOUTHS ESCAPE FROM TERROR SCHOOL
Tell Fantastic Tale of Underworld Horrors.

WERE THE BOYS DRUGGED?
OR IS THERE SOMETHING DOWN THERE?

They decided we were drugged.

Like some diplomat said, "Truth is the best deception, because nobody will believe it."

The jovial "Captain" Craig, we learned, had suddenly left the country. Fleeing from somebody. More likely from his former partners than from the Police.

THE JOURNAL OF MITCHELL LARRABIE

I, Mitchell Larrabie, am now the legal father of these twelve youths. People praise me and make jokes about my twelve sons. "What a splendid deed you are doing! What charming lads! What a delightful family!" No one senses the cold fear that lies inside of me.

I curse the day when I sent Jaymie and Daniel to that grotesque school. Something happened there in the last weeks. Something sinister and dreadful. The boys told me a wild yarn. I doubt if anyone will ever learn the truth.

I fear these boys. I am a front for them. A figure head parent. A puppet on their strings. I am in their power!

Outwardly, they treat me with respect and courtesy. "Good morning, *sir*. How are you today, *sir*? May we go out tonight, *sir*? We'll be home by three. We'll all be together, *sir*."

I try to shout, "No, you may not!" But it always comes out, "Yes, of course."

"May we have a party next Saturday, sir? Just our friends?" That means all the young hoodlums and roughnecks of the neighborhood.

"Next Saturday is not convenient," I snapped.

"Next Sunday, then?"

"Well, keep the noise down and no rough stuff," I ordered.

"We will, sir." That was the closest I ever came to defying them. Each day, I fall deeper under their control.

"May we have a ten-speed bike, sir? One for each of us?" A hifi. A computer. A movie projector. . . . Typewriters. Tape machines. Guitars. Cameras. TV's. Bowling balls. Bobsleds. . . . The list is endless. I never have the power to refuse them.

To outsiders, they appear as model young men. Always friendly. Always helpful. They work hard keeping the house in order. But it is their house now. No longer mine.

Our friends and neighbors seem enchanted by these street boys. Pamela, too. I have never seen my wife so well and happy. Constantly doing things for the boys and ignoring me. In the evening, we were deluged with phone calls from one silly girl after another. I had to get the boys their own phone so I could have some peace.

They would not attend the public schools from which most of them were expelled or suspended. Instead, they bade me hire them a teacher. None other than that ridiculous poet, Rodney Desmond. He teaches them in *Naghallah School Number Two.* Some school! Always filled with noise and laughter. It is hard to believe they will ever learn anything.

That silly poet sent me report cards. One for each of the boys. Of course, they are all *Excellent* or *Very Good.*

A silly ass, that Rodney Desmond! He has just won some poetry prize. For a lot of unmitigated drivel. The judges must be asses, too. Here is his picture in the *Greenwood Trumpet* with the boys. My twelve new sons shouting and yelling. Says the caption:

Poet Desmond cheered by young poetry fans.

What a laugh!

The boys drink beer openly and help themselves to anything in the house. Oddly, all twelve of them refuse to eat meat.

They have converted Pamela to their peculiar ways. She knocks herself out preparing them choice vegetarian dishes. If I want meat, I have to go to a restaurant.

They wear black leather jackets, with their gang mark on the back, trying to look tough. But real leather violates their weird taboo against killing animals. Pamela wore herself out shopping, until she found them some fancy artificial leather jackets. . . . Real expensive! Costing more than the real thing.

They never quarrel, these youths, as normal brothers do. They decide everything behind closed doors in secret conclave. Their rooms are always locked. I wonder what secrets they have inside. . . . . . .

*   *   *   *   *   *   *

I must confess the boys can make money as well as spend it. Some weeks ago, Jaymie and his brothers told me to buy stock in a near bankrupt mining company, then listed at $2.00 a share and going lower. Annoyed by their nagging, I purchased thirty thousand shares, more to show the boys how foolish they were than with any expectation of profit. In fact, I fully expected to lose, which would give me an excuse to put the boys in their place.

To my surprise, there was a tremendous new strike and the mining stock has more than tripled in value. The profit is enough to maintain my expensive whelps for many months.

I cannot believe this was just luck. It is the kind of thing Karl Hasserman used to do. What strange power do these boys have? It frightens me. What will happen if they decide I am no longer useful to them?

*   *   *   *   *   *   *

I had lunch today with Commander Bartlow. He will not come to the house any more. He fears the boys, perhaps with greater reason than I do.

He started out by handing me a check for fifty thousand dollars. It was a refund of the tuition payments for Jaymie and Daniel and also in compensation for any injuries they and the other boys had sustained at the *Kaah Naghallah* school. In return, as the boys' guardian, I would have to waive all claims to further damages on their behalf. Since we had no intention of suing the school, this money was quite a windfall.

Bartlow had heard about the jewels and offered to help me sell them. He has international connections and asked only a very small commission. Bartlow's generosity, however, had a purpose to it. I could tell he was leading up to something.

The boys, he said, are holding something that they took from Karl Hasserman. It is something that could be very

dangerous, particularly in the hands of immature youths.
If I could retrieve it, Bartlow would buy it from me for
twenty million dollars. He would also set up generous
trust funds for the boys. "How much did the boys tell
you?"

I said, "You know more than I do, Bartlow. Lay your
cards on the table and then I'll lay mine."

"What do you want to know?" he asked.

"What really happened to Karl Hasserman? What happened to Dr. Mehary? And who were these people who
tried to kill the boys?"

Bartlow claimed he didn't know. I think he is lying.
Pamela says not to trust him. We must protect the boys.

These are my sons, I keep telling myself. Not punks and
guttersnipes out of reform school. I must learn to love
them and I will try. ... Bartlow has called me several
times for another luncheon date, but I put him off....

BELOVED SONS

Sneaky Jaymie was the one who found out Father was
keeping a Journal. I saw him writing something and he
tried to hide it. Stealing Father's private papers and reading them on the sly was a dirty, rotten, sneaky thing to
do. But we were dirty, rotten, sneaky kids. That's how we
lasted this long. And we had to find out what Father
really thought about us. That's why Cameron pulled another burglary, right in our own house. Father never knew
it. His Journal was back by morning.

If Father really felt like he wrote in the Journal, we
were in danger. If Dad really feared us, he might betray
us. Next time around, he might succumb to Bartlow's
blandishments and help him take the *Vrrooohn* away
from us. Without the *Vrrooohn*, we would be helpless. Our
enemies could waste and destroy us. With the *Vrrooohn*,
we could stand up against any threat.

We had sworn we would never use the *Vrrooohn* unless the twelve of us consented. Strangely, it was Donald who balked. He didn't say *No;* he just grunted. You would think Donald was still the retarded boy, if you didn't know the hidden powers of his mind.

"Why not, Don Don? Why don't you want us to use the *Vrrooohn?*"

Donald said there were Lemurians on Earth who were watching us. Who? He didn't know. He had just picked up their thought waves.

"Why should they care? We won't use it for anything bad."

"Do what you want."

"We can't without you. You're our Gangleader, Don Don. You and Cameron. You got to agree, too."

He paused for a moment as if getting a signal. I thought maybe Donald was the Lemurian keeping watch over us, to make sure the *Vrrooohn* was not misused. "Donald agrees," he announced. The guys cheered.

Mitch was in his study. He looked alarmed when the twelve of us entered. "Don't you knock, boys?"

Cameron said, "I thought we did knock, Sir. I thought you told us to come in."

"Oh, did I?" Dad appeared weary. "Just what do you want?"

Keith said, "We're sorry to have disturbed you, Sir. It isn't important. Some other time——"

Our parent looked into Donald's yellow eyes with fear and fascination. Donald said, "You are very tired now, Sir. Why don't you lie down on the couch and take a nap?"

"Yes, I am tired." We took his shoes off and laid a pillow under his head. Mitch closed his eyes. In another moment, he was asleep.

We formed a circle, locking our arms together. It didn't matter who held the *Vrrooohn*. We let Jody hold it.

Cameron spoke. "We are your beloved sons. We are your hope, your joy and your dream."

The sleeping figure raised up his head. *"You are my beloved sons. My hope, my joy and my dream. . . ."*

"We are loyal and true. You trust us and believe in us."

"You are loyal and true. I trust you and believe in you. . . ."

"We will be first in your heart forever."

"You will be first in my heart forever," said the Sleeper. And he added, unexpectedly, *"Nothing will ever turn me against you."* Then our brainwashed parent fell into a deep sleep.

Mitch woke up several hours later. Rummaging through a drawer, he found a picture of the twelve of us taken when we returned from *Naghallah.* Now he dusted it off carefully and put it on his desk.

We had left the door open and Father came into our bedroom. We were all asleep or pretended to be. Father stood for a moment before each of our beds and smiled a little.

Young Roger lay sprawled off the mattress, half way to the floor. Mitch lifted Roger back up and covered him. It was getting cold and he closed the big window. He emptied out our overflowing garbage cans and brought us up some new cakes of soap and clean towels.

Maybe that *Vrrooohn* did too good a job. Now Mitch would be messing around and fussing over us. Pamela's fussing was bad enough. A devoted parent could be a pain. But the other guys didn't know that yet. They sort of liked to be fussed over. Even Cameron and Stevie.

Mitch asked, "What did you want to talk to me about last night — before I fell alseep?"

"A party, Sir. For Cameron's fifteenth birthday."

"Sure. You pick the date. But call me *Dad,* won't you, instead of *Sir.*"

"Okay, Dad."

THE BABY NURSE

Miss Ferris was my old baby nurse. She was also Danny's baby nurse. Back in my kindergarten days, she had a blow-up with Father who, she felt, wasn't treating Danny right. She left and me and Danny felt bad. I think Mother felt bad, too, but in those days she let Mitch walk all over her. Danny would never have gotten in trouble like he did if Miss Ferris had been around. But then we would never have gone to *Kaah Naghallah* and never met our Coyote brothers.

Anyway, Mother called her back now to help out with her twelve sons. Father made no objection. He was glad to have someone around who could handle us.

Miss Ferris was a take-charge person. She acted like she was everybody's baby nurse. She bossed us around like a drill sergeant. She combed Bobby's unruly hair, made Keith wear a sweater and made Troy change his wet clothing.

At night, she chased us all to bed or at least to our room. "No, you cannot go out! It's a school night." And on week-ends, "Come back before midnight! No prowling around at night."

Miss Ferris barked out orders. "Donald, get a hair cut!" "Jaymie, clean your nails!" "Steven, wipe your feet!" "Roger, wipe your nose!" "Jody, wash your face!" "Daniel, pick your coat up! Don't leave it on the floor." "Do you have a fever, Brandon? Let me take your temperature." "Raymond, take your vitamins!"

Raymond really got the works. He had to take three different pills. And no getting out of it. Miss Ferris stood there and made sure all three went down.

"How old are you, Cameron? Young boys should *not* be drinking beer!"

"This ain't beer. It's ale, Ma'am," said Cameron, downing his glass. Cameron ended up getting a pill, too.

"And where did you get that big knife, Steven? That's much too dangerous for a little boy!"

"What knife?" asked Stevie, concealing the shiv in his

shoe. Miss Ferris searched him, but didn't find it.

Somehow, the guys didn't resent it. They seemed glad to have someone looking after them. Like a stray dog who finally finds a home. They rather enjoyed being bossed around — up to a point.

But one thing we would never do is to let Miss Ferris into our rooms. We kept the doors locked and bolted. Miss Ferris poked around trying to get in, but never could. A couple of times we locked ourselves out and had to climb in through the window.

Miss Ferris insisted on washing and sorting our clothes. She made four piles:

> *Size One* — Jody and Roger
> *Size Two* — Troy, Jaymie and Brandon
> *Size Three* — Bobby, Raymond and Keith
> *Size Four* — Stevie, Danny, Cameron and Donald

Miss Ferris washed our sheets, too; cooked our breakfast; darned our socks; mended our ripped pants and sewed on buttons. She made us lazy.

She cut our toe nails, too.

THE DEADLIEST POISON EVER KNOWN

Rodney Desmond was a real good teacher. He once taught in a private school. I don't know if he quit or got kicked out.

Rodney would read us poems and stories and teach history like it was an exciting drama. He showed us movies and brought in slides and pictures of faraway places. But none of them were as beautiful as *Glow Malomba*.

Rodney would act out a character in history. He was General Custer, General Braddock and King Richard III, being defeated; Columbus crossing the Atlantic; Marc Antony at Caesar's funeral; Napoleon invading

Russia; Nat Turner in rebellion; and Socrates condemned to drink the poison hemlock. Rodney would get us into the act, too. We were the soldiers, the enemy or the crowd.

Rodney even made math interesting to Stevie and Danny. With dice, roulette and cards to teach probability and numbers.

I think Rodney Desmond was the only one who sensed we had the *Vrrooohn*, or something like it. Some device that would give its possessor tremendous power. He kept warning his students about the dangers of Power:

> *The deadliest poison ever known*
> *Comes from Caesar's laurel crown.*

The Poet spoke with such eloquence and passion that Bobby opened up his mouth. "It's okay, Rodney. We'll never use the *Vrrooohn* to hurt people.——"

Cameron socked Bobby to shut him up. Rodney pretended not to hear it, but I'm sure he did.

Actually, we got a kick out of all kinds of mischief we could have done with the *Vrrooohn*. Especially tricks on our Grouchy Neighbor, who called the cops when we played music on our electric guitars. Like making his sewer run backwards.

We could form an anti-mirage and raise hell all over Greenwood. But we resisted the temptation. We got our laughs just thinking about it.

We found just having the *Vrrooohn* smartened us up. We didn't have to take it out of the *Quayne*. Rodney was surprised. He expected us to be stupid.

We discovered we could telepath and clairvoyant to a degree and see things at a distance. Especially if a group of us linked our minds together. We found lost dogs and cats and kids and things. Even a lost husband, who was in an accident. We never charged any fee. But if people insisted on giving us a reward, we took it. We were going to start the Larrabie Brothers Detective Agency. But things began to happen again. . . . . .

THE PHONY INSPECTOR

It started innocently enough. A bunch of characters came around to the house. An "Inspector" came to inspect the electric, though no one had asked him to inspect it. Another man came to repair the telephone, which didn't need repairing.

A "lady salesman" called, but didn't try to sell anything. She asked a lot of questions about "the boys in that picture." *Us,* that is. And a "real estate agent" made a visit. She had a client who wanted to buy "this beautiful house." Mother showed her through all the rooms, but said she didn't want to sell. Not even for a very fancy price. "We have twelve sons. It would be too much trouble to move."

Finally, the Fire Insurance Company sent an agent around. At least, he claimed to be from the Company. He looked through all the rooms, pretending to check for fire hazards. Especially the boys' rooms, which we opened up for him. He examined all our cubbyholes and closets. Of course, he couldn't spot the *Quayne* with the *Vrrooohn* in it and went away disappointed.

There was a wall safe downstairs and somebody cracked it. But the joker Larrabie kids had taken the contents out and put in a fancy metal box, sealed and locked. We filled the inside of the box with horse shit and smelly garbage. What a laugh we had when the safe cracker stole it!

We still dunked each other in the shower, roughhoused and threw pillows, rotten apples, water and mudballs at each other. Our parents seemed relieved rather than annoyed. Mother said, "I'm glad they're acting like children, instead of——"

"Instead of what?"

Mother didn't really know. Something not quite human. Unnatural.

We made up a new Coyote law that a guy got doused for *"messing the room up"* or for not doing his share of the cleaning. In consequence, everybody got dunked or doused at least once; excepting Don Don, who always made his bed neatly and cleaned up.

Donald was distressed rather than pleased. He doesn't like to be left out of things. So we charged Donald with *"being too clean"* and found him guilty. We poured a bucket of water down his trouser legs and another bucket through a funnel down Donald's sleeves. That made him happy.

While they were at it, the guys doused Jaymie and Troy and Keith, too. They didn't even bother to make up a reason. Don Don laughed.

Then the guys doused Cameron for his fifteenth birthday. And Raymond for his fourteenth birthday. And Roger for his eleventh birthday. Miss Ferris came running up and pounded on the door. There was water coming through the ceiling.

THE BUG

The Larrabie urchins took over the top floor of the house. That was four rooms and a porch, besides our double bed room. Mother worried about us being crowded. Cameron assured her that was more than enough for a bunch of guys who, not many months ago, had been sleeping in the streets or in some juvenile jail.

"This is great, Mom! The kind of place we used to dream about."

We held our gang meetings in what Mother called "The Boys' Sitting Room." We called it *The Coyotes' Den.*

"Scribe, call the roll," ordered Cameron.

We called the roll every night. It had become a Coyote ritual.

I called the roll in our old alphabetical order, even though now everybody's name was *Larrabie. Bobby ...*

*Keith... Troy... Jody... Danny... Roger... Ray Ray
... Stevie ... Don Don ... Cameron ... Bran.... All
"Here" or "Present."*

Excepting Don Don. He just sat there with his eyes
shut.

"Hey, Don Don! Wake up!" Still no answer. Stevie
socked him.

He opened his eyes. "Bug!" said Donald. "See——"
Someone had placed a small metal object inside a lamp.

"Holy shit! They wire-tapped us." I don't know who
said that. It was an unspoken thought. We got now so
we could often read each other's thoughts without talking. The bug was something like a radio that broadcast
and recorded at the other end. One of those phony in-
spectors or visitors must have planted it.

"Take the *Vrrooohn* out of the *Quayne!*"

We had sworn never to use the *Vrrooohn* unless we all
agreed. That way, perhaps, we would never use it for any
trivial or evil purpose. We were the masters of the
Vrrooohn, yet also afraid of it. Releasing it was like letting the genie out of the bottle.

We called the roll. No one objected. We formed a circle,
crossed our arms and closed our eyes. Then we threw out
our mind power and the *Horned Crystal* came into being.

When we first found the *Vrrooohn*, it looked like a fortune teller's crystal ball, with whirls that resembled eyes
and two shining horns welded in at the top. The horns
were delicate, but you couldn't break them or even make
a mark on them. Hard and solid like a diamond, yet
warm to the touch. Throbbing and pulsating as if they
had a life of their own.

What an astounding thing the *Vrrooohn* was! Every
time we used it, it seemed different. Sometimes just like
ordinary glass, sometimes like a shining jewel, blue sap-
phire horns set in a ruby globe. Then, a phantom gossamer in a midsummer meadow. A whirling cloud, covered
with shimmering rainbows. A kaleidoscope of ever
changing colored patterns. An eerie lantern that glowed
and glittered like it had a moonbeam locked inside.

Now it was bobbing up and down like flotsam in an ocean wave and slowly turning. Donald said, "Don't touch it. Let it move!" He said it with his mind, not with his voice.

The *Vrrooohn* seemed to be growing larger. Shapes were forming on the surface of the Crystal, like images on a television screen. Faint shadows, vague and out of focus. And strangely, the images each guy saw were different. The *Vrrooohn* works on our minds, not on our eyes and ears. Now, it all came out a jumble.

"Talk to it," urged Raymond. "What do you want to know?"

"We want to know what's on the other end of the wiretap. Who did it and why?"

Raymond said, "Oh, *Horned Crystal*, make that bug work backwards. Let us see our enemies!"

I figured when you talked to the *Vrrooohn*, you were really talking to yourself. It was just a way of concentrating your mind. Raymond didn't agree. He thought the *Horned Crystal* was a real Being. A kind of spirit. That belief worked for him. Raymond could do more with the *Vrrooohn* than anyone else, excepting Don Don. It began to work for Raymond now.

The shadows on the surface of the Crystal became sharp and clear. This was inside the house of Mr. Bartlow. I had been there with Father. I recognized the room by the tapestry on the wall. *The Hunting of the Stag.* The young stag fought bravely, but the hounds and hunters finally got him.

Were the Naghallah boys like the stag in the tapestry? We fought hard and escaped again and again. But in the end would they run us down? I forgot we could read each others' minds. I got a punch from Brother Danny and a sock from Stevie. That was for even thinking about defeat. We fought them off and beat them when we were weak. Now we were strong. Unconquerable!

The *Vrrooohn* spread around us in every direction. It seemed we were now right in the middle of the picture. This was the living room of Bartlow's mansion, crammed

Oh, Horned Crystal, Give us power! Reveal!

with all kinds of expensive junk. There were three men gathered around a table. We saw them clearly, but they couldn't see us. We knew them well. "Major" Powell with his bristling moustache, in a military uniform of his own private army. "Captain" Klayborne, with his hard, cruel mouth and nervous manner. And "Commander" Bartlow, suave and smooth, in expensive evening clothing. Three *Masters of Naghallah.* We got a picture of them, but couldn't tell what they were saying.

"Can you hear them, Don Don? What are they talking about?"

"Us," said Donald.

Now we could hear them. Donald's mind must have acted as a kind of amplifier. . . .

"I can't understand how they could do it. Twelve low grade juvenile delinquents of sub-normal intelligence."

"Except that Jaymie. A clever but obnoxious little punk."

(*A punch and a laugh from Brother Danny.*)

"In some way, we lost control of the boys."

"You were too soft with them," declared Klayborne. "You should have put some fear into the boys. You had to break them before you sent them on a mission. If you had let me handle the boys the way I wanted to——"

"Lammington handled the boys," said Powell. "The collars should have controlled them. Someone helped them get the collars off. Some Outsider. Whoever it was is using the boys now."

Klayborne's face gave a nervous twitch. "How long are we going to wait before we move?"

"We are moving now," said Bartlow. "We will act as soon as we are ready." Bartlow found the situation not unfavorable. "We know now where the *Thing* is. In the hands of a group of ignorant boys. It should not be too difficult to get it. Whoever is directing the boys can be disposed of. It will be easier to deal with the boys alone."

(*Now the visions of the Vrrooohn began to fade.*)

MURDER FOR HIRE

Keith noted a headline in yesterday's newspaper:

MYSTERY MAN VANISHES

Stanley Klayborne, an associate of the missing billionaire, Karl Hasserman, had left his house abruptly and had not returned. Apparently, his departure was voluntary, since he had taken his car and his personal possessions.

Klayborne was wanted by the police for questioning in connection with "several violent crimes," including the death of Dr. Mortimer Mehary, "Director of the ill-fated Naghallah school for delinquent boys. . . . ."

Klayborne had been accused of heading "a terrorist group that would commit *murder for hire.*" He strenuously denied this and said his own life had been threatened by criminal elements.

"Klayborne is a licensed detective and holds a permit to carry firearms. . . ."

The Police had searched the missing man's home to no avail. They found no clue and were baffled. "Captain" Klayborne had now been missing for a week, "vanished without a trace. . . ." But we had just seen Klayborne at the other end of the wire-tap. Hiding out in "Commander" Bartlow's house.

Powell and Bartlow, however, had not gone into hiding. They were still very much around. There was nothing to connect them directly with the killings. The late Masters, Striker and Lammington, and now Klayborne and his henchmen, had done their dirty work for them.

Bartlow and Powell might be suspected, but they were too powerful to touch.

Now that we knew about the bug, we decided to have some fun. We rehearsed what to say and said it in front of the bug. About a safety deposit vault in which we pretended to put the *Vrrooohn.*

We took out a safe deposit box at the local bank. The Manager thought it was a big joke. "What are you going to keep in here, boys? Your baseball cards?"

"No, sir."

"No dirty pictures now." Said with a wagging finger.

We filled the box with cheap imitation jewelry and a magic store crystal that might be mistaken for the *Vrrooohn*. We wrote messages in invisible ink that would show up if you treated the paper. *Fuck you, creep!* Stuff like that.

We made up phony maps and wrote stuff in meaningless code. We came back four or five times, adding more and more junk. The Bank Manager laughed each time we came in. But he stopped laughing a few days later. Someone had broken into the vault and ransacked our deposit box. They had even knocked a wall in. But the Larrabie kids were laughing. We had put them to so much trouble for nothing.

"They got themselves a bunch of shit!" said Stevie.

We forgot we weren't playing *Capture-the-Flag* or *Ring-a-levio*. This was a grim game, played for keeps.

*   *   *   *   *   *   *

HASSERMAN "WILL" FILED

A document purporting to be the Last Will and Testament of the vanished billionaire, Karl Hasserman, was filed today in the State Supreme Court by the law firm of Meyer, Greenbaum, Perkins, O'Leary and Untermeyer.

The alleged Will is written in long-hand. Hasserman's writing and the signatures of three witnesses have been authenticated by a group of handwriting experts. . . . .

WILL CALLED HOAX

Commander Bartlow, Chairman of the Hasserman bank, branded the Hasserman Will to be either a hoax or a forgery. Bartlow insisted the missing billionaire is still alive and has merely "gone into seclusion". . . . .

The Masters of Naghallah
Major Powell, Captain Klayborne and Commander Bartlow

DANGEROUS CHILDREN

The Horned Crystal was a-glowing and the images came back. This time there were only two men. Klayborne wasn't there. The others didn't trust him. Both Bartlow and Powell seemed afraid of Klayborne. They wondered if he had become a little mad.

Bartlow said, "We can't get rid of him yet. Right now, we need him."

Powell said, "You can't control him any more."

There was a pause. The two men now were trying to read the bug. To watch *them*, we had to let them watch *us*. Each guy took a turn watching, hidden by the *Vrrooohn*, while the rest of the guys fooled around. Now, it was my turn.

"What are those boys doing?"

"Playing some stupid game. Hide-and-go-seek or something like that. Wrestling and throwing eggs.

"They act like children."

"They *are* children. *Dangerous children*. As dangerous as a horde of vipers."

"As long as they have Hasserman's *Thing*. That's the fangs of the viper."

"They are too stupid to know what power they have."

"If Klayborne should ever get the *Thing*———"

"We must never let that happen!"

They were uneasy confederates, hating and fearing each other. Too bad the interference came again and the *Vrrooohn* went dead.

Somebody turned the room lights back on. Then Brother Danny hit me with an egg.

THE MISSING WITNESS

Rodney Desmond, our teacher, told us, "There's a state police officer outside to see you. What have you guys been doing?"

"Nothing," said Keith. "We've been good boys. Honest."

The police officer was a Black lady in a bright blue uniform. With a big shining badge, *Detective Inspector General.* "I'm Officer Caroline." She didn't say if that was her first or last name. She smiled disarmingly. "Sorry to interrupt your school, boys. We just wanted to ask a few questions."

"We take the Fifth Amendment, Ma'am," said Cameron Anthony Westcott Larrabie.

"We need your help, boys. You're not being charged with anything. Nothing at all." She smiled again. We gathered around her in a circle and sprawled on the floor.

"Inspector Smith has spoken well of you."

"Inspector Smith?" None of us could remember any such person.

"We all have a police record — excepting Jaymie."

"You have a record for telling tall stories," said Officer Caroline. "Going down a tunnel into a labyrinth and coming out eight weeks later. But that isn't what we want to ask you about.

"What do you know about your school Director, Dr. Mehary?"

"He's dead," said Brandon.

"How do you know?"

"We saw his body in the school. It looked like he had been murdered. The body disappeared."

She made some notes. "How about Karl Hasserman?"

"We heard he was dead. We found his Will," said Raymond.

"Is that why they tried to kill you in the Ranger's cabin? Because you knew about Dr. Mehary and had Karl Hasserman's Will?"

"That might be the reason. They didn't give us any explanation, Ma'am."

"Now what do you know about Franz Johannes Has-serman?"

We looked blank.

"An older man. A distant cousin of Karl Hasserman. He stayed at the mansion at Kaah Naghallah while you were in the school. We think he tried to impersonate his cousin."

Cameron thought he knew Old Franz. "A white-haired old gentleman with false teeth who signed Karl Hasserman's name on checks. I saw him a couple of times through a window in the mansion."

"He disappeared some time in late September."

"Is Old Franz dead, too?"

"Inspector Smith" — she spoke his name reverently — "Thought he is still alive. And hiding out somewhere not far from here. Why should Franz Hasserman go into hiding?"

"I guess," said Bobby, "he knows where the bodies are buried."

"He knows many things that we would like to know," said Caroline. "Inspector Smith thought maybe you boys could give us some clue. You may have heard something."

There was a mystery about Inspector Smith. He, too, had been a victim. Inspector Smith had been taken violently ill after eating rice pudding. He had recovered, thank the Good Lord and was now on leave, convalescing.

There was no proof that the Inspector had been deliberately poisoned. But Officer Caroline didn't think it was accidental. There were people who didn't want Inspector Smith around. Powerful and important people. An honest cop could be a menace.

Meanwhile, Officer Caroline was carrying on as his deputy, investigating the disappearance of Karl Hasserman. "If we could find his cousin, Franz! He's the clue to the whole affair. Will you help us?"

We all looked at Cameron. The Gangleader looked at Donald. Then he said, "We'll help you any way we can,

Officer. If we find him, what would you offer him to get him to talk?"

"Immunity. And protection. If he tells the truth."

Neither Bartlow's money and influence, nor Powell's connections nor Klayborne's ruthless cunning could long protect them, if the old German forger decided to spill the beans. The authorities might not believe the fantastic stories of the Naghallah boys, nor take the word of runaway juvenile delinquents. But Cousin Franz, who had been in the center of the conspiracy, could provide clear proof of massive fraud and perhaps of murder.

It was with good reason that Old Franz had gone into hiding. He knew too much.

"Goodbye, Inspector Caroline. Don't eat any rice pudding."

Caroline said she didn't eat anything they served at the station house. She brought her meals from home.

Cameron was the only one of us who had actually seen Old Franz. But Donald was the one who had the power to make the Horned Crystal work. Could we get Cameron's memories into Donald's mind?

Cameron and Donald held the *Vrrooohn*. The rest of us formed a closed circle around them. After a while, Donald thought he could see the Old German. He was on a balcony on a rickety old three story house.

"Where?"

Donald couldn't tell. "Not far from here."

"Can you see any more?"

He tried again. It was a white house with green shutters on a narrow street. Donald got the idea of a pet shop on one side and a music store on the other. There was an Eating Place on that same street and a church yard.

Donald strained hard, but that was all he could get. One thing we learned about the *Vrrooohn*. If an image doesn't come right in the beginning, it don't come at all.

A white house with a balcony . . . a pet shop . . . a music shop. . . . Somewhere near here. That didn't give you much information, but maybe it was enough.

Look up the music shops and pet shops in the phone

book, suggested Jaymie. There were some sixty music shops and forty pet shops listed in the local Yellow Pages. Cut out stores in a shopping center or in a wide main street. That reduced the numbers by half. Now see where there's a pet shop and a music shop close together. There were four pairs in the tri-county area. We found by phoning that one music shop and one pet shop were out of business. That left two pairs. We decided to try the nearest one first.

It was too cold to bicycle. Too risky to take a car with no driver's license. We were still on the J.D. list of the Greenwood police. We took a bus to South Greenwood and then walked.

It was mid-afternoon, but the light was already fading. Flurries of snow descended from the darkening sky. The thermometer had hit zero and was still falling. We shivered and wished we had listened to Mother when she told us to get ourselves thermal underwear and a warm winter coat.

Twelve noisy youths crowded onto the South Greenwood bus. A short man with heavy glasses followed them, then took a rear seat and buried his face in a newspaper. When they got off several miles later, he followed the youths, pulling down his wide brim hat. He moved aimlessly, but kept about a block behind his quarry. To anyone who noticed him, he seemed just a bit drunk.

Donald led us down a narrow, curving street called *Hemlock Lane*. We passed a church yard and came upon an old-fashioned white house with green shutters and a balcony. It was wedged in between two commercial buildings. Sure enough, one of them housed a pet shop with parakeets and tropical fish. The other a music shop, with harps and guitars. Just as Donald had envisioned it, except there was no Eating Place across the street. Donald had hit the target, but not the bull's eye. His score was less than perfect and that left him unhappy.

"Why did I get the wrong image?"

"Maybe you were hungry," suggested Troy. "That's why the *Vrrooohn* made you see an Eating Place."

The old mansion had been divided into small apartments. There were twelve mail boxes in the hall downstairs: *Wolozczak... Perrota... Malakoff... Fong... McNulty... Vanderlyn... Levy... Yamamoto... Aristides... Schultz... Gonzales... Jackson...* A truly all-American roster of tenants!

But no Franz Hasserman. Of course! If he's in hiding, he would change his identity. Old Franz would take a different name. Probably a German name. "Try *Schultz*," suggested Cameron. "Top floor, East." There was a light in the window.

"If we all go up," said Danny, "we'll scare the shit out of him. He may take off."

"Brandon go up," decided Cameron. "Talk to him in German. Tell him we have good news for him."

"What good news?"

"That he'll get immunity and the Police will protect him."

Brandon climbed the stairs and knocked. "Herr Schultz?" he inquired.

An elderly German lady opened the door. "He isn't here now."

"*Wir sind Freunde. Wir bringen Herr Schultz gute Nachrichten.*"

"*Er ist nicht hier. Geh' weg!* Go away."

"*Es ist sehr wichtig das wir mit Herr Hasserman sprechen.*"

The name *Hasserman* momentarily floored her. She stared at Brandon with frightened eyes. "Who are you?"

"I told you. We are friends. We have good news——"

"Come back in an hour. *Nein. Zwei Stunden.*" She held up two fingers. "*Er wird denn hier sein.*"

Brandon wrote a note in German and departed.

We didn't want to stand around for two hours. "There must be an Eating Place around here somewhere." There was. Back at the bus stop. A sign said *BUSY BEE CAFETERIA*. But it wasn't very busy now. The place was almost empty. And pleasantly warm.

We killed about an hour eating pizza, hot chocolate

and pie. Bobby and Raymond remembered getting thrown out of here once. Back in the days when they were homeless street kids. "We had no money. We were eating the leftovers on other peoples' plates." Bobby was still mad at the Manager. "He didn't have to throw us out. He could just have talked to us and asked us to leave."

Bobby called the guy a *Fucking Queer* and Raymond said we'd get our gang and wreck the place. The Manager called the cops and the boys ran away.

Anyway, the jerk wasn't around any more. At least we didn't see him. Instead, there was a red-headed lady who gave us free cookies.

We thought we had shaken off that short man with the heavy glasses. But here he was now sitting in a corner, reading a newspaper. He appeared to be reading the same page over and over again. Every now and then, he would look at his watch and then at us.

Stevie and Danny walked over to him. Stevie grabbed the newspaper out of his hand. "What do you want with us, Mister?"

The man got up. "I don't believe I know you."

"We seen you, Mister. You've been following us. What do you want?"

"You got a big mouth for a little punk."

"Get out of here," said Steven, angrily.

"Get out of here!" echoed Danny.

Now Bobby, Keith and Raymond, and Cameron too, came over to back Stevie up. The man had put his hand into his pocket. I thought for a moment he might draw a gun. Instead, he smiled. He got up and walked out the back door.

Cameron said, "*We* better get out. That guy might come back and bring his mob with him."

We paid the bill and started for the door. Suddenly there was a loud noise, like the shot of a rifle. Then another. A scream and the screeching of brakes. The crash of two vehicles colliding. A series of angry shouts and frightened outcries. Then horns blasting, people yelling and general havoc.

We rushed for the exit. "Hold it!" ordered Cameron. "Stay together! Form column of twos and follow me." He said it with his mind. Otherwise, we couldn't have heard it above the din.

Outside in the square, a huge crowd was gathering. A young policeman was frantically trying to hold them in check. Traffic was blocked in all directions.

A man lay dead in the middle of the street. Without looking at the man, I knew who he was.

"What happened?"

"He got off the bus. He was crossing the square. There was a shot or a couple of shots. The old man turned and put his hand up.

"Then this car hit him. Went right through the light, sideswiped two other cars and kept going."

"It was a hit and run?"

"No, it was murder. He had a wound in his shoulder, but it was the car that killed him. They were waiting for him in ambush."

An Oriental lady, with a scarf around her neck, pushed forward; then gave an anguished cry when she saw the body.

"Do you know him?" asked the young officer.

"Yes. It's our neighbor, Mr. Schultz."

"What is your name, Ma'am?"

"Edna Yamamoto. Such a nice man he was! Poor Mr. Schultz!"

Now an ambulance pulled into the square. *Too late!* The white-coated doctors came rushing out. *Too late!* And we had come and found Old Franz, *too late!*

Now a police car pulled in. Then another. And another. Watching in the crowd, we saw once again the short man with the heavy glasses.

"Do you think he fired the shots?"

"I doubt it. He would have been waiting in the square and not in the BUSY BEE watching us. But I think he was in with the killers. He had a gun. If the car didn't get Franz Hasserman, he was a follow-up."

"It's our neighbor, Mr. Schultz!"

Cameron signalled. "Let's get out of here. We won't take the bus. There may be a death car at the other end, waiting at the bus stop.

"We'll hike back. I don't care how cold it is. We'll jog. That'll keep us warm. Get away now, while no one is watching us." Cameron said it all with his mind. We scattered and broke away separately. Then came together six blocks away.

In *Bane N'Gai* we had learned to see in the dark. We went home now through darkened alleys and dimly lit side streets. Nothing was following us, but we zigzagged back and forth like a ship evading a pursuing submarine.

Half way home and half frozen, we hit another Eaterie. We telephoned Dad from there and he came and picked us up.

"We were worried about you guys. Why didn't you tell us where you were going?"

"We got lost," said Jaymie. "Sorry, Dad."

"One day sooner," said Cameron, bitterly. "One day sooner and we could have saved him!"

"We might have saved him today, if we had the *Vrrooohn* along."

"If we had it on us, they could have taken it away from us." In the *Quayne*, nobody could touch the *Vrrooohn* but us.

We didn't tell our parents about Franz Hasserman. We said we didn't want to worry them. But the real reason was we were ashamed at having failed.

A MINOR SKIRMISH

We hadn't felt fear since the day of the adoption. Now, it came back again. We took the *Vrrooohn* out of the *Quayne* at night and put it in the middle of our circle of beds. We set the *Vrrooohn* to trigger an alarm, if an attack were coming.

Our Enemy, we thought, might try to set the house on fire. That would force us to take the *Vrrooohn* out of its hiding place and they would get a chance to seize it.

If we got a fire warning, two of us would go down and rouse our parents and Miss Ferris. Two others would rescue the two kittens Donald and Roger found abandoned at the shopping center. They roamed by day, but at night they stayed in what Mother called *The Cat Room*.

The rest of the guys would form an anti-mirage and escape with the *Horned Crystal* over the roofs and down a rope ladder; then counter-attack the arsonists with our hidden weapons. For a while, we took turns guarding at night, like we used to do in *Bane N'Gai*. But nothing happened, so we stopped.

Perhaps fortunately, Father was very jittery about fires. He installed all kinds of alarms and extinguishers, including a direct line to the fire house.

Our parents sensed we were in danger, though they didn't talk about it. Father hired a night watchman, a young man named Larry, who used to work in Father's company. Larry got put out of his apartment and Father gave him the rooms above the garage. Father sort of expected the boys to complain. But we all liked Larry. He was a good guy.

Larry and his poodle, Topper, would walk the grounds at night. Larry had a loud police whistle. Topper had a bark that was even louder. Between the two of them, that was enough to scare off most intruders. Every four or five days, Larry routed an intruder. So he claimed; but I really think he was making them up. You can't blame a guy for trying to make himself important. If they asked us, we backed up Larry's stories. Then he, in turn, would back up our stories.

Rumors of the intruders aroused our nervous neighbors, who excitedly telephoned the Police. The Fuzz, in turn, promised to patrol our street at night. (But didn't. At least not very often.)

Indeed, the only time the Fuzz seemed to come around was when the Grouchy Man next door complained about the noise the Larrabie kids were making. Especially when we played rock music.

One evening, there was a suspicious-looking van, with phony license plates, parked outside our house. The Larrabie boys all grabbed our electric guitars and played as loudly as we could, with the window open. Sure enough, the Grouchy Neighbor called the cops.

When the Fuzz came, the suspicious-looking van took off. The cops chased the van and lost it. Then they came back to the house and started yammering about the Larrabie boys.

Miss Ferris told the cops we were *not* "a bunch of rowdies," nor "a gang of punks." We were fine young men and a credit to the town of Greenwood. So the Fuzz got back into their car and drove away.

It was another minor skirmish won by the Larrabie kids.

A DAY OF JOY AND FEASTING

Christmas came and we forgot about the *Masters of Naghallah.*

The guys started to feel like they had always been Larrabie kids. Young Jody really began to think so. Jody wished it and thought it so hard he began to believe it. Dad became confused with his stern stepfather who had sent him away. But now had changed and welcomed Jody back.

Jody told Father, "I made a lot of trouble, didn't I? That's why you sent me to *Kaah Naghallah?*"

Dad smiled. "What trouble did you make, Jody?"

"I told the cops about the pot you were selling."

Father was embarrassed. "Well, no, Jody. I didn't sell pot. I---er---sent you to the school so you would be with your brothers."

"Me and my brudders made a lot of trouble for you, didn't we?" said Jody. "But we're not going to do it any more."

Dad smiled again and put his arm around Jody. I do believe that Jody is his favorite son.

We decorated the tree and strung lights all around the house. We hung up wreaths and garlands, ribbons and mistletoe. Mother had us all hang up a stocking by the fireplace. In each, she put a wrist watch, a pen knife, a flashlight, a wallet and various goodies. That made Bobby cry a little. He hadn't had a stocking or any kind of Christmas since his grandmother died.

We all made something for our parents and for Miss Ferris, Teacher Rodney and Larry. Strangely, the *Vrrooohn* not only sharpens the mind, but gives you skills. Five guys painted pictures, memories from our adventures. Raymond, a Goblins' cave; Brandon, the silver woods; Donald, a Lemurian city, with rainbow arches and gleaming towers; Keith, the ghostly river we called The *Styx;* Troy, the *Garden of Eden.*

People said, "What a fantastic imagination these boys have!" "Remarkable talent!" "Such gifted youngsters!"

The pictures got exhibited at the Greenwood Inn.

The rest of us made tables, book shelves, chairs and benches and grew potted plants from bulbs. Lillies, tulips, amaryllis and hyacinths. The *Vrrooohn* made them grow like flowers in Lemuria.

We had a family dinner on Christmas Eve. Father made a toast. *"To my twelve splendid sons!"* I could see a smile on Brother Danny. In a year, he had been transformed from a *juvenile hood* into a *splendid son.*

On Christmas Day, we had a merry party. Miss Ferris was a great cook and prepared a truly Lemurian feast. She chased us all out of the kitchen excepting Brandon, whom she selected as her assistant. Cooks always seem to like Brandon.

"You boys can set the table," said Mother. Even with all the extra boards, the dining room table wasn't nearly big enough. We kept adding on odd tables and brought down most of the chairs in the house. All in all, we had thirty-six people, two cats and a dog.

The relatives came in force; Aunt Laura and Uncle Leon, Uncle Oscar and Aunt Rosa, Cousin Katie Weisman and her husband, Cousin Michael. Also, Wilma Weisman and Billy, her fiance. Billy brought along a saxophone, but nobody asked him to play.

There was also our teacher, Rodney. And Larry, the Watchman with his poodle, Topper. And our good neighbors, the Meyers and the Weinbergers.

There were seven girls: Wilma's two younger sisters, Cousin Karen, Joyce and Marjorie Meyer and Dr. Weinberger's two daughters. And, of course, Miss Ferris and the twelve Larrabie boys.

We rolled back the rugs and danced or tried to dance. The grown-ups, mostly, just sat around gawking. Old man Meyer, though, was hopping and whirling all over the place. After a while, everyone got lively. We sang carols, square danced, break danced, rock danced; and the Poet did a jig.

Cousin Katie had us all walking around bearing pine boughs to celebrate the winter solstice, *The Turning of*

The Light. Joyce Meyer, bearing the mistletoe, paraded around on Larry's shoulders. Uncle Oscar played a squeaking fiddle. Aunts Laura and Rosa tried to sing. Billy, the fiance, grabbed the chance and broke in with his saxophone and Uncle Leon pounded loudly on the piano, as if trying to drown out the others.

It was a great and happy time. The kind you wish would happen all over again, exactly the same way. If I had to choose a time to last forever, it would be that Christmas day. . . .

At the end, Mother looked exhausted, but happy. "We can clean up tomorrow."

But Miss Ferris insisted on cleaning up tonight.

HIGH JINKS AND CHOCOLATE SAUCE

On New Year's Eve, we went to the Greenwood Inn. Our cousin and good neighbor, Innkeeper Weisman, gave us a front line table. Meanwhile, Larry and his friends guarded the house and held a noisy celebration. The Grouchy Neighbor complained, as usual; but for once the cops paid him no heed.

Miss Ferris struggled into an ancient evening dress too tight for her and a new set of false teeth that kept coming loose.

Mother looked beautiful and never stopped dancing with one son after another. Miss Ferris didn't want to dance at all, but we persuaded her. She was rather hefty to push around. Her shoes were too tight, but she kept going gamely until her heel came off. Then she went limping back to the table. "Go dance with the girls, you boys. That's enough for an old lady."

"You're not an old lady!" declared Roger. "You're a---a---" *A dowager,* Roger decided, not quite knowing what the word meant. Miss Ferris took this to be a high compliment.

There was no lack of dancing partners. The Weisman, Meyer and Weinberger maidens and Cousin Karen were all there. Most of the guys were kind of shy and only danced with the girls we knew. Cameron, however, was all over the place, approaching strange young ladies years older than he was. "I'm Cameron Anthony Larrabie. Would you like to meet me?" Everyone always said, *Yes, they would.*

When Cameron broke the ice with a girl, the other guys would get up the courage to join in. Now Danny and Stevie, and Keith, too, were hopping around clumsily with three elegant young ladies. They paid little attention to the music, doing a break dance, while the orchestra played an old-fashioned waltz.

Donald was leaping around with Marjorie Meyer. He was Whirling Boy again, swinging his partner through the air. Marjorie seemed to like it. The other dancers all got out of the way. All twelve Larrabie boys were on the floor most of the time. Father started to dance, but pulled a muscle and limped back to the table.

We ate a course. Then the Master of Ceremonies lined everybody up for the *Bunny Hop,* the *Leapfrog* and the *Conga.* Round and round and round the floor. The exhausted grown-ups dropped out, but we kept going.

Now another dinner course. It was almost midnight. Cheers and celebrations. Corks popped and balloons burst. Old man Meyer, trying to reach a balloon on the ceiling, climbed up on a chair and broke it.

"Get ready for midnight!" Father proclaimed a toast, "To the Future!" The champagne flowed freely. We filled our glasses. Miss Ferris gave us a reproving look.

A lady sang. Miss Ferris thought the song was rather vulgar. *Rolling in the Grass With You.*

The New Year's gong went off. The band played. Everybody sang *Auld Lang Syne.* Then another naughty song. *It Happened Under A Cherry Tree.* Miss Ferris looked shocked.

"What happened?" asked Jody.

"Never mind!"

A Family Celebration:
The Larrabie Parents, Miss Ferris and the Boys

Now came the final course of the dinner. Ice cream and chocolate sauce. A tall man in formal evening dress was coming over to the table. He looked like an ad for an expensive clothing store. It was Mr. Bartlow. "Well! Good evening Larrabie. And Mrs. Larrabie."

Father said, "Good evening, Commander Bartlow." Which is how he liked to be addressed. We still hadn't found out what he was supposed to be Commander of.

He gave us boys a look of disdain, mingled with curiosity. "Well, Larrabie, I see you have the whole family here. Quite a change for the boys, isn't it? You took quite a task for yourself, didn't you, Larrabie? Taking all these rowdies in."

He pointed at Donald who was staring at Bartlow with his mouth open. Rather like a peasant boy looking at a king. "You even got this one, too, Larrabie? Has he learned to talk yet?"

I don't know what happened. I swear nobody touched that chocolate sauce. Yet it ended up all over Bartlow's stiff shirt and white vest. Donald and Raymond looked at each other meaningfully. Then that chocolate sauce just flew up, all over Bartlow.

Jody and Roger started to giggle. Troy and Bobby burst out laughing. "Oh, dear!" cried Mother. "Let me wipe it off!" But the Commander turned on his heels and walked angrily away.

An attentive waiter brought us another pitcher of chocolate sauce. We ate and danced some more.

HER FAVORITE BURGLAR

"She's here!" cried Cameron excitedly. That girl he had met in her bed while he was burglarizing her apartment. He told us about her back in the dungeon at *Kaah Naghallah.* We thought then he was bullshitting.

He gave her his usual line. "I'm Cameron Anthony Larrabie. Would you like to meet me?"

"I'm sure we met already," said the girl. "Who are you?"

"Your favorite burglar."

"Oh!" She looked at the handsome, well dressed youth and remembered the ragged, dirty house-breaker. "Where have you been since we last met?"

"In reform school."

"Really?" She smiled a little. "Did they reform you?"

"No. They threw me out as hopeless."

"Do they let you just run around loose?"

"Well — They decided I wasn't a public danger. Just a public nuisance."

She smiled again. "Are you still in the same occupation?"

"No. I have new parents and eleven brothers now. And a very strict nurse. They're all here."

"Do they let you out at night?"

"Not very often. I have to break out." Cameron put his arm around her. She didn't pull away.

Her name was Gloria. She didn't reveal her last name. "I suppose you still have my telephone number?"

"Alas, no. The Fuzz confiscated my address book. They have been pestering all my girls for dates."

'I have a new phone number ——" She didn't tell him and he didn't ask for it. Instead, he wrote on the back of a menu:

Cameron Anthony Larrabie
479-2358

The guys all laughed. "Bet she don't call," said Stevie.

"Bet you a buck she will."

We all bet. Cameron's eleven bucks against one buck by each of his brothers.

Sure enough, she did call. Cameron played hard to get. "Tell her I'm out. But I'll be down tomorrow morning at Greenwood Lake." That was a long C-shaped lake where the town kids liked to go ice skating. "Want to bet I have a date with her? Within three days. I'll give you guys a chance to get your money back."

The girl arrived in an all red costume that you could spot from the other end of the lake. Cameron called us over. "Gloria, I'd like to have you meet my brothers."

"Pleased to meet you," said Brandon, Jody, Donald, Roger, Jaymie, Raymond, Bobby, Keith, Stevie, Danny and Troy.

She nodded. "And I'd like to have you meet my fiance. My future husband."

He was a real big guy, with a police detective's badge on his coat. Tough and mean-looking. And he didn't seem a bit pleased to meet us.

Cameron decided to forget about the date.

MISTER X

The holidays were a glorious, magic time. But now that they were over, I had a curious feeling in the pit of my stomach. It took a while to figure out what it was. *It was Fear!* The last few weeks had been too quiet. Somehow, the lull seemed ominous.

We resolved once again to stay together when we left the house. That sort of cramped Cameron's style on a girl date to have to drag his eleven kid brothers along. Cameron would bring his date to the *"Boys' Sitting Room"* in the house and chase the rest of us until it was time to take the girl home.

The girls didn't seem to mind coming to the house or travelling with an eleven-youth bodyguard. We blamed it on Father. *His orders.* We weren't allowed to go out alone at night. He was afraid we might get into trouble. Or be kidnapped. That always made the girls laugh.

We had seen nothing on the *Vrrooohn* since the death of Old Franz. That made the headlines for a week, but now had become just another unsolved murder mystery. For the moment, our enemies were lying low.

It was *Martin Luther King Day.* The other schools all had a holiday. But Teacher Rodney had an inspiration. He introduced himself as Martin Luther King who would speak to the assembled crowd. (Us, that is). Then he presented some of the Reverend's most famous lines. *I have a dream. . . . Let Freedom ring. . . . We shall live in peace. . . .*

Rodney spoke well, in a vibrant, powerful voice. He knew his stuff by heart and never looked at his notes.

Then he went on to give speeches by other great orators. Lincoln at Gettysburg. Patrick Henry: *Give me Liberty or give me Death.* Franklin Roosevelt: *There is nothing to fear but Fear.* William Jennings Bryan: *The Cross of Gold.* Each time, Rodney spoke in a different voice and made some changes in his costume. He should have been an actor.

We thought he had finished and applauded. That was a mistake. For, as an encore, he gave us speeches by the great Roman orator, Cicero. First, he gave the speech in English translation. Then he repeated it in Latin "so we could get the musical cadence." Cicero sure was a windy guy.

Rodney stopped abruptly when he saw his pet pupil, Brandon, *the urchin bold with hair of gold,* had fallen asleep.

"Sorry, fellers. I'm afraid I got carried away. I always wished I could become an orator——"

Stevie said, "Why don't you?"

"Looks like my talking puts guys to sleep."

"Maybe the other orators did, too."

"Any questions?" asked Rodney, hopefully.

Now Brandon opened his eyes and his mouth, trying to make Teacher think he had been listening carefully. "What did Cicero mean when he said *This is the time!* The time for what?"

"Time for lunch," said Brother Danny. And that was the end of school for the day.

*   *   *   *   *   *   *

That night, the visions of the *Vrrooohn* came back. . . .

Once again, the Masters of Naghallah were in conclave, in the living room of Bartlow's mansion. Two strangers were present. One was a bald-headed man with large ears. The other was a thin man with dark glasses. Keith thought he had seen Big Ears before. He was some kind of a police officer. "An undercover detective." We had been wise not to trust too much in the Police. Bartlow had his agents there.

"Commander" Bartlow was talking. He was explaining something to the two strangers. A picture, but no sound came through. The effect was rather like an old-fashioned silent movie. Gradually, Bartlow's voice became audible. Once again, he was talking about *us*.

"These urchins have in their hands tremendous power. A power which, fortunately, they are incapable of using. They are like a jungle tribe, holding an atomic bomb."

"They may, however, learn to use the *Thing*," said Klayborne. "In fact, they *did* use it back in the cabin."

"We don't know what happened there. There was a loss of nerve by the men you hired. Or maybe they turned on each other," asserted Bartlow.

"I don't believe the boys on their own can handle Hasserman's *Thing*. But some outsider — some adult — could get to them and use the boys."

"Some one may have gotten to them already," reflected Powell.

"Not Mitchell Larrabie," said Bartlow. "I am sure he knows nothing. He is frightened of the boys."

"That Rodney Desmond sees them nearly every day——"

"That milksop poet? The Gay Scribbler? He is a weak-kneed clown. The enemy I am looking for is somebody strong and dominating.

"Look at these boys as a pack of vicious dogs. Some-where, there is a man who controls them, or will control them and sic them on his enemies. Until he destroys all opposition or is destroyed himself.

"We'll call him *Mr. X*. We must hit hard and soon and cripple *Mr. X* by taking Karl Hasserman's *Thing* away from him. Draw their teeth and the vicious dog pack will be turned into yelping puppies."

"He uses the *Thing* to control the boys?"

"I suppose so. Assuming there is a *Mister X*. The boys seem to follow him quite willingly. There is no sign of any rebellion."

"We may be looking in the wrong place. *Mr. X* is more likely to have Hasserman's *Thing* than the boys are."

"No. These boys are not altogether stupid. They won't give up the *Thing* to an outsider and *Mr. X* knows better than to ask for it. Let the boys keep Hasserman's *Thing*. He will show them how to use it. *Mr. X* will gain power and will reward his punks with toys and goodies."

"And who then is this *Mister X*?"

There was a moment of silence. Then Powell turned to Klayborne and asked a question; and Klayborne turned white and shaky. The question was, "Are you sure Dr. Mehary is dead?"

*   *   *   *   *   *   *

They must have feared Dr. Mehary wasn't dead. They went to the trouble of digging up his bones. We boys were unworthy of being taken seriously. It was *Mr. X* they feared.

"Let's give them a *Mister X*."

"You mean a real live one?"

"A real man," said Jaymie. "But he don't have to be

alive. As long as they don't know he's dead or can't be sure."

"Not Karl Hasserman. We already said we seen his body and found his Will."

"Remember *Treasure Island*," said Troy. "This old pirate, Ben Gunn, was marooned on the island and left to die. And he swore to get vengeance."

"So what?"

"There was a guy the Masters marooned in *Bane N'Gai*. Remember our old beloved Teacher Smeer?"

"We told them Smeer was dead," objected Brandon.

"We were lying. Smeer told us to say that. We rescued Old Smeer and brought him back with us. Now he is *Mister X.*, scheming vengeance by siccing his vicious dog pack against the Masters of *Naghallah*. His twelve vicious attack boys, the Larrabie kids."

"Hey!" said Cameron, "That's a great idea!"

"What do we do now?"

"Nothing. Until we get orders from Mister X."

"Mister X. is really *us*."

"I know. We got to wait. The Lemurians will be watching us. We can't use the *Vrrooohn*, except in self-defense. Right, Don Don?"

"We could shake them up a bit. Let them think Smeer has come back by talking about him in front of the wire tap."

Our whole conversation was carried out in silence. All in our minds, without a single spoken word. Strangely, Donald could talk better in telepathy than by actually speaking. When Donald talked out loud, he just said a couple of words. In mind reading, he gave out complicated messages.

"Come, brudders. let us rehearse what to say in front of the bug."

"Hey, somebody ought to be Smeer. We could have him visiting us."

Keith was a pretty good mimic. Smeer always sounded hoarse. Like he had a cold.

"Let him have a real bad cold and whisper. Or maybe

his vocal cords got damaged by the swamp-worms."

Keith croaked, "I can't talk too much, boys. My throat hurts me."

"We're sorry, Captain Smeer."

"You don't have to call me Captain Smeer, boys. You can call me *Ed.*"

"His name was Albert."

"Call me *Al* then."

"Yessir. Yes, Captain Al."

"Okay, you vicious hounds of *Bane N'Gai.* Show your teeth and growl!"

"G-r-r-r-r-r-r-r!"

"Very good, boys. Captain Al is pleased with you." And darned if Keith didn't start acting like he really was Teacher Smeer.

"Remember what I did to you punks in the schoolroom? I thrashed the twelve of you."

"You got the worst of it, Captain Al. You ran off without your pants."

"You were a bunch of hoods then," continued the phony Smeer. "And you've improved very little. I tried to turn you punks into gentlemen. I tried to teach Roger what a denominator is." (*Loud laughter from everyone but Roger*).

"I promised not to beat you punks any more. Although sometimes I feel tempted ———"

"Gowan, Captain Al. You couldn't even beat up an egg!"

Keith put his hands to his head in pretended alarm. "Where's my wig? Which of you hoodlums took my wig?"

Raymond yelled, "You're sitting on it!"

But when the pretended Captain Smeer spoke in front of the wire-tap, he was a mysterious, sinister figure. We all treated him with great respect and a bit of fear.

ALADDIN'S LAMP AND THE GOLDEN FLEECE

Rodney Desmond would tell us stories and legends from all over the world. His favorite tales were the myths of ancient Greece. Among them, was the story of Jason and the Argonauts who sailed into the Black Sea to gain the Golden Fleece.

In his mind's eye, we, his students, were modern Argonauts who had crossed into some unknown realm to gain our mysterious treasure. Rodney himself was like Chiron, the Centaur, who taught the sons of heroes and heroes in their boyhood, enhancing their courage and physical power with skills and wisdom.

In truth, though, we weren't at all like the Argonaut heroes. Just a bunch of dumb kids who didn't know what we were looking for and stumbled onto our treasure by accident. We were more like Aladdin, sent into the enchanted cave by the Evil Magician. The Magician dumped Aladdin and left him to perish in the cave. The Masters of *Naghallah* dumped us in *Bane N'Gai*. By lucky accident, Aladdin found the Lamp. By lucky accident, we found the *Vrrooohn*. But we had to work for it longer and harder than Aladdin did.

The Lamp was magic, but the *Vrrooohn*, Jaymie believed, was just a tool to enhance the natural powers of the mind. It released clairvoyant forces, so weak in ordinary humans that most people didn't believe they existed. The same powers that the Lemurians had without the *Vrrooohn*. So held Jaymie Larrabie, who had been taught to believe in Reason.

Most of the other guys didn't agree. They believed the *Vrrooohn* was a kind of creature with a life of its own. So held Raymond and Troy and Bobby and Brandon and Brother Danny. Donald, too. He asked the favor of the *Vrrooohn*, instead of using it as a tool.

The Evil Magician didn't give up. He gained control of the Lamp and its Genie when Aladdin's foolish Princess traded it away for a fancy new lamp.

The *Horned Crystal* was securely in the *Quayne*. Nobody could touch it but *us*. Nobody could trade it away. But the Masters of *Naghallah* didn't give up either. They had a plan. Their scheme involved not a lamp nor a crystal, but something more modern — a motor bike.

* * * * * * *

It was mid-afternoon when the Express Company delivered a Grensen Motorbike — an elegant and expensive model. It was addressed to: *Thomas Larrabie, Jr.*

Mother said, "I have twelve sons, but I don't have a *Thomas*. At least I don't think so——" She counted us off. Cameron, Steven, Raymond, Brandon, Daniel, Troy, Roger, Robert, Donald, Jody, Keith and Jaymie. "No, it must be a mistake."

The delivery man insisted it was no mistake. "This is 369 Meadowbrook Lane. And here are the ownership papers made out to Thomas Larrabie."

"Maybe one of the boys ordered it. Maybe he didn't give his right name because he thought his parents wouldn't like it. Is it C.O.D.?"

"No, ma'am. It's paid for."

"Really? It couldn't have been my husband. He wouldn't approve the boys riding around wildly on these dangerous things."

Perhaps it was the eccentric poet? He would do anything the boys asked him to do. Or perhaps Uncle Leon? He liked the boys. Uncle couldn't afford to buy more than one motorbike. He sent it to a youth who didn't exist. Then his twelve real nephews would share it and nobody would feel left out. "Just leave it at the door. Thank you."

The expressman coughed discreetly. There was a sixty dollar delivery charge. Mother thought this was a bit steep. She borrowed forty dollars from Miss Ferris who viewed the motorbike with stern disapproval. "That thing is much too dangerous for the boys!" She would have preferred to see "her children" riding kiddie cars and tricycles.

Mitch disapproved, too. "You can't ride that on the highways, boys. You have to be at least sixteen."

"Cameron is fifteen."

"That's still too young. The police will arrest you. You don't want to go back to Juvenile Court again."

"We could make a bike path on the property."

"You can't do that until the snow clears." In the meantime, Mitch locked the bike up in the garage closet. "Leave it there until Spring. If there's any fooling around, I'll take the bike away."

Strangely, ever since we had brainwashed Mitch with the *Vrrooohn*, he had started laying the law down to us. We had transformed Mitch into a devoted father. Somehow, fathers couldn't be devoted to their sons without being bossy.

Uncle Leon hadn't sent us the motorbike. Nor had the Poet, nor anyone else we knew. We checked the bike out and found nothing wrong with it. No hidden explosives. No defective brakes. Some man had bought it and paid cash for it.

We decided it must have been Dad after all. Good old Dad! Father thought it must have been the kids. "They put someone up to buying it for them. They didn't quite dare to do it openly. That shows the boys are becoming a little afraid of me; or at least respect me." Father was pleased.

"And when I locked the bike up," Father reported, "the boys didn't give me any argument." He added with a big smile, "These kids are beginning to learn who the boss is around here."

Father should have known that accomplished thieves like the Larrabie urchins could open that garage closet lock with a pen knife.

Thus the Larrabie kids acquired a Gremsen Royal Champion motorbike, a magnificent and unusual vehicle. This particular model was especially unusual. For, concealed inside the frame, was an electronic tracer.

KIDNAP

It was a warm day at the end of January. One of those days of false Spring that is followed by two more months of frigid winter. The snows melted and the brooks and creeks ran high.

The Masters of *Naghallah* had surmised correctly. Two wheel-crazy teenagers could not long resist the lure of the motorbike.

We had sworn never to split up. Always to let the other guys know where we were going. And never go off alone at night. We voted that into the *Boy Law*. A loyal Coyote could break the laws made by the grown-ups. But the commandments of the *Boy Law* were unbreakable.

Bobby and Stevie broke the *Boy Law*. They cut out while everyone else was asleep. Silently, they cracked the lock on the garage closet. Silently, they rolled the motorbike down the driveway. Then they went speeding down the road. Stevie was driving, Bobby clinging on behind. They took off about two in the morning and for ninety minutes raced all through Greenwood and the surrounding towns.

Bobby and Stevie were on their way back when a police car ordered them to "Pull over!" Bobby was driving now and put on speed. If he could make it for another two miles, they could cut into the woods, down a rough path where no police car could follow them.

These cops had a gun though and pointed it. *"Pull over, you!"*

"Go, Bobby! They ain't gonna shoot us. They ain't gonna shoot a couple of kids just for riding a motorbike!"

Stevie was wrong. These guys *did* shoot. One of the bullets tore through a tire. The motorbike careened crazily and ran off the road. Almost miraculously, Bobby managed to miss a pole and a tree and landed against a pile of ice-covered dirt and rocks.

Bobby felt a sharp pain in his arms and legs. Stevie's head was injured and he was bruised and dazed. The motorbike was bent and twisted out of shape, never to be ridden again.

The police car pulled up alongside of them. The men surrounded the two youths. Their guns were pointed and their faces were grim.

Stevie lay limp against the dirt pile. Bobby turned to face the police. He felt anger rather than fear, expecting nothing worse than to be taken to Police Headquarters. "You almost killed us! Just for riding a bike without a license!" That's what Bobby started to say. But he found it hard to talk. The blood was coming out of his mouth.

Bobby sank down on one knee. They pulled him up. A pair of handcuffs were fastened on his wrists. Stevie got it, too. Both were thrown roughly into the police car. They would get out of it, Bobby was sure, with nothing worse than a bawling out and some embarrassment.

Stevie groaned. "I'm hurt! Take me to the hospital!"

"Shut up!" Somebody smacked his face.

Bobby got mad. "What kind of a cop are you!"

"I said *Shut up!*" Bobby got a crack with the night stick. *For this was no police arrest. This was a kidnapping.*

"Don't start yelling, boy! Not if you want to live!"

THESE PEOPLE ARE NASTY

We awoke in the morning to find Bobby and Stevie gone. Their beds were empty. Roger saw them go out during the night. Stevie told him, "Go back to sleep, Roger. And don't tell nobody. Don't snitch, huh!" About two o'clock. Roger thought they were going to ride the motorbike. Yes, it was gone. And the garage closet was open. The boys should have returned long before now.

Cameron was worried. We all felt something bad had happened. Usually, if we tried hard, we could read each other's thoughts. We could send out a message and get an answer, which might just be "Get the fuck out of my mind, Crumbum, and leave me alone!" But we probed and got no answer at all from Bobby and Stevie. Even Donald got nothing. Just a blank wall.

"Get the *Vrrooohn* out of the *Quayne!*"

"Wait!" cried Keith. "Make sure first. Is there anyone outside, Don Don? In the house or on the roof or lurking around the property?"

Donald stood for a moment in silence. "No. No one."

"Who's around the house besides us?"

"Just our parents and Miss Ferris. They are sleeping. And Larry. He's sleeping, too."

Our powers were weaker than Don Don, but we all probed, too. There was no trace of any Enemy outside. After we materialized the *Vrrooohn*, it would be vulnerable. An armed force could break in and seize it.

We pulled down the shades and darkened the room. We crossed arms and formed *The Circle*, with Donald in the middle. A smaller Circle than usual. Just nine guys instead of eleven.

We sat in silence in the darkened room. Then the *Vrrooohn* appeared out of Nothing. The *Rainbow Crystal* with the *Shining Horns*. Donald reached out and grabbed it.

Donald strained and struggled as if trying to lift a great weight. Then he shook his head in failure. A stream of colored images appeared around the *Vrrooohn*, flickering like a television set that is out of order. Wheels and motors. Ice and rocks. A gloved hand clutching a revolver. Roads and streets and a darkened highway. Then handle bars twisted out of shape. Nothing that made any sense. . . .

"Help me, Ray Ray!" Of all the Earth kids, Raymond was the one with the most power.

Raymond joined Donald in *The Circle*. Each of them gripped one of the Horns of the *Vrrooohn*. Those Horns were flaming red now. Each became a burning fire. But a cold flame that gave no heat and caused no pain.

Raymond called out, "Oh, Horned Crystal! Help us

find Bobby and Stevie! Reveal!"

There was a flash like lightning, and the Crystal went completely dark. I had a horrible feeling our brothers were dead. The *Vrrooohn* can do many things, but it couldn't cross the boundary between the Dead and the Living. The room had suddenly become very cold.

Donald and Raymond kept staring into the darkened Crystal.

"See anything?"

"Shadows," said Donald. "Just shadows."

A faint silver glow now was coming out of the *Vrrooohn*, starting at the Horns and spreading downwards.

All at once, Raymond broke into a grin. "They're alive! They're in a dark place, but they're alive!"

Again and again, Donald called out their names. "They can't hear us."

"Wait!" cried Raymond. "They're coming in! They can hear us now."

"Bobby! Stevie! What happened?"

The answer came in very faintly. Only Raymond and Donald could hear it. "They were kidnapped."

"Who did it?"

"Cops. Or guys dressed up as cops. They ain't cops really. They are hired mobsters."

"Are you hurt?"

"They gave us a deal. They muckled us and threw us in here. Everything aches. But I guess it's not too bad. We can both move."

"Where are you?"

"Don't know. Down in a cellar somewhere."

"Are you cold?"

"No. It's hot as Hell here. Right near the steam pipes."

"They got water but no food," said Raymond. "They don't feel like eating anyway."

Cameron asked, "What do they want? Why did they grab you? Was it for money?"

"Not just money. They want the *Vrrooohn*. But don't give it up. We ain't worth it."

The images were growing weaker. Cameron yelled,

"Bobby! Stevie! Can you give us any clue to where you are?"

"Not far from Greenwood. Out in the country. Some place with a big gate and a stone wall around it. And a big house."

"Did they ask you any questions? Did they torture you?"

"No. Not yet--"

"If they ask you where the *Vrrooohn* is, tell them. It won't be there any more. Tell them anything they ask. It won't help them any."

Stevie was saying something, but you could no longer hear it. Cameron shouted, "Bobby! Stevie! Hang in there! Your brothers are coming. We're going to get you out!"

The *Horned Crystal* had become dark again. The horns stopped shining. The power of the *Vrrooohn* had run out.

*   *   *   *   *   *   *

There was a frantic pounding on the door and Father's voice, "Boys! Open up!"

We opened the door cautiously and concealed the *Vrrooohn* under the bed sheets. Father's voice trembled and his hands were shaking. "Do you know where Bobby and Stevie are?"

"No, sir."

"They aren't here?" He looked around the room, a faint hope turning to despair. "When did you last see them?"

"Last night, sir."

"I received a very alarming telephone call. From Mr. Bartlow. Your brothers have been kidnapped."

Bartlow claimed he had been contacted by the kidnappers and asked to act as an intermediary. As a friend of the family. A transparent and flimsy pretense. I don't think even Father was deceived.

"They want two hundred and fifty thousand dollars ransom. In ten and twenty dollar bills.

"They are giving us until tomorrow night. Bartlow warned me not to tell the police. Or anyone else outside the family. *'These people are nasty!'*

"Believe me, boys, Steven and Robert are my own sons now. I shall do everything I can to get them back safely! I know that's what you want me to do." Dad thought he could raise the money in time. He would have to put up the house and business for collateral.

It seemed clear that the men behind the kidnapping were Bartlow and his partners. But why the quarter million dollars in ransom? Why would they bother with such chicken feed?

Perhaps it was to pay off the expenses of the kidnapping and to keep Mitchell Larrabie busy so he wouldn't interfere while the Masters of *Naghallah* collected the real ransom — *The Horned Crystal.*

Now Father asked, "Do you know a Captain Al?"

"Captain Al?"

"He means Smeer," said Keith.

Our trick had worked. They were convinced that Smeer was alive and had returned. But that wasn't much help to us now.

"He said, " Father continued, "If Captain Al calls this number, he might receive some useful information." It was a local number.

'I'm sorry, boys." Father laid his hands on Danny's shoulder. Then on Jody's. Then on Brandon, Troy and Donald. Then on Roger, Cameron, Raymond, Keith and Jaymie. "We'll fight this thing, guys! We'll get them back!"

There were tears in Mitch's eyes when he left the room. For the first time since I was a little kid, I loved my father.

A CONTEMPTUOUS LAUGH

"Hello, Bartlow. This is *Captain Al.*" Keith spoke in a hoarse whisper.

"Yes, Smeer. We know you."

Keith expressed surprise. "Smeeah? Who is Smeeah?"

"We know who *Captain Al* is. Now listen, Smeer. We have two of your boys. You will hand over Hasserman's *Thing*. If you want to see your boys alive again."

There was no pretense and no dissembling. Apparently, Bartlow didn't care if the phone was tapped. Bartlow was shooting for all or nothing. If he got the *Vrrooohn*, he would be unstoppable. He held the police in contempt.

"Did you hear me, Smeer? The boys for Hasserman's *Thing!*"

Keith sputtered. "Do you think I would give it up — for *them?*"

"You don't have the *Thing*, Smeer. The boys have it. Those hyenas are going to want to save their friends. Talk it over with your boys, Smeer. Tell them about the deal. Their friends for Hasserman's treasure. They will tear you apart, Smeer, if you hold out on them."

A bit of silence. Then a boy's voice. "This is Jaymie Larrabie. Captain Al has trouble talking. He asked me to speak for him."

"Go ahead."

"What has happened to Stevie and Bobby?"

"Nothing has happened — *yet.* But you and your brothers won't see them again, Jaymie. They will die miserably. Unless——"

Jaymie gave a gasp of horror. "If we give you the *Vrrooohn*, will you release them?"

"Yes, Jaymie. We kept our word when we released Cameron, didn't we?"

(*They didn't release Cameron. They imprisoned the rest of us.*)

Jaymie, however, said, "Yes, you did, sir."

"Then you and your friends broke your word and ran away."

"We didn't break our word, sir. We took the slave collars off. We almost died down there a dozen times. Then your people tried to kill us back in the Ranger's cabin—"

Bartlow broke in, "If you had given us Karl Hasserman's *Thing*, it wouldn't have happened. The Treasure is no good to you, Jaymie. You boys don't know how to use it.

"Smeer isn't your friend, Jaymie. He is just using you. Return the *Thing*, and we will leave you alone."

"If we return the *Vrrooohn*," asked Jaymie, "will we still get a million bucks each?"

A contemptuous laugh. Somebody said, "What a nerve that little squirt has!"

Bartlow continued. "You are not in a position to bargain, Jaymie. We are offering you the lives of your friends and that is enough."

"How can we be sure they are still alive?" asked Jaymie.

"Listen:"

> *Hello. This is Steve Larrabie.*
> *This is Bobby Larrabie.*
> *We are okay so far. But we ain't gonna last very long. They are gonna waste us, if they don't get the Vrrooohn.*

That was just a recording made hours ago. Our brothers might be dead by now. But that was all the proof they would give us.

"You will bring the *Vrrooohn* tomorrow evening twenty minutes before midnight. *All ten* of you will come and you will come alone. *Alone*, remember. Bring no weapons and don't try any tricks. Then we will trade goods. Your two brothers for Hasserman's *Thing*."

"Why not tonight?" asked Jaymie. "Can't we make the trade tonight?"

"Tomorrow night!" ordered Bartlow. "Stay in your house! All of you! You will be watched. Tomorrow, you will receive further instructions. Don't try to contact the

police or anyone else. You have just *one* chance to get
your brothers back. You know what will happen if you
double-cross me!" A click and a disconnect.

We looked at each other in silence, each trembling with
fear and helpless anger. At length, Troy spoke. "Why
not tonight? You would think they would be in a hurry to
trade."

"I think I know why," said Cameron. "They want time
to set up an ambush."

"You mean——?" Brandon's eyes bulged with horror.

"They want to get rid of *all* of us. That's why they
want us *all* there. Stevie and Bobby are the live bait to
hook the *Vrrooohn* with. After that, the Larrabie kids
will just disappear."

Troy still could not believe it. "You mean kill all twelve
of us? How could they get away with it?"

"With the powers of the *Vrrooohn* and us out of the
way, Bartlow and his partners can get away with a lot of
things. It will be very hard to stop them.

"These guys are shooting for the moon. They're not
going to put the *Vrrooohn* in storage and go out and play
touch football, like we did. They're going to use it to gain
Power. Perhaps to gain control of the whole World."

THE DEATH LIST

One of the worst mistakes our enemies made was to wire-tap us. Of course, they didn't know how the *Vrrooohn* worked. We didn't either, in the beginning. But with the *Vrrooohn*, it became possible to reverse the bug and spy on them.

"I don't like it," said Powell. "It's cold-blooded murder. Worse than that, it's a massacre. I don't have any high regard for these boys, but after all they are human beings."

"A dubious assumption," said Commander Bartlow.

"Why couldn't we just take the *Vrrooohn* from them and let them go?"

"And let them blab to the Police? And finger the kidnapping? Are you crazy?" That was Klayborne.

Bartlow said, "There are now three separate investigations into the Hasserman business. The County Prosecutor, the F.B.I. and the State Police. Any day now, everything is going to blow up. Those kids are a walking time bomb."

Klayborne pulled out a paper and muttered something you couldn't quite hear. It was, apparently, a list of those dangerous to the plotters and were destined to be "terminated."

At the head of the list, *Franz Hasserman* had been crossed out.

The Larrabie boys was the second entry. Third, was their former partner, *Captain Craig*.

"Craig has left the country. We think he's in England. Craig is lying low, but he's a menace."

Next was *Old George*, The Gardener at *Kaah Naghallah.*

"I can't believe *he's* any danger," said Powell. "The old man is half cracked. No one will pay any attention to his ravings."

"You can't be sure of that," contended Klayborne. "Old George is a wino and talks too much. Next time he gets drunk, he will meet with an accident. Old George will fall down a flight of stairs."

Bartlow chuckled. "Klayborne, you are an excellent prophet. Your predictions always have a way of coming true."

A lot of mumbling. Then somebody said, "What about the cooks? Johanna and her sister, Minnie?"

"They're scared stiff. Too frightened even to claim Karl Hasserman's legacy. The Police are looking for them."

"How much harm could they do, if they talked?"

"The old bitches could do a great deal of harm. We will have to find them before the Police do."

Powell had a man working on it. "He thinks he has located them." The Sisters were in a retirement Home down in Riverport. *The Golden Age Hotel.*

"Is your man — *dependable*?" Bartlow spoke the word in a somewhat sinister tone.

"I don't know what you mean by *dependable*. The man is a licensed professional detective. He wouldn't touch anything criminal. He thinks he's working for a collection agency."

Bartlow said, "He's served his purpose. Lay him off. Klayborne and his people will have to finish the job."

"Do you really think it is necessary——"

Bartlow did and so did Klayborne. "But there can't be any blundering. There are *two* of them. You will have to get *both*. It would be disastrous, if one of them survived."

There were more names on the list. Several that we didn't know and two we *did* know. One of them was the non-existent Teacher, Smeer. The other was the Nurse, Lyandra. "She disappeared right into thin air. Nobody's been able to find a trace of her."

"Is the Nurse dangerous?"

"Lyandra could be very dangerous. Almost as dangerous as the Larrabie boys."

"We will have to track her down at all costs," Bartlow told Klayborne. "Spend whatever you have to."

We laughed inwardly. Lyandra, on the other side of the Gateway, was one victim the Conspirators could never reach.

"But let's put first things first. Get the *Vrrooohn* and get rid of the Larrabie Boys.

"There must be no slip-up this time, Klayborne. No matter how backward these boys are, as long as they hold Hasserman's *Thing,* they are a menace. Like apes with a hand grenade. They just might pull the pin and throw it."

(Some inaudible mumbles.)

"That's why I wanted these oafs to come alone, without Smeer. By themselves, the boys will be much easier to deal with. We can take care of Smeer later."

Klayborne said, "We have found no trace of Smeer at all. No evidence that he ever came back from the Labyrinth. If the boys were not so stupid, I would almost think they made him up."

They kept on jabbering for a few minutes. Then "Captain" Klayborne departed. Bartlow and Powell were left alone. Bartlow studied the List of dangerous characters destined to be "terminated." Then he added another name to *the Death List.*

"*Last,* but not *Least.*" He chuckled.

The name was that of "Captain" Klayborne himself.

MOBILIZATION

"We have to find out where Bobby and Stevie are," said Cameron. "And then get them out of there fast."

"But how?"

"If we can do the first," said Cameron, "we'll figure out how to do the second."

It wasn't easy to discover where Bobby and Stevie were being held prisoner. Reading their minds wouldn't help, because they didn't know themselves. The *Vrrooohn* couldn't or wouldn't answer the question we most wanted to know. We had to drag it out in little pieces. "Like the Greek Oracle," said Keith. "It never gives you a straight answer."

The *Horned Crystal* never seems to work if you're just fooling around. But if the pressure is on and you feel desperate, that triggers something in the brain that unleashes the *Vrrooohn*.

We were getting better at it. Eating meat, said Donald, weakens your mindpower. We gave up meat when we came back from *Bane N'Gai*. We gave up other things, too. *No meat. No booze. No drugs. No smoking. No hunting for sport. No hurting other people, if they didn't hurt you.* We wrote all this into the BOY LAW. Or what we now called THE COYOTE GANG LAW. That was to keep our minds sharp and clean. And we couldn't cheat, because the other guys could read our minds and know we cheated.

Raymond thought the *Vrrooohn* might get mad, if we broke the Gang Law. "It wouldn't help us next time we needed it."

"The fucking *Vrrooohn* is turning us into good boys," lamented Keith. "Sometimes I wish I was a juvenile delinquent again."

"At least," said Cameron, consolingly, "There's no Gang Rule against cursing or fucking."

"When did we pass that law against booze?" demanded Brother Danny. "I must have been asleep."

"We all voted *no booze,*" said Cameron. "But beer don't count." That satisfied Danny — for now.

"But nothing until we get Bobby and Stevie free."

"We got to eat." We'd need a lot of strength for what we had to do. We ate pancakes, English muffins, hot cocoa and jam. Stevie and Bobby would be lucky if they got stale bread and water.

Donald had stripped all his clothes off. The clothes seemed to get in his way. He motioned to Raymond to join him in *The Circle* and the rest of us gathered around them.

When Donald talked to the *Vrrooohn,* he spoke silently with just his mind. When Raymond talked, he spoke in words. "Oh, *Horned Crystal,* bring us Stevie and Bobby! Reveal!"

It was much easier this time. A silver glow spread over the Crystal, starting at the horns and moving downward. Then the images came. Raymond said, "Bobby and Stevie are sleeping. They're okay for now."

"We have to wake them up. We have to focus on them to find out where they are."

Bobby woke up. Stevie groaned in his sleep and turned over on his side.

"One guy is enough. Hey, Bobby. It's us again. We have to find you. We think we can do it with the *Vrrooohn.* Think of something real hard."

"About *What?*"

It could be anything that aroused powerful emotions. The *Vrrooohn* was a Thing of the Mind. Strong feelings could draw the *Vrrooohn* like iron could draw a magnet.

"Think about the motorbike."

Bobby did. He felt deep shame at his deception and anger at the mistreatment he had received and fear for the future. Now you could sense the Shame and Anger and Fear rising through his body. Bobby's pale face grew red. A few tears trickled down his cheeks and his body sweated.

"Compass," said Donald. Keith had a compass. The same one we had carried in *Bane N'Gai.*

Silently, Donald commanded it. Moved by the *Vrrooohn*, the needle of the compass turned from the North about a hundred degrees to the left.

"West Southwest," said Raymond. "That's where Bobby and Stevie are."

"How far? Can you get the *Vrrooohn* to tell us?"

"Oh, *Horned Crystal.* How far away are Stevie and Bobby? Reveal!"

There was no answer. We had to find a different way of asking.

"How far must we go to find our brothers? *Twenty miles?*"

The needle jumped.

"*Twenty-five miles?*"

The needle jumped again.

"*Thirty miles?*" This time, the needle did not move.

"West Southwest, between twenty-five and thirty miles."

Jaymie looked at the map. "*Echo Lake.* That's where Bartlow has his country place." It was an area with large estates and few people.

So far, Bartlow had always remained in the background, letting others do his dirty work. It would be a high risk to bring the kidnap victims to his estate. But he was in too deep. The roof was caving in. Only by the *Vrrooohn* could he escape the closing net. Charges of fraud and embezzlement, if not murder.

Besides, Bartlow didn't trust Klayborne. If Klayborne had control of the prisoners, he could make a separate ransom deal and keep the *Vrrooohn* for himself. Bartlow would want to keep the boys where only *he* could get the ransom.

Last time, Klayborne and Lammington had loused things up and let the Larrabie kids escape. This time, there must be no blundering. The Larrabie urchins would have to be disposed of properly. Bartlow would have to do it himself.

He had a large estate of nearly two hundred acres. If the prisoners were stashed somewhere underground, there would be little risk of anybody discovering them.

"We got it, Bobby. We think you're on Bartlow's estate. Can you hear any noise?"

Stevie was awake now, too. He heard water running. "We're deep underground."

"Can you smell anything?"

"Yeah. A lot of things. Chlorine, I think. And there's a sewer somewhere near."

"Hang on, brothers. The Coyotes are coming! We won't let you down!"

"Please!" pleaded Bobby. "Come tonight."

"We will. Go back to sleep."

"Dad," asked Jaymie, "does Bartlow have a heated swimming pool?"

"Yes, he does, Jaymie. Why?"

"Just wondering." I left Father wondering, too. . . .

We formed an *An-Mir,* an anti-mirage, as much to evade our protective adult guardians as to escape our enemies. We left our room door open and a note on the wall:

GOING OUT. WILL BE BACK SOON

We couldn't explain any more.

Father found the note several hours later and was filled with dismay. "They're all gone now. Every one of them!"

But Mother said, "We have to trust the boys, Mitchell. They have their own way of doing things. They came through before and they'll do it again!"

We would hit them in the dark. In January, it gets dark early. About five o'clock. The Coyotes were night kids and the darkness gave us power.

We gathered our tools and weapons as well as the *Vrrooohn.* Once again, the Hunted turned Hunter. And we hung our heroes' medals from the Queen of Lemuria around our necks to give us luck.

COUNTER-ATTACK

We were right not to confide in any grown-ups, no matter how well-intentioned they might be. The adults would have tried to help us by calling in the police. We were sure that Bartlow had his agents there, perhaps in high places. Stevie and Bobby could be disposed of long before anyone could rescue them. Our brothers then would never be seen or heard of again.

This was a job the Coyotes must do alone. We would have to strike hard and strike by surprise. The Bartlow estate was heavily guarded, even more protected than the Hasserman mansion. But we had tools now that we didn't have before.

Of the Masters of *Naghallah*, only five survived. Smeer, Eberle and Vedemore perished in the Labyrinth. Striker and Lammington in the Ranger's cabin. The jovial Captain Craig was in hiding outside the country. Teacher Matthews, who really didn't know anything, was in a mental hospital. (Honest! It wasn't teaching the Larrabie kids that put him there.)

The trio, Bartlow, Powell and Klayborne, were the ones we had to fear. The others on the estate were hired guns who were paid to do the dirty work. They weren't mad at the Larrabie kids and wouldn't kill us for nothing. They wouldn't risk murder, unless they got paid for it.

Donald scanned the *Vrrooohn*. There were at least nine people on the estate now besides the prisoners. One was the butler or the Gate-keeper. The other eight were probably Klayborne's hired mobsters. Except for that old man, all Bartlow's regular servants had been dismissed.

Bartlow and Powell had left the estate. Perhaps they felt uncomfortable in the presence of the vermin Klayborne had imported to do the murders. Or perhaps they feared that one or both of them might be included among the victims. One less to share the power of the *Vrrooohn*.

Bartlow and Powell would not return until the following night, when the *Vrrooohn* was being traded. They
would return with reliable body guards, perhaps meanwhile having established an alibi for the murders.

Klayborne was still in the mansion. He was in his room
behind locked doors and heavily armed. Perhaps he
didn't trust his hired killers either. Those men were armed to the teeth and deadly. Professional murderers, selling their services to the highest bidder.

Bartlow's estate was at the end of a long private road.
They would be watching for a car — any car. An intruder
would set off an alarm.

Would our anti-mirage cover a car? Donald didn't
think so, not completely. And if it did, you can imagine
all the accidents that could happen on a highway to a car
that people couldn't see. We couldn't walk twenty-eight
miles in an *An-mir*. It was getting cold again. The
Vrrooohn didn't tell us that. The radio did.

*"A cold-front, descending from the arctic region, will
put an end to our early Spring. . . ."*

The storm clouds were gathering. *"There will be a blizzard. . . ."* You could never be sure of the *Vrrooohn*. Mental
power might be able to keep us warm, but you couldn't
count on it. The snow was beginning to fall already.

Donald gave us a signal. Parked on the street outside
the house was a moving van that wasn't moving anything. "They're watching the house."

"Can you tell, Don Don, who sent the van?"

"The kidnappers."

There was only one guy in the van. He was armed and
had a spy glass and a two-way radio. We made sure he
saw us in our room before we formed the *An-Mir*.

"No activity in the Larrabie house. The boys are still
upstairs. No one has been going in and out, except that
big, stout woman who bought some groceries. . . . (He
meant Miss Ferris.)

"How long do I have to sit here? When is my relief
coming?"

"You're getting paid for sitting. Stay awake and quit

bitching." (Click. Sign-off.)

The man shivered. He pulled out a bottle of rye and took a slug. He took several slugs. He heard a noise and saw nothing, but had an uneasy feeling there was something lurking outside the van.

The Larrabie boys had learned to move silently and send out confusing waves of thought. The watcher still saw nothing when a noose tightened around his neck and a knife was pointed into his back.

"Don't touch that!" His hand was reaching for the transmitter. "If you move, you're dead!"

"I —— I ——"

"Shut up! Don't turn around!"

The man did turn a little and what he saw frightened him even more. *He saw nothing!*

"Take that whiskey bottle and drink it!" He didn't argue. We held the *Vrrooohn* over him and put him to sleep. Not permanently, but out of action for a good long time. We could just have thrown him out of the van and left him there. But he might have frozen to death in the blizzard.

Next door, was the house of the Grouchy Man who kept complaining about our electric guitars. He called the cops five or six times on us. We owed him something. The Grouchy Man was out now. His car was gone.

Still in an anti-mirage, we carried the sleeping jerk to the Grouchy Man's residence. The doors were locked, but there was a window open. We lifted the mobster into the bedroom of the Grouchy Man's wife. We laid him on the lady's bed with the empty whiskey bottle beside him. Troy found a bottle of gin and we spilled that over him, too.

We retreated hastily, when the Grouch's car entered the driveway. He had a couple of fancy-dressed visitors with him. What a scene! The Grouchy Man yelling, Mrs. Grouchy screaming and the visitors yammering and going batty! What a trick on the complaining neighbors! What a laugh! If only Bobby and Stevie had been there to enjoy it with us!

We were afraid our nasty neighbor might blow his top and shoot the drunken thug. Instead, he called the cops and the mobster ended up in jail, with no idea how he got there. One enemy out of the way. Another triumph for the Larrabie boys.

We hijacked the van, or let's say we commandeered it and the mobster's two guns. Jaymie and Troy studied a map and planned a route by the side roads. We had to evade the cops as well as our enemies. The snow was coming down fiercely now. That ought to empty the roads and keep the cops in the station house.

Twenty-five miles to the Echo Lake line. "Then we'll check the compass with the *Vrrooohn* again. The last couple of miles we'll cover by foot," Cameron decided.

"How are we going to break the guys out?"

Cameron didn't know. "It all depends on how the land lies. We'll do what the *Horned Crystal* tells us."

The radio crackled with an urgent request for an answer. Instead, Cameron wrecked the equipment.

"They'll know now something has happened."

"But they won't know what. If they send a man to find out, that's one less enemy we have to deal with."

The Coyotes drove onward through the falling snow. Twelve miles . . . nine miles. . . . Now just six miles to Echo Lake. The shock and terror we had felt before was gone. Instead, we had a rising sense of strength and power.

The Coyotes are coming! Let our enemies beware!

Donald yelled, "*Lanna Hai!*" The ancient Lemurian cry of battle.

"*Lanna Hai!*" shouted the Coyote kids.

MEMOIRS OF A PROFESSIONAL KILLER:
"A MESSY JOB," BUT IT PAID WELL.

They called me *The Creeper,* because I can move without any noise. I like that name. It gives people the jitters. Just hearing it is enough to make them tremble.

I'm in the Exterminating business — not insects, but people. In California, I got rid of a dangerous witness. Down in Florida, it was a meddlesome reporter who knew too much. In Indiana, it was the Head of a business muscling in on my Boss's people. In Texas, it was a drug dealer who wouldn't pay for his stuff. And I knocked off a rich but stingy husband on the side.

Somewhere along the line, things got loused up. I got put on the F.B.I.'s *Most Wanted* List. I went into hiding and got a new identity. The Boss is clever at arranging things like that. Hair and skin transplants. Fingerprints altered. Then I went back into practice.

I knocked off an old German named Schultz. He was hiding out. I had to track him down. The Boss collected ninety G's on that one. That seemed a lot to pay for that nutty old goat.

This time, it was a job for Klayborne, a big shot who worked for the billionaire, Karl Hasserman. It was "a messy job," but would pay well.

Was it Karl Hasserman who was making the pay-off? The Boss said, "You know better than to ask things like that."

"It's just that there are rumors about Karl Hasserman. I heard he isn't around any more. Someone on the inside knocked him off."

The Boss said, "Don't let that worry you."

"It won't," said me, "as long as I get paid."

"You will be." And this job paid well. Two hundred and fifty G's. Enough to retire on.

"What do I have to do for that? Shoot the President?"

The Boss said, "Karl Hasserman's people are loaded. A million bucks ain't nothing to them. But this is a dirty job and not for squeamish stomachs. There are twelve kids who have to be terminated."

I don't have a squeamish stomach. Still, I don't like the idea of wasting kids. But the Boss says, "This is a gang of teenage punks. Juvenile hoods who have made a lot of trouble for people. And they're likely to make a lot more trouble if they keep on running around loose. More than one good man is dead on account of *them.* They're not worth any sympathy.

"And, if you do the job right, besides the two hundred and fifty G's, there might be a bonus."

He was giving me Buggsey as a partner. They call him *Buggsey* because he's been in the bug house. He's weird, that Buggsey. People call me *The Creeper,* but Buggsey sometimes gives *me* the creeps. When he blows his top, there is no telling what he will do.

I hate to be around Buggsey when he has a gun. I'll never turn my back on him or get him mad. Buggsey is about the last guy I would choose as a partner. But when the Boss says something, I know better than to argue.

The first part of the job was easy. We have to kidnap two punks who would be riding around on a motorbike. But be careful. No rough stuff. At least no more than necessary. These kids had to be in one piece when they were traded for ransom. Klayborne says they're two nasty little squirts.

"What if they resist or start yelling?"

"Give them a deal, if you have to. But don't cripple them. At least, not before the ransom trade." The kids, of course, weren't going to be turned loose. They were among the twelve to be wasted.

Snatching the kids was simple. The Boss had it all figured out. The boys had no license and would be driving the motorbike illegally. We would be detectives in a cop car and bust them. Handcuff the snots and throw them in the back.

Buggsey knew how to play a cop. He had once been a real one, but got thrown off the force. The cop car would be real, borrowed for the occasion. Our employer had connections.

When we got the signal, we hunted these kids down. Me and Buggsey in the cop car. Fish and Wires, playing detective in an unmarked car, followed as a back-up. Those kids didn't yell or resist at all. They thought we really were cops.

They were younger than I expected. Two fourteen year olds. I couldn't help feel a little sorry for them. But only for a minute. When you're on a job, you can't let your feelings interfere. It's like a war. You can't start feeling sorry for the enemy.

Buggsey smacked them around a bit and called them names. Like "shitty punk" and "dirty little fart." Then one kid started cursing and Buggsey punched him in the face.

I just said, "Keep your mouth shut and don't start making trouble, boy, or we'll make a lot of trouble for you."

We drove the punks to the estate of a guy named Bartlow. A real fancy place with a high fence around it. And we stuck them in a lock-up underneath the ground. A dark hole with no windows down below the pool house. It was a lonely spot, a long way from anything. Those kids could shout their lungs out down there and nobody would hear them. Still, we warned them if they yelled we would turn the heat off and freeze them or turn the heat up high and roast them.

That lock-up was more like a tomb than a room. But no matter. The boys were only going to be there for two days. Tomorrow night would be their last.

Tomorrow night, the boys would be traded for that ransom Thing. Their friends and brothers — ten of them — would come to Bartlow's estate with the *Thing*. They would want to see the prisoners before handing over the ransom.

The exchange would be carried out in a building containing Bartlow's heated pool and private gym. When the ten boys were all inside, the prisoners would be brought up from below.

Bartlow warned us the teenagers would be carrying something dangerous. Keep out of sight with your weapons until that ransom *Thing* was safely in Bartlow's hands and he was out of the way. The ransom trade was to appear as a friendly exchange. He would ask the boys if they wanted to take a swim in his heated pool. If they did, that would make things easy. We could get them right there in the water.

In any case, we had to make sure that none of the kids left the building. *Twelve* boys in. *Zero* out. And clean up all the traces. That's why Bartlow and his partners were paying for professionals, instead of doing a bungling job themselves.

Each of the kids would have a marker sprayed on them without their knowing it. The Boss is clever that way. If any of the punks should manage to get out of the building, the attack dogs and Buggsey would be waiting for them outside. To make sure that none of them escaped from the estate.

"Then," said the Boss, "you will dispose of the bodies and collect your money."

"What if we don't get paid?" demanded The Fish.

"Don't sweat about it," retorted the Boss. "Commander Bartlow was — or rather is — the partner of Karl Hasserman. He can use hundred dollar bills for toilet paper. You'll get paid. I'm trusting him for my share. Just do your job right. And don't start getting stoned until it's over."

The Boss didn't tell us what *he* got for the job. If I know the Boss, it probably ran to seven figures. A cool million. And he got half of it in advance.

That seemed like an awful lot for anyone to pay to get rid of a dozen shitty teenagers.

THE HOUSE OF HORROR

The Boss always said when there's a job to be done, the fewer people in on it, the better. That's why I didn't like this Bartlow set-up. Too many people. Besides Bartlow's two partners, Klayborne and Powell, there was a whole mob around.

There was the Boss, with me, Buggsey, Wires and The Fish. Bartlow had sent most of his servants away, but he left two. There was that snoopy old Caretaker who poked his nose into things. He wasn't supposed to know about the kids in the Hole, but he could tell there was something smelly going on. The Fish caught him poking around the pool house and pulled a gun on him. Scared the Old Man half out of his wits. I thought maybe we ought to eliminate the Old Snoop. But the Boss says don't kill nobody unless I tell you. We can't have too many bodies around.

Then there was the dog handler, a red-headed guy with a big nose. Bartlow had five nasty attack dogs. Three Dobermans, a Great Dane and a German police dog. They roamed the estate at night and would tear an intruder to pieces. At least that's what Red said and I believe him. Red's the only one who can handle them.

There was a short, thick man with heavy glasses. He worked for Bartlow, too, and sent and received messages. He looked like a hop-toad and hopped around like one. And there was a phony cop — or, for all I know, a real one — to turn unwanted visitors away. He was Powell's man, that cop. He reported to Powell and wouldn't take orders from anyone else.

There was also a man in woman's clothing or a big, muscular woman. It was hard to tell which. Klayborne had put her (or him) here. Everyone had their finger in the pie. The Boss rightly figured they were checking up on him. For some reason, that Man-woman got on Buggsey's nerves. He claimed she had poisoned his coffee. I had to drink the coffee to show him there was nothing wrong with it. Buggsey is getting bad again. This is the last time I will ever work with him.

Then there's Harry, who is watching the Larrabie house. That's thirteen people I know who are mixed up in this business. Usually, these things are a two-man job. With a crowd like this, there's bound to be a weak sister somewhere.

The Boss had a private meeting with Bartlow and came out with a big smile. It looked like he had made another million dollar deal. Maybe to protect Bartlow, who was afraid somebody might try to hijack the boys' ransom. Or maybe to terminate some other people Bartlow had on his list.

The rest of us never did see Bartlow. He drove off in his limousine saying he would be back tomorrow for the ransom collection. Bartlow avoided us and kept a scarf over his face.

That Powell guy left, too. He wouldn't talk to us either. I don't know why they think they're so much better than we are.

Klayborne said not to mind him. We had about thirty hours to kill before the *You-know-what.* Just go in the house and make yourselves comfortable. Help yourself to food and drink, but don't take too much. Do your job, but leave the Caretaker alone. Bartlow would be real mad if you waste the old man.

The Boss said, "You hired me to run this show and that's what I'm doing. I don't leave any loose ends around. That's why I'm still alive and still in business."

"Suit yourself," said Klayborne. The old man had gone upstairs and locked himself in his room.

"We won't bother him for now. As long as he don't try to leave the estate." We had the phone cut off, except for one line that the Boss controlled.

Klayborne couldn't resist tormenting those kids. He had them dragged out of the Hole and made them dig a good size pit in the half frozen ground. That, he said, is where you're going to be buried if your friends don't come up with the ransom pronto. That wasn't true. They were going to be dumped in a swamp upstate. Bartlow didn't want any bodies on his property.

It was real cold, but those kids were sweating. They were real glad when we put them back in the Hole. Me and The Fish stood over them with guns pointed. Klayborne kept telling them to dig harder, dig faster. And, for no particular reason, he began punching them, cursing them and smacking them around. This seemed quite unnecessary. There was no point in beating the kids when they were being terminated tomorrow.

That's when the first thing went wrong. That Hop Toad guy told Klayborne something. He called the Boss in and the three of them looked worried. Harry, the guy we left in the van to watch the Larrabie house, didn't answer our signals. Communications were broken and the van was gone.

Harry is a lush. That stupid bum, we found out, broke into a neighbor's house and passed out cold. The cops grabbed him and locked him in the Greenwood jail house. Klayborne said, "We'll have to get him out, before he talks."

Klayborne couldn't do it himself. He had to see a guy who had to see a guy to get Harry out. Klayborne right now is lying low. The State Police are looking for him. He has to be awfully careful. I think Bartlow has set him up to be the fall guy, if things go wrong.

Harry don't know too much. He don't know where the kids are stashed or about that swamp upstate. But he could finger the Boss and Klayborne; and maybe Bartlow, too. Harry drinks and blabs and might try a spot of clumsy blackmail.

Some lawyer got Harry released and he drove off somewhere with Klayborne. And, as far as I know, nobody ever saw hair or hide of him again.

We ate the best from Bartlow's pantry, then sat around in the parlor. And it was Wires now who became the Weeping Mary. He was really a safe cracker, but there were no safes here to be cracked. Wires said he had signed up for the kidnapping, not for the killings. He wanted to get out of it and said he didn't care about being paid.

The Boss told him off. "No one quits under me. Just try it and you'll end up in that swamp, along with the kids."

Just after it got dark, the first alarm went off. The whole estate is rigged with these alarm signals. The board showed someone was crossing the wall to the Northeast. The dog handler went out and found nothing. But before he got back, the alarms went off again. South this time. The Fish went out with Wires. Still *nothing*.

Now the alarms were blowing off all over. The searchlights swept across the grounds. The grounds were empty.

A dozen signal lights were flashing all at once. Intruders North, East, South and West. An army of Invisible Men. The Boss was getting jumpy. His iron nerve was gone. "I'll be glad after tomorrow night. This place gives me the creeps."

Buggsey paced up and down the driveway. He started shooting wildly, shooting at shadows. The Boss told him to cut it out. He might hit one of us.

The Hop Toad started screaming over the walkie-talkie. We couldn't understand him. He came in all shaky. He had seen something cross the wall, like a big grey cloud. The cloud split open and was moving around on many legs. The Boss cursed him for an idiot. If there was anything out there, the dogs would find it.

There was still no sign of anything. The searchlights showed only emptiness. But I had the feeling of a *Presence.* Something deadly. You couldn't tell if it was man or beast.

Wires was seeing things, too. Gigantic wolves. Huge grey things with crocodile jaws and deadly yellow eyes, howling like demons.

The dogs were yelping now. They had cornered something and were attacking it. When we got there, we found it was The Fish. He was badly chewed up. We had to carry him back to the house.

Now that phony dame started yelling. She screamed like a woman and maybe she was one. She had opened a door and seen a spider larger than a man. We looked and found nothing. Something weird was happening at the Bartlow estate. We were seeing and hearing things that weren't there.

The Fish groaned. He was cursing the dog handler and everyone else. Those dogs were now in full hunting cry. Like they were on the trail of something big. Suddenly their excited barks turned to yelps of terror. There was a series of whines and whimpers. Then silence. One of the mastiffs came cowering in. The dog handler took his gun and went out into the night. He didn't return.

The phony cop went out after him. He didn't come back either.

Buggsey said he wasn't afraid of anything, man or beast. He took his automatic and vowed he would drill that Terror-Thing, whatever it was, between the eyes. We heard the wind howling and we heard Buggsey shooting, and then silence.

That fool woman started screaming again. She claimed there was a cloud of yellow gas coming out of the cellar. It was leaking through the floor. The smoke alarms were going off. The Boss broke off the connection. He didn't want the fire department to come nosing around.

We searched the house and found no sign of fire. Just that oozing cloud of yellow gas. It was all over now, coming through the ceiling and the walls as well as the floor. The smell of Death was in that yellow cloud; something between burning rubber and a decaying corpse. *The Bartlow mansion had become a House of Horror.*

We abandoned the mansion and took to the Gate House. The Caretaker was still locked in his room. We left him there. If the gas got him, said the Boss, that would save us some trouble.

There were six of us now. The cop, Buggsey and the dog handler were all missing. There was just the Boss, Wires, the Man-woman, the Hop Toad and me. And The Fish with his bitten leg, hobbling on two canes.

We could hear the wind howling. But there were noises now that weren't the wind. Like the shrieking of a hundred wolves stalking their prey. The Hop Toad wandered off and came back yelling. He had seen wolf tracks in the snow. Enormous footprints of a horde of gigantic beasts. The Boss cursed him and said they were just tracks made by the guard dogs.

We reached the Gate House. Buggsey had been here. His red scarf lay on the table. His smelly cigar was still burning. An empty whisky bottle had been dropped on the floor. But there was no sign of Buggsey himself.

The alarms started going off again and the red lights were flashing on the signal board. The Boss said, "There is an enemy out in the snow. They want to draw us out to look for them and get us one at a time. We'll stay here. Hang on to your guns and get ready."

Now there was a frantic pounding on the Gatehouse door. It turned out to be the Caretaker. He was in a panic. He had fled from the yellow gas that was oozing through the walls and ceiling. Outside, he had seen things moving through the air. Dark shapes of something enormous and horrifying. Not wolves. No wolves could cross the wall. These were more like a pack of demons. Something was terribly wrong. He wanted to call Mr. Bartlow.

The Boss didn't trust him. "You're not calling anybody!" he shouted. And he pointed a revolver at the trembling caretaker's head. "You call, Creeper."

I tried. "The line is dead, Boss." And that short wave radio on which we sent and received messages was dead, too.

Now we heard those wolf howls again. There was a volley of gunfire followed by a terrified scream. Then silence. Wires seemed to think it was Buggsey. He had to help the guy.

"Let him be," the Boss ordered. "We'll stay together here."

"I can't let Buggsey be wasted," insisted Wires. "He owes me a hundred bucks." That was like Wires who couldn't do a good deed without an excuse.

The Boss is a suspicious guy. He didn't trust Wires

since Wires wanted to quit. "Go after him, Creeper." I tried to follow him. Something hard and heavy hit me in the face and I lost him.

I found Wires later. He was lying in the snow, unconscious, but still breathing. His flashlight and his gun were gone. I half carried, half dragged him back to the Gatehouse.

After a while, Wires recovered. He claimed he had seen the wolf pack. Huge, nasty brutes with eyes like burning coals. Wires had started to shout and a big rock hit him on the head. There was no sign of any rock where Wires had fallen. Just a heap of snow.

The Man-woman had cleaned up and bandaged The Fish's wound. He could stand up and limp around. There was still no sign of the three missing guys, the Cop, Buggsey and the dog man.

The Boss said, "We better check up on those kids in the Hole. If we lose them, we won't get paid."

We walked to the Pool House, where the Hole was. We were all armed except the Caretaker. Wires had a club. The rest of us had guns. The Boss ordered the Caretaker to go first. The Boss, who had the keys, went next. Then me and Wires. The Man-woman and the limping Fish followed behind.

The wolves were still howling in the distance. Clouds of that yellow gas were creeping over the ground like gigantic beasts. The Fish started shooting at them wildly. The Boss ordered him to stop.

We reached the Pool House and went down the dark, narrow stairs. Here was a heavy, metal door. The Boss unlocked it and flashed the light downward. Two bodies were lying on the concrete floor. Their hands and feet were bound and they were stripped nearly naked. But these were not the bodies of the boys.

The bodies twitched. They were alive and breathing. One was the red-headed dog handler, with his arms and legs bound behind his back. And hand-cuffed with his own hand-cuffs was the phony cop. Both men were gagged.

"Where are the boys?"

The policeman anwered with a muffled groan. The dog man shook his head in bewilderment. The Boss cursed angrily and slammed the metal door shut, leaving the two men still hogtied and imprisoned in the Hole.

"They got away! They got away! A million bucks I was supposed to get!" He turned his anger on the rest of us. "You stupid lazy bums! Why weren't you guarding them?"

We all knew better than to answer him.

Then he yelled, "Creeper! Wires! Fish!"

"Yes, Boss?"

"Find those kids! They may be still on the property. If they're over the wall, they can't be far. Get 'em! Otherwise, you'll get nothing, do you understand? No pay at all."

"That Bartlow has money," cried the Fish, angrily. "He has to pay us. Otherwise we'll terminate *him!*"

We saw now that the Caretaker was missing. In the confusion, he had slipped away. The old man knew the property and could move around in the dark. The Boss thought he might head for the garage and try to grab a car. "Go after him! Don't let him get away!"

Monstrous shadows hung over the snow-covered ground. Something was moving through the night with glowing eyes. We shot at it. We shot at the shadows and at anything that moved.

In the distance, we could see a pin point of light. Something was running through the snow like a frightened rabbit. It zigzagged, ducking behind trees, moving toward the garage. The Boss aimed his gun and fired. The light went out. *"Got him!"*

Once again, we could hear that howling sound. Only it was different this time. More like the wailing of a siren.

The Boss was standing there, holding his gun. All at once, a wild figure came tearing in out of the darkness. It was Buggsey and he had blown his top. "You lousy bastard!" he yelled. "You tried to kill me!" And he aimed the muzzle of his gun right at the Boss' chest.

The Boss tried to shout. But before he could get it out,

a burst of purple flame exploded from Buggsey's gun. The Boss' chest split open. His legs caved in and he flopped backwards, almost split in two.

"You fool, Buggsey!" cried The Fish. "You killed the Boss!"

"He tried to kill me first."

The Fish yelled, "You're crazy, Buggsey. That was the Boss you killed. Now how are we going to get paid?"

Buggsey went nuts. "Crazy am I? I'll show you who is crazy!" And he blasted down The Fish.

I shouted, "Don't shoot, Buggsey! I'm Creeper." But I knew he wasn't going to stop. I leaped away and so did Wires. But I think he got the Hop Toad. The Toad was crawling away, leaving a trail of blood.

All at once, those sirens broke into a shrieking blast. A stream of police cars were smashing through the gates. These were not locals. They were State Police. They were storming in in overwhelming numbers.

Crazy Buggsey turned his gun on the Troopers. But they blasted him and shot the gun out of his hand. Buggsey dropped in his tracks and I guess he was dead, too.

The Boss, The Fish and Buggsey lay there cold. The Hop Toad was badly injured and maybe dying. The Manwoman threw up his/her hands in surrender.

The State Troopers shouted out a warning. Wires had thrown his gun away and fled. I tried to follow him. I was running over the snow in the darkness and forgot about that hole the kids dug. I ran right into it, fell about five feet and lay there crippled.

The dog man and the phony cop were released from the Pool House dungeon, and taken into custody. Both of them claimed they had nothing to do with the crimes. They just worked on the estate.

The dog handler changed sides, denouncing Bartlow and his partners. He rounded up his five still terrified hounds. They found the frightened caretaker hiding in the pump house. And they found me.

I lay there helplessly with a broken leg, while the State Troopers closed in on me.

Death of The Boss

* * * * * * *

(The Creeper was sentenced to 50 years to Life for his part in the murder of Franz Hasserman. He was not tried for the kidnapping. He plea-bargained and testified against the Higher-ups in so many trials, he became known as *The Singing Canary*.

In prison, he wrote a novel that became a best seller. It was called *The House of Horror*.)

THE TRIUMPH OF THE COYOTES

The Larrabie boys stowed the van about two miles away and approached the estate in an anti-mirage. We would have liked to send a message to Bobby and Stevie that we were coming. Cameron, however, decided not to. There was a chance the message might have been intercepted and put our brothers in danger.

The only reason Bobby and Stevie were safe now was because the kidnappers figured they had plenty of time to kill them later. They were being held as live bait to get the rest of us and to capture the *Vrrooohn*.

In open combat, the weapon power was overwhelmingly on the side of our Enemies. We would have to hit them in a surprise attack. "Oh, *Horned Crystal*," called Raymond, "give us strength!" And it did. For a few hours, we could read each others' minds completely and we threw all our mind force behind Donald to give him power.

The Bartlow estate was ringed with electronic alarms. There was no way we could make sure of silencing them. Just one alarm could be a fatal giveaway. Cameron and Donald decided on a diversion. By the *Vrrooohn*, we made the alarms go off all over.

The Enemy ran around frantically, trying to locate the intruders. We waited a while before crossing the wall. I don't know if we made any waves. But by this time our enemies were puzzled and disgusted and thought it was just another false alarm.

The dogs found us though as we approached the Pool House. The guard dogs were unexpected. The *Vrrooohn* hadn't told us about them. It only tells you the things you ask. Donald has a way with animals and could make friends with almost any bird or beast. But these mastiffs were attack dogs, trained to kill. They didn't sniff around and give you a chance to make friends.

Donald didn't wait to be sniffed. He used the *Vrrooohn* and projected an image. Whatever it was, it scared the daylights out of those hounds and sent them off yelping, with their tails between their legs. We knew now that the *Vrrooohn* worked on beasts as well as people.

"Howl!" ordered Donald.

We gave the Coyote howl. But Donald said we weren't Coyotes any more. We were a pack of gigantic wolves. Werwolves who could take the shape of human boys.

Think like you're a pack of giant wolves. We projected the werwolf image and scared the shit not only out of our enemies, but out of our imprisoned brothers. Stevie and Bobby had forgotten about the *Horned Crystal* and its mind projections. They saw a flock of monsters coming at them and began to yell. They almost keeled over when Cameron's voice came out of nowhere. "Shut up, you stupid crud! We said we were coming. And we're here."

Our enemies were aroused now and they had guns. In an *An-mir* or not, we could still be shot. Donald tried to project clouds of yellow poison gas. That should keep them away from us. We couldn't see or feel it ourselves and couldn't be sure if it worked.

A couple of guys were coming down to check on the prisoners. We ambushed them, jumped them, tied them up and stuck them down in the Hole. One of the guys was dressed like a cop. Maybe a phony. We took his uniform and gun.

*We Terrified our Brothers Almost as Much
as we did our Enemies*

Two more guys came prowling around. We threw
snowballs at them and made them think they had been
hit by rocks. We stunned one guy and knocked the other
out. We took his gun, too.

"Let's get out of here."

There was shooting now. We hoped our enemies were
shooting at each other. We resisted the temptation to
shoot back. That would give our position away. All our
enemies could see of us at all was a faint yellow cloud.
Donald cunningly projected a whole flock of yellow
clouds. Some of the clouds shone in the dark. Ours — the
real one — didn't. The kidnappers were shooting wildly
at nothing. First, at a pack of imaginary wolves; then at
the empty air.

We didn't fire a shot or use a weapon. But the men who
died that night were of our doing. This was War and they
were trying to kill us. *They* started the war. But instead
of twelve helpless kids, they fought the Warriors of the
Horned Crystal, the Coyote Terrors. The most dangerous youth gang on the face of the Earth!

We withdrew and crossed the wall. After we got over,
Donald did something, blowing out all the lights and the
electric in the Bartlow mansion. That blew out their car
batteries, too. There was no way they could pursue us.

All at once, we could hear the frenzied shriek of the
police sirens. An attack force was moving on the Bartlow
mansion. There were more than a dozen police cars and a
couple of trucks.

There are only about six cops in Echo Lake. But these
weren't locals. They were State Police. Like an assault-
ing army, they crashed through the gates and into the
Bartlow estate.

We decided to get the hell out of there. Still in an anti-
mirage, we started down the road toward our hidden
van....

A man was coming down the road behind us. He slid
on a patch of ice and took a flop. Stevie said it was one of
the kidnappers, fleeing the police. We broke the anti-
mirage and grabbed the guy.

Danny started to kick the shit out of him. The guy looked terrified. His name was Wires. Bobby said yes, he was a kidnapper but not one of the worst. He had brought them food and water, when everyone else forgot about them and stopped another guy from beating them. We decided to let him go.

Keith had been holding the *Horned Crystal.* He was only kidding when he told the guy, "You're a crow! You're a crow! Flap your wings and caw!" And Donald added, "You're a royal crow. Go sit on a queen!"

It wasn't our fault the jerk went bonkers. I guess these hired guns are half bonkers anyway and this one flipped his lid completely. Wires ran around flapping his arms and yelling, "Caw! Caw! Caw!" Maybe he was looking for a queen to sit on. That *Horned Crystal* packs a galaxy of power. You can't fool around with it.

We went off and left him. The cops picked him up and he still thought he was a crow. That Wires ended up in a funny farm just about the time our old teacher, Mr. Matthews, was getting out.

When they finally did get him to talk, all he could say was a lot of gibberish. No one believed his story about a pack of invisible boys popping out of the snow.

Maybe we did him a favor in the long run. Wires had a pile of charges on him and going bonkers like that helped him beat the rap.

RETURN OF THE LARRABIE SONS

Father had toiled all day and late into the night and managed to raise most of the ransom money. The balance should be forthcoming tomorrow. Bundles of twenty dollar bills were piled into two heavy sacks.

Father had recruited two men to help him, Larry the Watchman and Teacher Rodney. Both were armed to guard the money bags. The trio, along with Mother and Miss Ferris, kept a vigil, drinking coffee and waiting for a telephone call that didn't come.

Mother kept making sandwiches that nobody ate. Larry paced back and forth, like a sentry on duty. Miss Ferris examined the bank notes and was listing the serial numbers. Father worried about hearing nothing and worried even more about receiving bad news. The Poet appeared the most cheerful of the group, somehow certain that the boys would return unharmed.

The front door had been latched and bolted and fastened with a chain. Now all at once it flew open. Larry and Rodney leaped up, clutching their weapons. Miss Ferris rushed to conceal the bags of money. The hostile growl of Larry's poodle changed to a puzzled whine.

The group all stared at the door. At first, they saw nothing. Then Jaymie and Danny entered the room. Danny said, "Are you paying out two hundred and fifty grand for Bobby and Stevie? That's a hell of a lot to pay for those two punks."

Dad look bewildered. "But——"

"If you want them, I can get them back for five bucks each."

Eight other Larrabie youths came in, forming a double line. A short pause, then the two missing sons, Stevie and Bobby, came hobbling in. Mauled and battered, but still on their feet.

For a moment, Dad was angry. "Was this some kind of a hoax? If this kidnapping was a joke——"

"A lousy joke," agreed Stevie. He had a black eye and a broken nose. Bobby had two black eyes and a swollen

The Poet, Larry and Topper

face and thought his wrist was broken. Their bodies were covered with welts and bruises.

"I see what you mean," said Dad. "How did you get free?"

"You wouldn't believe it, Dad," said Keith. "But they're home! We got them home!"

Mother threw her arms around Stevie. Miss Ferris embraced Bobby. "My poor little boys! How did it happen?"

Stevie said, "We went out last night, riding the motorbike. We promised not to and we broke our word."

Dad looked at the two battered youths and smiled a little. "Whatever happened, you've been punished enough."

Miss Ferris surveyed the two injured boys with growing anger. "Who did this awful thing to you? We should get the children to a hospital."

"We better stay here for now. Some of our kidnappers are still around."

"If they try to come here, we'll stop them. Won't we Larry?" The Poet brandished his rifle, like a sharpshooter in a Cowboy movie. But, if the truth be known, he had never shot a gun before.

"Come, boys, let me bathe your eyes. And protect that nose and wrist so they don't get any worse." Miss Ferris was always happy when she had someone to nurse. Bobby and Stevie followed her obediently.

All at once, the telephone broke into a shrill jangle.

"Don't answer it!" implored Mother, fearfully. It kept on ringing thirteen times and then stopped.

Raymond made a mind scan. "It was Bartlow, I think. He's trying to find out if we got home."

A moment later, the ringing started up again. We disconnected the telephone and piled the ransom money into Father's safe. Larry and Rodney, joined by the poodle, Topper, determined to stay on guard. The rest of us went to bed.

*　　*　　*　　*　　*　　*　　*

They say no man is a hero to his valet. And I guess no

boy is a hero to his baby nurse. Miss Ferris wept over Bobby and Stevie. And she wept over Brother Danny and the rest of us. But next day she was yelling at us again:

"Daniel Larrabie, you are tracking mud all over the carpet! Can't you wipe your feet before coming in? . . . Pick up your coat, Jaymie! Don't leave it on the floor! . . . Raymond, tie your shoe laces! . . . Jody, you'll break that chair leaning backwards like that! . . . .

"Keith, wipe your nose with a handkerchief, not with your sleeve! . . . Cameron Anthony! Don't *throw* things in the trash can. *Put* them in!

"Donald, you have dirt on your face. Let me wipe it off. . . . Brandon, don't leave those dirty dishes in the parlor! Pick them up and bring them into the kitchen. . . . Roger, put those eggs back in the refrigerator! Young gentlemen don't throw eggs! . . . .

"No, no, Troy! Young gentlemen don't slide down the bannisters! Don't jump! Walk down nicely. . . .

"No, you are *not* going out, Steven! Nor *you*, Robert! The doctor said you should rest. Be good boys now and no more monkey business!" And she combed Bobby's unruly hair and sewed Stevie's much ripped pants.

We were the wild Coyote Terrors, the most dangerous youth gang on the face of the Earth. But we let the ladies lead us around by the nose. The guys seemed to like it and enjoyed having someone bossing them around.

Still, it took a while for that Giant Wolf image to wear off. Our two kittens kept out of our way. It was two days before they would rub against our legs and purr again.

*　*　*　*　*　*　*

Cameron used to say, "*Never trust anyone over twenty.*" But we knew now we had at least three grown-up friends whom we could count on no matter how rough things got. Now that we had saved the ransom money, I hoped Dad would do something for our friends. Especially for Larry, who was getting married. Larry didn't have to tell us. Today, we had the Power and could scan his mind.

Troy asked, "When are you getting married, Larry?"

He looked surprised. "How did you know?"

Mother said, "It's amazing. The boys sometimes pick up vibrations. Can you tell the name of Larry's bride?"

"Rosalind Turner," said me. "She works in a bookshop. And she has a poodle, the sister of Topper." And then I bit my tongue and so did Troy. We had sworn to keep our mind powers hidden.

Larry just grinned. "Aw, your Dad told you."

We didn't have to urge Dad to help our friends or even send him a mind message. Dad was as generous now as he had been stingy before. And Mother thought how lovely it would be if Larry had his wedding in our house. And keep that garage apartment, rent-free, of course. Apartments were real hard to come by nowadays. We could finish off the attic and make two more rooms.

Mother had some lovely furniture in storage from her great-aunt. Just right for a young married couple. . . . .

It looked like Larry was going to be bossed around, too. Benevolently, of course.

QUEEN HECATE'S EXPEDITIONARY ARMY

Miss Ferris knocked on the door of our bedroom. "Inspector Smith is here. From the State Police. He wants to talk to you boys."

Cameron looked at Donald. "Probe, Don Don. See if he's alone. See if he has a weapon."

Donald's body stiffened. His yellow eyes gleamed as he stared into space. Then he grinned. "It's okay."

Inspector Smith had a pointed beard and a bristling moustache. He wore dark glasses and heavy woolen gloves. "This is Inspector Smith," announced Miss Ferris, unnecessarily. Then, discreetly, she withdrew.

There was something oddly familiar about the Inspector. His English was impeccable, without any trace of a foreign accent. But it had an unusual musical quality. Each word was pronounced carefully. He sounded more like a voice teacher than a cop.

The Inspector's hair was black with whitish streaks. It didn't look quite natural. I had a feeling it was dyed. Except for Donald, Keith was the first to spot him. It was our Lemurian friend, Ral Garyon. "Hi, Ral!"

"I am Inspector Smith," he insisted. There really was an Inspector Smith. He was stricken ill and returned to Lemuria.

"Inspector Smith" was a Lemurian mole planted over the years in the American police. There were other agents like him, scattered over the face of the Earth. The Lemurians were supposed just to report, and not interfere in Earth affairs, unless there was a serious danger to Lemuria.

When there was a grave threat, the agent was permitted to act; provided he acted secretly, without revealing his true identity. Ral had convinced Queen Hecate that such a threat existed, if the *Vrrooohn* were to fall into the wrong hands.

Ral Garyon as "Inspector Smith" had led the attack of the State Police on the Bartlow mansion. Officer Caroline, wounded in the shoulder, had gunned down the mad killer, Buggsey.

The original Inspector Smith had been looking into the Karl Hasserman business. "Somebody poisoned him."

"The rice pudding?"

"Either that or the mushrooms." The vegetarian Police Inspector had been eating mushrooms for lunch instead of meat. "If he wasn't a Lemurian, he would be dead." Lemurians are hard to kill.

Ral had taken over Inspector Smith's identity. "It was a rush job. I didn't get a chance to change my fingerprints." But most Earth people weren't too hard to fool.

"We knew you were in trouble. We came through the Gateway as fast as we could. We had to get the Queen's permission."

Unfortunately, there was no such thing as teleportation. At least, the Lemurians hadn't discovered it. The mind could jump around anywhere. But bodies had to follow physical laws.

"We arrived too late to help you. But the *Great Mother* protected you." Ral made a circle around his heart.

Queen Hecate had sent a six-man expeditionary force to Earth to save the Larrabie kids. One was the nurse, Lyandra. She went to *Kaah Naghallah*. "Old George was almost killed last night." They didn't wait for George to fall down a flight of stairs. Somebody shot him with a deadly arrow. "He is in the hospital, but will recover."

Lyandra got there almost too late. However, she captured the hired killer and turned him over to the local police. You wouldn't think a frail woman could overcome an armed murderer. But these Lemurian women could be deadly. They knew all the tricks of judo and karate and a lot more, including mind power.

A third Lemurian had gone down to Johanna and her sister, Minnie, at the Golden Age Home in Riverport. "They were on the *Death List.*"

"How did you know about that?"

"We scanned your minds. When you use the *Vrrooohn*, you broadcast it.

"Want to meet my deputy? The rescuer of Johanna and Minnie?"

It was Prince Frain, dressed in a state trooper's uniform too small for him. He, too, had dark glasses and dyed hair. The Prince looked unhappy. This was his first trip to Earth and he decided it would be his last. "It's so cold here!" He needed all his mind power to keep from freezing.

"You would like it better, if you came in the summer."

"I'd get used to it in time," said Frain. "After all, our ancestors lived here for thousands of years. How's my English?" He wanted to practice his English, instead of thought reading.

"I get mixed up on Earth languages. Why do you people have so many?"

Frain had talked to the hunted women in German. *"Ich bin ein Freund von Brandon Zuchtig.* When I mentioned Brandon and Lyandra, they believed and trusted me."

The Lemurians were concerned that the *Vrrooohn* might fall into hostile hands. Some tyrant might gain domination over Earth, then break through the Gateway and overrun Lemuria. "Earth has many billions. We have maybe a million, counting everybody."

Once, the Lemurians had been scattered over thousands of planets. But today, their survivors liked to live close together in extended families. Despite their long lives, their population hardly grew at all. They had few kids and shared them like they did most other things. One kid might have a dozen parents and guardians. Being a Prince, said Frain, he must have about fifty. The Elders all gave him presents. But they also gave him advice and Frain had to listen to it.

We told Frain, "You ought to build up the population of Lemuria. Have another hundred cities like *Glow Malomba*," A billion Lemurians would be safer than a million. They had so much land, they had never even explored most of it. They didn't even know where *Bane N'Gai* ended. If it ever did.

Prince Frain liked that idea and would tell it to the Queen. The Lemurians should start having more children.

"And set them an example, you and Ral. As soon as you get back."

Would you believe it? Prince Frain got all red and embarrassed.

* * * * * * *

"I got three more deputies," announced Ral Garyon. Three more members of *Queen Hecate's Earth Expeditionary Force*, disguised in the uniforms of the State Police. Part of the cohorts that attacked the Bartlow mansion.

And here were the three cadets, Gledd, Kollen and Corporal Tramm. Now Sergeant Tramm and Corporals

Kollen and Gledd. They had been promoted.

"After this Earth mission," said Kollen, "we ought all to be officers."

"What will you do," asked Troy, "when you have an army all full of officers and no privates?"

Keith had a suggestion. "Recruit some Earthmen in your army. Then you'll have somebody to boss around."

"Are you guys volunteering?"

"Not right now. Wait until your next war."

"Are you going to win the next war for us, too?"

"We'll try."

"We'll stick you guys in the reserves," said Ral. "And mobilize you when we have our next war. Which we hope will be — *Never.*"

The five Lemurians joined us for dinner. Our parents and Miss Ferris were real hospitable, but rather curious about how we came to know "Inspector Smith" and his young assistants. We didn't tell them.

"Now," said Ral Garyon, "I'm afraid we'll have to be going." The others, I thought, would have liked to stay. Gledd, Tramm and Kollen still looked wonder-eyed at Earth, not quite believing the place was real.

Mother said, "What charming policemen!"

They thanked our parents and bade us *Goodbye.* They hoped to see us again, but couldn't be sure. Ral said, "Farewell, friends. Guard the *Vrrooohn* well. Keep it in the *Quayne,* unless you need it badly."

Cameron asked, "Do you want it back?" I don't know what we would have done if they had said *Yes, they wanted it.*

But Prince Frain said, "No. You have earned it." And Ral added, "We think the *Horned Crystal* is safe with you."

Now the five Lemurians departed. So fast it almost looked like they vanished. Their cars vanished, too. I think the Lemurians still have a few tricks they didn't tell us.

FINALE

"Commander" Bartlow received the news of the police raid and did not return to his estate. Instead, he made a few telephone calls and instructed his chauffeur to drive him to the South Logan airport. Here, a private plane and crew awaited him to fly him out of the country.

Bartlow had his Swiss bank accounts and South American connections. He had passports from four countries and could take his choice. Even without the power of the *Vrrooohn*, he could look forward to a rich and luxurious life.

The chauffeur was speeding. Bartlow ordered him to slow down, so as not to attract attention. The pilot was waiting and the plane prepared for a take-off on the darkened runway. Bartlow congratulated himself on his foresight and careful planning. Survival of the fittest! He would go on. Powell and the hired mobsters would be thrown to the wolves.

As Bartlow stepped out of his limousine, a flashlight and a gun were pushed into his face. Bartlow was arrested by Inspector Smith of the State Police.

"Major" Powell turned his station wagon eastward. He had connections in New York City. Powell, too, had prepared a new identity. He would take a cruise to the Caribbean and then drop out of sight.

Powell never made it. As he approached the State line, the phony Major was pounced on by the ubiquitous Inspector Smith and his men.

"Captain" Klayborne had few connections and very little money. Unable to contact his associates, he received the ill tidings from the radio and newspapers:

STATE POLICE RAID BARTLOW MANSION
4 MOBSTERS DEAD, LADY COP WOUNDED

There was no immediate mention of the kidnapped youths who, in some incredible way, had managed to escape.

Someone was a double-crosser and had tipped off the police! Klayborne thought it was Powell. He was a weak sister and had balked at getting rid of those worthless boys.

Unfortunately, Klayborne was now himself a suspected traitor. He had left the estate a few hours before the raid and failed to return.

Up to now, Klayborne had managed to evade the police, who were hunting him. Now, however, his former allies and partners would be searching for him, too. The Death Mob, or what was left of it, did not take kindly to defeat and would be looking for someone to blame.

Klayborne was in a trap and the trap was closing from two sides. There was only one way out. He decided on a last, frantic drive to seize the *Vrrooohn*.

It was in the room of the Larrabie boys. That much he had beaten out of the kidnapped youths. It was hidden in something they couldn't quite explain. But a pointed gun would open up the lock.

Klayborne had a pistol in his belt and was carrying an automatic. He was driving a red sport car, a real fancy Hermes, which still had not been paid for. We knew he was coming and we prepared for him.

Again, we formed the *An-mir,* but an anti-mirage won't work unless you are close to the *Vrrooohn*. We couldn't spread out. We had to stay close together. Klayborne was heading for our bedroom. We were waiting for him in the entrance hall.

The grown-ups were sleeping in their rooms upstairs. We would smite the Enemy before he could harm them. We forgot about Larry, our protector and watchman. Night watchmen are supposed to sleep at night, not go around patrolling the grounds and getting shot at.

Larry watched the red Hermes come in, swerving a bit, as if the driver were drunk. A family friend, thought Larry, who has had too much winter cheer; or a neighbor coming to the wrong house. As Klayborne reached our door, Larry confronted him. "Stop! What are you doing here?"

Larry had a gun, but didn't get a chance to use it. Before he could draw, Klayborne shot him in the chest. We could see it happening in a mind scan. Too late, we yelled out an alarm to Larry.

Cameron flashed us a warning. *Stay in formation. Don't break the An-mir. The Creep is armed and he's coming in.*

Klayborne threw open the door. He didn't see the twelve youths gathered in ambush. A dark shadow with a hundred arms and legs hung over Klayborne like a colossal crouching insect. Its twisted limbs were reaching downward. The last of the Masters of *Naghallah* raised up his gun and fired wildly at the empty ceiling. Then he panicked and fled out of the house.

Klayborne raced to his car, shooting blindly behind him. The red Hermes sped away. Keith seized the *Vrrooohn* and tried to blast its tires with mind power. But it didn't work.

Larry was in a bad way. He was unconscious and bleeding heavily. His breath came in short, anguished gasps. The dog, Topper, stood over him, whining and howling, desperately calling for help.

"Don't move him!"

"We'll have to. He'll freeze out here." Larry's face was turning blue. We improvised a carpet stretcher and carried Larry into the house.

Donald took the *Vrrooohn* and held it close to Larry's heart. He was pleading and calling with an inner, silent voice.

Oh, Horned Crystal! Heal! Heal Larry! Bring Larry back!

The *Vrrooohn* gleamed with an orange flame. The rest of us formed a circle around them. The life flowed back into Larry's body and his feeble heart beat became strong again.

Awakened by the shots, our parents and Miss Ferris watched us in bewilderment. Then Dad called an ambulance and our good neighbor, Dr. Weinberger. By the time they both arrived, Larry had recovered consciousness and his bleeding had stopped. They hauled Larry off to the hospital, though Larry protested and insisted he was "All right." Father and Miss Ferris went with them. Topper stopped trembling and lay down by the fire.

Inspector Caroline also arrived belatedly, with four police cars and a bandaged shoulder. They had been sent by "Inspector Smith" to protect us; welcome, although somewhat late.

Officer Caroline started making frantic telephone calls. Yes, the red Hermes had been spotted coming out of Greenwood, going North, South, East and West. The Police set up roadblocks in every direction, but the villainous Captain had vanished without a trace.

We got a telephone call from Larry at the hospital. He was having a fight with the doctors who were trying to keep him there. Larry wanted to get out.

Would we call Rosalind, his bride to be. He forgot her new number. Tell her he was shot, but was okay now; before she heard about it on the radio.

What a shitty place this hospital was, said Larry. He wanted a gin and tonic, but all they would give him was tea!

Everyone congratulated the doctors for saving Larry's life. That was all right with us. We didn't want any credit. We had vowed to keep our powers a secret and put the *Vrrooohn* back in the *Quayne,* as soon as Larry was out of danger. But our parents, Miss Ferris and Larry, too, were all sure "the boys did something."

Mother told Donald, "You have a wonderful healing power. You should be a doctor."

Donald smiled and said nothing.

* * * * * * *

Captain Klayborne changed cars and was now driving a yellow Cadillac, registered to the late Karl Hasserman. He prided himself on his cleverness. The police, who were looking for a red Hermes, let him slip away. The

Hermes lay wrecked at the bottom of a hill, in a frozen lake. Hopefully, the police would think he died in it.

Klayborne was heading north, toward the Grey Mountains. The roads were empty, but somehow he couldn't escape the feeling of being pursued. Something impelled him to hurry. *Faster! Faster! That thing is coming up behind you.*

Now Klayborne entered the Grey Mountain State Park. The roads here were twisting, narrow, unsafe for winter travel.

He reached a barricade. A sign warned:

ROAD CLOSED. DANGER
DETOUR TWO MILES BACK.

Klayborne suspected this was a trap. He crashed through the barricade and kept going.

There was something wrong with the brakes. Klayborne reached a sharp turn and tried to slow down. The Cadillac skidded on the icy road.

The yellow car broke through the railing and catapulted down the side of Panther Mountain. Within a minute, it exploded and became a smoking wreck two hundred feet below.

The police believed it was an accident. It is better that they thought so and maybe it was. Just about that time, Donald was holding the *Vrrooohn.* His yellow eyes were staring into space. He was chanting something in an unknown tongue, ending in a cry of triumph. Donald-of-the-yellow-eyes has *Power.*

Did Donald make that car crash in the distant mountains? He wouldn't say. I tried a mind scan, but he blocked it. *"Trust me, Brother Jaymie. Donald is loyal."*

I sure would hate to have Donald as an enemy. I sure am glad he's on the same side as me!

CAMERON'S AUNT

Brandon never did find his folks. I guess his people must have dumped him and sold him to that pimp who was so mean to Brandon.

Danny said, "We ought to get even with that lousy scumbag." But Brandon said forget it. If we started paying back all the creeps who had injured us or one of our friends, we'd be doing nothing else. Brandon don't care any more. He's *Brandon Larrabie* now.

Cameron did locate the aunt who dumped him. "But I can't blame her. I gave her an awful lot of shit.

"After I got kicked out of military school, she sent me to a Home for wayward youth run by the Reverend Blabbermouth, or something like that. One of those places where they read the Bible all the time, work your tail off, feed you slop and beat the crud out of you.

"Every Friday was public confession. I confessed my *sinful thoughts*. How I thought the Reverend Blabbermouth was a *louse* and a *crook* and a *phony*. They ended up sticking me in the *Meditation Room*, which was a closet down in the cellar."

Cameron, however, broke out, stole a bunch of stuff and ran away up north.

Cameron landed in Riverport. "I burglarized a grocery store. All I got was six lousy bucks and a box of crackers. The cops were looking for me. I jumped on the first bus out of town and landed here in Greenwood." That's how Cameron came here.

On Valentine's Day, Cameron got sentimental and called his aunt. He called her person to person, because he didn't want her husband to take the call. "Last time, he hung up on me. It wasn't collect either. It was my own money." Cameron's last dollar.

After several tries, Aunt Myra came to the phone. "I don't know any Cameron Larrabie," she told the operator.

"Tell her it's Tony Westcott."

"Oh, Tony! I thought you were in jail! I heard you ran away from that Boys' Home they put you in."

"I got a real home now, Aunt Myra. With my eleven brothers I wrote you about."

"You mean those same boys you were with at that Naghallah school? I'm surprised they let you stay together after causing so much trouble. Is this another Boys' Home, like the other one?"

"This is the Larrabie Family home. They adopted me. They adopted all twelve of us. But I'm *Son Number One* and the leader," said Cameron, boastfully.

"I hope they make you go to school, Tony."

"Sure. We got a private teacher, Mr. Desmond and he's real good. I'm learning all about — about orators. Cicero and guys like that. I'm gonna be an orator myself."

"That's very nice," said Aunt Myra, who didn't have the faintest idea what an orator was.

"And we got a baby nurse."

"A baby nurse?"

"Yeah. Miss Ferris. She takes good care of us. Want to talk to her?"

Miss Ferris got on the phone and told Auntie what a wonderful child Cameron Anthony was.

"Want to talk to my teacher?" Rodney Desmond also praised Tony highly. "A born leader. . . . A very promising youngster., . . . It is a privilege to teach him!"

Uncle, who was listening on the library extension, wondered if they were talking about the same guy.

"Want to talk to my brudders?"

"Some other time, Tony."

"We could all come down and visit you." Tony winked.

Aunt Myra gulped. Uncle gasped. "We have a very small place, Tony. And no extra room."

"We don't mind. We could sleep on the floor." Uncle's frantic *No! No!* sounded clearly over the phone.

"Maybe you could come up here," suggested Tony. "We got a big old house with twenty-six rooms.

"Want to talk to my parents? Some other time, huh? Oh, here's Larry. He's our bodyguard. Some people kidnapped a couple of my brudders, but we got them back—"

"Cut it short!" whispered Uncle, loudly. "Don't get involved."

"You must tell me all about it, Tony. But I must go now. Goodbye." And Auntie hung up.

A few days later, however, Cameron received a check for $65.00 "A belated Christmas present."

"Ten dollars for you, dear Tony. And five dollars for each of your dear brothers. Please give my love to your dear parents and your teacher and your nurse and your bodyguard.

"Your devoted, Aunt Myra."

I guess we got ourselves a new aunt.

THE RITES OF PASSAGE

I'm beginning to think Raymond is right. The *Vrrooohn* is a Thing in itself and has a life of its own. If we use it for evil, it will turn against us, as it did with Karl Hasserman. If we use the *Vrrooohn* for trivial or petty things, it will fritter away its power and become impotent.

Donald thought the *Vrrooohn* was a shard of *The Great Mother*. We swore never to abuse it. The twelve of us formed a circle around it and took an oath :

We will never use the Vrrooohn for conquest or destruction. Nor to injure others. Nor for selfish wealth or power.

We shall use it only to protect our friends and family from dire peril. And to protect our country and our World against deadly war or catastrophe. We shall never use the Horned Crystal, unless the twelve of us agree.

We shall try to be worthy of the Horned Crystal and shall never knowingly do evil.

We swear this by our lives and souls. And by all that is or ever was or will be. Now, Always and Forever.

We wrote the oath on parchment and we cut our hands and signed it with our blood. Which was about as sacred as we could make it.

Now the *Horned Crystal* was shining with a blue aura. The two horns gleamed with a golden glow. Raymond said the Spirit of the *Vrrooohn* was satisfied.

*   *   *   *   *   *   *

We concealed the oath among our valued things. However, we made a copy. Accidentally on purpose, we let the copy fall into the hands of our Teacher, Rodney Desmond. For he was the only one who had guessed the secret of our hidden powers.

Grown-ups always remember how happy their childhood was. But it don't always seem happy to a kid. The Naghallah boys didn't have too much fun being kids. They were kicked around as far back as they could remember.

But there is no one to push us around now. No pimps, no kid-hating bullies, no slave-masters or assorted creeps; no phony youth correctors or disciplinarians. We can enjoy the golden youth the poets sing about, but never have themselves.

Much has been written about the *Rites of Passage* from adolescence to adult. We decided to make a *Rite of Passage* the other way. We had become men in *Kaah Naghallah* and *Bane N'Gai*. And in the Grey Mountains and Echo Lake. Now, *Right about face! To the rear, March!* Back to Boyhood!

We put the *Vrrooohn* in the *Quayne* and went bobsledding. We toasted marshmallows and had a snowball fight. . . . . .

*   *   *   *   *   *   *

The Goblins' Bread that we brought back to feed the hungry is all gone. We tried to grow it down in the cellar where it is warm and wet and dark, like in the caves of *Bane N'Gai.* But something was missing. We put all kinds of things in trays to grow it on; sawdust and soup and grain. But nothing worked too well. It hardly grew at all.

Then someone threw all the trays out, and all the Goblins' Bread, too. My stupid father. "You shouldn't leave rotting food around, boys. It draws rats and bugs."

We didn't tell Dad he had ruined what might have been one of the great experiments of the century. He wouldn't have believed it anyway.

We tried to rescue some of the Goblin's bread from the dumpster. But the garbage had been carted away.

Maybe that stuff we seeded grew in the caves up in the Grey Mountains. But I doubt it.

Danny said, "Don't fret about it, Jaymiebrudder. Some day we'll all go back to *Bane N'Gai* and get some more. And while we're at it, we'll bring back some unicorns and pterodactyls. And maybe a couple of Brontosaurus and flying trees."

"How can we? They closed the Gateway."

"We'll find a way. We got the *Vrrooohn*, don't we? And we got our heroes' medals. They can't keep us out!"

THE THREE HUNDRED YEAR PLAN

Donald received a mind message. Ral Garyon will be the father of quads — two boys, two girls. Prince Frain is going him one better and will become the father of quints. Two boys, three girls. Neither Ral nor Frain is married yet. The Lemurians work these things out ahead of time.

Ral is wedding the great-granddaughter of the High Priestess. High Priestesses don't have to be celibate in *Bane N'Gai* (And never are).

Frain's bride will be the Lady Rana-Loo, a raiser of giant riding frogs. Now she will be the Princess Rana-Loo. Will she keep on raising frogs? "Certainly. I love my frogs almost as much as I love my Prince."

Queen Hecate has launched a three hundred year plan to raise the population of Lemuria to one billion souls. That's for a start. "We must catch up to and pass Earth. Then we won't have to worry if they discover us." The Oreads, Goblins and Animal People are also launching population drives to keep from falling too far behind. I guess there's plenty of room in *Bane N'Gai.* No one has ever come to the end of it.

Lyandra is expecting triplets. She is planning to wed the real Inspector Smith. Maybe they will come to Earth. I hope so.

Sergeant (now Lieutenant) Framm has a bride picked out. (Or, rather, she picked him out). A lady cheese-maker. They are having twins. Just to begin with.

Lieutenant Kollen (He was promoted, too) got hooked by a lady dentist. Lieutenant Gledd got hooked by a lady math teacher. *Everyone must do their duty for Queen and country!*

Ral says at the rate we're going, we'll finish the three hundred year plan in less than two hundred years.

BOOKS AND PLAYS
By James S. Wallerstein

THE DEMON'S MIRROR

TOMMY AND JULIE

ADVENTURE: FIVE PLAYS FOR YOUTH
Windigo Island
Raymond and the Monster
The Cactus Wildcat
Johnny Aladdin
Bobby and the Time Machine

OVER THE HILLS: FOUR PLAYS FOR YOUTH
The Curse of the Larrabies
Laura and the Magic Trumpet
The Terror of Hoostack Mills
Jimmy the Werwolf

THE TRAIL OF DANGER

THE OUTER DARKNESS

NO TRAVELLER RETURNS